Nothing is easier than self-deceit.
For what each man wishes, than he also
believes to be true.

- Demosthenes

Däm'Um:
Song of the Vam Pŷr's
BLOOD JUNKY

Written by Stavros
Edited by Carol Russell

CRAZY DUCK PRESS

Library of Congress Catalog Number: 2010910115

ISBN: 978-0-9828121-1-2

Published by Crazy Duck Press, PO Box 946, Poolesville,
MD. 20837-0946

The Upanishads
Translation by Juan Mascaró; Penguin Press
©Juan Mascaró, 1965

"Wishing"
Written by Buddy Holly & Bob Montgomery
©MPL Communications
©Wren Music Company

"Down on the Street"
Written by Iggy Pop & The Stooges
©Rhino Records

"Ring of Fire"
Written by Merle Kilgore & June Carter
©Painted Desert Music Corp.

Illustrations and Graphic Design by Stavros
Typeset in Garamond, Bleeding Cowboys, Scythe, Blue Highway,
Preston Script, & Marvelouz DSG

Printed in the United States of America

To the memory of my Father:

Rodney L. Cockrell
1946 - 2010

A Novel in Eight Parts

PART ONE:

Social Contract

In dreams the mind beholds its own immensity. What has been seen is seen again, and what has been heard is heard again. What has been felt in different places or faraway regions returns to the mind again. Seen and unseen, heard and unheard, felt and not felt, the mind sees all, since the mind is all.

-The Upanishads

Lin looked out over the tawdry lights of the city of lost angels. A million pinpricks that filled the moonlit night with brilliant noise. *There's no real dark anymore. The earth is crowded; guttersnipes and trash.* Breathing smoke, a tattooed dragon on the slag stone balcony, she pulled hard from the cigarette. Its glowing red tip briefly added to the twinkling as Santa Ana winds grabbed the ashen embers and ferried them through the streets like little glowing devils seeking fuel to ignite the desperate pith of the city. The cancer-stick was stale, at least three years old. Stuffed in a drawer the last time her thoughts fell on Dominique.

Dull bitterness, in mind and body, a steady ache; the smoky flavor sent spasms through her parasite in angry shudders. It despised the smoke and pushed it out of Lin's nostrils, screaming for blood. Her thin, white robe floated on a breath of air.

From up here, where all the smog gathered around this west coast haven, in her castle in the sky, her deluxe apartment far from the throttle and choke of the world, she could hear the chaos clashing below. Crushed under the soles of her bare, waxen feet, sounds drifted up to her. Called to her. Pleading for scant recognition, each lonely voice clamored in the din, each a single cell in the red tapestry proclaiming its mortality. A cacophony: pointless conversations, bleating car radios, hookers on their knees in alleys, police thrusting a robber to the ground, a baby's cry, a drug addict haggling price from the meager metal protection of an idling car, and an old man's last breath – all circulated into the drumming mood of this sanguine night.

One hundred years ago it wasn't like this. The town still held some glimmer of magic. Hell, it wasn't like this fifty years ago. But who's counting? Who even notices that the magic is gone, leaving in its wake the lingering remains of an extinguished black wick on an old dusty candle held waiting in the breast of one who still mourns its passing? Lin sighed. *This used to be such a fun town. Now there's just too many people breeding like a damn disease, infecting every living cell, spreading out like a well-fed cancer. Viral.*

Dreaming of bygone nights lit by the pale glamour of the same moon blinking down time after time, Lin placed her alabaster hands on the stone railing of the balcony terrace as she jettisoned the soft cotton cargo of the cigarette into the Santa Ana air. She watched it tumble and turn, spiraling to the fetid street below. The blood parasite within writhed along her spine and ribs. It caused her jungle tattoo to quiver into inked life. Toucans took flight across her back, into that blank spot where Lin was thinking of putting a city scene. *Nature vs Man. The epitome of progress.* Living on the Pacific Ring of Fire, nestled into the big shoulders of skyscrapers and movie stars, it only felt right to finish the elaborate design with a monument to the civilized state. *Not until Three Hundred, though. That'll be a seminal year. I will finish it then.*

Lin curled a finger around the hand-carved spirits glass, swishing the red liquid within. Her parasite, her Jadaraa Soo*, wound around her wrist, pushed into her fingertips with love, and cradled the cup. It was hungry. It wanted to go out into the illumined night and drive its tendril features into a warm body. It yearned, unceasingly, to be fulfilled. Lin opened her mouth and kissed the cup for a hefty dose. The parasite cringed at the blood's cold temperature. Withdrawing at first into its veiny legs, it receded back to its full girth, seeping throughout Lin's body like a wave on a beach. To the painted host, the chilled hemoglobin felt good against this warm, dry night. It cooled her stillborn flesh and fucked with the Jadaraa Soo. A 'lil kick for the bastard to make her smile. A not-so-brutal reminder to the beast within that she does what she likes despite what it wants. Lin didn't feel like going out tonight or calling The Service to have a Sanglant delivered. So, this cold plate would have to do for them both.

A few seconds after ingesting the blood, the veins of her captor began to purr like a giant, caged cat. Softly. Just softly, mimicking the jungle beast tattooed on her left calf. *After all, blood is blood.* That's all the thing wants: blood. An endless cycle of self-consumption from the day that Lin let it consume her vital fluids, let the vile thing be born in her body, let the blood become beast and beast become being; the Jadaraa Soo ended one life, and began another.

"Blood. Blood eats Blood. That is the rule. It is as simple as that."

That is what Dominique told her when Lin was on her knees before the woman. Before she uncorked the cylindrical crystal vial and ingested the black blood of Ornn Däm Mu. *His dark fluid. Bottled night.* Before she became what the world would call a vampire. Dominique said it was *"as simple as that"* in her soft voice with that perfect lilt. It sounded simple and easy, basic and one dimensional to Lin then. It was, after all, what she wanted – to be resurrected in the thrall of her lover's arms.

"Love?" she huffed and a scowl twisted her cheeks. *I deluded myself, believing in its utter simplicity with a child's naiveté, so that I could be with the gorgeous woman for all time. Live with her and her dark gift, endlessly affectionate and kind. Foolish!*

*See Lexicon on pg. 369 for assistance
with definitions and pronunciations.*

Lin ground a flat tooth against the veiny canine staring through the noise of the bright night. A small quiver shook her jungle leaves, uncoiled around her shoulder blades, and moved serpent-like through the base of her neck and down her spine to where the ram horns connected around William's name. Her Jadaraa Soo trembled and cracked the last cold element of digestion, like a yawn, and stretched Lin's muscles and fleshy tissue. It held her like a lover. *Like Dominique used to.* But the parasite is no lover! Most of the time it's just there. Out of mind. On autopilot, gliding through its urges with its limited slideshow of transmitted images from its old life, directing Lin when to feed. She hardly paid attention to it anymore. Blood memory dripping down the pedestal of time through her creeping veins. It's all become so ordinary. Mundane. Hard to recall when the epochal creature became like so much white noise to her being. *But, tonight…*tonight, it's as agitated as she is.

Perhaps, it too, knows.

Her hand wandered to the silver locket around her neck. It felt heavy. *My albatross from the desert.* Anxious fingers fidgeted with the antique jewelry as she glared out across the flat landscape of lights. Her vampiric veins pulled back from the surface of her skin as fingertips touched the silver ornament. They retreated from the vile mineral, deeper into the cavity of her digits, and coiled around the bones in her hand. It was a warm night. A dry night. The kind of night that told Lin that hidden in this city somewhere, someone was going to be murdered. *Feelings boiled to the surface in violent tempests.* She tasted it in the wind, distinct as rain. And, when one has lived as long as she had, one tends to pick up on the little things like that. Besides the thin sheer robe, decorative tattoos, and arid Santa Ana breeze, the locket was the only thing she wore to guard herself from the murderous intent roaming through the streets of this city of lost angels.

It feels like only yesterday we made the trip. Lin chuckled softly, letting her dead breath roll off her lips, and pulled another dose from the crystal chalice to numb her frustrating maw. *Another decade has passed* – in the blink of an eye, disappearing like candy. Time ate her heels with longing; Lin shook her foot. Time pushed on her shoulder blades and flitted through her legs; she felt like launching herself into the air beyond the balcony, floating weightless to the ground. Lin felt the veiny fingers of her Jadaraa Soo coil around her esophagus. It felt like bile racing up the back of her throat and she mashed her teeth hard against the bitter memory of desert winds and death. She didn't want it. *Not now!* She didn't want to go. *What's the point? What's the use?* The constant drumming of the city below pounded through

Lin's head like a hollow tube as she reached for another stale cigarette.

"Fuck," Lin uttered.

Her clumsy fingers, devoid of the puppet strings, having only left the confines of the silver locket a second ago, were useless tools. The Jadaraa Soo hadn't filled the little round digits of flesh yet and she knocked the old cigarettes off the banister. She watched them tumble and turn, spiral down... down. *Some lucky bum will find 'em.* Lin sighed. She knew it was time, but she didn't want to go.

Dominique will be expecting me to stop by. Lin pursed her lips after another refreshing repast. The two old lovers were colder than this red dish. Lin huffed and shook her head as she thought on it, adding her discord to the muffled cacophony and spit. She watched it tumble down too, weightless and falling, a red speck against the painted drama of Los Angeles. *Down. Like she was, on her knees, before the Persian beauty with her mouth opened. Waiting. Wanting. Willing. Down.* Lin watched the red spit fall all of the way. Then...

Splat!

Lin grinned and her mirth died. *Dominique?* Too much unsettled baggage with that one. Unpacked, wrinkled feelings left in their confines; stored in the dustbins of her soul. She recalled the flutter that filled her belly on that evening when she was first introduced to the Vam Pŷr. *Milan. 1772.* She was a guest of the Conte and Contessa De Luca, having vacationed with them throughout August. Linnet and the Conte's wife, Carmela, got on so well that she was encouraged to extend her stay throughout winter.

Conte Antonio De Luca was a business associate and friend of Linnet's father, and the two of them devised the arrangements to broaden the young lady's matrimonial opportunities that brought her to the noble home in the Austrian Duchy. A lovely girl, Linnet had long, coal black hair with eyes so bright they ignited a room. She had a slender European figure that had filled out nicely enough over the past few years, but for all of her charms her social prospects in England were less than advantageous. Reluctantly, Emerson Pevensey agreed to Carmela's wishes and his youngest daughter remained abroad with the hopes of landing a husband.

There were suitors in Italy for the highborn buxom broad and chiefly among them was a minister's son, Donatello Adessi. He was fair-haired and handsome, a seminary student who had left to join the Cavalry and achieved some small notoriety. Carmela took great joy in playing matchmaker with the lurid lass, thinking it her duty to find Linnet an apropos spouse since the young woman's own mother was several years dead. Carmela felt akin to the

English maid, having lost her only daughter to the cot death as an infant. She and Antonio had raised and wed boys, and having the young Pevensey girl with them had bridged that long-suffering gap in her soul.

The prodigy's return to Milan was the perfect excuse to show off the young lady and orchestrate a chance meeting with the fair-haired soldier. It was the twenty-sixth of December, and though the winter had been unexpectedly warm a spot of rain lingered in the heavens of the mostly starlit sky. Intermission was letting out and Carmela quickly pulled Linnet into the grand ballroom of the Teatro Regio Ducal as the Conte wandered over to the Faro table to test his luck with the cards.

"Only sixteen years old and he has already composed his third operetta." The Contessa explained, leading Linnet along. "One would think his father helped him with the mature nature of the theme, but I assure you, once you meet the young man his talent is most evident. He is quite capable, though I do prefer the soprano tone of the castrato to the natural pitch of Mrs. Amicis-Buonsolazzi. There is just something lacking in a woman's timbre.

Antonio and I were at the gala premiere of Mitridate, re di Ponto, two years ago to the day. The carnival was in town then – Oh you should have seen it Linnet! It was magnificent. You would have loved it. And, of course, we attended the festivities of Ferdinand's wedding last year when the Maestro performed his second opera." She leaned in and patted the young woman's hand. "Did you know, it was on the advice of the Conte that he obtained the commission?" Carmela shook her head and raised her eyebrows. "With the apparent age of the Archduke and the extraordinary gift of Herr Mozart it seemed an appropriate fit. Ah…" Her gaze swept the room. "This way my dear."

"Are we to meet him now?"

"Do not be silly. Only those of lesser breeding would introduce themselves during an interlude when everyone knows it is best after the encore; and besides, I told Antonio that we simply must entertain the young man this time around. It would be a travesty not to. He is going to speak with his father, Leopold, tonight and you can be introduced to him properly, tomorrow."

"Introduced to whom?" a young man asked as he clicked his heels and bowed at the two women turning to him.

"The Maestro," announced the Contessa. "You do recall my Goddaughter,

Linnet?"

"Yes, of course." He took Linnet's gloved hand in his. "How could I forget." He kissed her fingertips lightly and smiled.

Linnet blushed.

Donatello's eyes were untraditionally blue. Piercing. He stood out among the rank and file of olive tones and dark hair, dressed in his light gray uniform, a neatly pressed long-skirted overcoat, buttoned waistcoat, breeches, and thigh high leather gaiters. His sword decorated his side and he carried his hat. Politely, he inquired on Linnet's thoughts of the play. As she began to tell him the Contessa excused herself, wandering over to an elderly couple that Linnet had seen the De Lucas' favoring socially on previous engagements. In the crowded room, the young couple was left to their own devices.

"There were many lovely arias," Linnet professed.

"It is within a comfortable range." He offered her his arm. "Though I must confess I fear that I have not the experience to judge the work. This is only the second opera that I have attended."

"Then let us educate you on the form so that you may feel more at ease in the second half."

The couple took to wandering slowly around the room discussing the libretto and plot-driven recitatives within the first half of the opera. The hem of Linnet's blue silk taffeta gown silently drifted above the floor, pressing gently against the cotton fabric of her chemise as they walked. The soldier let her fill his ear as he kept his eyes on the shape of Linnet's mouth. He dreamed of kissing her lips. Neither one realized that they were being watched. As they neared the southern sloping staircase the Contessa returned at their elbows.

"Linnet? There is someone I'd like you to meet." Both turned around. "This is the Madame De'Paul. She is a spirited woman. Maintains her *own* fleet of ships. Can you believe that? A female Quartermaster. When I heard I simply knew that I had to introduce the two of you."

Donatello clicked his heels and bowed his head slightly. "Madame."

A corner of the pale stranger's mouth slightly upturned toward the young man and Carmela continued her introduction, sounding the young man's achievements, more for Linnet's ear than for the fascination of her unique guest. Linnet was immediately struck by the beauty of the lush burgundy gown worn by the woman. It was cut to the French letter with a brocade intricately crafted to match the veil that fell from the elaborate headdress and crossed the woman's eyes. Linnet felt the room tilt, absorbing into the splendid rose of the gown and the sublime nature of the woman's bare shoulders. The subtle curve of her neck, the cut of her jawbone, and her powdered tan skin was captivating. The man at Linnet's arm faded as the woman smiled, warmly, at her. Full and bright. The English lass became flush in the moment, and slowly the Contessa's high-pitched bray took hold of her ears once again.

"...That is just what we were discussing earlier. It is an age of youth that compels us. More and more the young are advancing in areas traditionally occupied by more seasoned gentry. Take for example our beloved composer, which I was just informing Linnet priory..."

"The splendor of youth," broke the soft, perfect voice of Madame De'Paul, "is not in one's age, but in the timbre of one's heart." She placed a hand to the maid's rosy cheek. "Wouldn't you agree?"

Linnet felt an intense draw upon her touch and leaned into the bowl of the woman's palm, sensing the majestic weight of her eyes through the thin concealment. Butterflies lifted in her stomach and she clanged the bottom of the antique chalice against the stone railing of her balcony and exhaled, bitterly.

The Vam Pŷr was an idea clothed in flesh that pulsated a burning desire, addled Lin's young mind in an endorphin rush that beat back her fear, canceled every cautionary warning and dived off the cliff to sprout wings like an angel and soar the heavens as a god. Lin knew it. Felt it with every beating pulse of her veiny parasite. *I am corrupted by the civilized state.* The manicured glitz of a million pinpricks of light danced within her hardened soul. She was spiraling down, a tattooed dragon curling into the void behind her breastplate.

Splat!

Lin yanked the locket's chain tight against the back of her neck. Her parasite whined as it fled from the silver. *That dark candle of the city in my memory was never lit. There is no afterglow from sex. Happily ever after never happens. The same putrid stenches of the streets below still invade my nostrils like Nazis, just like they did fifty years ago. That little girl who dreamed is dead, consumed in the fire of her passions. Everything. Every moment. It's all a bitter, acid-tongued lie. Every act of life, living, screaming in this mess of noise, lost in the throttle and choke, to attain the slightest glimmer of some divine destiny for its self is but a foolhardy pursuit. There is no truth to the hopes one breeds within the mind. Everything is shit. Everything decays. It is the way of things. It's how the universe is spun. Everything recycles into its own quiet death. Yet…*

I'm still here…and Dominique will expect me to stop by for a visit.

The veiny blood parasite wove through Lin's fine muscles, curled around porous bones, and slithered under her flesh as it caressed its host with a devoted embrace. Resilient, its tough interior hide was the pulley and the wheel of the symbiotic meat machine. Through its will the vampire drank again from the hand carved crystal, replenishing her death over and over. Lin's death, like the universe, was constantly expanding. She, a willing victim in the everlasting freak show that had become her flimsy excuse of a life, trapped like a hostage in her own corium castle.

Lin let the antique locket go. It plummeted against the hard valley of her chest, knocking against the painted lock of her sealed, winged heart. Dark crimson veins spread out like a ripple under her inked skin, travelling deeper behind her breastplate, away from the vile silver. *My own private albatross. An heirloom from a time of harsh, bitter winds and dirt so thick I could swim through the sky.* It was a time of savage loss, and death so replete in its appetite that it still haunted the vampire to this day. The locket was the scale in her soul, tipping with the weight of her passions. The memory of her dark mistress burned just as brightly as the garish lit horizon of Los Angeles. It was the commencement of the journey, the crack in the impenetrable wall behind her eyes, the augury to behold.

Lin peered down and saw a lucky vagabond pick up her fallen, stale cigarettes. *The universe is smiling down at him tonight.* The taste of murder filled Lin's mouth and she gagged on the dust-collected reflections, forcing them back down her gullet with another swallow of cold hemoglobin and days of yore.

Another decade has passed. It's time.

Z let Manuel drop the e-pill onto her outstretched tongue. It wasn't the first time that he saw her teeth, the protruding fang-like canines. He thought her obsession with vampires was a bit trendy. Blasé even. He never considered the possibility that they weren't retrofitted Halloween memorabilia. It never really crossed his mind to ask her about them either.

The two of 'em were always too busy dancing, or drinking; partying until dawn. *Everyone's a freak*, thought Manuel. *Who am I to judge? The only thing that mattered was…getting freaky.*

Manuel could handle freaks. He fit right in; snuggled like a tight-fitting condom. From his close-cropped, blond dyed hair with its tufts of color shooting out in long plumes like a peacock all the way down to his platform shoes and leather underwear, which he hoped some classic built sailor was going to be pulling off with his teeth tonight. Manuel always felt at home with the misfits. It was all the normal people that worried him. All the Regular Joes, the common shopper folk, out there turning the world into a shithole, building a better bomb; they were the ones that were going to kill him. They were the ones that just didn't get it.

The lights of the disco gyrated like a spinning top. A heavy bass pulse triturated. Z couldn't stop moving, even if she wanted too. And she didn't want to. She felt the tablet of ecstasy melt on her tongue and felt the angry twinge of pain from her blood parasite within. She figured the thing should have been used to her excessive alcohol and drug use by now. *Fuck it if it wasn't.* She fed it. And she fed it well. All the in-between moments were hers and hers to do with as she damned well pleased.

It pleased Z to dance. To dance among the crushing throng of the living, wrapped in their luxurious warmth, their collective heat. She moved among them soaking up the vivacious energy. She let them press upon her a vivid impression of living so that she could become like a Phoenix, an imitation of life, and rise to the top of the heap a perfected being of the curse, a reflecting pool of radiant, effervescent energy, bristling on the edge of possibility. So that she could dive into this humid sea of flesh without losing control. Z twirled. She let the music take her like a lover, place its hands on her hips, and drive her inhibitions wild. Her teeth twittered on edge. She was on the verge of some pure movement that her limbs had never concocted before.

That guy to my left, behind the chatty brunette, is still watching me. Z loved it when someone watched her. She was a divine spectacle of brilliance. A thunderclap of god light. *They should all fuckin' watch me! Z's amazing. They should bow down to my every whim. Submit to my devilish merriment. Bow. Bow. Bow.* Her thoughts echoed to the beat as she cut her sway into a sensual, syncopated rhythm. Her hands slowly traversed the landscape of her undulating body. She imagined that she knew what Eve felt like on the night that she seduced Adam. She felt her snake coiling along the curves of her spine, down past the small of her back, to those two luscious mounds of her perfectly formed ass. Z embraced the stranger's eyes as if they were kisses.

She reveled in the fact that if he was going to watch her…then she was damn sure gonna give him a show!

Ryan Silva watched the girl dance. She slithered up her spine and cast her eyes at him as if they were dice. This wasn't the first time that he'd seen her at the club. But it was the first time that she appeared to have noticed him. It usually didn't take that long for a girl to notice Ryan. Getting girls to notice him wasn't his problem. With his strong build, square jaw, Hollywood good looks, and confident swagger, it was usually getting rid of the girls that was the problem. And it was a problem that Ryan Silva didn't put much mind to. Once he was done with 'em, that was that.

Yet, this one…

This one had a vibe like a razor and a cut along her curves that made his chest ache. This one had been coming to his club, walkin' his turf for the past three weeks and hadn't paid him any due until now. He'd seen her dancing and talking with that Mexican faggot. Ryan even knew her drink. Whiskey. *A strong tongue for such a lithe female. Bet she'd taste like a freshly plucked peach, she would. The girl has done her best to stay off my radar. That is… until now.* Once Ryan Silva had a girl in his sight…well…that never was his problem.

Mindy wandered up to him and stroked her silver-ring-fingered hand through Ryan's chiseled blond hair and kissed him hello hard on the mouth. He bedded her tongue with his and stared into her heavy eyeliner eyes.

"Thought you'd show at Mickey's. Me and Theresa scored and been looking for you."

"Mickey's a fucker."

"True enough. Whatchya doin?"

At Ryan's silence she followed his line of sight.

"Wanna jet?"

"Maybe later."

Mindy watched the skank twitch her skinny ass to the beat like a dog in heat. She knew Ryan's appetite and could tell this girl fit the bill, that her long legs filled his eyes. She could taste his want in their kiss. She also knew that no woman truly satisfied his itch. Ryan's heart was a wanderer, never steady, never settled, searching. Mindy accepted that fact about him a long time ago. She didn't take offense to him eyeing the skinny twat. Ryan was a great lay – *definitely not the marrying type*. And he probably never would be.

"Mmmm," Mindy whispered softly into his ear. "You want that?"

He looked at her for a moment. "You in a giving mood?

"It could be arranged."

Mindy's smile slid across her face, a worm spinning silk, as she slid her jacket off. Exposing her bare shoulders to the gyrating lights she handed her soft leather coat to Theresa, whom Ryan had not even noticed until now. Then, without another word, Mindy turned toward the crowded dance floor. She moved with a slow, smiling walk and entered the writhing horde as if she owned the joint. Her fine, svelte body cut a luscious path toward the intoxicating punk and Ryan leveled his gaze drawing them both in. He breathed slowly. Mindy slithered up to her and the mysterious, vibrant punk fell instantly into the girl's tempting, revolving curves. Ryan's lips parted. His tongue felt thick and wet as he watched them, dancing together.

Z sensed the stranger's eyes on her as she approached. She could feel her heat and smell the liquor of her sex as she smoothed up beside her. She was pretty. Petite. Had a licentious grin as she wiggled her hips. She wanted to play, like a kitty cat with a ball of yarn. Z immediately fell into her and the room disappeared.

The vampire placed her hands on the girl's rolling hips and their bodies leveled, in sync with each other, in sync with the down beat of the rhythm, and in sync with the live girl's steady, thumping heart. It was the drum that the surrendering bloodsucker danced to and the beat that finally made Z's blood parasite, her Jadaraa Soo, crave the lewd girl's flush, pink flesh and mellow out. Her sensual rhythm made Z's beast lull into the calm of hunting. Made it open and receptive like a sponge. It was exactly what Z needed.

Within a few seconds the full effects of the ecstasy hit the prancing addict harder than a wave. It hit her like a feather hammer to the temple, like she was touching the sun or falling in love for the very first time. The heat off every sweat-laden body twisting and turning on the dance floor dazzled her hypersensitivity. She was drunk on their flesh. Smashed to the collective rhythm of their circulatory systems. Inebriated from the stink of their panting breaths. She was infused with their life force.

This moment…

This moment was better than blood. Better than sex. Better than anything else she could recall. *Happiness in a little, white pill.* From across the room Z could detect the palpitating flutter of her voyeur's heart racing as he swallowed hard his searing desire.

1774. London, England.

The painter told her not to move. Linnet had been sitting with a stiff back for the better part of the afternoon. Her corset dug deep into the soft, malleable flesh under her arms and pressed in to the bones of her ribs. He told her, warned her in fact, on a few occasions, to remain still. Yet, she required further prodding and had learned all too well the sharp consequences of both Master Reynolds's tongue and lash if she did not obey.

Her eyes frequently wandered to the timepiece on his worktable. Evening approached, and with it, her Dark Mistress. The light was already beginning to wane in the Englishman's studio. Yet he continued to work, mixing the pungent linseed oil and powdered pigments with the flat slap of a knife and swirl of a brush, distilling real life onto the flat canvas. This meant, of course, that Linnet had to remain sitting no matter how excruciating it became. A woman's life, after all, was one of sacrifice and patience, waiting on one man or another.

"This is the way of things," her Mother had told her on several occasions as they performed the duties of the house when she was growing up.

This general temperament was clearly expressed in Master Reynolds's sister, Frances, as she hurried about the studio, a quiet church mouse, lighting the candles and removing the uneaten plates of food, prepared so lovingly, from her brother's bench. Craftsman and Form had been talking vigorously throughout the day. Rousseau's treatise, Du Contrat Social, was the coat rack from which the day's conversation hung and the reason Joshua had neglected to eat the bread, fruit, and cheeses his sister had brought him earlier. In the week that Linnet had been posing for the painter, this subtle forsaking to nourish his body proved regular. He was quite a gregarious man and often held no quarter with his tongue. Having found it intriguing that the young girl and her benefactress had only recently arrived from Paris to pose for him, the artist took it upon himself to impress upon the young maid his vast knowledge of all things French.

Being a child of Britannia herself, born in the little town of Abingdon, merely twenty leagues and a day's ride from where she posed, Linnet found Sir Joshua Reynolds's ideas on their southern neighbor quite stimulating, if not archaic. He was a learned man replete with all of the finery that his education and station in life afforded him, and often told Linnet so. Frances barely looked upon her at all, and Linnet wondered if he beat her too if she displeased him. It did not miss her fair judgement that like most men, from either the English Isle or the adopted home of her Mistress, that he preferred the company of a woman who lent her ear to modern ideas more so than her lip.

"There is no duality about it," the artist interrupted. "The nature of man is untainted, of singular purpose, when left to the devices God intended for him."

"Devotion is not an inherent trait but a learned…"

"It is when Man divines for himself this social contract of cities and marketplaces, building upon the grand schemes and ideas of his youth, that he looses all aspects of his intended purpose." The celebrated artist continued, unaware of the protestations escaping out of the young woman's mouth. "He at once gives into vice, corruption roots, the heart becomes callous, and is forced to compromise his spirit. Thereby transforming God's free man into the chained slave of his own social will."

"Surely," Linnet interjected, raising her feminine voice to match Reynolds's heightened vibrato, "the heart of Man still retains some semblance, some origin of its true nature, or all societies would fall to ruin instantly."

"That, my dear girl, is the precise reason why it succeeds. If you are to learn anything, outside of the humdrum of your age, then let it, at least, be that modern man thrives in corruption."

"But, what of the noble pursuits?"

"Mere gallivanting vanity," he said, dismissing the question with a wave of his pigment stained hand.

"Surely, Sir, that cannot be said of the arts and sciences? You of all people should easily see how man's nobility far exceeds his cruelty."

"Ha!" He alighted. "Even more so!"

Linnet switched her tact and suggested that her fair sex possessed purity and grace if man did not. The artist dismissed these notions away with the flutter of his occupational hand as he stood defiantly behind his easel, gruffly complaining. He would hear none of it. Reynolds rebuked her naïveté, claiming that females were without a doubt the more cunning and conniving members of the species. Their actions far surpassed any atrocities perpetrated by any man written about in the annals of history. He pointed to Eve's perpetual damnation of their race and Helena's destruction of Troy as proof of woman's curse upon man's erudite souls.

"Perhaps, if women were allowed to govern themselves," Linnet shot back, "instead of being mere pageantry of a man's estate, held as possessions, then such ideas of conquest would not permeate our culture."

The artist scoffed.

Linnet was ablaze in defense of her sex and rallied to continue. "If women governed alongside men, as equals, a better judgement and temperance might be cast in the affairs of state and the true natural order of things could be preserved in civilized company."

Though, before all of the words finished tumbling out of Linnet's small, well-shaped mouth the painter's laughter filled his studio. She drew quiet, slighted by Master Reynolds's jeers. Pride felt hot within her bodice, but she held her tongue. It was, after all, a woman's role to practice a triage of graces. The fair sex knew what men could not practice: *patient espionage sustained polite social circles where arrogance paraded proudly and with gall.*

Lin culled the frilly thoughts from her raven's nest. She hadn't considered the painting in such a long time and proposed that it, along with all her other relics, was still sequestered in the darken hovels of the attic off Rue Abel, collecting dust. She looked up to the bright orb flowing down blue lines of gray and could think of nothing else now, but her. *Dominique.* Her Jaci, her moon spirit shining down. *Thought I was liberated in your arms.*

"You don't know shit about anything!" Yelled the vampire at the moon. "You were never there."

She buried her tired complaint into the bottom of her cup, draining the vessel of its red bounty. Gloom filled her eyes as she looked to the street below. *Been here too long. Nothing's new. Nothing.* Her Jadaraa Soo slid under her breasts and squeezed her ribcage. It writhed over her stomach, wanting more. As she stepped away from the balcony's ledge to refill her cup she vaguely heard the bum below asking every passerby if they had a light. *Seems the universe is not without its dull retractions.* Lin snickered as she stepped into the kitchen, thinking of Queen Elizabeth I. All that power at her fingertips, a commander of vast armies who struggled and fought to actualize her royal destiny, and yet, she could take no lover into her bed without spoiling the runes of her country. Fate twisted. Fate connived. *What good is a fucking cigarette if you don't have a lighter?* Fate withheld.

You left me to build your Council.

Lin punched in the code on the refrigerator's electronic lock and opened the huge stainless steel door when she heard the little pop. The quiet of the house moved around her. Comfortable, standing in the hard glow of the cold machine's inner sanctum, she filled her cup with the ruby contents in the plastic container. The Jadaraa Soo planted itself deeper within Lin's body away from the utility light. Wind blew the hem of the curtains through the opened patio door softly grazing the glass. She tried to recall the face of the pockmarked artist, but it was lost to the channels of time. The staunch sound of his voice remained, however. Barking in the back of her mind for her to sit up, drilling her to *Turn this way, and that way, hold your breath like so...*

Lin chuckled quietly and a police siren erupted several blocks away when she had returned to her nightly perch. On the street below, the vagabond was gone and the pariah's gaze fell onto the taillights of cars, drawing red lines, like blood, through the veins of the city. Lin felt the road tug at her gut and she closed her eyes. Pulling on the silver ornament, gritting her teeth against the corrupt thoughts from the desert she turned her musings on her father. *You never listened either. You, a capitalist and I a reformer.* Lin smiled and lifted her cup to the moon to toast his bones.

For all his labors, Emerson Pevensey was never so near to the King of England than when his progeny sat all those long hours for the celebrated artist. Emerson toiled, the son of a lesser nobleman, trading textiles and goods for His Majesty in Oxford. Though the Pevensey house was a respected establishment of the realm, he was never invited to Court.

Seven Pevensey ladies were ushered out from under the broom and married by the time Linnet was born. She was the eighth daughter to a family that could sustain no male heir. Emerson's only son, Linnet's only brother, William, died of consumption the year before her birth. Though she never knew the young Pevensey master, the weight of his death bore down upon her throughout her upbringing. William was the silent opponent she reckoned with daily. He was the ghost that haunted her Mother's tears and framed her Father's chin with firm anger. William usurped their kind love. William was the length of the yardstick to which Linnet could never live up to. She grew up feeling like a disappointment simply because she was the child that had survived, and was yet another female.

The affect of femininity permeated the Pevensey clan, and on more than one occasion Linnet overheard her Father claim that his ruin was due to a house of women. Ironically, it would be a woman that stole his only remaining child at the twilight of his years and took her to the regal courts of princes and kings; kept her embroiled in a rich circle of lords and ladies whereas he could not.

The mutated odors of the concrete sea drifted past her nose as she drank from the spirits glass in memory of a man long since dead. She could not recall his face either. The cerebral labyrinth in her head was as pockmarked and faded as the artist's features. It did not escape Lin's fine attention that she'd been spending more and more time of late thinking about days gone by, staying indoors, refusing to dress, sequestered away from the constant crush of life. It's always a precursor to the tune of spinning tires. Lost admiration for the now, counting years, wanting nothing more than sullen isolation, buried above the city's lights to take the time, *the god awful time*, reminding herself as to why.

Lin sighed, bowed her head, and let the desert memories take her. *They'd come sooner or later, anyways.* But she began to shake. A vile torment of flesh rocking her, Lin felt queasy. It wasn't a spasm from the enigmatic creature, so she boxed the desert back up choosing instead to fall on the ease and cold forgotten comfort of the painting.

1774. London, England.

Linnet's bruised ego settled into her quiet knowing. The timepiece on Joshua's table was accurate and sure. Dusk had descended. Her Dark Mistress knew freedom the likes of which Master Reynolds could scarcely comprehend. *Nay! Even artistically conceive of as possible!* His frail ramblings on the nature of good and evil in Man were ineffectual at best. He boasted to stand on the forefront of modern thinking, but was, in fact, a dullard to the true mechanics of the world. Linnet had been shown things that the master artist would envy. He prattled on. He liked the sound of his own voice. Linnet listened, raised on the good graces of a silent tongue, until she tried an altogether different track. Her statement was simple and clear.

"Love is man's salvation from himself."

Unexpectedly, her well-timed retort bore strange fruit. It caused Master Reynolds to reflect. He fell silent as he worked, leaving only the rough grate of the coarse horsehair brush to speak in his defense. This silence, in and of itself, surprised the eighth lady of the House of Pevensey. It was not an unfamiliar truth in a Christian kingdom torn by Catholics and Protestants, but the painter was caught dumbstruck, and after a time, the instrument that he worked with earnest diligence paused on the rough fibers of the canvas. Master Reynolds returned from his internal communion and boasted loudly through the room as if cracking a whip.

"Love is merely a temporary delusional state by which the species can propagate."

Typical. The inert model rolled her eyes. *The thinking of men halted at the swollen, protruding belly of a woman producing kith. Obviously, the harder sex was stunted by nature.*

"Love is just a socially accepted opiate," pressed Master Reynolds with renewed verve, "that deludes the heart more than it could *ever* care for it. I have personally witnessed more unions of marriage destroyed by the ideals of love or from awakening from the Love State than the institution could scarcely claim success." He stepped out from the protection of his easel, "which is a travesty when one considers that the house of marriage is an empty house, whose walls are the vessel of duty, where no seed of love could ever flourish or take root, because, the institution itself is in motion."

Linnet's mind pulled her dead brother from the grave and felt the stagnancy and foul silence that she had grown up with. It was the ballast of despair. "In motion, Sir? It no more resembles motion than a statue in the garden. A marriage grows docile and inevitably dull by its lack of movement."

"It is a constant engagement," the Artist explained. "It produces dependency, instead of freedom, and requires obedient reliability in the submissive pursuits of husbandry."

"I beg to differ, Sir!" Linnet challenged with a snort, raising her voice as she spoke. "A woman is far more submissive in role and character than a man in the institution of marriage. And she is without entitlement! Managing the affairs of a household usually fall upon her broad shoulders while the man busies himself with matters of State, drinking, and war."

Master Reynolds cackled a braying, loud laugh. He loved the girl's passion. She challenged him. Whereas so few patrons dared to even comment, she freely spoke her mind. Frances cut a well-worn path through her brother's studio behind them.

"Joshua," she said quietly invading. "The Lady De'Paul has arrived. Should I make room for her and Ms. Pangbourn at the table this evening?"

The pock-faced man shook his head as he spoke. "That will not be necessary. I am meeting with the Academy tonight."

"Very well. I will send her up."

He wiped his hands on a soiled rag and Linnet finally relaxed her posture. Her spine bore fruit baskets of pain. Her joints were cramped and weary from inactivity. It hurt to stand. Yet, it all seemed worthwhile once the young maid spied her Dark Mistress drifting into the darkened room.

Dominique De'Paul was elegant and graceful. The epitome of mystique and beauty. She seemed to glide on a cushion of air. The hems of her petticoat and gown did not whisper as she walked. A five-foot seven-inch Persian goddess from the Timurid Dynasty, she was shrouded in the allure of night. Her skin was the timbre of unspun silk and Linnet was sure that the woman's water swayed the tide of the moon itself. In Linnet's doe eyes Dominique was perfection personified. Beauty unbridled. Upon seeing her illustrious inamorata the model felt a fire ignite in her belly.

The benefactress was attired simply in a French, striped Poplin dress and quilted petticoat. The stomacher was gracefully refined and immediately caught the eye, which traveled upward toward the exposed neckline that cradled the olive bleached complexion of the woman's once dark skin. The Lady De'Paul wore a fetching hat that matched the delicate Poplin and a thin veil fell about her face and neck, obscuring the Persian woman's pallor. The soft tones of Dominique's skin balanced the colors cascading through the dress.

However, it was the woman standing in the center of the room who held Dominique's attention. Regally garbed in a shell pink calash and white silk de chine brocade dress of hand-splayed floral bouquets, Linnet watched as the master artist delicately took Dominique's hand in his, pressing her gloved fingers to his lips. Dominique's eyes lingered on the warm face of her paramour as her Jadaraa Soo reached up to the plum of the man's mouth.

Master Reynolds was careful not to transfer any oils from his paints onto the Lady's glove. Such an accident would be indecent and rude. He so cherished the generosity of his patrons. As he greeted her graciously, he complimented on the charm and wit of his model for her Lady's pleasure.

"Yes," Dominique agreed. "My dear Linnet is quite outspoken. It is a trait, I wish, you could capture on canvas."

Reynolds humbly alleged his lack of talent at such a task and offered poetic endorsement that the vibrant energy of their conversations infused each stroke of his brush. The pale angel was not listening to him, though. She drew silently closer to the canvas on the painter's easel, captivated by the image that was emerging from the thick, earthen stench of paint.

"Sir Reynolds, you surprise me each day with your progress."

"Thank you. The subject makes it easy."

How does flattery fit into the uncivilized state? Linnet scoffed. *It is no natural accommodation of the soul!*

"You are without equal." Dominique's eyes followed every line and curve of the portrait of her darling Linnet.

"My lady flatters me," he boasted to Linnet with his usual social grace. "But, do tell me Lady De'Paul, when will you allow me to discern the complexities of your complexion on canvas? I am ever so intrigued. Your pallor pales even the glow of the moon."

"Monsieur," Dominique smiled. "It is I who am flattered. But I am afraid that only my fair Linnet will have the joy of your brush. We are set to travel immediately after you are done."

"Oh." His hope was crestfallen. "Where to?"

"The arrangements are still being finalized. My condition hampers me from securing the details of our affairs, and with Linnet sitting for you this past week, I fear I have allowed a good many things to lapse in her absence. I do so depend upon her abilities." She cast a warm smile on her consort and began to meander through the studio. "My holdings in Brazil need attention. I believe we will be travelling there by the rise of the next full moon." She stopped and turned to the man. "Do you think you will have completed the painting by then?"

"Of course," he offered as he crossed the gulf between them. "More than enough time. Though, I feel it is a grave injustice to the world that I will not have the chance to immortalize such a raving beauty as yourself."

Dominique slightly curtseyed, feigning an embarrassed blush.

"At least allow me to paint you from my memory," urged the Artist.

"As long as it is of your memory and not some creature that walks the earth, then let it be so."

Master Reynolds chuckled. "You are too fetching a woman to be so innocuous to your glamour. But, if my memory is all that there is to serve, then it will have to be enough."

"I am sure that it will."

A natural silence descended upon them. Reynolds took the opportunity to take his leave and wash up for the evening, saying he would find Frances to escort them out. The air of pretense in the room vanished with the master painter and the ladies fell casually into each other's comfort.

"So you are set on São Paulo then?" Linnet moved slowly toward her mistress.

"Yes," the enigmatic woman said, resolute. "I think it best considering all the mess Peter Plogojowitz had caused. It's turned into quite the frenzy with Arnuad, you know." She raised her eyebrows, thoughtfully, and turned toward Joshua's table. "Europe is steadily declining and I fear another war is on the horizon. There is nothing more tedious than another war." She picked up an unused brush and placed it within a jar that held many other implements of the artist's craft. "There also has been no reply from Isabela. I fear the worse."

Dominique moved to the window as something caught her eye beyond the tempered glass. Linnet was confused by her mistress's worry over the Habsburg incident. It had all happened decades before Linnet's own birth, yet the former Vam Pŷr was still on edge about it. In the early days of their relationship Dominique went so far as to make Linnet read the 1732 Chief Medical Examiner's Report, Visum et Repertum, and Dom Augustine Calmet's 1746 Treatise on Vampires and Revenants. Her strained voice still stained her ears.

"It is important for you to know for yourself," she told Linnet at her house off Rue Abel. "How the world is shaping us into being. We must be careful. You can not risk exposing what I am going to share with you to others. It is for you and you alone. There are elements at large that would destroy everything if our existence came to light."

Dominique explained that it was the Dalam Kha'Shiya J'in that created the debacle in East Prussia and the Habsburg Monarchy when they tried to reinstate the slave trade. They failed, of course, which was why events had lit a candle to the nocturnal habits of creatures like Linnet's Dark Mistress. The incident sparked fear in the common folk. It became lore. Recent German poetics from Ossenfelder and Burger capitalized off this burgeoning spark and reclaimed a foothold in people's minds in the form of macabre literature.

The former blood slave often criticized the works of these writers. Yet, while managing the sale of some properties a few months ago Linnet found financial documents that allied the Vam Pỹr as a secret contributor to the publication of Gottfried's Lenore. *If Dominique were truly so vexed by public opinion and afraid of its backlash, then why would she seek to have Gottfried's work published? His quaint vampire tale had mass appeal. Why not just kill him and be done with it?*

Linnet watched the woman peering out of the window. There was obviously something that she was keeping from her. Though, the young maid could scarcely find a reason to ask. Her Lady's habits and secrets were her own vessels to keep. Since she had joined her Dark Mistress's entourage nothing had been what it had seemed and Linnet figured that nothing ever would. It was like looking at the world anew. "I was hoping we might venture to Asia this time."

"No," Dominique said, peering out of the thick ripples of glass. "Emperor Kangxi said he'd have my head if I ever stepped foot in China again." She turned and smiled at her consort. "I have grown rather fond of my hat collection."

"But, that was nearly a hundred years ago…"

"The memory of an imperial decree is very long, my dear…and besides," she said pausing, indicating outside of the window with a nod of her head, "I believe we have more pressing company that must first be attended to."

Linnet pulled alongside Dominique and gazed out of the spiral pane of glass to the street below. Standing under the frail wax-and-oil-light of a street lamp stood a tall Moorish fellow. He was as black as the night itself and offset the conservative, light beige suit he wore. Thick grooved scars decorated his face. He was striking under the canopy of stars.

Dominique gazed down too. Not at the tall African gentleman who looked up at them in the window, but to the swinging curve of Linnet's tempting flesh and the protruding vein that bulged in the bend of her neck. The woman's visceral warmth caressed the cold flesh of the Vam Pŷr's face. It excited the parasite within. The thing shimmered throughout Dominique's limbs as the copper scent of Linnet's blood coursed like a racing river through her body.

Just then, the front door to the secure penthouse burst wide open and an explosion of noise, jocularity, and laughter intruded upon the quiet memories of the eighth daughter to the House of Pevensey. Lin turned around and saw Z leading a ragtag collection of oddly dressed freaks through the house. The obtruding vamp drank from an opened bottle of Vodka, held tightly in her left hand as she escorted the pack toward the accessible entrance to the terrace.

The ruckus ceased in snickering hurdles as Z stopped short, her gaze falling all over Lin's frame in the opened doorway. The men behind the punk fell into her lanky stance and the women, oblivious, stepped on the heels of the men. None of them, saved for the peacock-dressed Mexican, had Lin met before. They all gawked at the splendid absence of clothing with which the pale, statuesque woman greeted them. Lin fused her sudden anger to her Jadaraa Soo and bid the veiny creature to recede deeper under her flesh.

High above the throttle and choke of the city of lost angels, alit like a pale tower jutting from the smog on the balcony, Lin slowly collected the sheer, white robe about her waist with unabashed dignity. Z looked up Lin's tattoo-clad body with heavy eyes, drinking the voluptuous vamp in as she pulled a steady swig from the clear glass Vodka bottle. Lin felt exposed. Raw. Her thin robe did little to conceal that which had already been seen.

"Hi honey," the inebriated vampire said. "I'm home."

PART TWO:

Bloodlines & Serenades

Two paths lie in front of man.
Pondering on them, the wise man chooses
the path of joy; the fool takes the path of pleasure.

-The Upanishads

1774. London, England.

"The story my grandfather's father told him was passed down from all those who had gone before. Many generations remembered so that we would never forget *why* we fight.

The sun was low in the sky as the three hunters, Aadii, Bala, and Suma returned home with a gazelle on their backs. As the sun dipped below the treetops, the hunters reached a part of the Savannah where the grasses grew tall. Aadii took the gazelle from Bala, who had been shouldering the kill. They laughed and spoke of the hunt, of their wives and children, of stories their elders spoke, as they waded through the towering grass toward the Marula trees on the far side. The three hunters thought to camp and build a fire under the protection of the trees and return to the village the following morning. But as they neared the outlying grove, wild beasts did set upon them.

A flash of white. The rustling of movement. A beast leapt from one of the Marula trees and landed on Bala who was behind the others. He was taken under. The grass came alive with his screams as Suma ran toward him. Even as his death cries filled the dawning night, the edge of the tall grass began to flap in the direction of Aadii. He cried out for Suma to come help him. He had given Bala his spear when he had taken the burden of the gazelle. Bala's cries grew faint. There was little Suma could do. So he turned to help his friend. Aadii dropped the gazelle, thinking that whatever it was attacking them would go for the fresh meat instead of him. But it did not.

Suma ran toward Aadii, shrieking to scare the unseen animal as the bending sedge revealed its path. He threw one of his spears, hoping for a good clean hit. He missed and the beast kept coming. As Suma reached Aadii he brought up his last spear, but the beast was faster and ripped Aadii from the sea of green spraying the young man's blood across Suma's face. When the hunter opened his eyes…there was quiet. Both of his friends were gone and the grass swayed ever so gently in a light, cool breeze.

Suma knew the beasts were still there. He could not run, for if he did, he might run straight into them. He had to wait for them to make their move. The beasts were in no hurry to reveal themselves and time passed. They were like no other animal the hunters had faced before. There was a savage cunning in their attack. Each advance brought their prey closer to them, instead of driving it away. Suma was frightened. He had just lost two brothers of the tribe in the blink of an eye and had scarcely seen a thing. He began sweating despite the coolness of the night air. He gripped the thin wooden shaft of his spear tighter as his eyes swept across the tops of the tranquil grass. Any second now they would make their move and he would know the face of death.

Again, it was sudden. One after the other bound from their cover toward him. In the light of the rising moon, as they glided through the air, he could now see his attackers as clear as day. Their bodies shone with a white luminescence. Their long arms reached out toward him, not like an animal, but like a man. Their thick legs were tucked up to their chests, ready to pounce. Their bodies were hairless and each had a mane of long black hair that flowed out from the tops of their heads. They roared...and it thundered as if the heavens itself had cracked. Suma had never seen men like these before, though he had heard tales of them. Far to the east where the forest still remained thick against the encroaching desert, a tribe of celestial beings was said to reside. They were known as Malaika. But Suma had never heard tales of how the Malaika hunted men.

When the beasts sprang from the brush, giving away their locations and the location they intended to be, Suma took off in the opposite direction away from them. He was the fastest runner of the three hunters and had gained a good distance from the beasts by the time they landed and began pursuit. But, alas, Suma was not as fast as the Malaika. They soon gained on him. He turned 'round just as one of them leapt at him. He brought his spear up and impaled the beast through the belly as it landed on top of him. Both he and the injured Malaika went rolling through the grass, tumbling over one another. Suma did not waste the advantage he had gained and quickly got to his feet and continued to run. He ran as fast as he could. He called on all the gods to carry him, to give him the legs of a cheetah and protect him from the white angels. When he reached the edge of the grasslands he looked back. The other Malaika had broken chase. Perhaps to take care of their injured brother or perhaps because they had enough food from their hunt, or perhaps because they had made the point that they wanted to make. Whatever the reason, Suma ran.

He ran all of the way back to the village and told everyone what he had seen and what had happened. Our elders took counsel with Suma and it was agreed. We would no longer hunt on the lands past the sea of grass. There were good grounds to the south and in the plains over the western mountain. We would hunt in those places more and perhaps the Malaika would leave us in peace as they had done until then. But it was not to be. Soon, the Malaika began raiding our villages and stealing our loved ones, taking them into the dark night never to be seen again."

Nsia Bah leaned against the high back of the chair pausing in his tale to give his empty teacup to Laurel, the servant girl, and to take stock of his audience, the Vam Pŷr Dominique De'Paul and her consort, Linnet Pangbourn. Linnet asked him how he had come to be a warrior in his tribe, and so the tale unfurled under the candlelight and hospitality of the Lady De'Paul. He was sure that Dominique already knew this story. She had been silent during their time together, letting her consort navigate the conversation. Perhaps his great grandfather, Musa Bah, told it to her, or she had heard it from some other source. Nsia had no doubt that she knew a great deal about his people and the beasts of which his tale told. Her countenance spoke of a deeper wisdom. Her eyes were calculating and he did not like it when she looked at him. None the less, he was delighted to see that the young maid, Linnet, was quite taken by the tale and enjoyed his telling of it.

"For many generations," Nsia concluded, "we were preyed upon by the Malaika at night and they became to be called the Kula Malaika, Shaytan Khalid. Which in your tongue translates as cannibal angel, devil immortal." He turned to the silent and composed Vam Pŷr and nodded. "You know them as Omjadda, others to the North and East have called them Annunaki."

"That is correct," Dominique affirmed, finally breaking her lengthy quiet.

"They are our waking nightmare." Nsia said, looking down. "So the responsibility fell to my family and the family of four others to stay behind and protect the village from the Kula Malaika so that our people could cross the mountain to live safely within the center of the great mother. For over nine hundred generations we have defended ourselves and protected all that we love from these beasts that have hunted us, stolen our women, and sought to disrupt the evolution of Man."

"Suma was your ancestor," Linnet said realizing the breadth of the man's lineage.

Nsia Bah nodded his head. "Yes."

"Can I offer you another cup of tea?"

Linnet signaled Laurel to come remove her cup, uneaten biscuits, spoon, and saucer. The tall, slender African, sharply dressed in a beige suit cut in the style of the Colonies, declined a second cup of the lady's hospitality.

"Then do please tell me Mr. Bah," inquired Linnet, speaking in a cordial tone, sitting up on the haunches of her gown, "how again you came to be putting a knife to my throat?"

It had happened earlier that night, as she and Dominique were leaving the residence of the artist, Sir Joshua Reynolds. Dominique had seen the tall African from the window of Master Reynolds's studio and thought it best to flush the young man out by walking home instead of taking the carriage.

He was gone from the dimming light of the wax-and-oil street lamp by the time they had turned the corner. It wasn't until they had left Leicester Square and crossed over the bridge that he made himself known to them, bursting from the mouth of a shadowed alley. He grabbed Linnet by the waist and pulled her to him pressing the blade of a very sharp knife to the exposed flesh of the young woman's throat. She did not scream.

Dominique heard the sole of the man's shoe scrape against the ground just before he grabbed her darling Linnet. She stood firm and let the young maid be taken. She had expected some kind of move like this from the stranger, and knew that the best way to find out what he wanted was to ensnare him with willing and eager bait.

"I will not hurt her if I do not have to," the dark foreigner shouted in English coated in the thick rhythm of his accent. "Fizza, I only wish to talk. Fizza, please?"

The man called Dominique by her true name. So few people had ever learned it and none were alive today, she had thought. A fragrant bloom of blood entered the air. It was obvious. The man's trembling hand had nicked the neck of her sweet Linnet. Dominique knew the bouquet of her lady's life essence intimately and the beast within quivered at the smell.

The African stranger waited for the elegant, pale woman to speak. His breathing bounced on his lips as his eyes tuned from the woman in his arms to the one in the street.

"And what if I do not wish to talk?" Dominique muttered casually, slowly moving to the man's right as she lifted the veil from her face.

She wanted him to see the steadiness in her eyes and the bleached complexion of her once darkened skin. She wanted him to see the Jadaraa Soo, her horrible veiny blood parasite, as it crisscrossed and mapped her decaying features. She wanted him to see the sharp tips of her fangs and know that he had found that which he sought: *a Vam Pÿr*. He had found a freed Slave of the People to the East. He had found the once prized property of the Rom Pŷr J'in and the Tien Däm Mu J'in. She was a swallower of souls. The erudite rebel who sparked a war to end the Eras of Slavery. She was the destroyer of Ornn Däm Mu, the once proud J'in Ankh of the Tien Däm Mu J'in. She was a creature of darkest night, born from the blood of his enemy. His idle threat and violent introduction did little to impress.

"I will kill her and you will be without your human consort." Nsia announced, pressing the tip of his blade harder against Linnet's throat.

"Then what would stop me from killing you?"

He did not know. His eyes darted wildly. It was obvious that he did not want to hurt the girl. Yet she was the only leverage he had. Nsia merely thought to grab Fizza's attention and stake his claim for an audience. He was confident in his great grandfather's words and was not prepared to grapple with the Vam Pŷr alone.

He gazed upon her ashen features, sickened by the pallor of death, which framed her countenance, and noticed that her shoulders were relaxed. Ready. The young man did the only thing left to him. He yielded the field and released the Lady Pangbourn. He immediately apologized and offered Linnet his handkerchief to wipe off the blood from her neck where he'd nicked her delicate white skin. It was not his intention to shed blood. The Lady Pangbourn did not accept his handkerchief. Instead, she wiped the blood off with her finger and offered it to her dark mistress without ever taking her eyes off of him. She was strong willed; Nsia could see why Fizza had chosen the woman as her consort.

Dominique sucked the still warm blood off Linnet's finger and took position behind her. Nsia Bah introduced himself, asked their forgiveness, and repeated that he needed to speak with Fizza. He explained that his great grandfather, Musa Bah, had told him when he was a young boy, that if ever there came a day that the tribe had cause to reach out to the old slaves of the Kula Malaika, then he should seek out the one known as Dominique in the European lands, and that he should call her Fizza.

"Tell me of your business with my Lady and I will consider whether or not it is pertinent to her attention."

Nsia's eyes sought out the taller, pale figure. Her silence was resolute. He lowered his head. "For several years now, I have gained education in this country and in France to learn modern things and the way of the western world. Many more years have I spent tracking you down."

He lifted his head and peered at Dominique. "Now, may I speak *to you* on behalf of my people about our growing concerns with the Vam Pŷr race? I beg you, these are not matters that go lightly or should be shared outdoors where those in earshot might overhear."

Linnet mulled over the man's request. He was slender, yet his body was hard with muscle. He was charismatic and appeared honest and sincere, and besides, as Dominique had previously explained when they set out on their venturous walk, *"Nothing will come of this stranger unless we present ourselves as willing."*

So she agreed that they would meet with him, and he joined them on their walk to the carriage, waiting just a few blocks away. During the ride Linnet inquired about his European education and they fell quickly into casual conversation.

It was when they retired to the lounge of one of Dominique's modest English homes that Nsia and the Lady Pangbourn partook of tea and biscuits and Nsia revealed how his family became warriors against the Omjadda.

Dominique had mentioned the ancient species to Linnet on only a few occasions, instructing her on the intricacies of their blood, rival power disputes, clan affiliations, and little else. Linnet had never met one. She was intrigued by Nsia's description and by the name he had called them: *Kula Malaika, Shaytan Khalid. Cannibal Angel, Devil Immortal.*

Linnet knew only what Dominique wanted her to know concerning her former masters, and had gleaned that her Lady was still tormented by the centuries she spent as their slave, working the mines in the dark underbelly of the earth. Linnet burned to know more about those dark days of her Mistress's life, but the young maid did not press the Vam Pŷr. She knew it would come when it was meant to come. She was, after all, a patient woman, just as her Mother raised her to be. It was one of the graces for which Dominique praised her on many occasions.

Now, after the pleasantries had been established Linnet dove into the meat of the matter, truly wishing she could hear more from this charming black man. His presence was captivating. But she knew her Lady's habits, and it was late.

"There is a growing concern among my people," he said with the utmost tact, speaking directly to his silent, pale host, "that the freed Vam population has grown unruly and too large in number, and that their dependence on living blood is causing hysteria in many cities, towns, and villages, just as it did in the old days of the Kula Malaika. I have been sent to assess the level of threat and to see if we should expand our hunts to include your kind as well." He waited for the ghost-colored woman to interject, but she only regarded him with an even, blank stare. "And, if you will allow," he added, "we would like to know all that you know of the Tien Däm Mu, Rom Pŷr, and Dalam Kha'Shiya J'ins."

There was a long silence before Dominique spoke. Linnet could feel the tension in the room, waiting for the sound of her Mistress's tongue.

"In the old days, the tribe did not have a problem cutting down Vam and Omjadda alike during their assaults. Why now is there a question of battle tactics?"

"In the old days, as you have said, Vam were used as shields and guards for Omjadda strongholds. They did their Masters' bidding. Ever since the days of slavery ended, however, fewer Vam protect Omjadda and we have had little cause to hunt them. As I know you are aware, my great grandfather had a lot to do with our neutrality toward your species. We have not sought out contact until now. Initially, we were curious to see how the Vam would integrate into human society. Though, lately with rumors and vicious tales circulating we have come to question our position on the matter."

"Then you are aware that the Dalam Kha'Shiya tried to reinstate the Vam Pŷr legacy and failed."

"That is what we have heard. But you cannot deny that there are members of your kind who seek for themselves all that the Omjadda once had. You yourself have attained wealth and prominence, wielding great power in both the human and Omjadda worlds. You state no allegiance to the Tien Däm Mu, yet you are their reigning J'in Ankh. How then can you claim that the Vam are neutral?"

"Since when is a Lady's prominence cause for doubt?" fired Linnet. "Are we, too, expected to cower behind the men of our species…"

Dominique raised her hand to silence her maid. Linnet turned to her Dark Mistress, hot in her defense.

"Please, excuse my Linnet. She means well."

Nsia nodded to the Vam Pŷr and eased back in his seat. It was odd for him to hear the Lady Pangbourn speak as if she were already a night creature, steeped in a grim sallowness with the blood of his enemy flushing through her veins. He wondered what kind of sway the freed slave of the Omjadda had on the young girl.

"Tell me, Nsia," asked Dominique, "how did Musa die?"

He stammered, failing to see the relevance of such an inquiry. "It is of no concern."

The wheelhouse of the Vam Pŷr churned silently, staring at the man. She raised the tips of her fingers, placing them together at the base of her chin. Moments squeezed by as night dripped away behind thick Polynesian curtains.

"Truly, I can think of nothing more relevant."

It was too human a thought, too human in its need to know. Nsia peered into the milky eyes of the creature before him and saw the red velum of the veiny Jadaraa Soo. She had fed on the black blood of the Ancients. It had metamorphosed her once human countenance into a shade of night. Her prying into his family's bloodline made him angry.

"The same blood that courses through the veins of the Omjadda resides in you now." Nsia stood, close to shouting. "What makes you any different from my enemy? Tell me. Tell me now!"

Quietly, Dominique folded her hands in her lap. Linnet's heart raced watching the gentleman suddenly flare like a fire's crackling. She found herself excited by his rash outbreak, and was surprised.

"Did not Musa tell you how he came to know me?"

It was a simple, innocuous question and tempered the young man's anger with calm. "No. He did not."

Dominique stood, lifting her eyes to the hot, flushed African. Linnet watched them both, only now understanding the huge weight that pressed down on her Mistress. Dominique's concerns over the Habsburg horror were justified; news of it had spread to the one place she did not want it known. The African Tribe were legendary hunters of the Omjadda. They could spell destruction for the symbiont race if they chose to wage war. A war between the species would plunge the world into terror, exposing not just Dominique and her kind, but the ancient species as well.

Strange, how this seemingly non-alarming man in a smart suit brought with him a tide of fury and the promise of death. Linnet was on the edge of her seat, her breath held tightly in her bodice, waiting for her

Lady to seal their fate.

"Then it is not for me to inform you. Though," Dominique inhaled a large, soft breath, "I still want to know how he passed."

"In his sleep." Nsia failed to see why it mattered. "He died in his sleep on an August day."

"Good." Dominique nodded her head, slowly. "That is a good death."

Linnet noticed a slight smile in the corners of her Lady's mouth. She was as confused by Dominique's position as was Nsia.

"He was a warrior," the proud man added. "He died past his prime. We are bred for the hunt. There was nothing *good* about it."

Dominique stiffened and graciously extended her hand to the young man. "Come tomorrow night and we will continue our discussion then."

Nsia Bah looked at the Vam Pŷr's outstretched hand like it was a dead rat. Anger rode his breath, tempered in a holstered box, as Linnet stood, gently fanning out the folds of her gown. Begrudgingly, he took the gloved hand of his host and bowed. Thanking them both for their hospitality, he affirmed that he would join them tomorrow evening.

Before Nsia departed he took Linnet's ungloved hand in his strong, black fingers, and befitting a man of manners, gently kissed her delicate digits. The young maiden became aroused by a sudden, radiant heat, her breath caught in the eaves of her throat. Dominique watched the change in her consort with growing interest. It took Linnet a minute to compose herself before she sent Laurel to inform the Carriage Driver to escort Mr. Bah to his hotel. Both ladies watched the handsome backside of the man as he left the room.

"He is an exciting young man, is he not?" Dominique eyed the aroused young maid.

"Yes. Fascinating."

Linnet's mind tarried on the evening, whirled in a rush of thoughts and flushed emotions. Eventually, one tenet in particular claimed center stage. "How did you come to know his great grandfather?"

Dominique smiled, remembering. "He was my lover."

Linnet was shocked. Words flittered from her mouth like sparrows, silent and small, disappearing. Dominique removed her gloves and drew closer to her maid. She placed a supple hand upon Linnet's shoulder, encircling the young woman, and absorbed the titillating bloom of heat, which rose off of her in bristling urgency.

"Tell me, Linnet," she paused, drinking up the woman's eyes, "have you ever been with a man?"

"No. I have not."

"You should," Dominique advised. "It can be a wonderful experience with the right man."

"Was Mr. Bah such a man?"

The loom of Dominique's memories ignited and she grinned. Crossing the room, the enigmatic shade left the question open to burn within her young maid.

"Have Laurel come to my chambers," Dominique ordered with the unpleasant dispassion of a lady of business. "It will be morning soon and I have yet to feed."

A knot staled in Linnet's bodice. Her brow curled and the word jutted forth. "No."

Linnet's response caused her Lady to pause in the room. Dominique turned as the eighth daughter of the House of Pevensey crossed the carpeted expanse and stood a few inches from her. Her consort's tone was resolute and her posture determined.

"Be with me this evening." Linnet mimicked the business-like dispassion of her Lady, belying the tender need in the hole of her heart. "I will send Laurel to bed."

Dominique, whom the strong and charming African had called Fizza, looked at the incalculable girl. Her smile broadened with impregnable charm. The tantalizing scent of Linnet's piqued flesh rose up between them, stirring palpable waves. It was as delicious as blood. Dominique did not want to forestall Linnet's passion. She took her consort's hand in hers. The live girl's flesh was hot and ready. Instinctually, the Vam Pŷr knew that this evening would not be like the others. More and more they had been growing closer. Feedings were becoming nothing more than a reason to shed clothing and embrace. The dark haired woman was steadily melting the cold strings of her ill-gotten heart and each time she gazed upon Linnet's radiant features her own lust flamed. Soon, she would not be able to resist the young girl's spell. Linnet squeezed Dominique's fingers as they left the artfully decorated room with none but the walls as their witness.

What gets into the head of that girl sometimes?! This was the last thing Lin needed right now, a house full of foolish riffraff. Their callous merriment intruded on her senses. Lin stared hatefully into the cold glare of the mirror, watching her necklace dangle back and forth like a pendulum. It was time. She should get going. Tune up the Caddy. Pack a dufflebag of clothes, a cooler of blood, and hit the road.

And, yet...

Lin slid a pair of faded jeans over fresh Hello Kitty undies and fell into the hard soles of her boots. She exited her bedchambers wearing frank disgust. She wanted to piss on everyone's parade, and kick 'em all, specially that tweaked vampire bitch, out of her building. And to think, Zia's crazy inhibitions used to be alluring. Her wild nature. Her carefree what-the-fuck. Her Howdy Doody anytime. Now, it was just another annoying trait in a growing laundry list of unpleasant attributes filling the spaces between them like rotting fruit. Time definitely had a way of wearing down the best intentions, eroding the beautiful to rust.

Lin felt as worn as a pointy rock that had been smoothed to a pebble on the beach.

When did I first loose interest in Zia's huck-a-buck beauty and reckless charm? The eighties? That self-styled ego boom of loud shirts, excess, and hidden wars. No, that decade was murder. Would have felt like a hundred years if Z wasn't there pulling me out of my funk. Sometime before that. Before the punk rock seventies and her return to music. Perhaps, it was the humdrum of the 60's as all the humans ran around injecting themselves with a wanderlust of chemicals, murder, and ideas. Perhaps, it was throughout it all...rising and falling like a wave, an ebb and flow of good times mingling with bad.

Lin sighed. *What did it matter?*

All the stupid people were gathered at her place anyway. *Pitch a fit or paint the town red?* Lin grimaced at her reflection in the mirror and drew down her veins. As she stepped through the portal, closing the door, she locked eyes with a handsome man. His crystal blue eyes swept Lin's clothed form like a broom. He smiled. Lin passed him, heading down the smoke-filled hall, letting her gaze linger on his beautiful body.

Music thrummed through her place like it was a discotheque. Lin passed the Mexican Peacock, whom she had run into a few other times while out clubbing with Z. He was making out with some bloke up against the wall. Lin laughed. *The bounty of flesh was appetite.* Lust perpetually devoured in nature's gaping maw. She spied her imprudent housemate dancing with two slender vixens in the livingroom. One of them saw Lin approach and began dancing toward her like a charmed snake, wiggling her empty womb as if it were an "Open For Business" sign.

Lin poked the wannabe Madonna between the soft flesh of the eyes and plastered her up against the wall, out of her way. The scowl on the woman's face cheered Lin up a bit. At least it was a start. The other girl moved out of Lin's way as she neared the dancing vampire. Z gave Lin a down-home smile, plying that charm of hers. Lin's stare was hard and cold. She felt like punching Z in the neck. Instead she grabbed the half-empty bottle of Vodka and overturned it on her lips. The cruel rush of alcohol filled her gullet as the parasite screamed bitter agony for her ears alone. The slacked crazed monkeys guffawed at Lin's excess, and there was Z leading the charge, howling into the gutter shutters of the moon. As Lin pulled the bottle from her mouth, panting from the sting of wet abuse, Z leaned into Lin's warm glow smiling like a Cheshire Cat.

"Here," she said, holding up a little, white pill. "You're gonna love this."

In her torrid two hundred and fifty-six years, Lin had done many things on impulse, on a dare, raging against the universe and time. But now wasn't one of those moments. She looked from Zia's tiny gift to her tweaked housemate and wondered again where the empty envelope of time had slipped to. How they both had wrangled themselves into this hackneyed moment of disappointment. Lin's eyes were stolid. She'd dealt with boredom the likes of which suicide queens could scarcely dream about in the folds of their homely journals. She'd imbibed endless parties that only those who walked by the moon's light could even remember. She'd done things that she was happy with and did 'em again and again until they lost their glamour, and then she'd done things that she wished she could forget. Horrid things. The kinds of things that psychopaths dream about in the folds of *their* homely journals. The kinds of things that never go away, recurring like nightmares without end. The kinds of things that forced one to chase after them for far longer than they should have because forgiveness was too easy a reality to remember. The kinds of things that housed themselves, after the horror, in the simplest of artifacts. The kinds of things that were bound, say, in a necklace.

As Lin pulled the silver locket taut against its chain, she built the exact size and shape of the little white pill in her gray matter. She didn't want to laugh. She didn't want to cry. She didn't even want to exact revenge anymore on Z for spoiling her quiet evening. She felt nothing, a blunt numbness circumnavigating her skin. Even her constant companion, her Jadaraa Soo, that ever present essence of Omjadda blood, binding her up like a marionette, now seemed far away and distant like undiscovered galaxies. Feeling nothing, Lin opened her trap.

Z placed the tiny gift on the vampire's tongue and excitedly watched as Lin closed her mouth around it. Grinning from ear to ear, Z let the hands of the music grab her hips. She began swaying, side-to-side, in front of the vampire becoming a ticking clock, a snake charmer. Lin curled her tongue around the small, white obstacle and her Jadaraa Soo whined. She swallowed and thought of Dominique again. *She'll expect me to stop by for a visit when I make the journey. It's become ritual.* Lin rubbed her tongue against the backside of her right fang as the pound from the music entered her.

Z howled at the ceiling as the first wave of ecstasy hit Lin like a soft shell. The room tilted. She was amazed at how well Z buried all the muck of living a drawn-out life behind a veil of excess and celebration. Lin wondered if Z even knew that it was time again. She shook her head, trying to let go of the velvet press of ego. Visions of bloody corpses and grotesque smiles invaded her high. Lin gritted her teeth. The noise of the sandstorm invaded ear canals. She reached out blindly, grabbed the dancing vampire, and pulled her close.

Z saw the tangled look on Lin's tightly wound bonnet. *She's cracking.* "Dance it out," Z hollered through the din. "Just let it go. You're here now."

The wild punk embraced her flatmate, helping her to move to the rhythm and the beat, helping her to vent all the muck through the porous channels of her flesh. Though inside, Z knew it was time too. She'd known it for quite awhile. She felt the stroke of the timepiece falling; felt fate's itchy fingers, its grabby hands hunting them down. *Always hunting them down.* She knew Lin felt time like the crosshairs on a sniper's rifle. Z did everything in her power to ignore it. To push it down and bury it under the most obscure, extreme recklessness she could think of. Z howled at the ceiling again and smiled until Lin followed suit. The raven haired beauty needed prodding, she needed to be poked and coerced into a good time. *She needed distraction, full tilt wonder-rama!* Her affair with the necklace was dragging her down. Z could see it. Slowly, Lin let go and began to dance, and Z allowed every fiber of her being to revel in the glorified bliss of delusion.

1774. London, England.

Dominique's bite marks were healed, yet Linnet still felt the scars. She lay in bed, staring at the ceiling, listening to the wind and rains pummel the house. Usually, she went to see Nsia after the bite marks had healed, but he saw them today. Along her breasts, it was glaringly obvious to the African warrior; Linnet was still her Mistress's jewel. The mournful look on his face as he grazed his fingers over the half-healed puncture wounds, his downcast eyes, he moved to get dressed until Linnet stopped him. He begged her to leave Dominique. She did not know what to say. Pulling Nsia closer, Linnet held his jaw, forcing him to look into the canvas of her eyes as he entered her. She wanted him to avoid her rendered flesh, have nothing between them, and hold his mahogany gaze upon her features. He was not as gentle as he had previously been. Linnet did not care. She wanted him. Whole and alive, inside of her, she wanted *him*. Her body spoke where her mind could not.

The Vam Pŷr's consort did not bathe before returning home or apply any perfume. Nsia's musk was all over her. Their mingled sweats and his seed in her sex were pungent to Dominique. Linnet wore it like a shield, brazen against her skin. She knew the Vam Pŷr would not touch her with Nsia's scent all over her. Aching and lonely in the quiet shell of her bed, Linnet did not want to push away her Dark Mistress, nor did she want to lose Nsia. She curled around the cavity of hurt in her gut, embroiled in the stink of their union, and cried.

"Open yourself to him." Dominique had told Linnet as they lay together that afternoon after they first met the dark-skinned man. "Embrace his character as you would my own. Entreat him to the munificence of your charms. Let him learn to see you as I do. Let him come to love you as I do."

A month later and Linnet still did not understand why Dominique encouraged the affair between them when their own love was blossoming. The invisible scars from her Lady's bites stung, not by the embrace of the kiss that she enjoyed, but by the words that the Persian woman spoke. Even after all of this time together the young girl's good innocence led her to feel betrayed. At first Linnet did not see how she could open herself to a man who had professed an interest and a desire to see the destruction of her dark mistress and all those of her kind. Nor did she understand how to embrace Nsia's character with the same heart, body, and mind that longed for and embraced the Vam Pŷr. It had made no sense. Linnet felt that what Dominique asked of her pulled her loyalties in opposite directions. Yet, she complied, and now Linnet did not know how to close herself off from him.

The feel of his Nembo under the touch of her thumb was encased within her hands as she held his face. Her body ached for Nsia in much of the same way that it ached for Dominique. Her heart was torn. *Why would Dominique want that?* She heard a creak from a floorboard in the hallway, beyond her door, and wondered if her Lady was coming to see her. She lifted up. Soft light flittered under the door, but the entranceway remained intact. Closed. Linnet sighed and laid her head back down on the pillow, recalling the evening when Nsia returned to their home as promised.

It was not what he had expected. Instead of the freed blood slave of the Omjadda greeting him in the marble foyer, Linnet was there, occupying his evening. Nsia's displeasure was obvious. The young maid smiled against his grim countenance and invited him to walk with her in the garden. A waxen moon alighted the night sky and the roses were in bloom. The hem of her gown shuffled softly along the stone walkway, rubbing gently against the leaves of flowers and bushes that spilled out of their boxes. After sitting most of the day for Master Reynolds, being on her feet felt exceptionally good.

"Should I take offense that you are not pleased to see me again or are you generally dower when in the company of a woman?"

Nsia apologized. "The matter I bring to Fizza's attention is most important and not for the likes of her understudy."

Linnet smiled. "I can assure you that I am well versed in the issues of which you speak and am more than just her second." She stopped walking and turned to the man. "My Lady trusts me emphatically. So I suggest that you do, as well." Linnet watched him as his eyes searched the easements of the house, surrounding the garden. "Are you looking for something in particular, Mr. Bah?"

A distrustful glance fell on her. "She watches us."

"I can assure that we are quite alone," said Linnet, offering him a warm grin. "As I have said, Dominique had business to attend too and will be away for most of the evening. Laurel is accompanying her. So, it is just you and I, good sir."

He held his ground, sizing the woman up. Her affluent manner suggested good breeding. "She is a clever adversary."

"Mr. Bah, Dominique is not your adversary." She crossed to him and slipped her arm under his and gently nudged him to walk. "May I be frank with you?"

"Yes. Please."

"I am here of my own accord. I manage my Lady's affairs and holdings. I was not coerced or enthralled to abandon my previous life for the company of the Vam Pŷr. I chose to be here; and I am free to leave when-so-ever I choose. I love Dominique. And I would do anything to protect her." She turned to Nsia and their walking fell stagnant. "Except, she has instructed me to be forth-right and open to all of your concerns and inquires. This goes against my nature to protect that which I love. But it is my Lady's bidding and I am here to serve. So, rest confidently that your position has Dominique's full attention and appreciation. As well as my own. We have nothing to hide."

Linnet took his arm again and they sauntered through the garden. The African warrior warmed to the young woman. Her strength flooded him and he respected her candor. Chambering his distrust, Nsia eased away from the serious nature of their engagement, asking about the history of the house. Halfway around the opened splendor, Linnet changed her tack.

"Are you hungry?" She did not wait for the man to respond. "I am famished."

She escorted him to the Library and exited to the kitchen to retrieve the delicate morsels that Laurel had prepared earlier. Roasted pheasant covered in mulberry jam. A half loaf of caraway seeded bread. Wine. A block of Port Salut cheese. When she returned to the book depository Nsia had found an intriguing manuscript.

She did not wait for the man and dug in, inviting him to eat at his leisure. He tarried over the handwritten tome, ever so careful with its brittle and artistic pages. The smell of ancient paper and ink excited the warrior. Linnet watched him. He showed his true heart, a student of knowledge in the world.

"Tell me of your home."

"It is on the eastern slope of the Great Mother, seventy miles north of Dakar and the Atlantic Ocean, along a dry Savanna." He set the old book down and took up his wine as Linnet carved a breast for him." It is only a day's trek from where my people originally dwelt."

"When was the last time you were there?"

"Oh…it has been some time. My studies have taken me far, and tracking you and Fizza had become a yearly occupation."

"I apologize." Linnet sat her empty plate on the dinner tray. "We move around a lot. It could not have been easy for you."

He smiled politely, sat, and took up his fork.

"Do you miss it?"

"Yes." He shook his head. "I have been away for many years. I hope to return soon."

"Then we will have to see that you do." Linnet stood and crossed to the bookshelves on the far wall. "The hearth of friends and family should never go unattended for too long." She scoured the books for one in particular. "Are you married?"

Nsia nearly choked on the tidbit of meat he was swallowing. "No."

"A lover or someone at home, perhaps, that waits for you?"

He was the one that was meant to discover. Yet this young woman kept him on his toes, firing questions at him faster than he could count.

"And what of you?" He was determined to gain an upper hand. "I already know your real name is not Pangbourn. You are not from London, but you are English. Where is *your* home? Your family?"

Linnet grinned, her back to the African man, continuing to locate the artifact. "True. My name is not Pangbourn. It is an alias." She found the rare hand-bound collected pages and carried them to where Nsia sat eating his pheasant. "I come from a good house of modest standing. So, in the business of my Lady I have chosen a name that would not attract attention to my family. My mother passed when I was just a girl. My father is a merchant for His Majesty and my sisters are well married. And since your business concerns my Lady, and not myself, the whereabouts of my home and surname are of no matter."

She handed him the book.

"This is Omjadda," he uttered upon opening it. The sharp wit of the woman constantly surprised him. "Where did you get this?"

"From the library of Ornn Däm Mu before Dominique burned it to the ground."

"Huh…"

He thumbed through its old pages. They were made from huge, pressed fan leaves, thick and stiff. In some areas of the book the ancient ink was faded to only a dull indentation of what it once was.

"Can you read Omjadda?"

"Some," he answered with his head bent into the crack of the unique document. "This is very old. The language has evolved since the production of this book. It would take some time to decipher."

"Dominique invites you to peruse her collection. But the books must remain on the grounds, in the Library."

"Yes…yes, of course." His mind turned on the primitive scrawl. "See this passage here…" he said pointing to a small phrase. Linnet sat beside him on the sofa. "This, I believe, speaks of the Lanz Gur Mae. It was their home, before the intrusion of Mar, and the climate shift that eventually forced them to migrate."

The look on Linnet's face told him that she did not understand, so he explained. Before the history of his people's songs, before the birth of man, and the encroaching desert of Nsia's homeland the Malaika thrived in a lush, immense forest where the leaves were so thick and the jungle so deep that the sun could not penetrate. This was the home of the Omjadda. This was the Lanz Gur Mae.

Nsia crossed to a map that hung on the wall. His strong, brown fingers caressed the Gambia and Senegal regions of Africa, indicating the whole protruding nipple of the Dark Continent and described the ancient homelands with such vivid detail that Linnet imagined him living there and walking through its dense foliage. The young, buxom beauty found it hard to take her eyes off the speaker's mouth. The way he framed his words. The way his lips perched on a thought and dived into details. Linnet was captivated.

"It was the Rom Pŷr J'in that began the ritual to create blood slaves," explained Nsia. "Rom Pŷr means 'Strong People of the East', and in the dawn of time when the world was still young and the Jad Tree first gave root, they were known as the Om Pŷr. Here," he indicated a page in the ancient book. "They were known then as the Sound from the East." He read ahead of his explanation and Linnet followed his finger as it traversed down the page. "Across the Onnaki River lived the Asli Pyl, First People of the West. As the legend tells, the two J'ins came to war against one another and the J'in Ankhs, rulers, of each clan came to the banks of the Onnak to face one another. Their armies stood ready, all brothers under Layal…"

"Who or what is Layal?"

"Their Goddess." Nsia turned to Linnet. She hung over his shoulder and her scent flooded him. "Has not Dominique told you of Layal?"

Linnet shook her head.

"The Omjadda worshipped the moon. Their culture was based around it. Layal is the female aspect, the sister/mother to her brother/father Rah, the Sun God." He could not stop thinking about the shape of Linnet's lips. "They…they feared him. He was like the Christian's version of the Devil."

"Oh." Linnet pulled back, thinking, intoxicated by his heat.

Slowly, Nsia recovered, surprised at the sudden warmth that the room had taken on. "It says here that instead of shedding precious däm, blood, each J'in Ankh recognized the power and authority of the other. The leader of The Sound called out to his brother and named him Jadda, which…by this text means father/mother…place of original source. The leader of The People saw strength in his brother from this…" He read a little further, struggling with the ancient text. "I think it says that both kings left the banks of the Onnaki River by placing their troubles in some kind of sacrificial boat, to float away in the waters." He shrugged, not very confident in his hasty translation. "From that day forward The Sound became the Rom Pŷr J'in and The People became the Jadda Asli J'in." He smiled. "My people only knew of the Malaika when they were divided into four distinct clans, during the dying days of their homelands. This book," he closed it and laid his hand upon it gently, "is without comparison."

Linnet found it hard to imagine that the creatures from this story, so regal and wise, were the same ones that had tormented her Mistress. That they could have sunk so low to where they changed her into a blood sucking revenant and terrorized Nsia's people, forcing them to flee for their lives.

"What happened to them?" she asked.

"The climate changed. It destroyed their paradise and forced them to begin hunting men. My ancestors have peaceful tales of the white devils before the Great Migration when the Kula Malaika referred to us as the Children of Marh.

"The children of…?"

"Marh. It is what they first called us. People. Though, the use of the term has changed over time. The 'h' has been dropped and all reference to the phrase's origins are lost. Perhaps, I will find its beginning here, in your books. But, it will take some time."

Linnet stood. "I do not wish to keep you from your home longer than necessary."

Nsia drew his face up, thinking. He set the book on the sofa and rose. "Before the dawn of Man, the Omjadda flourished and were many. In the beginning, the world was made for them and they worshipped the moon and the water. But God spoke. He sent man to walk upon the Earth, to balance the day. He caused the waters in the Onnak to dry up and the forests of the Lanz Gur Mae to die. The Kula Malaika chose their fate when they raided our village.

Five warriors were chosen. Each were picked for their speed, their agility, their skill, stamina, and strength. They were chosen to stay behind with their families to protect the village as it moved deeper into the Great Mother. Hundreds of generations upon generations, my ancestors bred and trained to do one thing. Survive. To survive among the terror and the beasts of night that preyed upon the flesh of Mar. To survive and protect our home and our right so that our spear would be the dominant force in the world. We did not choose this fight. We merely accept its burden."

"Then, by your own admission your fight is not with my Lady and her people."

Nsia smirked. "We will see."

Night after night, Linnet did her Mistress's bidding, talking with the African until the small hours of dawn. Sometimes, they sojourned until morning, gathered in the Library or traversed the garden paths.

Occasionally, the conversation would be particular to the habits of the Vam Pŷr and Omjadda J'ins. For these matters Linnet took instruction from Dominique and it placed a cumbersome toll upon her engagements with the artist, Sir Joshua Reynolds.

By day, instead of posing for the portrait that Dominique had commissioned, Linnet apprised her of all that she and Nsia had said and done the night before. Dominique was intently fascinated. Asking, at what first seemed like ridiculous questions, about how she felt towards the handsome tribesman. No small amount of detail was too insignificant to go examined. Often their daylight retreats far outlasted the hours of the day, wrapping the two of them, Vam Pŷr and consort, in exhilarating exchanges. All of the curiosities that burned in Linnet's core began to find answers and she found herself with very little time to sleep, never wanting to leave the embrace of the ashen lady.

Many times Laurel was sent with a dispatch requesting the Master's pardon in the Lady Pangbourn's absence. On one such delivery Master Reynolds fumed at the indignity of being stood up so often that he commanded Laurel to return wearing Lady Pangbourn's dress, so he could, at least, attend to the detail of the brocade.

At first, Linnet could not wait to embroil herself within the catacombs of Dominique's chambers and press upon the symbiont her evening with Nsia. Her Dark Mistress lavished the woman when they were together and Linnet felt as if all the stars in heaven were brightly lit, standing in the sky for her. The task of indulging Mr. Bah became nothing more than a reason to spend more time with Dominique. It was the division bell between one elating affair and the other.

Laurel was in the kitchen as Dominique lit the candelabra in the lounge. Linnet fastened the curtains over the window and pulled out a tin of rolling papers and Turkish tobacco. She set about rolling cigarettes for the three of them.

"He wanted confirmation last night that it was Ornn's blood that you used to transform mortal men and women."

Linnet licked the edge of the thin paper.

"What did you tell him?"

"I told him that it was. Though, I was not sure. That particular detail was not clearly expressed." She set the wrinkled cigarette down. "Was I correct?"

"Yes." Dominique blew out the wooden matchstick. "Did he ask about my involvement as J'in Ankh of the Tien Däm Mu?"

"No. He is satisfied that your role is perfunctory. He called you a dilo fata ketu." She thought about it. "I believe that is what he said."

Dominique raised her eyebrows and pursed her lips. "Do not trust his satisfaction, Linnet. He is waiting."

The consort sprinkled the dried, aromatic leaves over another rolling paper. "What makes you think that?"

"He referred to me as a deceiving death-dealer."

"Ah."

Linnet ran her tongue over the edge of another thin paper and Laurel returned with a tray, carrying several hollow gourds, metal straws, Yerba Maté, biscuits, grapes, and a pitcher of hot water covered in a thick insulating cloth. The doe-eyed girl began pouring the steaming liquid over the finely ground leaves and twigs that she had placed in the gourds.

"Dominique?"

The Vam Pŷr lifted her hand to Laurel and shook her head no.

"I want you both to be aware." They turned toward their mistress. "The threat here is very real. I witnessed several Tribe attacks on the Rom Pŷr Keep when I was there. They are swift, cunning, and shrewd. Decisive and without mercy. If they decide to turn against…"

"That is not going to happen," interjected Linnet.

Dominique motioned for her to listen. "If…they decide to focus their hunts on the Children of Evensong then I want both of you to flee. No, hear me out." She saw the look on their faces. "I have set up several accounts with sufficient funds here in England and in Venice for the both of you. Return to your old lives and then move on from there. I want, more than anything else, to see that you both are safe."

The thought of leaving Dominique under such vile conditions stung both of the women's hearts. Linnet hid her scowl and Laurel wiped tears from her eyes.

"He said the Tribe has tracked and kept number of most of the Vam who survived the war."

"I would be surprised," said Dominique, "if they had not."

Linnet offered her Mistress a cigarette, but she was not in the mood for the comforter. Laurel passed her adopted sister the spice tea, quietly, taking one of the hand-rolled sticks. The room was thick in the rich bloom of tobacco leaves and Maté. Linnet stirred the steeping beverage, placing it to the side, and finished rolling another cigarette. The two dark haired beauties lit up as Dominique leaned back in her chair thoughtfully.

"I did not plan to kill Ornn or his wife, Ele." The Vam Pŷr bit the inside of her lower lip and frowned. "I was a slave for nearly three hundred years. Most of which, as you know, was spent in the mines of the Rom Pŷr J'in. Things were different among the Tien Däm Mu and under Ornn's tutelage I learned many customs of the Omjadda, without which I would have never known to claim Ornn's body and blood as victor." She paused with a nagging hurt tugging at her soul. "I did not set out to usurp Ornn's throne. During the sedition he sought me out. I had little choice." Her eyes searched her loyal consorts. "Once he had fallen, Ele's fate was sealed. She would have hunted each and everyone of us down had I not interjected myself in the line of succession and defended the Shrij´Ţęk Aŭr."

"What is that?" Laurel asked, sipping from her Yerba Maté.

"The Shrij´Ţęk Aŭr is the Omjadda call for challenge. Though, Val'Kir Däm Mu did not initially make the challenge when he first attacked. I called the Ohanao as was my right as victor and in his rage he lit his knife upon me. I left a scar on his cheek for his insolence, besting him in front of his elders, and displayed the proper ceremonial rites, which he did not. He humiliated himself in his grief to the likes of a Vam, and in his stupor, as J'in Ankh I decreed that a proper call for challenge could not be named for five hundred years hence. So until that time Val'Kir can only rule the Tien Däm Mu J'in in proxy. And I can, if I so choose, overrule any proclamation or judgment that he makes."

"But you do not wish the Omjadda throne," voiced Laurel, breathing out a pillar of tasty smoke. "Surely, Nsia can see that."

"He is biased by his people's history," Linnet added, resting the butt of her Turkish cigarette in the ashtray. "They fear a war on two fronts. But fear contamination of the Omjadda strain more." She picked up her guampa and held it close. "We simply need to show him that we are different. That our traditions and customs are not aligned to that of the

Omjadda."

Dominique stood and crossed the room, standing by the closed window. She folded her hands behind her back, pensively staring forward. Laurel pulled from the hand rolled cigarette, burning the flame down to a stub.

"Do we have any traditions and customs?"

Laurel's question went unanswered as she rested her butt on the tray and picked up her tea. Linnet sipped from her metal straw, imbibing the grassy brew, confident that she could prove to Nsia that Dominique and those of her kind were not akin to the ancient species.

"Laurel, would you please fetch some flowers for the room?" Dominique turned to her attendant. "The yellow roses would be nice."

"Yes, of course."

She set her tea down, exiting toward the garden as Dominique turned to the shielded window again. The Vam Pŷr could feel the heat from the daylight outside and imagined that it was a fine day beyond the thick, dark curtains.

"Is it true that by your intercession of the line that the Tien Däm Mu J'in was forever altered to mean Clan of Ill Blood?"

"Yes."

Dominique remained fixed, gazing upon the closed blinds that protected her from the sun.

"Nsia said that the Tien Däm Mu came about from a split of the Qamar Däm J'in during the Great Migration, and that they were the first J'in to leave the Lanz Gur Mae."

Dominique did not readily answer. Linnet's eyes played across her back and bare shoulders. The black dress she wore fell to the ground in a gentle slope, offsetting her pale olive-drab skin. She watched the veins of her Mistress's parasite slither across her shoulder blades and wondered what it felt like to have something like that moving within.

"The Qamar Däm was torn. They, along with the Dalam Vala'Shiya, did not wish to hunt Mar any longer. They believed that by doing so they caused the death that ate their homelands." Dominique turned to Linnet.

"Ornn told me about it one night." The Vam Pŷr wore a face that stung from a longing pang. "The Qamar Däm was a large clan, faithful to the Jadda Asli. They believed that through prayer and sacrifice they could heal the Lanz Gur Mae from the encroaching desert. Ornn was a child when his people made their exodus. He told me that it took months for them to cross the desert at night and that many died." She turned back to the nothingness of the curtain. "They were the first to flee of their own volition and Layal did not weep. That is what he said...*Layal did not weep*. Ornn said that the Qamar Däm was named after a blood moon from a time of great strife among his ancestors, when Jadda Marh and his followers were banished from the Lanz Gur Mae..."

"Marh? Nsia spoke something of him on our first night."

Dominique turned to her consort again and watched as she lit another Turkish delight, pondering the channels of her memory.

"Some Omjadda legend though...he did not go into any detail." Linnet puffed a cloud of smoke that curled above her head. "What do you know of Marh?"

"A little bit." Dominique moved away from the covered window and crossed to where Linnet sat in one of the huge crown-backed chairs. "Not much actually." Dominique reached out for Linnet's hand. "He was the heir to the Jadda Asli J'in; he rebelled and was banished."

"He rebelled about what?"

Dominique squeezed the young woman's hand and smiled. "More important than some old story is how you enjoyed Mr. Bah's company last night."

The Vam Pŷr let Linnet's hand go. The young woman grimaced as her Dark Mistress sat on the sofa, curling her legs along the cushions of the two-seater and leaned against the armrest.

"He is charming." Linnet looked down. "Educated. He is more of a scholar than a fighter, which is why I think he was chosen for the task of tracking you."

"How does he make you feel?"

Just then Laurel entered, carrying a bouquet of freshly cut flowers. Linnet's thoughts lingered on the tall African and the sharp point of Dominique's question.

"I picked some white peonies and lavender also. I thought they looked nice with the roses."

Dominique sat up. "Here, let me see them."

Laurel handed the Vam Pŷr the loose bundle of flowers. She closed her eyes and held the colorful garland to her face and inhaled. Opening her eyes, she thanked the girl for bringing them into the house. Flowers were so radiant and fragrant during the light of the day. Their bloom enlivened Dominique's soft pallor and the drab ambiance of the room.

"I will procure a vase," Laurel said, turning to Linnet. "I found this over by the chrysanthemums." She handed the item to her. "Were you not wearing this last night?"

Linnet took the ribbon and looked down at it. She was wearing it last night and recalled stroking her hair when she caught Nsia looking at her. She had blushed and turned away from his luring glance, running her fingers through her coal black tresses to hide her face. The ribbon reminded her of how the man had made her feel.

"Did you lose anything else while you were out there?"

Laurel did not wait for Linnet to answer. Teasingly, she smirked and left the room. Linnet followed her with her eyes, pushing disdain on her back. Dominique chuckled, smelling her flowers. Her consort's affection for Nsia was as plain on her face as the light blue ribbon that dangled limply in her hand.

"It is evident that he has made quite an impression upon you."

Linnet's eyes fell on her mistress weakly and she was embarrassed. She looked away and grabbed the tin that housed her smoking paraphernalia, uneasy under the gaze of her paramour.

"He is a handsome and virile man. I would be worried had he not left an impression."

Linnet's eyes flicked up to her Dark Mistress. She said nothing. A sinking feeling pulled at the uneasy buoy in her gut. Laurel entered the room carrying a vase filled with a quarter of water. Dominique set the flowers in it and arranged them to her liking, leaning in, every so often, to engorge herself with their scents and brush their petals against her face. The raven haired woman offered her adopted sister another smoke as Laurel refreshed their tea; and to avoid the strange matter of her heart, Linnet dived into the meat of the matter that occupied the majority of last night's conversation.

"Nsia is curious if the Vam have complete recall of Omjadda memories from their blood."

Dominique laughed, preening her flowers. "Of course he is."

Laurel moved to the edge of her seat, pausing to light her cigarette. She was unaware that the potential for blood memories even existed. Her mind reeled, tantalized by the thought. The prospect of there existing a way to reach far into the gaping jaws of time was fascinating and propelled the young maid's desire to imbibe the dark drink even sooner.

"He claimed that they have, for some time now, believed that the Omjadda consume their dead in a ritual called," Linnet paused and thought, "Tet Däm'vah," she spoke hesitantly. "They think their blood retains some essence of the creatures life force, maybe even retaining their memories."

Dominique merely smirked, paying all her attention to the inside garden that Laurel had gotten for her. Both girls waited.

"They think their blood contains the memories of its owner," prompted Linnet after a time, also eager to see if the Tribe's speculations were true.

"The memories of the Jadaraa Soo," spoke Dominique finally, "are not so clear and focused as one might think. Visions come in broken swells of distorted experiences. They are haphazard, and though they may appear random, one quickly learns in time, that this is the way the blood communicates. Through imagery and pain the Jadaraa Soo demands to be fed. Through imagery and pleasure it shares its contentment. One simply cannot access the lively episodic adventures of the Omjadda's life as if they could peer into a trunk for old knickknacks or shoes."

"But, how…how does…" Laurel could scarcely get her thought out. She was too excited.

"The Tet Däm'vah is sentient." The looks from her consorts told Dominique that they did not understand. "Blood. It is not a ritual. It is what they call their blood. The Jadaraa Soo uses the memory housed within its essence to coax and acquire nourishment from us. The majority of our blood memories are of basic carnality – food and sex – sustenance in one form or another. Much of the Omjadda's heart, will, and mind are never expressed through the cravings of the blood. Much of the being's life, lived, is not transferred in the Ja Rủ Tộk. If the blood had revealed anything above and beyond its craving for food the revolts that ended the Eras of Slavery would have happened eons before it did."

"Did you ever meet the one whose blood you were forced to drink?" asked Laurel, only now recalling the unlit cigarette in her hand.

Dominique thought about it, remembering an encounter with an elder Omjadda a few decades after she had been turned. As usual, the creature did not notice her. Like most of the noble race they did not look upon the Vam as equals. They were property. Mar was used chiefly as food and those that were not eaten suffered the Ja Rủ Tộk. All Omjadda that she knew believed humans were nothing more than an eyesore on Gai'Anâka that was best kept unseen, unheard, and enslaved. The beast she recalled was on a tour of the gold mine where she labored. He was being escorted by the mine's Overseer. His aged features felt familiar to her. His eyes appeared to be the perfect window for the theater in her mind. When she looked upon him she was whipped, told to keep her eyes down and get back to work. No real confirmation existed, other than Dominique's own musings. So she told the young maid, "No."

The anonymity and barren isolation that Linnet inferred from Dominique's answer struck her chest like a hot poker. To be stranded with alien thoughts rattling around in one's own mind did not seem appealing. It was nightmarish and sad. Even if the memories were only spurred by the parasite's hunger, it was still not an inviting prospect. *A millenium of experiences, lives lived; loves and pains felt, all bound within the cellular logic of the blood clamoring inside of one's head…*

"How do you live with it?

Dominique smiled at her darling Linnet. "How do you? They act no different than your own memories. You become accustomed to them and they fade like all remembrances do."

"But what do you see?" Laurel still had not lit her tobacco stick.

She pressed the Vam Pỷr to tell them more and share what visions she had from the blood. Once Dominique began unfurling her accounts Laurel finally ignited the hand rolled comforter. One such memory, frequent in Dominique's early days as a blood slave, was of the beast's conquest of a female by a pond. The reflection of their hairless, luminescent bodies rippled across the black-strewn waters as they clawed, groped, and bit each other in their copulating postures. The vision was melded with a driving desire to consume and Dominique remembered that the sensation of lust was quite overwhelming for her tender age.

Her servants were shocked by the raw emotion transported by the blood and asked the night mother to regale them with more. This Dominique did until the day's light broke, hazy and dark, on the thatch and beams of London. Once again Linnet had to cancel her portrait sitting with the master artist, opting to send her regrets through a courier service so that Laurel might remain within the comforting abode of their strange family. Sleep tugged at Linnet's bones, but she was too enraptured by the primal nature of the visions to force herself to bed. Their fellowship was a warm retreat gathered around the gentleness and plum beauty of the Vam Pŷr. As the day wore on, Dominique supped from them both, and the draw of blood from Linnet's bosom sent her consort dreamily to sleep.

When evening sang and Nsia returned to the house, it was quiet and dark. Laurel greeted him and woke Linnet. The raven haired consort found the young man in the Library and shared with him all that Dominique had imparted to her on the subject of fluid recall. He was not less fascinated by the prospect of blood memories as Linnet had been. On the contrary, he was ecstatic. Captivated. It was as if he had been taken backstage to a carnival caravan and shown how the wooden pulleys and gears worked their magic on the audience. His joy became her joy and she found herself, with ease, favoring the man.

"Dominique could not add any insight as to how the Omjaddas interacted with their own blood." Announced Linnet as they spoke over a meal that Laurel had prepared once she had fallen asleep earlier.

"We know it is their custom to consume their dead and share the amen of their blood," confessed Nsia. "Blood to the Kula Malaika is precious. A sacred vessel. We have seen this and believe that the essence holds some secret. If she could enact some influence on the Tien Däm Mu so that we might better understand this process, it would be greatly appreciated."

Linnet knew that what he asked for could be achieved. Though by procuring it, any reason that existed for their rendezvous might dissolve. "Is it more important to know about their culture than to eradicate the creatures from the earth?"

Nsia smiled, a curved, sideways grin. He leaned back in his seat and sipped his wine. "I see a fierce heart in you." He shot forward. "But you must understand, the Kula Malaika Shaytan Khalid have spread throughout the whole of the world and infected their language, their art, their culture, and religion upon our growing, infantile species. Their influence bled through all aspects of our development and way of life. They were the hidden masters to a race of puerile people. They were the lineage that gave rise to Gods and the diversity of agriculture, fetishes, and stately cycles. One cannot so easily eradicate such a force of nature."

Linnet considered what he had said, twirling her wine around the bottom of her glass, knowing that he watched her. Judged her every move. His gaze held weight. She felt torn. "If blood is so revered among the Omjadda then why would they waste it on transforming Mar into slaves? Wouldn't it be, in effect, a transgression of their most sacred sacraments?"

Nsia's grin grew wide. "Ah, you see. Yes, something else we wish to know. Why would they do such a thing? It fractured their people, sent them throughout the whole of the world."

Linnet saw the opportunity in the man's words before she spoke and a nagging guilt tugged at her chest that she did not understand. Usually, she enjoyed the art of negotiation, but here she felt bad about capitalizing on their connection of the moment. "Then surely you can see the benefit of an alliance between us. That there would be more to gain in friendly concord than the devastation of sustaining another war."

He stabbed his meat with his fork, cut a sliver off, and ate it.

"The possibility of an alliance is not for me to decide. I hope you know this." He set his cutlery down, folded his hands as he put his weight on his elbows, and stared across the table at the woman that sat at the other end. "The benefits could mutual. Yes. But you and I, we are merely pawns." He paused gauging her. "Surely, you know this to be true."

"Mr. Bah…" Linnet held her empty wineglass. "I am no pawn in the construction of this alliance. I create my own destiny. And…I am out of wine."

The man grinned, her affect admirable. He wiped his hands on the cloth napkin, rose, and crossed the breadth of the dining table. He liked her confidence. It reminded him of the women at home. He attended to his hostess's empty vessel. Refilling the pale red liquid, he noticed how the Vam Pŷr's consort could not keep her eyes off of him.

"Tell me then," he said as he returned to his seat, "if you are not a pawn in this affair, when will Dominique grace us again with her presence? I have not seen her since the first night we met."

"When I deem it necessary you will speak with her. But until that day, let's you and I become better acquainted." She leaned forward, resting her elbows on the table. "Because, I believe that it is in our grasp, more than any others', to forge a respectable alliance between our peoples."

Nsia raised his glass, offering this gallant lady a silent toast.

Over the ensuing days, Nsia stopped asking when Dominique would meet with him personally and Linnet discovered that she looked forward to his visits just how she cherished her moments with Dominique. Each encounter with the beautiful man was rich and sweeping and filled Linnet's bonnet with the buzz of a billion thoughts. She neglected to inform her Lady of Nsia's interest to have her gain information by exerting her influence as J'in Ankh of the Tien Däm Mu. There was something between her and Nsia that she wanted time to ferret out. Giving her Mistress the bargaining chip she needed to secure a deal with the African would end any chance she had at finding understanding as to why the man confused her so.

As the days wore on, Linnet felt that her heart betrayed her Dark Mistress. Worried, their daily aggregation to go over the evening's details took on a new face. Each question of Dominique's, as to Linnet's mood and temperance toward Nsia made her angry, sparking ire of rebellion. She withheld more and found Dominique's pleasure and constant expedition into her fluxed state vexing. One day, as they explored the previous night's rendezvous, in the dark seclusion of the house, Linnet could contain her rage no longer.

"I will not meet with him again!" She yelled. "He has learned enough as it is. You meet with him, if you want, and let us be done with the whole fiasco and go to South America as we have planned. I've grown tired of this."

Laurel listened from a shadow in the hall.

"Will you not miss him if we slip through the night and leave?" the Vam Pŷr inquired gently.

"What difference is it if I do?" Linnet shouted to the rafters. "You asked me to become open to this man, obviously to lure him into some sense of false trust, and I have done so. I did not ask you why you wanted me to do this. You requested it and I gave. Now, I ask you to leave me out of these ridiculous pursuits. I will not meet with him again!"

Linnet's eyes burned with tears on the dam strokes of her lashes. Dominique looked at the woman who so recently had become a fixed point in her soul. Her lover, her confidant, and friend. She saw how her playful manipulations had worn her strong Linnet down. Dominique crossed the room to her and gently stroked her hot cheeks with the backside of her fingers. The dams of Linnet's eyes could not hold back the water. They broke and tears streamed down her face.

"Why have you not taken sustenance from me for several days now?" Linnet asked meekly, falling into the melodious pillow of Dominique's touch.

"Oh, my child," she pulled the hollow girl to her bosom. "I love you like no other. Surely, you must know this by now?"

Linnet slid her arms around Dominique's waist and held her tight. She heaved great big sobs, never wanting to let go of the woman. Fearing that if she did she would float away. There was a thief that kept chipping away at her, kept tearing her heart to pieces.

"If you love me so much, then why do you want love to bloom between Nsia and me?"

Laurel gasped from her hidden perch, quickly covering her mouth with her hand lest the sharp ears of her Mistress detected her intrusion. Dominique felt the hard patter of Linnet's heart against her belly and recalled the first time she had seen the woman at the Teatro Regio Ducal in Milan.

It was an exceptional night for the opera, despite the rain. Linnet sat in a boxed tier with the Conte and his wife. She wore a French blue silk taffeta dress brocaded with silver thread. The young woman was gorgeous, a stunning distraction to the play on the stage. Riveted, Dominique spent the entire production watching Linnet, instead of the performers, through her spectacles. During intermission she sought her out, noticing how the Contessa De Luca kept the young girl close as she negotiated a rendezvous with a fair-haired soldier.

The elder lady's motives were garish and obvious, pandering to her own hidden desires as she played matchmaker. A simple prelusion from some of Milan's more prominent folk, a few carefully dropped phrases and names, a statement of wealth, and soon the Contessa thought it her own idea to forge an introduction with her Goddaughter. Dominique knew the moment they first met that the girl would one day come to her. And she did. Seven months later in what appeared like a meeting of happenstance in Oxford.

They had shared several letters in the interim since Milan and Dominique could wait no longer. With the memory of the girl, she was sleeping with ghosts. Reunited, after a brisk summer rain, they each quickly found that the bond, which they had forged in the Austrian owned, Celtic born city, had not been severed or disillusioned by time. Dominique should have seen it coming. Though, in that initial preface she was too wrapped up and simply unaware as to how deeply she would fall for the English lass. For all of her advanced years nothing had prepared her for the bounty of Linnet Pevensey.

Daintily, the symbiont peeled the woman off of her and regarded her at arm's length. Laurel eased closer to the door of the chamber as her Mistress's voice dropped.

"You crave this life with me. Just as much as I crave a life with you." Linnet looked up at the Vam Pŷr, hearing only distance slowly slicing her eardrums. "I want to give you something I never had. I want to give you a choice. I want you to be able to decide for yourself if this is what you truly want." A red tear broke upon Dominique's cheek and slid off her face. "Because once it is done, Linnet…you can never go back."

The raven haired beauty stared at the earnest love etched in the woman's timeless face. She was yet a babe in her arms. The rhythm of the Vam Pŷr's years gave weight to her stare. Linnet had never seen her cry before. She felt small. In her heart, she felt that Dominique knew the terrain of the course of affairs she undertook with Nsia. Her Dark Mistress had given her trust while all she gave her in return was anger and fear.

"You'd have me sleep with him then?"

The words tumbled out of Linnet's mouth like an accusation, even as they provided an answer to the burning in her groin and the confusion of her faculties. She voiced her true conscience and knew that she had been denying herself to speak of her lust for this man to the woman who had stolen her heart. The affair was tangled and tainted by motivations that Linnet did not readily understand.

"I have only given you the time to cultivate the feelings that were already there. I hold no sway over your desires. If you choose to bed him then that decision would be yours and his alone."

Linnet watched her Lady speak arriving at a disheartened feeling. "But you want me to." Numbly, Linnet moved away. "You want me to sleep with Nsia."

Laurel pressed her ear to the cold, wooden door.

Linnet's mind churned. It was hard for her to understand the dispassion and perspective that several hundred years afforded one. Dominique had always made her feel like a treasure set above all others. She believed that what they shared was not for the likes of any one else. The valley of their flesh was sacred ground. Even Laurel was not elevated to the role Linnet occupied. Dominique was hers alone. Linnet felt her naiveté cracking like a child in the womb of Christmas.

"I want you to experience life, my girl. To know the touch of the sun on your face or feel the embrace of a man or read poetry in a garden." Dominique placed her hand upon Linnet's shoulder, turning her around to face her. "I was twelve years old when I was taken. I knew nothing of life before I was enslaved. How could you ever be sure that you had made the right decision unless you've tasted all that life had to offer first?" The freed blood slave shook her head with deep consideration. "Death is easy to come by, my love, and lasts much longer than this brief expanse."

Linnet brooded. "But what if I love him?"

Dominique smirked. "What do you think it will be like a hundred years from now? Or even fifty? Hmm? All that you know and love will be gone. The world will have changed, moved on, and there you will be, the same as ever, with only the consistency of the thirst to anchor you, berth you. Tether you to the strange and the unfamiliar like a star within the heavens. How do you expect to survive such an ordeal if you cannot even pacify the clamor of your heart?"

It was an epiphany. Linnet's Lady tested her! She conspired to forge the metal of the young woman's spirit so she could weather the storms of eons. Her Dark Mistress was giving her centuries of truth in the vial of a man. This was a trial to see if she could handle all that she had asked for. Linnet felt dazed. The sudden rush of understanding was profound. If the young woman could conquer the desire of her heart with her will, then she would flourish in the bloom of eternity! There was a daredevil spirit required to survive that Linnet had not gleaned previously. Everything in this moment seemed so mountainous and vast, like some undiscovered country fell before her feet in the iron furnace of her soul.

Linnet yearned for the man in a natural way. In the way God had intended his flock to flourish. Yet, she also craved Dominique with a desire so voracious in its appetite that the virginal woman was scared of her own passions. Awakened, Linnet looked to her Dark Mistress with new eyes. She understood now that she was growing too quickly into the flesh of her love with Nsia. She needed to slow things down, gain perspective. *He was, after all, just a man.* Linnet took Dominique in her arms and kissed her hard on the mouth. The Vam Pŷr embraced her with equal passion and Linnet could scarcely remove her garments fast enough.

The voices on the other side of the door grew faint again and Laurel strained to hear the rustling of clothing beyond the door. She pushed against the wooden edifice. She did not fully understand the exchange between Dominique and Linnet. It all seemed too elaborate for her. If she fancied the man then she would have him. It was all very simple, in fact. That was the one thing that Laurel loved about her servitude to the Vam Pŷr. It made all of her fantasies and desires attainable. Linnet was, yet again, complicating matters that could be better handled with a straightforward approach. The servant girl shook her head and scurried quietly along the hall, returning to her duties.

That was less than a week ago; Linnet held the fearful epiphany like a jewel and had made love to Dominique for only the third time. To slow things down, she cancelled her meeting with Nsia that evening and chose, instead, to sit for Master Reynolds. But, the earnest man had found her again outside of the artist's abode and invited her to dinner. This time he did not greet her with a knife, and in his good company Linnet found it hard to decline his invitation. Before she retired to her home with the symbiont and Laurel, Linnet invited him to visit her the very next day. It was rash and impulsive, but the young maid felt alive.

When Nsia arrived she did not linger around the house, choosing instead to take him horseback riding along a neighboring farm. They rode over the rolling hills to a forest where she knew game was abundant for hunting. She wanted to show Nsia the fertile green of her homelands, but found instead that his dominant presence overwhelmed her with hidden sensations. He was a skilled rider and looked magnificent upon his steed. The golden bloom of the sky shone down on them as the beasts' hooves tore into the ground during a playful chase. Under a fervent blue canopy, amid the gentle sway of rustling leaves, to the babbling music of a brook, Linnet allowed the man to take her and they made love. He held her after and they talked of nothing about ancient races or blood slaves or tribes that had fought for millennia. Their time was simple and pure and Linnet felt comfortable and whole.

That evening she told Dominique everything. Quietly, the Vam Pŷr sat on the couch in a Spitalfield silk dress, listening. The achievement of her machinations was won and she felt wretched. Linnet's words numbly washed over her as she waited for the knell of her heart to stop breaking. The woman was blossoming in front of her and there was nothing she could do about it, but wait.

"I will always love you," whispered Linnet to her Dark Mistress.

The Vam Pŷr placed her fingers to the woman's warm lips and stopped her from making anymore foolish proclamations. Each word sounded like goodbye. They retired to her chambers and Dominique silently held Linnet. She supped from the young woman's breasts at her maid's request even though she did not crave the elixir in her veins. It was important for the freed blood slave to keep everything between them as normal as possible. She had done too much already that could push the girl from Abingdon away. If she lit Linnet a window to the pain in her heart then all that must yet be done would fall to ruin and ignite a war.

Now, Linnet could not bring herself to slumber as the shale of rain beat against her window. Her mind was turning, too busy on all that had transpired over the past month. The easiness of last week had vanished somewhere in the tangled limbs of days and nights gone by. Linnet felt a spiral twisting in her gut, when only yesterday she felt so high, embroiled in the joy of two wonderful loves. Then Nsia had gone and asked her to leave Dominique and come away with him.

What am I to do?

Linnet grieved and stretched out on her bed. She heard the distinct creak of the floorboard in the hall again and guessed that Laurel was teetering outside of her bedchambers with matters pertaining to one thing or another.

"Go away or come in. But do not stand in the hall like that."

Nothing happened. The rain knocked against her window. Linnet sighed. She figured her active mental state was making up the presence outside of her room. Beyond her door, Nsia waited for her. Beyond her door Dominique yearned for her. Beyond her door…Linnet did not know what to do. She craved them both and lying awake, thinking about it was not helping. Moments dragged by on mud-covered feet.

Frustrated, Linnet rose and got dressed. She was shaking. She could not get the look of Nsia's face out of her mind as he glared at Dominique's bite marks. He was hurt. He loved her even though he had not said the words. Linnet felt it in her heart, but she needed to know if it was true. He had asked her not to return to the Vam Pŷr's house, and to stay with him. But she wouldn't listen. She had to get back. There were business matters that only she could attend too. Linnet lied. She had lied to Nsia. And it was easy. She withheld from Dominique. Her body ached and her heart was a weapon set against itself. Linnet felt as if she were falling down a tunnel of which she did not know the length and width.

Leaving her room she thought she would talk it out with Dominique but decided on an altogether different course of action when she took the stairs. She did not see Laurel standing in a doorway to the hall, spying on her, when she walked pass. Nor did Linnet see Dominique standing on the easement of the roof watching her as she ran from the house to the stables. The Vam Pŷr was drenched. Wind beat against her pallid skin and the sky cried for her. Water poured off her sublime shoulders and ran down her nose. Below, on the cobblestone and pebbles her love fled from the house. Linnet mounted a fresh mare and took off into the blinding, wet night.

Dominique knew where she was going, but it still felt as if a knife churned in her belly. She knew Linnet was destined to leave since that first moment when she sniffed out her consort's budding desire for the tall African. Though, knowing did not make it hurt any less. *Fate was a cruel mistress, predictable in its heartache.* Linnet's plum organ was being ripped apart and it was her fault. Dominique knew her lover's turmoil and hated the fact that she had to put her through this madness. She knew of no other way to pacify the drums of war beating in the Dark Continent than to sacrifice the girl. Lasting alliances were forged in bed. It was how she quelled the tide of fury the first time around when she became Musa Bah's lover. Her darling Linnet followed too closely in her own footsteps. *It is all my fault.*

Shame wreaked havoc on the shores of Dominique's spirit. The rain was a slow baptism. She could completely lose Linnet to Musa's great grandson. The possibility of it teetered on the elevated easement with her. *It would serve me well, sending my lover to do my bidding.* Dominique stood at the top of the house as the weather thrashed her for her great sin. She could not bring herself to stop the delicate drama that unfurled between Linnet and the African warrior any more than she could have stayed the blade in her hand from Ornn Däm Mu's thin, white throat. She felt both deaths of love and time, slipping through her grasp. She played a vile game and it ate at her denuded soul.

He called himself Joy, the man explained, yelling over the blaring music of the stereo. He was as effeminate as a 1940's pin-up girl and Lin could tell that it was nothing more than a side show act. He, like his self-proclaimed moniker, was a slapped together ruse against which he frequently leaned an elbow.

Lin half-heartedly listened to Joy as she eyed Z gawking it up with Manuel by the Greta Garbo portrait. Suddenly an urge overcame her to touch Joy's flapping lips. Instantly, she ran her fingers over the man's face and squished the soft mounds of flesh that the Mexican had been kissing earlier that evening. Joy stopped jaw wagging, laughed, and rolled his eyes expressively exclaiming that somebody had had too much to drink.

It wasn't alcohol that rippled through the vampire's body. It was the ecstasy. After the initial hiccup of distaste from Lin's Jadaraa Soo, the little white pill dissolved into an easy flow that hit her in soft pulsating waves. The waves were followed by tiny shuddering aftershocks. Wave and then… shock. Wave and then…shock. Her teeth jittered. Her body hummed. She was on cruise control, floating. Lin laughed and hugged the man feeling the music dreamily wash over her and stroke her hips.

Theresa finished her bottle of water and tugged at Mindy's shirt as the svelte, ornery vixen attempted to smooth up to Ryan Silva. She rubbed his inner thigh with her hand. But his attention was elsewhere, fixed on the tall, slender back of the magnetic chick from the club.

"C'mon Min," Theresa nagged. "Let's go. This is nothing more than a clam bake."

"In a minute."

"Better be. I'm starting to get hungry."

Lin listened to the whiny girl who came slithering up to her earlier. *Food sounded good.* The liquid of her being drifted amid the rolling waves of the Pacific Ocean as the parasite painted the image of a blood tide from its dormant memories. Lin felt connected to the giant body of water; out there beyond the dirty streets of the city. She placed a hand to her belly, recalling the sensation of standing on the deck of a galleon as it pushed through high seas. The sweat and blood sugar from all the people at her place flooded her nostrils. Her head swooned. Her hypersenses were razor sharp, buzzing like a hive of bees, and she wondered what Joy would taste like. Lin giggled at the thought of sucking joy.

"...So, is that some kind of prosthetic or dental implant or do you always walk around like Bela Lugosi's crazy half sister?"

"What?" Lin looked up at the man suddenly aware that he was still talking to her.

"Your grill." Joy waved his hand in front of his mouth. "What's with the freak show?"

Lin laughed. The music pushed through her. "I'm a vampire."

The sound of truth, in the low light interior of the sharply decorated penthouse suite, was nothing short of surreal and comical.

"No really, are you in a show?" He asked like a steamroller on a diving board. "My cousin Charley was in the Broadway production of Dracula last year and he wore his teeth everywhere he..."

"No, really." Lin leaned in, cutting him off. "I'm a Vampire."

Joy laughed at the girl's earnest impart as the music pounded around them. Lin opened her mouth and lifted her head. The room tilted. She told the man to look and flicked a fang with her finger. It was as hard as rock candy.

"Go ahead," invited Lin. "Touch it."

Joy reached out and grabbed one of Lin's protruding canines. He gave it a little tug and felt it squirm under his thumb. But it didn't pull off like Charley's teeth did. Joy gasped like a little girl, flexed his fingers against his chest, and wrinkled his freshly plucked eyebrows like a silent screen diva.

"Are you going to eat me?"

Lin giggled at the dainty man. *Drinking Joy...* "You're perfectly safe." She slapped him hard against the shoulder like a fair weathered sailor. "I don't eat where I live and I don't shit where I eat."

The axiom was a modern day expression of Dominique's second rule. As Lin uttered it she popped her soft, papery lips. They felt bouncy and she recalled her Mistress's instruction on surviving with the condition of evensong. They were leaving England on a short holiday before going to Paris. Only recently they had been reunited since their introduction in Milan. The young maid was taken by her present company in the county town of Oxfordshire and the two had spent time touring the famed city, visiting lush botanical gardens, exquisite shops, viewing the dreaming spires, and walking along The Isis under the magnificent charm of the moon. After a week of courtship, the enigmatic Persian revealed to Linnet her fearful inclination and the young woman found, with ease, that she was not put off by Dominique's rare condition. Linnet embraced it. The world was far wider and fuller than she had ever imagined.

They were going to Vienna together. Linnet was surprised at the lady's request for her to come away. Though, she was more surprised at her eagerness to suspend the duties that her father had charged and travel with the strange woman abroad.

"Monsieur Blouchard was a scribe," explained Dominique during their long carriage ride. "A mathematician, astronomer, and self-styled philosopher. He was nearly blind by the time I met him and had a kindly disposition. I was in such a wretched state, reduced to the back alleys and gutters of the Villa de Nicé.

I had washed up on the beach a few days before and was wandering through the city looking for food. It had been days since I had last taken sustenance. Most of which were spent floating in the cold waters of the Atlantic. I was forced to abandon my ship at the hands of a band of cutthroat pirates who showed me no due kindness."

Dominique's young companion gasped at the horrific prospect.

"I was being pursued by local authorities having been discovered killing a farmer's sheep." Dominique raised her hand. "I know, it is awful to imagine, but it was true. Circumstances as they were. To evade capture I hopped a fence and hid among the drapery and laggard construction materials that littered the yard. Nicodemus found me there and took pity on me. He invited me in despite my earnest protests, saying that no child of God should go forsaken or denied.

I was cold. Starving. I had no where else to go. I knew no one in the city and my impression so far was less than advantageous. All I could do was rely on the kindness of strangers. I bared my soul to him that day and I was sure that he would send me away. But, he did not. He arranged for several butchers in the neighborhood to furnish his household with fresh sanguine fluid. He revived me. Educated me in the ways of arithmetic and writing language. He taught me the rules of the stars and how to guide myself by the archetype of their constellations. He was more than a teacher."

Dominique drifted off dreamily for a moment and Linnet watched her, captivated by the woman's rich history.

"What became of him?"

"He succumbed to pestilence a few years after we met."

"I am sorry."

The Vam Pŷr smirked. "Do not be. He died contented. Before Monsieur Blouchard I prevaricated my circumstances to my benefit. I was no better than the soiled urchin that he found hiding in his back yard. Though, under his tutelage we crafted the persona of Madame Dominique De'Paul." The symbiont bowed graciously to her guest as a carriage wheel hit a rut. Jolted, the two women fell into brisk laughter. "That is why I unveil myself to you." The pale, olive-tan skinned woman snickered. "Truth can sometimes be an adversary. It is a righteous path infrequently applied, though when utilized its fruit is ameliorate." Dominique leaned forward and took Linnet by the hand. "I want nothing between us that could hold us back from what could be. The stars have decreed it. You and I were destined to meet. They foretold of your arrival."

They held each other's gaze.

"What you speak of is without comparison to the life I know. I hear tell of stars and mysteries, wrapped in adventures centuries past, and I find it difficult to conceive that you are over five hundred years my senior." Linnet squeezed Dominique's hand and sat back. "I must confess, my eyes deceive me."

The Vam Pŷr regarded Linnet for a spell before she spoke. "It is quite simple actually. The moon follows the sun and the sun follows the moon. The heavens are a pinwheel in God's playhouse. Each day comes after the next and eventually one finds themself sitting in a carriage with a beautiful woman on their way to one of Earth's most fabulous cities."

The raven haired beauty blushed. "That is not what I meant."

"I live by three very natural rules: Never kill when you can devise a method to feed without injury. Do not feed where you live and you will live to feed. Ingratiate yourself with your city; you are the eternal guest. Nicodemus helped me forge those simple proverbs and they have served me well, or else I would not be here this day, and I would never have known the

81

wonder of meeting you."

Linnet could not contain her smile. Nervously, she pulled at the stomacher of her dress, brushing her fingers along the top of her breasts.

"Should I infer that you intend to drink from me?"

Dominique's lips grew wide and embracing. She nodded her head, slowly, up and down, and whispered, "Oh yes. You are a budding flower, ethereal in design; a potion of ten thousand stars and honeysuckle dew. If you would but acquiesce to favor me with the bounty of your charms I would be deeply honored by your gift. "

Fear tickled her belly. "Will it hurt?"

Dominique stared at her for a terse minute. "Into every sky a little rain must fall."

A sudden heat and shiver rose in the confines of the carriage. Linnet could not stop thinking about what it would be like to have this mysterious woman sup from her, she like a chalice. Every learned notion told her that it was wrong. The pulpit preached in her head, expounding how she should not be joining Dominique on her trek through Austria, or become party to the dark habits of which she spoke. But Linnet could not help it. She was not afraid or offended by Dominique's need for blood. Curiosity poked at the fine edges of her skin and she wanted to know what else lay beyond the brink of the horizon with this woman.

"And if I should decline your sweet proposal?"

Dominique tingled. The girl toyed with her. "My rules are steadfast. You are safe." She grinned, knowingly. "You will come to me when you are ready."

The Lass was ready now. Dominique could smell the blossom of her sex ripening under the folds of her floral painted gown and sense the heat of her rising as her heart thrummed loudly in her bodice. Though, she would not take her along the sides of the road like a common Highwayman. She would endure the lady's company until the passion between them became too unbearable. In all of her years the Vam Pŷr had not met anyone who made her feel the way that this unbelievable girl was making her feel. She was scared and fascinated at the same time, beside herself that such delicate possibilities of love existed for her still.

A quickened heat filled Lin. It started from her toes and climbed upwards. She shuddered, standing before the man called Joy, rung as if her body was a bell. *Dominique's rules*...they had served her well too. Though, over time, the symbiont's last rule developed secondary precepts: seek out the weak and corruptible in power and make them dependent on your financial generosity. Give back to the community, from which you take; maintain balance. And lastly, always remain a foreign traveler, never staying in any one place too long.

The rules allowed one to be present, but invisible. To come and go like the wind, to leave no footprint that would raise suspicion. *To hide in plain sight.* Over time, as civilization progressed, Lin adapted Dominique's tenets to the climate and conditions in which she found herself. She added stipulations while forsaking others, never forgetting the invaluable luxuries of the lady that had instructed her.

"Oooh honey, are you dead?"

Joy sucked in a breath. His lips quivered and he squished up his face as if he'd been sucking lemons. Lin stood back and twirled around.

"Do I look dead to you?"

"No," he confessed and shook his head to affirm the negative, "you have a tight little tushy. Oh God! How do you stay so trim?"

"That's what I'm talkin' about!"

The vampire clinked the near empty Vodka bottle against Joy's glass in good drunken cheer.

"Hey, sugar."

Manuel slid up behind Joy, draping his arm over the young man's neck.

"Did you know she's a vampire?" Joy boasted as the Mexican kissed his neck. "A real one. Not faking it like those weirdoes at Club Orpheus."

"Is that so."

Manuel's eyes drifted up the hard tumble curves of the raven haired beauty, thinking Z's life partner was just as far out there as Z was, and that he couldn't care less. Even if she threatened to drink his blood right here in the hallway, he wasn't phased. Other things pulled at the motor in his mind.

"Yeah. She said that..."

But Manuel kissed him. The rest of Joy's explanation fell into the soft gyrations of their tongues. Lin watched them for a moment. The energies of their auras rippled out from them in orange, red, and purple lines. Lin felt as if she could reach out and scoop them up like water. She smiled at their passionate display and felt her own lips tingle. Even after their kiss broke her lips continued to feel like fresh pressed velvet.

"Stop it." Joy toyed. "I was in the middle of a sentence."

"And that was the exclamation point."

Manuel rocked him by the hips.

"He's such a sad, well-hung man."

Manuel kissed him on the ear. "Well," he breathed, "I can tell you want I wanna suck."

The Diva's face lit up like an 'O'. "You did not just say that!"

Lin left the couple giggling in her wake and wandered into another room of her house. Mindy and Theresa floated past, bickering. Inspired by the kiss, her memories clashed to that of Dominique and Nsia. Her mind's eye filled with lovely scenes of appetite. The Vam Pŷr was stretched out, naked in their bed. Lin traversed her pallid skin planting kisses. They groped and pulled at each other. She felt Dominique's teeth as her hand reached the inside of her thigh. The ecstasy fueled each delicious time capsule. She felt Nsia piercing her, enveloping her, and she grew wet. She remembered the way his dark skin framed her peach nakedness. How his mouth suckled her nipples and engulfed her breasts. The way he took her lovingly, placing his hand in the small of her back as he laid her down on the silk sheets of his bed, entering her in an explosion of wonderful pleasure and pain.

Time undressed itself as she felt both ancient lovers play against the canvas of her flesh. Her memories mingled, a ménage à trios. Lin staggered and leaned against the wall. Her cheeks were flushed and her forearms and hands tingled with the pricks of a thousand tiny pins. She breathed and calmed her nervous Jadaraa Soo. Inflamed by her recollections of the African warrior and her Dark Mistress, Lin scoured the house for the light haired stranger with the crystal blue eyes that she had seen earlier. *He could scratch the annoying little itch that had cropped up and curled in my belly now!* Lin imagined a plethora of nasty things that she was going to do to him as she turned a sharp corner and neared Ryan Silva. But he veered away. Instead of walking up to her, as her look beckoned him to do, he wandered onto the terrace where Z lounged in one of their reclining chairs. Lin's passion was a sudden car crash.

"This is a great place you have here." He spoke to Z as he crossed to the railing and peered out onto the vast landscape of the city of lost angels.

"Is this small talk?" Z toyed. "I saw you watching me. I was wonderin' when you'd get the nerve…up."

"Fuck." Lin breathed. *There goes that.*

Ryan turned and absorbed the brash tease. Her tongue played with the tip of a very large tooth as her eyes danced on him like a worm on a hook. The girl was a sample of night pressed into tight fitting clothes. Confidence reeked off of her like a corpse.

"Are those real?"

"Is what real?" Z raised her eyebrows.

"Your teeth."

Z laughed. *She's a hellcat. The poor boy doesn't have a clue at what he's getting himself into.* Lin shook her head and turned away. She'd already been to that conversation. She was thirsty. She hungered. Her flesh pounded with appetite. Her memories had awoken her Jadaraa Soo and it craved blood. As quickly as it came, this intrusion of merriment had lost its brief appeal and she decided to return to her room.

Strolling through the kitchen, Lin stopped at the refrigerator. She punched in the security code on the lock. In anticipation of its meal, her blood parasite quivered, buzzing like a motorboat. She released the hold she had on the veiny freeloader and a thousand tiny fissures crisscrossed her pale flesh like a roadmap. She didn't care if anybody saw the veins now or not. Her breathing cadaver was warmed by the onslaught of memories that still danced in the drive-in theater of her brain. Recollections were all she needed to guide her to the dawn. Lin opened the cold-storage door and retrieved a packet of blood. She closed her eyes just as Nsia leaned in and kissed her.

"Is your dick real or a rent-a-rama dildo?"

"Ahh…what?" Ryan wasn't sure he heard her right.

"Is it live or Memorex? The poor boy wants to know if I bite."

Z gnashed her teeth and stared at Ryan, drinking up his statuesque physique. The night was arid and he leaned against the railing, high above the shuffling madness of the city below.

"Oh-kay," he stuttered and smiled.

He enjoyed the offbeat brashness of the sexy punk. But before he could make any sense of her flipped response or capitalize off the toothy invitation, their attentions were quickly diverted by the rapid succession of several deep-pitched gunshots splintering the predawn night. Z raced out of her chair and joined Ryan by the railing's edge. She climbed up onto her tippy-toes, leaning out over the beautiful nothingness of Los Angeles, as Santa Ana winds gently brushed her dyed red hair. There was a sting of silence. Then, two more blasts erupted with fury into the warm twilight.

"Hmmm," mused Ryan. "A shotgun serenade."

"Sweet Jesus that was beautiful." Z turned to the man, grinning. *He's a damn Adonis.*

Up close, the girl's canines were evident. *A vampire groupie.* Though, despite this fact Ryan was mystified by Z's awkward beauty and excited frivolity. *She was a unique being all right. A Mona Lisa. The Statue of fucking Liberty! The tits on a cherry topped ice cream.* Ryan's eyes traveled to her curved hips as they pressed against the railing. In the small of her back, poking out of the top of her denim jeans, was a tattoo of two revolvers jutting out of a colorful bed of flowers above the face of a girl. Cursive writing wove through the lush floral bed, disappearing into her jeans. He could just make out the name, Simon Ray.

"Nice ink."

"Thanks." Her eyes poured all over him like molasses.

"So ah…you trying to tell me you're a vampire?"

Z scrunched her lips. *He was scrumptious all right, a forty-two watt light bulb.* She wanted more from this colt than to just lick him up. She tingled. Slowly, she peeled off the railing as the normal drool of the city fell back into its odd shaped spaces, noticing how her curious, little fish had finally taken the bait. Z smirked, turned, and walked away, leaving him alone on the balcony to boil in his growing desire.

"I'm not trying to tell you anything."

She entered the house, knowing full well that he watched her perfect little ass like a tool.

1774. London, England.

Her feet were bare, dirty, and stuck with tiny wet leaves. She wore only her chemise and wandered her garden path. Dominique fidgeted with a knuckle on her left hand. Retracing her steps through the opened atrium, she traversed endlessly around the finite walkway, and paid no attention to the splendor of her flowers.

"Mistress, please," urged Laurel from the house. "Come away. It will be light soon."

The young maid yawned and pulled at the blanket around her shoulders. She had awakened early and found the Vam Pŷr in a pitiful state.

"You need not worry. Go back to bed." Dominique twisted the flesh of her digit as if turning a metallic band. "It will be a cloudy dawn and with it rain. I am fine."

The faithful consort watched her Lady feeling ineffectual against her sullen moods.

"I will make a fire to warm the house and put on a pot for tea. You have gone too long without taking nourishment. I will expect you this morning."

Dominique's feet slowly padded. She listened to the bugs digging in the earth, to the horses in the stables. She felt cold burrowing down past the thick rings of muscle and flesh. Worry plagued her mind. She had not eaten since Linnet went away.

Laurel waited for a response, but none came. She reentered the house feeling dismal that she alone could not pull her Mistress's attention away from the absence of the girl. She restocked the hearths with fresh logs and lit the kitchen stoves. When the Vam Pŷr finally came in the sun was invisible in the sky, buried behind a thick gray of morning rain clouds. A fair sprinkle had watered the ground and Dominique went straight to her chambers.

She refused, again, to feed when the young maid went to her later that morning. She did not even bid her entry into her room. Each day Dominique grew darker as the obvious manifested, withdrawing into seclusion. Dejected, Laurel set about turning down the house as her Lady had requested the day before. There were plans to return to Nicé by week's end.

An afternoon sun stapled the sky with light and Laurel was beating the carpets when she heard the carriage on the gravel drive. She went to the front of the house just as the raven haired woman stepped from the boxed cage. Linnet noticed Laurel, standing there at the top of the steps, and weakly smiled. The young maid wrinkled her brow as a claw of anger gripped her stomach. The carriage drove off as Linnet climbed the steps.

"Come to collect your things?"

Linnet stopped and stared at her adopted sister. "Is it *that* bad?"

Shame and jealousy cast the maid's eyes downward as Linnet entered the empty house.

"I will go to her."

Linnet walked at a brisk pace to her Lady's chambers. The clicks from her shoes echoed in the main hall against the flurry of her gown. She noticed white sheets covering the furniture in the lounge and study. *They are preparing to leave.*

"When did she last take blood?" Linnet asked the maid without turning.

Laurel stepped lightly into the house, closing the door.

"Nothing since you have gone."

Linnet's face pulled into a scowl. "You should have sent word to me."

The claw in Laurel's belly unfurled a quickened tension and she gnashed her teeth. Stabbing a taught fist toward the floor, the girl huffed and removed herself from the room lest she utter something wicked at Linnet's retreating back.

Climbing down the stairs, Linnet did not pause to light a candle. She made her way through the near dark to Dominique's closed door. She knew her Mistress was already aware of her presence in the house, so it did not bode well that her door still remained closed. She knocked lightly.

"Dominique?"

She waited. No reply came, except the quiet shifting of a metal lock. Pressing down on the latch, Linnet pushed the door open. Dominique stood in the center of the room. Her hands were folded and calm against her stomacher and she was fully garbed. Her hair was done up and her shoulders were squared. She appeared as regal as ever, except for the gaunt nature of her skin, hollow and sunken around her bones. There was a meekness that darkened her eyes and Linnet could see the Jadaraa Soo slithering over Dominique's breastplate and shoulders at her presence. She had never seen her Mistress in such a dilapidated state. Linnet entered the room.

"Laurel tells me you have not eaten once since I left four days ago."

"She worries. I am fine."

Linnet's eyes quickly flicked around the room. The candles had just been freshly lit. *She was sitting in the dark before my arrival.* As she neared her Dark Mistress, the woman bade her to come no further to her by the simple gesture of raising her hand. Linnet stopped, looked upon her, and wrinkled her brow. Sorrow tugged at her shoulders.

"I had to go."

"I know."

The Vam Pŷr stiffened her back and Linnet could tell that she was holding it in for her behalf. She despised the pretenses on which they acted. The woman crossed the lone expanse to her waiting paramour.

"Do not look upon me with such distance and disdain…"

"I could not. Not ever."

Linnet grabbed Dominique's cold hands and lifted them to her warm lips. The elapse of night still lived within her fingers. Dominique's veiny companion pulsed against Linnet's grasp, eager for a welcoming taste of the girl. Tears broke upon the consort's cheeks.

"I am sorry. I…"

"Hush. You have nothing to apologize for. You've done me no wrong. It is I who have let you down."

"No. Do not say that."

Linnet fell against her Mistress's chest. A sudden pang to rip into Linnet's neck stayed Dominique from placing her arms around the woman and embracing her.

"You mustn't…" Dominique pulled away. "I am too weak."

Linnet stepped back, and reaching behind herself, began to unlace her dress. "Then you must feed. Here, have of me and we will put this absence behind us."

Dominique violently turned away. "No, I can not."

Linnet grabbed her by the wrist. "Do not feign such modesty with me. I am yours. Bleed me."

The young woman's eyes were a conveyance of desire, mortal and loving. She offered up her veins on the altar of their union, but the Vam Pŷr refused and Linnet begged. She wanted Dominique's teeth. She had craved her Lady's embrace every day since she fled from the house to go to Nsia. Away from her dark mistress, Linnet's hunger grew like a fire within. She needed the comfort of Dominique to take blood from her. Linnet felt fat. She was too ripened like a peach, unplucked. She felt as if she would wither and die on the vine without being tasted.

"I want you too." Linnet urged. "I need you."

She pulled at Dominique's dress. Mother Night crumpled to the floor and held the woman around her waist. She was close to tears. "I can not…"

"I trust you to stop before the beating of my heart fades."

"You do not understand…"

"Then teach me. I am yours…"

Dominique looked up at Linnet. The fragrant bloom – so rich near the presence of her womb. She blurted out what only she appeared to know. "You are with child, Linnet. I can not."

The Vam Pŷr turned away as blood tears broke upon her face. Linnet's body went limp and her mouth hung agape.

"I am what?"

PART THREE:

The Story of a Guitar

He is seen in nature in the wonder of a flash of lightning.
He comes to the soul in the wonder of a flash of vision.

-The Upanishads

Ryan pulled at the scruff of his stubble, watching the green fingers of dawn wiggle through thick, prismatic smog, bleeding purple and orange trails before fading into smoky brilliance. Yellow opalescence illuminated architectural gaps between behemoth landmarks, herding elongated shadows away from the pale blue fireball rising out of the water. The sirens had faded and a hush permeated the wakening city. Only the waning edges of music blaring in the far room of the condominium drifted onto the balcony terrace.

Suddenly, a mechanical whine and hard clank of metal behind Ryan startled him. He turned and saw the ridged flaps of dense metal blinds descending behind the glass of the portico doors and windows. The entranceway back inside was slowly shrinking. He made a hasty run for it and dipped under the blinds, like a slacker Indiana Jones. Inside, he saw Lin with a remote control in one hand while the same thick veil crept over all the windows. What he didn't recognize, but his eyes detected, was how the lighting in the immense house automatically compensated for the difference in atmospheric illumination, so that the room's tone remained constant as the shields descended.

"Don't like sunrises either, huh?"

"What can I say," Lin shrugged. "I live the nightlife. I like to boogey."

The mysterious woman smirked and walked away, leaving Ryan alone to take stock of his enclosed surroundings. The penthouse was now quiet, tomb-like with its fastened shields and the stereo dead in the other room. He tried to remember what he knew about vampires. Both of these girls had oddly shaped canines and they were paler than most. The crowd that Ryan hung out with was not the most suntanned group one could meet. But these girls made that crowd look like Malibu Beach Barbie.

Ryan looked about. Polished, inlaid stone filled the halls to thick, plush carpeting that was in every room. Where there wasn't exposed brick, a darkened eggshell color coated the walls. Lacquered Brazilian wood trim offset the soft luster of the eggshell and brought out the rich allure of the old, red bricks. Yuko-e prints hung throughout the house. They were mixed among abstract designs, pop art, and Impressionists. These girls were obviously rich, or they were camping out at Daddy's luxurious hideaway. On one wall alone was mounted a huge wooden sculpture, roughly fifteen feet in length, of sea coral and fish. But there were no mirrors. Nowhere in the house had Ryan seen any looking glasses. Without the silver-backed reflectors the would-be vampires could avoid the awkward situation of not having their reflections cast.

Curiously, he went in search of the vibrant punk, keeping an eye out for any other telltale signs of vampirism. The place appeared empty. Manuel and his boy toy, Joy, weren't anywhere to be found. Mindy and Theresa were vaguely absent. *Had the vampires attacked them and drunk their blood while I listened to the city sing violence? Am I trapped in the middle of some midnight movie madness, with dawn bristling behind an inch of heavy steel?*

Ryan doubted his own musings. *Vampires…*

Even entertaining the thought was absurd. Ryan knew real vampires. They were just like everyone else, except that they liked to show off the fact that they drank blood, usually from some insecure groupie, who became enmeshed in their sacred harem. Those folks were flashy about it, downbeat to a fault, thinking it made them special and unique, something that Teen Goth Magazine would give two shits about. *But…these two?*

They were just two over zealous, geeky fan chicks with a hard-on for the genre. At least they weren't all Gothed out, drowning in Bauhaus and The Cure, drenched in black velvet leotards, pining after the gloom of Tim Burton animation. Ryan shuddered at those losers. At least these girls downplayed the whole vamp thing. It wasn't some trendy aspect of their DVD collection that they blogged about. He hadn't even seen a TV or computer in this place yet. Except for the weird teeth, sun shields, and lack of mirrors, Ryan had no other reason to follow this absurd train of thought any further. As far as he knew, they could be some rich heiresses in seclusion from their custodial family, or witnesses under FBI protection.

But, Vampires?

Ryan shook the thought from out of the tufts of his dirty blonde hair as he wandered through what looked like a kitchen. It was all modern and science fiction, had a sterile feeling and an electronic lock on the enormous stainless steel refrigerator. *No. These girls were definitely different. Bizarre to a fault.* They were both rough and elegant, like spitting on silk. Z had her own way about her and that's what he liked. She wasn't a carbon copy screaming an I-gotta-be-me-episode of the nightly news or the Gossip Girls. She was strong and powerful; a real woman with her own mind. *Sure, she was a bit eccentric,* he'd give her that. *But, a vampire?*

Ryan turned the corner and found that he was staring himself in the face. His blue eyes penetrated. His chiseled jaw reflected. His dirty blond locks were messed up in just the right way. At last, he'd found a mirror. As he moved away from the handsome man in the glass it occurred to him that Theresa wore a few crucifixes around her neck. He remembered seeing them when she was dancing earlier that night, and Mindy had that small gold cross. She usually kept it tucked under her shirt, though, because her Grandmother had given it to her. Neither Z nor the sable-haired chick freaked out at the sign of the cross, and their dancing earlier bordered on pornography - *for the most part*. It was something Ryan took a particular interest in watching. *No.* Ryan shook his head. *Vampires, like the ones in the movies, don't exist.*

He crossed the livingroom to an attached den and spied a door ajar. Pushing it open, he entered the unlit room. The smell of incense, perspiration, and old vinyl greeted him. Ryan searched for a light switch along the wall and eventually found one, thinking that he'd finally done it... *stumbled onto the room where the girls kept their coffins.* Flipping on the switch, fluorescent lights flickered as they buzzed to life, igniting a long chain, one after the other, across the concrete ceiling. Rows and rows of shelves filled the rectangular room, interrupted here and there by alcoves and careful setups.

Dust threw a party everywhere, except on the stacks of albums that filled the racks closest to the entrance. The out-of-date jacketed discs were packed tightly, from the floor to the ceiling, row after row, shelf after shelf, nothing but vinyl records. Ryan thumbed through a few of them. Punk Rock, mostly. The majority of it was pretty obscure. All of it was out of print.

Ryan looked down the long shaft of the room. Old Victrolas poked out from their dust-covered hovels. They were smashed against other aged stereo parts. Ryan poked through the junk. Phonographs and unused Hi-Fi sets. Eras of sound were thrown together on the same shelves, from the early days of radio past the invention of the boom-box. Interesting, if Ryan were a history buff. But he wasn't. He opened boxes filled with personal documents and photographs. A small lawn jockey lay on its side next to the bones of an ancient Indian. It appeared to Ryan that he had wandered into the condo's storage space. *Or...treasure trove?*

Ryan noticed a hundred dollar note sticking out of a billfold. The wallet sat on a plate that was filled with old pocket watches and keys. More plates, filled with more wallets, wristwatches, and personal effects came into view. Ryan turned toward the doorway to make sure no one was watching him. When he didn't see anyone he took the wallet from off the shelf, opened it, pulled out all of the cash and stuck it into his back pocket. He returned the billfold to the plate. Ryan was so eager to stash the cash that he failed to notice the dates on the bills were from the 1940's. Nor did he look at the photo of the girl, decked out in Big Band Era attire, in the wallet.

To Ryan it was just easy pickings, and with the scent of cash close by his fingertips, he began poking through the odd collection of artifacts with even more interest.

There were lots of bowls filled with dust-covered jewelry. Some of the items looked particularly pricey. If Ryan knew a fence he would have taken a few of the more expensive looking items. But as it was, he left the craft-works alone. That was until a petite diamond encrusted crucifix caught his eye. He checked the door again, and once more pocketed something that didn't belong to him.

The curious kid moved deeper into the room until he came upon something that truly caught his eye. It was a two-color starburst finished Fender Stratocaster. The guitar was in good condition. It only had a few nicks and dings. It sat on a stand in front of an alcove. There was no dust on it and the strings were new. Ryan ran his fingers up the solid one-piece maple neck to the uniquely wide dogleg-style headstock. His fingertips bristled over the inlaid black dots of the fret board, traversing the bridge claw, and wound along the smooth, cold metal of the Kluson machine heads. It was a beauty. His heart ached for the sleek, double-horned instrument, and he was sure he'd never make it out of the apartment with it stuck down his pant leg. Ryan had only ever seen pictures of this legendary guitar in magazines. Now here it was, tucked away in this odd room among this smash collection of kooks – *a hidden surprise.*

"I see you've found my Hot Box?"

Ryan turned and Z was standing right behind him. He hadn't even heard her approach. He wondered how long she'd been there. *Did she see me take the necklace?*

"Is, is this a '57 Fender Strat?" he asked, stuttering.

"Fifty-eight actually."

"It's…" Ryan paused, staring at the musical instrument with gilded awe, "…beautiful."

Z smiled at his boyish charm. She liked that he appreciated the hunk of carved wood, metal and wires. It was cute. She could feel his joy as heat radiating off of him just if she were standing in front of a dryer at a Laundromat.

"It belonged to Buddy Holly."

"No Shit. Really?"

"Really."

"How'd you, I mean, when did you buy it? I've never even heard of an original Holly Strat available at auction."

"I stole it."

Ryan laughed, a disbelieving chuckle. "Right. You stole it."

Z shrugged indifferently as the boy slowly took in the guitar's surroundings. Pictures of the late Buddy Holly and original album covers adorned the hand-painted alcove. There were reel-to-reel tapes stacked near a candle and incense; ticket stubs were stuck to the wall with a tack, a pair of black plastic, horned rimmed glasses hung close by; there were gas receipts, restaurant menus, and original photos of the plane crash that killed him, Ritchie Valens, and the Big Bopper. An old newspaper article about the crash was pressed between glass. Napkins from the Surf Ballroom, dead flowers, and a broken wristwatch had been placed in the alcove with loving care. Everything pulled in sharply, drawing the eye to the erect object of the two-color starburst Fender Stratocaster, centered amidst the artifacts. It was a shrine. Ryan had found a damn shrine.

"Ok," he chuckled. "I get it. You come from money." He turned to the dyed-redheaded punk like it was all good. "Though, you don't have to impress me. I already think you're hot."

He placed his hands on the licentious curves of Z's hips and pulled the slender flirt to him. She smiled, going with it, and Ryan thought for sure that he had mad game. But when he leaned in to kiss her plum junky lips, she titled her head up and to the side. The moment crashed like Buddy's plane. Feeling foolish, Ryan let his hands fall off her icy, smooth shape.

"I come from a cold night in the motor city," the not-so-easy fem explained. "My Daddy was a butcher and a factory worker and my Momma washed clothes to get by. I left home when I was fourteen, was arrested for stealing food, and returned as a runaway. I ain't never had shit unless I took it. And here you are knee deep in all my pirate booty and you're gonna call *me* a liar." She leveled her gaze at him and ran her tongue over her teeth. "Boy, ain't your Momma raised you with a lick of sense?"

Ryan grinned at his foolishness. She was an odd bird all right. He ran his hands through his hair, sparking an idea. "You play?" He indicated the guitar.

She shook her head no. "Never learned."

He wrapped his fingers around the maple neck, pitting the hard wood in the palm of his hand. "You mind if I play you a little something?"

Words were a train wreck in Z's mouth. She couldn't believe her eyes. The audacity of the boy! First to call her a liar, secondly to touch Buddy's fiddle – *he was hastening himself to the grave.* In her mind-numbing stupor he'd hoisted it from the stand.

In almost fifty years no one had ever touched the guitar except her. *Lin hasn't even held it!* Z had kept it locked up in her special little room since they returned with it from Iowa. It was safe in its case until 1971, when she finally opened it. A few years after that she erected the monument to her fallen icon. Now this skinny, sexy boy with less sense than what God gave a gnat held the vintage wood between his manly fingers and folded the curved body of the guitar to his abdomen.

He took a knee to play. It was like watching a car accident. Ryan strummed it a few times to get the feel of the instrument and sucked in a slow breath. It cut like butter in his hands.

"Sweet."

He began playing a song. A song that he knew the hot redhead would know. He played it slower because it fit the mood. He didn't want to cheat the piece until he began the melody. Watching the brazen boy's fingers move along the frets reminded Z of watching Buddy. She heard the maestro in her head and the hunk of wood, metal, and wires became alive again. In Ryan's tender care the guitar lived.

His voice lifted in the rectangular room as if it had wings. It pulled Z back into the present and she focused on him. *On him?* Melodious and angelic. His windpipes were gorgeous. Ryan sang Buddy Holly's *That'll Be The Day* with such soulful power and grace. Z felt a chill ride her spine. He was beautiful. This handsome, young nobody stored a songbird in his chest. Immediately, Z became aroused. He took shape and space in her dark soul. Her earlier musings of fucking him, killing him, and draining his corpse dry of every single drop of blood fled from her mind as he put his own delicious style to Buddy's classic. She enjoyed every sweet earful. When Ryan finished the song he looked up at Z and he knew he had her. He felt the hook in place.

"It wasn't how Buddy did it," he downplayed his effect. "It's such a great song. I couldn't help myself."

"He always pounded that one out." Z fell out of her stupor. "Usually as an encore." She grinned, reflecting. "He had this cute little twitch as he stepped back to play a solo, and he'd push his glasses back with the pick between his fingers…"

"You sound like you actually saw him."

Ryan returned the Fender to the stirrups of the guitar stand.

"How do you think I got the guitar?"

Ryan's head snapped in Z's direction, and she felt the hook set.

Clear Lake, Iowa. February 2, 1959.

Lin waited in the motel room, grinding her nails with a file. She sat on the bed agitated that Z hadn't come out of the bathroom yet. It took all her will power to ignore the disinfectant mothball and cotton candy stink that strangled the ashtray aroma embedded in the brownish carpet and yellow tile. Lazily, the sun set behind the cloud swirls that dominated the flat plain peaks as snow hardened over farmlands.

"Are you coming?" she whined. "It'll be over by the time we even get there."

Lin heard Z's sigh barrel through the small room and rolled her eyes.

"Are you sure I look all right?" The apprehensive vamp asked, emerging from the small checkered-tiled facility with a face twisted in worry. "I don't think this looks right. Do I look ok?"

She'd been like that all afternoon, trying on one outfit after another. Lin thought the pink Paige dress was elegant, but dialed down enough that the strumpet would blend well into the human crowd. Z wanted to look normal. But the vampire had thought the Paige dress made her boobs look flat. So, she traded slim elegance for the firm uplift of a conical bra and had begun trying on a whole bunch of sweaters and blouses. Her beatnik look of 4:30 – black Stella slacks, wedges, and a turtleneck jersey – was short-lived when Lin couldn't stop laughing.

The raven haired woman was sure that Z was going to go with the sexy fitting Houndstooth Check Lexy, but that was quickly replaced by a plaid, cherry red Lolita dress. But, Z decided that she was showing too much skin. She didn't want to be covered from head to toe in pancake make up. The star print prom mini disappeared into a white poodle skirt with a net petticoat support, pink saddle shoes, and a cardigan. It was adorable, but soon yielded to a stunning variety of polka dotted skirts and dresses.

As dusk waned, the pent-up Lin, waiting in a black bombshell dress (from her 1930's collection) over a strapless marquise corselette with a deep plunge, had had enough. The night had finally arrived, and there was no longer any reason to be locked up with a girl who couldn't make up her damn mind.

"What about the veins?" The insecure vampire asked. "Its too much make up, isn't it?" Z didn't even wait for an answer. She flung herself on the bed in a defiant pout as Lin got up. "Maybe I should just stay here. You go."

As Lin slid her wonderfully manicured hands and peach-colored nails into black gloves she turned to her annoying friend.

"We didn't make the show last night in Green Bay because you chickened out at the last minute, and we drove all of the way to this godforsaken nothing so you could catch him here.   I mean, Jesus Z, what's the big deal? It's just some skinny little troubadour with thick glasses."

"How can you say that!" Z was flush, rising to the man's defense. "Buddy Holly is the foremost important musician of his day. He's single-handedly changed the landscape of American music. He's…"

"Yeah, yeah, yeah," Lin chimed, breaking off Z's erratic rant. "God, you're so unabashedly smitten with this creep."

Lin put on her thick satin Melton cloth overcoat and grabbed her petite purse. She was going and that's all there was to it. She'd been cooped up in the Impala and crammed into motel rooms for days now, surrounded by suitcases of shoes and a menagerie of clashing prints and dress patterns. She was overloaded, aching for a night out, and a warm heart to pump blood through her parasitic veins. Lin walked toward the motel room door as the last gasp of desperation sighed behind her.

"What if…what if he sees me and…and…he *notices*…"

"No, no, no," volleyed Lin, turning on her heels. "I'm not going through this another night. Zia Jean Bell, you either come with me now or so help me God, I'm going to leave you here in Iowa for the fucking birds! I mean it."

"But what if...what if he notices that I'm not like everyone else?"

Z's small smattering of fear fell with the delicate thunder of a pin drop, soft and sincere. Lin couldn't help but feel sorry for her.

"Is that what's bothering you?" She crossed to the woman whom she'd come to know and rely on over the past twelve years as the bravest and most brazen person she had ever met. "You're afraid that he'll see you for what you are?"

Sheepishly, Z nodded her head up and down.

"When have you ever given a rat's ass about what anybody thinks?"

Z thought about it. "Never."

"Ok, then." Lin uttered squarely as truth, and before the moment had a chance to sink in, she added, "I'm leaving."

Just like that the buxom, raven haired beauty turned and walked out the door. Z stood in the havoc crashed motel room, wearing a blue and pink poodle skirt and matching pink polka dotted blouse, socks, a cowboy tied scarf, saddle shoes, and a bra that pressed her tits to her chin. She knew Lin was right. She never cared what anyone had thought of her before, not even her husband when he was alive! She always embraced the unknown with a kiss and a slap on the ass. To hell with open arms. Though lately she'd been acting like a train wreck. A walking catastrophe. *My god! I am smitten by this geeky troubadour.*

The dance floor of the Surf Ballroom was huge. Murals on the back wall depicted a beachfront ocean vista, complete with pounding surf, swaying palm trees, sailboats, and a lighthouse. The Tiki furnishings of bamboo and rattan gave one the sensation of lounging on a South Sea island. Hand-painted palm trees framed the stage under clouds that blended into a starry night that peered down on the wood tiled floor. The warm design of the Ballroom was a stark contrast to the blustery winds and snow that had begun to fall across the Iowa countryside.

The joint was packed. Cigarette smoke choked the painted sky. Ritchie Valens had just left the stage to a throng of screaming girls as Lin nestled into a Tiki booth with a drunken cowboy. She was well on her way to liquoring him up for a little light feeding. Z wandered near the back of the stage, straining for any glimpse of her musical heartthrob, who was sequestered somewhere backstage. She wasn't alone. If her goal was to appear as a normal American teenager, she succeeded, clamoring around the stage entrance with all of the other bobby-socked groupies.

When Holly finally hit the stage Z couldn't move. The whole place was a flutter and shake of bopping bodies contorting to the wild sounds of rock-n-roll. The bloodsucker was thunderstruck. She felt exposed under the painted canopy of night. Her heart raced in her throat. Not just because she was in the presence of Buddy Holly, but that the heat and perspiration of all the close-quartered bodies excited her Jadaraa Soo. Z wanted blood. She wanted to dive in, pick a poor soul, and have a good time. Usually, that got her off. Usually, all the heat and vibration from a packed crowd of people enticed Z's wild nature to let go and see what trouble she could find. But under Buddy's horn-rimmed stare every normal urge and compulsion felt sinister and wrong.

"Snap out of it," Lin said, dragging Z onto the dance floor.

She began to dance. Z stood still, gazing up at the man on the stage. She felt the kick drum in her chest in a way that she never heard on his albums. His guitar pierced her, a cold shower cutting across her skin, and the snare rattled in her head. His voice sang alive, bright like a sun, full with breathy brilliance.

"C'mon," Lin shouted. "Have a go." She pushed on Z. "Hey?"

Her eyes were glued to the young musician. Lin rocked her smitten flatmate by the hips, prodding her to move. She wouldn't take. Z just stood there staring up at the stage. Eventually, Lin gave up and danced alone to the twangy sounds.

Z felt mesmerized, transfixed like she was witnessing something god-like. She didn't know how to explain it. There was a power and a presence, an energy that surrounded him in an aura of majesty. She had never felt anything like it, yet she knew it had always been there. When she listened to his LPs on the turntable, she felt his magic spark through the record needle. But, here...now, amid the tropical trappings, palpitating hearts, and dank scent of the crowd, she knew she was in the presence of greatness. *True greatness.* She felt mediocre and small. Vulnerable and weak. It was all she could do to stop herself from trembling under the weight of his horned-rimmed stare from just a few feet away.

When Buddy Holly left the stage for the last time, after his second encore, Z rushed to the backstage entrance as if she were caught in an invisible fishing net with all the other groupies, pulled along by the wake of the rock-n-roll sensation. A swarm of sweaty pressed bobby socks and boobs kept the vampire from getting close to the artist as he signed autographs. Lin ran up behind her and grabbed her arm.

"C'mon. This way."

Z was pliable, a mess of dough. She let Lin lead her by the scruff of her polka dotted shirt out of the masses begging for a scrap of their favorite rocker. They headed toward a slouching man named Hank, who held Z's coat and a bottle of beer. Lin took Zia's coat from the Hank rack and gave it to her. Before she had even finished putting it on, Lin thrust the beer bottle at her.

"Here, drink this. It'll give you courage."

Z took a sloppy swig before Lin jerked it out of her hand and gave it back to the guy Lin had been baiting all evening.

"Wait for me," she shouted to her inebriated blood bank. "I'll be back."

Lin planted a friendly kiss on the man's lips to remind him of what he wasn't gonna get and dragged Z out the front door of the Surf Ballroom. Outside, away from the warm painted landscape, snow drifted above the iridescent glow of floodlights. Cold winds blew. Lin turned to her worship-addled friend and told it to her straight.

"You are going to meet him. We are going around back, away from all the other Betties and you are gonna suck it up and see that he's just a regular bloke with a banjo. You can do this. You have to do this."

Z stammered, wanting to tell her no. But Lin kept on, trying to amp Z up to meet the man that grounded her to the earth with melody. Lin's words rolled over her as if she were listening to them through a filter of cellophane. Z wondered why Lin couldn't see in Buddy what she saw. Wondered why she was so blind to his power and presence? To Z it was as clear as day and a striking bell. Buddy Holly was set apart from the rest of them, he floated above the world.

They were off again. Lin pulled the hapless vampire by the arm like a kid to the doctor's office. Z didn't resist. She ambled along after the elder vamp, watching the action unfold as if it were a motion picture show.

Around the back of the ballroom a handful of musicians huddled for a smoke. Buddy Holly was not among them. A few other fans had had the same idea and stood shivering in winter's embrace. Several of the musicians and stage crew were complaining about a plane that Buddy had chartered for himself while they had to endure another night on a bus with a broken heater. After awhile of standing around, waiting for the object of Z's teen obsession to wander outside for a quick nip, smoke, or chat with his crew, Lin got restless. This little brainstorm of hers was taking longer than she thought it would. So, instead of losing the meal that she had been working on all night, and given a strong assurance from Z that she could take it from here, Lin went in search of her own good time.

In the lonely cold, Z spied Waylon Jennings loading up his and Buddy's guitars into a storage compartment on the bus. He left the compartment door open when the Big Bopper walked up along side of him with the collar of his coat flipped up, grabbing it around the front of his neck with one thick hand to shield himself from the blistering winds. She overheard Jennings kindly give up his seat on the chartered Beechcraft Bonanza to the Bopper, who was running a fever and looked piqued.

A few of the other groupies couldn't take the cold any longer and gave up, leaving Z in the shadow of the building. She watched snowflakes fall from the dark abyss above. Tiny white dots falling down. Down. She stuck her tongue out, waiting for the fluffy flakes to land. Each one sizzled on her tongue. *Lin's so adamant that I meet him. She's grown confident since we got back from New Mexico. Knew a 'lil bedlam would purify her soul, get her on her feet again, get her out of that funk in which I found her.*

Z started humming a tune played earlier that night, swaying back and forth, and pictured Buddy up on the stage. *He was a dream. An apparition of harmony.* Z never noticed the eyes of the last two groupies as they watched her, walking back to their cars. She lazily played with the snow, feeling its wetness on her cheeks. Her eyes were closed and didn't see the songwriter when he finally came out into the cold, cursing the damnable weather. But she could smell him. His scent was unique. Pure, as the snow on her tongue. Z opened her eyes as he pulled his yellow leather jacket more tightly around himself. He called to his drummer, Allsup, saying that he was ready to roll.

Now's the chance! Z found herself pulling great, big gobs of cold air into her lungs, breathing out a smokestack. Her Jadaraa Soo shivered from the chill, and her feet hadn't moved an inch. *C'mon, girl. Easy.* She watched him. He consorted, talking it up with his mates. *All I have to do is run up and meet the man...meet the man that's shaping American Music!* Z shivered. *Simple. Easy. C'mon...*She took a few steps in the wrong direction, drifting back into the shadow of the building. It was obvious that he was eager to get going. *Now or never, sweetheart. Now or Never.* Then it rolled through her head that she could do it tomorrow night at the concert in Moorhead,

Minnesota. That she didn't have to do it now. It wasn't even her idea anyway to be flung to the wolves of her desires. This was Lin, again, trying to force her into doing something that she clearly didn't want to do.

But I want to see him. I wanna talk to him. Alone in the shadow she shook her head up and down. *All the other girls had left. I stood through it.* Her brow knotted as she followed every movement he made. Her arms wound around her shoulders and she held herself. *What if he looks at me and all he sees is a monster? What then, huh?* Z gritted her teeth, feeling her sharp fangs poke into her bottom gums, and for a brief moment she could hear the impact of each snowflake as it hit the ground. A pain seized her chest and Z wished that she were somebody different, wished that she could will the vampiric parasite away. If she could have made the veins recede, just a little bit, under her skin, the way that Lin did, that would've been something. That might have worked.

"Horrible freak, horrible freak, keep your face in a jar by the sink." Z sang quietly on blue-tinted lips.

Even if all the Max Factor fooled his eyes, Z knew it in her parasite-addled heart that he would sense how unnatural she was. Her veins were slithering under her skin from the prolonged exposure to the weather, trying to stay warm. They were the unbearable truth that plagued her brain. Her thoughts were cancer. Her body was a duplex. It was usually something she celebrated in a slaughtering frenzy or going out dancing. But here… *now*…was a man with all the stunning brilliance of a shooting star in the heavens. Z was a freak. *He'll know.* Despondent, she leaned back against the hard siding of the Surf Ballroom, giving in to fear, cursing Cross for the abomination that he had created.

Holly was gathering up his band to make for the plane when a tired and frozen Valens tried again to persuade Allsup to trade seats with him. He was sick of the bus and couldn't take another night shivering.

"Come on man," Valens pleaded. "Look, I'll flip ya for it."

He sneezed and held a quarter between a numb forefinger and thumb. The look in his eyes was desperate. Allsup took pity on the poor kid and agreed to the toss. The members of the Winter Dance Party Tour gathered around the pop sensation. Z noticed that the compartment door on the opposite side of the bus was still open, and just like that an old, familiar urge struck. It was a thought she couldn't ignore and set out at a brisk pace.

The coin was rocketed into the falling sky as Z walked to the opposite side of the tour bus. The twenty-five cent piece twirled in the air, rotating end over end. It fell heavier than snow as Z snatched the case that housed Buddy's Fender Stratocaster. She simply strolled off in the direction of Lin's fin-tailed beauty as the legal tender fell into anticipating hands. Z heard laughing and taunts behind her. On the other side of the bus Valens had won the toss.

"Well, I hope your old bus freezes up," Holly shouted as he inched through the backdoor of the Ballroom.

"Well, I hope your plane crashes," Jennings responded in friendly banter as he boarded the bus.

Despite the cold, Z waited outside of the aquamarine Chevy Impala for Lin to reappear. The snow had picked up and was falling harder. Holly's stolen guitar rested in the back seat of the car while she leaned against the rear window thinking about how insecure she had been. It wasn't like her. *Lin was right.* She needed to confront him and see for herself. He was, after all, just a man. *Just another human male.* Regardless of how he made her feel he was like Simon Ray. Meat. *And he was married meat at that!*

"Wishing. That I could see you everyday," Z sang to the night. "Wishing. That I could steal your heart away. Dreaming. Of the times I could hold you tight. Wishing. That the time would come tonight. That things would turn out right. I'd been hoping all along. Wishing. Then I would spend the night. If I could find the wishing star..."

"Could the wind blow up the backside of my dress any further?!"

Z turned as Lin scurried out of a shadow that fell across the parking lot. She headed straight for the driver's side door, looking rosy and flush.

"How 'bout I drive?" Z asked, moving out of Lin's way.

"Just want to get back to the motel."

Lin opened the door and climbed in. Z watched her for a second, shook her head, and went around to the passenger side of the vehicle.

"You always do that," complained Z, climbing in.

"Do what?" Lin peered into the rearview mirror, wiping fresh blood from out of the corners of her mouth.

"You never let me drive. You always have to be in control."

"I do not."

"Do too."

Lin spied the top of the guitar case propped up in the back seat in the rearview, and turned around.

"Where'd you get that?"

Z shrugged. "Just picked it up."

Lin tossed her a blank face, eyebrows raised.

Z met her gaze, staring impassively. "How's Hank?"

Lin stuck the key in the throat of the steering column and fired up the blue-green luxury car. "Left him passed out in the front seat of his truck; heat on, motor running, pants down around his ankles." The girls passed a quiet laugh. "He'll wake up by morning, thinking he cut himself while getting lucky."

"Much too kind." Z tossed her head from side to side.

"So?" The curious kitten asked, pausing as she pulled on the switch that turned on the headlights. "Did you do it? Did you finally meet the great Buddy Holly?"

Z turned and looked at her. "Yeah."

"Just another bloke, right?"

Z nodded the affirmation. "Just another bloke."

The raven haired woman moved the steering column gearshift into drive. "So, after you met him you just had a sudden urge to steal his guitar?"

"Something like that."

Lin pulled out of the parking lot, laughing, taking the street. The snow had begun to stick to the road.

"How long do you think it'd take us to drive to Minnesota?"

Lin turned to Z, mouth agape. "No."

"C'mon, it'd be fun." Z gave her that huck-a-buck smile of hers. It was hard to resist. "I'll even let you drive."

"Well, it is my car," chuckled Lin at the strange vampire, liking her easy way and cavorting nature. *Never a dull moment with this one.*

"We can even leave tonight."

Lin tossed her a look, *like there was any other option.* "You planning on giving him back his guitar."

"Oh, no, no. That puppy's mine."

Snow fell on the cold metal roof of the Impala as it buzzed down the frost-covered streets of Clear Lake, Iowa. As the wind picked up, the two vamps laughed, planning the trip to Moorhead.

Ryan wasn't convinced. It was an exciting tale and all, but there was no way this brazen, little hottie was a sycophant bloodsucker.

"So, like what…" the naive hustler taunted, "you're a couple hundred years old or something?"

"Or something."

She's stickin' to her guns. He wandered over to the shelf with the lawn jockey. "You nick this too?"

Z smirked, remembering.

"What?" Ryan asked, wanting to know the lie that had lit up her eyes.

"Lin and I crashed a party at Errol Flynn's place, back in '48. She started a fight and we got thrown out."

"Well, you had to take it then; just wouldn't have been right to leave it."

Ryan's cheeky smile cut through to Z's hips. His blues were two lights. He stirred her innards as his eyes swept the room. The place was loaded with junk and Ryan figured that Z had a story for everything in here. *Must work props in the industry.* He wandered over to another shelf, noticing the black faded lettering on an aged gray canvas bag that rested next to a set of tarnished silverware. The lettering on the bag spelled Winter's Bank. Ryan picked it up. It had weight and the jangle of coin.

"I suppose this is from some fearless bank job or train heist from the old west?"

Z rubbed her chin. The boy's vibrato egged her. "You ever hear of Bonnie and Clyde?"

"Yeah," he answered, setting the bag down and wiping the dust off his hands. "Some married bank robber couple back in prohibition days. Got all shot up like in that movie. Lemme guess…you were in their gang?"

Z grinned, finding his smart-ass pleasing. "They never married. In the whole time they were robbin' banks and raisin' hell they never netted more than fifteen hundred dollars. My husband Ray and I stole damn near ten times that and you ain't never heard shit about us."

"Huh." Ryan considered it for a minute as if it were factual. *The girl was steeped in it. If she wants to play a centuries-old vampire then who am I to argue with her? It really doesn't matter how she sees herself or what pair of shoes she decides to dance in. People put too much energy into trying to bend others to their ideas of life and what not. I'm not pressed. If she wants to act like a Goth whore, what does it hurt?* "So, why do you think that is?"

"Think what is?"

"Why they went down in the history books instead of you?" He flipped through more items on the shelf.

"Probably, 'cause they killed fourteen cops and kidnapped some asshole. Or, that the cops could lay claim to makin' 'em pay for their life of crime by shootin' 'em all to shit like snakes in a barrel. Whereas, they never got close to catchin' us." Z stepped toward him as she talked. "The point is…"

He turned into her and she ran her hand up his chest on the outside of his shirt. He was so close his breath hit her face. Warm. Z felt the nag from her parasite to have a taste, just a little taste. She recalled the beauty of his voice and swooned from the aphrodisiac of his scent. She leaned into him, opening her mouth just a bit by his Jugular vein. It sounded as if she were standing next to a brook in the forest. "I…I…" Z pushed herself back. "I think its time we said good night."

Z turned away. Her teeth thrummed and the bottom of her belly tingled.

"You do know its morning, don't you?"

A shiver raced up her flesh. "It's always morning somewhere, sunshine."

Her Jadaraa Soo protested vigorously in her ears like a cloud of gnats nesting in a vile temper. The blood parasite had been teased all night, taunted with live bait. It wanted to climax, to get off on the vital fluid coursing through the songbird's body. It didn't help any that Ryan was dawdling, trying to weasel his way into Z's denim.

"Yeah, guess it is," he said and moved in behind her, ignoring the wide swath that she had left for him to navigate his way out of her Hot Box. "But I can wait until tonight to say goodbye."

Cheeky bastard. Z turned around and looked up at him. *His shoulders were the perfect size to hang off of.* Her doughy, honey brown eyes were as hard as nails. "Aren't you at all concerned that your little friends have gone and left you all alone?"

Stupid. Z meant to be intimidating, but she only succeeded in enticing him further. So, before he could complete his grin, Z flexed her hand against his chest and stopped him from leaning in. His lips looked delicious. "You really need to leave. *Now.*"

Z grabbed the lip of one of the shelves with her other hand and looked away. The tension between them was palpable. His desire for her was strong. Ryan relaxed, conceding to not push it, knowing full well that she wanted him too. After a couple of breaths, he started for the door.

"So, what happened to your other half?"

Z exhaled. "Lin retired to her chambers."

"No," he corrected, turning to face her. "I meant your husband."

"Oh," Z replied daintily, her mind occupied on quelling her own piqued hunger. "I shot him in the head with his revolver."

It wasn't an answer that Ryan had expected and he stopped short. "Guess that could be easier than counseling."

Z chuckled strangely, gazing into Ryan's ocean blues. "We're all the cosmic shit machine, honey. That's just how it goes. He got his plot of dirt," she shrugged and presented herself with her hands, "and I wound up here."

Full blown delusion. Maybe an actress studying for a role? "Sounds tragic."

"Yeah. Cry me a river."

Z strutted to the opened door, stopped, and turned. Ryan had concrete shoes. He pulled gravity into the presence of his form, still occupying her treasure trove, drinking up more details from all of the artifacts that the supposed vampire had collected. *There was a spark, definitely a spark.* But, the boy kept her bound to a parade of unwanted memories and hard driving lust.

"You comin' or what?"

1775. *Tangier, Morocco.*

Unbelievable. Simply unbelievable. Linnet was in shock. Her eyes were deceiving her. She turned and saw Nsia walking through one of the ruined doors, out into the market air toward her. She had said her good-byes to Nsia in Nicé, before boarding the ship. It had been unbearable to tear herself away from him like she had done. It felt as if she were peeling flesh from off her arm with a dull knife. *He had said he was going home, back to his people.* Yet, here he was in Tanja, and he had found her. Linnet knew it was a mistake to stop along the port in the Strait of Gibraltar, but Dominique wanted to show her the city where she and Ramielle Eirinhas had spent many nights after their escape from the Tien Däm Mu.

"Of course, it is not as grand as it used to be." Dominique kept saying as they made their way up the sloping paths to the hilltop where the decimated city sat. "It was once spectacular and opulent."

The English had destroyed the town from the waters of the Strait as they withdrew from the blockade in 1684. After the Moroccan victory, Sultan Moulay Ismail had ordered reconstruction of the port town to an extent, but since then the city had just gradually declined. The Vam Pŷr's reminiscing admiration was evident on her face. She recalled structures and thoroughfares that no longer existed.

Along the Market Square, tucked in the ruined shoulders of Dominique's memories, a few vendors peddled by moonlight. The ship's Captain needed time to finish stocking the galleon with supplies and crewing the vessel so there were no plans to leave the harbor before midday. In the interim, the Lady De'Paul decided to entreat her consorts to a stroll through the town. That was when Linnet had seen him, in the darkened bazaar. Their paths had crossed on the shore of the African continent. Linnet's knees crumbled, her shoulders sank like an avalanche. *He cannot see me like this. Dear God, he cannot.* Linnet placed a hand to her protruding belly, blackness swirled around the edges of her eyes, and she fainted.

A butterfly flitted through the garden thistle. Linnet chased after it with the net her papaw had given her last Christmas. The child's small, stubby legs moved excitedly, giggling after the tiny orange-brown winged nymphalid along the pebble path eager to net the creature and show it to her mother. She followed the black spots because the sun-colored hue kept disappearing among the flowers.

They were walking the garden again today. The sun was high, bright and cheerful. Her mother had dressed her in a simple Poplin dress instead of her nanny, and Linnet had spent the majority of the day in her mother's care. She flung the net at the spectacular migrant when it landed on a flower. Missing it, she caught the butterfly on the upswing when it had taken flight. Linnet checked the net for her prize and ran over to her mother.

"What kind is it Mamma? What type is this one?"

"Well, let me see Linnet and I will tell you."

The child held her net up, holding it by the lap of fabric as her father had shown her so as to keep the critter from escaping.

"Careful," her Mother prodded, "you mustn't hurt it."

"I won't."

The Lady Pevensey knelt so that she could see more clearly through the mesh. "Oh, that is a pretty one. See the orange and black?"

"Yes." Linnet beamed.

"And how the white spots are only among the dark patches?"

"Yes. What kind of flitter-by is it?"

Audrey coughed and cleared her throat. "I believe you've captured a Painted Lady."

"Really, Mamma, really? A Painted Lady?"

Another cough erupted from Audrey's chest and she stood. Linnet watched her mother as she produced a handkerchief and placed it to her mouth. The uneasy chortles did not cease. Audrey's bosom heaved with violent shudders, pulling the cloth away from her mouth there was a red globule of blood dotting the pristine fabric. In her worry, the child had relaxed her hold on the instrument's lattice, releasing the Painted Lady to flutter among the glade.

Linnet woke hard coughing, unable to breathe as the salts stung her nose. She stared into the bearded face of Doctor Rohmer. She was in her cabin onboard ship. Laurel stood behind the disheveled physician, concern cutting her face.

"She seems through it now," the doctor added. Linnet tried to sit up and speak, but the middle-aged man put his hands to her shoulders. "Rest. Just lie back." He turned to Laurel. "See here girl, fetch me some water. The salts can bring on a thirst."

Linnet's eyes darted around the room, looking for him.

Laurel approached with a wooden cup of liquid. "Here."

"Drink this," the Doctor ordered. "You've had a nasty fall."

Linnet took the water and gulped it. She did not see Nsia in the cabin. *Was he aboard?* She attempted to move again, but her hip smarted. Disoriented, she did not see Dominique.

"The baby…"

"Yes, the baby is fine," commented Dr. Rohmer, wiping his hands on a rag. "But you need to rest. You've collapsed due to stress. I will speak with your Mistress about a remedy…"

Linnet fidgeted and tried again to sit up. "Is Dominique with him?"

"Mind yourself," Rohmer urged, becoming ill content. "You mustn't worry or take to the air anytime soon; plenty of bed rest. You hear me? Recuperate. I will keep my eye on you."

Linnet eased down, her breathing was an engine, heavy and panicking.

"Keep her sedate," the doctor informed Laurel. "Restrain her if you must, but no duties for a time." He closed his bag and picking it up, "I will look in on her later today after I've tended to my primary patient."

The young maiden nodded and the doctor left, spilling bright shades of daylight into the cabin. Linnet was befuddled. Her back ached.

"Is he on board ship?"

Laurel did not know what she was talking about. "Linnet, you must mind the doctor. That was the second time he was forced to use the salts to revive you. You've been unconscious for quite awhile, had many of us worried."

Laurel tucked the pregnant lass in, tightening the sheets around her with frustrated pampering. Slowly, Linnet began to feel the sway of the ship on the water.

"Have we left port?"

"Aye, 'bout an hour ago." She fussed with a pitcher, bowl, and a cloth. "Dominique was with you 'til daybreak. She had to return to her cabin or else…"

"I know."

An awkward silence descended the room. Linnet could clearly see the strain that she had placed the poor girl under. The past few months had been intense for everyone. Leaving London after completing the commission, traveling through France to the Villa de Nicé, the continual association of Mr. Bah prying into the affairs of the Vam Pŷr, and Linnet's romantic relationship with him. It had disrupted the balance of their strange family. Laurel had taken on more responsibility, shouldering the brunt of Dominique's welfare than either of them had previously suffered. The discovery of Linnet's pregnancy had placed even more strain upon the three of them while the favorite consort labored to keep her condition hidden from Nsia.

Heavy decisions framed the period before they boarded the ship and all the while social pretenses had to be maintained, business had to be looked after, and Dominique required blood. The withdrawal from and care of Lady De'Paul's properties while they were away needed to be tended to. The arrangements of the voyage had to be made. A mountain of detail stared the three ladies in the face and through it all Linnet vacillated on whether or not she would accompany her dark mistress and Laurel to Brazil or sojourn with Nsia to his African home. It was only at the last minute did Linnet finally decide to join them, using as a pretext for her decision the absence of communication from Dominique's ward, Isabela da Nóbrega.

The woman's holdings in South America were in serious trouble, anything could have happened in the waning years between letters. The lack of attention from Isabela could only mean one thing: affairs were not in order. Linnet relied upon dire circumstances abroad as the sole reason why she would not go with Nsia to his homeland. She felt like a liar and a fool the whole time that she was with him in Nicé, knowing full well that inside of her grew a child of their lovemaking. But she could not imagine abandoning the dark mistress, especially in her time of need.

As Laurel stepped up as the chief supplier of Dominique's source of blood jealousy rode Linnet's bones like a river. The Vam Pŷr could not take her or else she would injure the baby. And Dominique would never do that. Though her teeth were sharp, her heart was kind. Linnet felt weak and ineffectual in their house together. She clung to Dominique's presence as often as she could, fearing that she would lose the Vam Pŷr forever if she went with Nsia. Encapsulated in the enigma of the man and the dominant pledge of his people, Linnet feared that she would lose herself. If she journeyed now with Dominique she could always return to Nsia at some later date. She did not have to imbibe the dark drink. She could bring their child home to him one day.

"I saw him."

Laurel turned to the woman in bed. "Whom did you see?"

"Nsia. At the marketplace. He was walking toward me when…" Linnet's eyes gleaned the look on the young maid's face and followed her as she crossed the tight cabin and sat on the edge of the bed. "He is not here, is he?"

Laurel shook her head, "No."

Linnet sighed. "I've made a mockery of everything." Tears ran down her face.

Laurel scooped up Linnet's hand and held it gently. "The heart deceives. Do not put yourself under such scrutiny. It is an unnecessary quarrel."

Linnet held the girl in her gaze. She was modest in her beauty, faithful, and had only joined Dominique's employ prior to the Vam Pŷr finding Linnet at the Opera. Laurel's eyes were fatigued, deep set with black lines. Her weight and color were pale. As the sole beneficiary to their dark mistress's feeding habits Laurel appeared weakened. Linnet placed a hand to her cheek, stroking her face with her thumb.

"I am sorry that all of the burden has fallen to you and…for the way I've acted."

Laurel nodded. "Yes, well," she tightened her jaw, agitated, "it appears I will have to keep it up a little while longer. The boy whom Dominique had contracted to join us failed to meet his obligation this morning."

"He did not show?"

"No." She stood. "Nor did he bother to write that he would not. Fair to assume that he has absconded with our money."

"I will talk with Dominique. She can not encumber you excessively."

"No, that will not be necessary," Laurel turned firm. "You heard the doctor. And besides, Dominique and I have already devised alternate solutions much like the manner in which we maintained the household in Nicé. You must get your rest." She placed a hand to the small bubble of Linnet's belly. "There is somebody else that requires your diligence."

It ate holes in Linnet's pride to be so easily assigned by her understudy. "What are your alternatives aboard ship?"

"I am off to prepare a chicken for our Lady."

Linnet chuckled. "Oh, she will not fancy that."

"Well," she tucked Linnet in. "It is what we've devised and we have turned a portion of the cargo hold into a livery."

"Then you two have decided?"

"Yes. It seemed prudent. Considering."

Linnet grabbed Laurel's hand as the girl moved away. A wellspring of feeling swelled within her breast, but she did not have a voice to transport it. The two maids stared briefly into each other's eyes and the jealousy that had been plaguing Linnet's heart melted away. They did not have to speak the words. They knew. They held secrets together, understood that the night had teeth, and they were the closest that either of them had to friends or siblings amid the Vam Pŷr's unusual company. They had bonded in sacrifice, years of service, sharing the Persian woman, abandoning all that they'd grown up knowing for the prospect of some hidden divine. Nsia's arrival had intruded upon their quiet collective and though Dominique had instigated the affair between them, it was Linnet that had placed so much weight upon Laurel's narrow shoulders.

In the subdued lull and lonely rocking of the ship after Laurel had left, Linnet sustained herself on her memories of the man. Drifting back and forth by the sway of the large boat the bloodsucker's consort staggered on the import of values on which she was raised. There was a dark knocking in her heart that told her that she had made a mistake. It was small and quiet, but it was there. It told her that she should have forgone her interests in the night creature and joined Nsia wherever he might have led them throughout their life together. Her Mother had birthed nine children and remained bound to one man for her entire life. Linnet housed her first child and was bound to no one.

The tiny, fearful voice that told her that she should have stayed with Nsia clashed with the love she held for Dominique, the love she held for a woman. Her heart was unnatural, black as ash; she did unthinkable acts with her. Acts her parents and pastor would condemn her for. Acts that went against nature that she hid from Nsia. She was but a pendulum within the ship, swaying back and forth between what she felt was right and what she had grown up learning. There was no one to council her on this path she walked. She traveled it alone. Except for Laurel, who did not share Linnet's carnal desire for Dominique, there was nobody around who vaguely understood. She was like this vessel – *a dot amid the sea.*

After all this time and dreadful circumstance since she abandoned the duties that her father had charged, Linnet still could not endure the thought of losing the Vam Pŷr. It pained her that she was not within the cabin when she woke. Linnet understood Dominique's reason. It was for the best. Pretenses had to be maintained. It was one of the codes they followed in their Transacting Directives for transporting Kind during sea voyages. But Linnet's passions were unreasonable. Her heart was a conflux of cravings. She was selfish. Even during her last tenure in her homeland she had not gone to visit with her papaw. She was too wrapped up in her affairs. And now she was leaving Europe for God knew how long. *I am a spoiled fruit.* Despite their codes of conduct she wanted Dominique with her now. *Damn the sun! Damn my mind. Why else would I labor under constant torment if I had made the right choice?*

Ryan stood there considering the enigma of the girl. He jangled the loose change in his pockets, weighing his thoughts with the coins. They had mirrors, saw crucifixes, sported sharp canine teeth, shielded themselves from the sun, and were just plain odd. *Really odd.* What did he know? *Really!* What did he actually know about vampires other than what he had seen in movies or on TV? He hadn't even read Bram Stoker's Dracula. These girls felt slightly out of touch, unattainable, off-kilter; there was something about them that was peculiar. Though, he couldn't quite put his finger on it.

"Are you an actress?"

"You ask a lot of questions."

"You avoid a lot of answers."

Z grinned. *He was a little worm. Wiggle. Wiggle.* The tattooed punk walked back into the room, slow and sexy. The warmth of his heat bathed her with each step. As she neared, Ryan began to notice the thin trail of veins that ran across the whites of her eyes and dived down her pupils. That seemed to squirm beneath her powdering of make-up and skin. Her eyes weren't deadened from too many pills and alcohol, like he had previously thought. They simply lacked a living luster that normal eyes had, and Ryan would know, having spent a good deal of time staring into the opened eyes of the women he'd had sex with.

"You know," the apple in his throat hiccuped, "I know a few *real* vampires too. They live down in the canyon. Got a club over in the valley."

"Is that so?"

He shook his head up and down, slowly. "Guy named Morpheus; you know him?"

Z chuckled and grinned, picturing the idiot with the name, and innocently peeled back her lips with wide mirth. Ryan saw that her canine teeth weren't just special dental caps. That there was a thin weave of tiny reddish veins that led from the tops of her fangs, breaking into the hard flesh of her gums.

"He ain't like you, is he?"

"Ain't nobody like me?" Z pressed up against him. Her eyeballs titled upwards, quivering toward the back of her head. The man's musk flooded her like an Incan village during the rainy season and she put her hands on his ribcage, along both sides. "It's rare I invite anyone to leave," she sucked a breath through the grate of her clenched teeth. "Are you fixin' to be rude?"

What? Ryan stared down at her, captivated by all the little imperfections of her nocturnal condition slowly unveiling itself to him.

"You have me at a bit of a disadvantage…"

"You don't know the half of it."

"Before I go, can I at least get your phone number?"

Z cracked up. Slapped her knee. *That was a good one.* Ryan failed to see the joke, picking his ego up from off the floor, where the sudden crush of chortles had left it. "Now, who's being rude?"

Z wanted that throat where the songbird lived. She tasted feathers on her tongue just thinking about it. *That'll be the day-hey-hey…that I die –* memories of Buddy. The boy was peeking through her, into her, that spark she felt between them was igniting. It would lead to a forest fire. Z didn't want the hassle of the man right now. "C'mon Romeo," Z nudged him toward the door. "Let's save the last dance for later."

Ryan gave in and began walking toward the door. Every round with the bright dyed-red punk brought him back to her escorting him out of the secluded hollow. He usually didn't have to work this hard to get a kiss. *Off-kilter, odd; just out of reach.* Ryan hated the thought of leaving with his tail between his legs, and a hard-on in his pants, so as he passed her by he leaned down and planted one.

It wasn't so much that Z didn't want him to kiss her or that she despised his forward nature. It wasn't that she was offended in anyway by his small smooch that made her react violently and plaster him up against the shelves on the opposite wall. It was the fact that Z felt the button of her sex unfasten too quickly that she had pushed him away. Ryan felt the bright sting of pain ripping across his back in solid hardware lines more than he'd felt the lush beauty of Z's lips.

"I said," Z glowered at him, "let's save the last dance 'til later."

Ryan started bitterly laughing. *Such an odd bird.* "Look whose all aflutter." He peeled himself off the shelf. "I think the lady doth protest too much."

"I think the lady asked you nicely to leave."

Her words said no, but her eyes, with all the veins, said yes, yes, yes. "Are you really a vampire?"

Z grinned, a hiccuping laugh, winding into her words. "Bela's the only vamp I know and he had a wicked bump for the junk. Me?" She shrugged her shoulders and tilted her head. "I'm just Z. And, that's all there is to know about me little boy."

"Is that so?" It'd been ages since anyone had ever called Ryan a *little* boy.

"Yeah. That's so."

It nagged his growing ego. He wanted to know for sure. "Bite me," he said as he stepped toward her with serious intent. "That's how it works, right? We've been alone long enough. If you're a vampire why haven't you bitten me?"

All the laughter left Z in a quick flap. He stood before her, calling her out like a gunslinger. *Cards on the table. Black Jack and bumpin' uglies between the sheets.* He wanted it serious. *Hardcore.* "Maybe I'm full. Not in the mood. Or, have a headache."

"What kind of vampire doesn't drink blood?"

"That tweaked Underworld bitch."

"I'm not talking about some bullshit movie." He was getting frustrated now. The teasing was fun and all, but he had called her out and she hadn't stepped up, continuing to dance through every little verbal snare like a greased snake. "I'm talking about you, here and now, supposedly the very real deal and I'm letting you know it's Ok." He tapped the vein on the side of his neck with a finger. "I like it rough."

"Oh. You do?" Z moved closer to him now.

"Yeah. I do." He stepped toward her too, excited that this was finally going somewhere.

They stood facing one another in the center of Z's Hot Box.

"Don't force it, bright-eyes." She matched the sincerity of his tone. "You might not like the consequences."

"I think I can handle it."

Z stared at him, long and hard. She wanted his blood in her mouth just as much as her Jadaraa Soo wanted it. She wanted to unpack the bulge in his pants and ride him around the apartment like a prize bull in a cowboy rodeo. But with the music in her head and the *e* drilling through her system, Z didn't know if she could handle herself or not, refrain from killing him, stop herself once all the juices started to flow and the fun began.

"So, ah…" Z laid a hand on him again and found her way under his shirt, "you wouldn't mind if I…" she pinched one of Ryan's nipples. Pulling and twisting, she enjoyed watching his face wince from the modest delectation. "If I go and…"

"Yeah?"

She pinched him harder and moved into his careening body, placing a leg between his two, sturdy supports. Immediately, she felt his hardened member pressing against her childless womb, hot and tempting. *God, that feels gorgeous.* "…get my strap on an' twirl you around on my plastic Willy like a sweet singing sister in the jailhouse shower?"

That wasn't exactly what Ryan had in mind. *She teased. Damn, she teased!* He moved to step away, gain some perspective, get her on the right track. But Z grabbed both of his nipples, twisted vehemently, and pulled him closer. The vampire had a hell of a grip. He tried to downplay how much he was gloriously suffering and a moan escaped his lips.

Ryan decided to return the favor and trailed his fingers around the curvature of her breasts, stroking her soft mounds with the palms of his hands. He applied a softer touch, all the while never disengaging eye contact with her dull honey browns.

"Ok, I'm only going to say this once." Her lips were so close to his that she could kiss him. The heat between them was electric. "Cause, you're just like every other guy out there. You think your shit don't stink and your cock's the holy grail; can make any girl famous, find god and call ya Jesus. But just because you've made a few girls cum does not mean you know the first thing about navigating your way through the pleasure center of a girl's heart." His moist, full lips brushed against hers like a match striking a tinderbox. She leaned back. "I'm not talking about that magic, little button they call a clit. I'm talking about her brain, you asshole. And if you had one yourself you wouldn't be here asking *me* to bite you. You'd be with that Mindy slut, pile-driving her face into the mattress considering yourself lucky that I left you with any balls for her to lick. But you're not smart. You're young, dumb, full of cum, and acting stupid, thinking you could hook it up with Jan Brady's crazy half-sister in the back room. But I can tell you this, Frankenstein…I'm definitely one party your dick ain't ever been to. So why don't you go home, find five fingers of love, and forget about me and everything you *think* you know. 'Cause you don't know Jack and you definitely don't know shit."

Z backed up, panting. Head delirious with lust, her Jadaraa Soo was pitching a fit, assaulting her senses with a visual escapade of carnality. Ryan's nipples throbbed as he glared at the punk. It all boiled down to one simple thing: *she was a fucking tease.*

He was *so* done with this. "If you are some sort of vampire then you're the strangest one I've ever met."

Z literally bit her tongue to keep herself from ripping the front of his throat out and freeing the caged songbird that he kept stored in his chest. Ryan huffed as he started for the door. There were so many other chicks out there that would gladly give him more than a nipple tweak. He didn't need this bullshit. "I know a lot more than you think and can handle everything that you've got."

Z's eyes narrowed to slits. "Look meat, it's simple." She cocked her hip at a dangerous angle. "I don't eat where I live and I don't shit where I eat. So strange or not, you're going home, unfulfilled. Unrequited. All alone. But at least you're going home."

Ryan reached the door, stopped, and turned around, displaying unprecedented gall. "Aaww..." his branded chaff mocked her sincerity, "you're crushin' me and breakin' my heart."

"Better than if I drained it dry," Z whispered.

"*Now* you're talkin' dirty." He gave it one last try, moving toward her again. "C'mon. Bite me. Bite me really hard?"

Z laughed. *He was adorable!* "Tenacious little fucker, aren't you?"

"I just know what I want." Even his words had swagger. "And, I won't give up 'til I get it."

She liked him. He was a hoot. Z leaned into his warm array of charisma, arching up onto her tippy-toes, and gently kissed him. It was only meant to be a friendly, neighborly kiss. A nice-knowing-ya-and-thank-ya kind of lip lock. But that didn't last. Despite their ebb and flow, their lackadaisical wind up, they wanted each other and the little howya-doin' kiss quickly developed into a groping, wanna-fuck-ya-on-the-cold-concrete kind of kiss, tying their tongues around one another, pressing pliant curves against firm extremities like the pages in a tightly bound book.

"You're sweet," she uttered once she finally broke the lip-smack, and straightening up her shirt, "you definitely know you're sexy." She was grinning wide, a live rendition of Carroll's Cheshire Cat, as a silly thought swam through her head. She wiped the slobber from off her chin. "I'm old enough to be your great grandmother." She giggled and swiveled on a heel. "I may be impulsive. But I'm not stupid." She patted his chest. "Go home."

The chick was mental. Fantastic kisser though!

Z headed toward the door. Ryan watched the two-moon caravan of her plush derrière, pining to mount those curves and go for a ride. *Fucking tease.* As the soulful songbird began to follow Z out of her steamy Hot Box, he was suddenly set upon and swept off his feet. Before he could make sense of what was happening he felt the sting again from solid metal shelving and the soft joy of Z's firm breasts crushing him as her legs intertwined around his own. Then, with more force than what he thought the svelte lady possessed she bent his head to the side, yanking him by his dirty-blond locks.

A sudden flash of fear ripped through Ryan's core. She held him there, splayed before her dark appetite, a willing buffet. He couldn't budge or lift himself away from her. He couldn't break out of the woman's grasp, even if he wanted to. Z smelled his unique musk and the copper tinge of his rushing blood that coursed just below his skin. She savored his scent and the parasite trembled in a violent shudder, eager to finally enjoy a repast from a twitching live thing.

All night it had been cavorting in a sea of warm flesh while its selfish host ignored it. The cold sustenance Z had taken before she went out clubbing was nothing but a bitter memory to the veiny parasite. It demanded raw food, pumped fresh from the grinding organ. Z's veins pulsed to the surface of her flesh as Ryan wrapped his arms around the lustful carnivore.

Against a tide of gnawing fear he pulled the vampire closer while Z ran her tongue along the ridge of his protruding jugular. It was the same one that Ryan had plucked earlier, so carefree and inviting, with a finger. The salt from his sweat-soaked flesh was titillating. She felt his penis engorge under her, pressing with mad passion into the soft, round thigh that rested between his legs. She liked the feel of his hardness and traversed a hand over the stretched denim jeans and began stroking.

"Do it," he moaned.

Z placed her ardent lips against Ryan's pulpy ear and whispered. "The one thing I've learned in all this time is that you do not rush the things you enjoy."

Before Ryan could respond to Z's timeless wisdom she sucked his earlobe into her mouth and bit down hard using only one fang. The pointy tooth, comprised of several knotted and woven veins, unwound in Ryan's hot flesh and began to wriggle through his ear, absorbing the blood around it. What sanguine fluid the tiny veins didn't drink Z swallowed. After the initial pain of rendered flesh the suckling was rather pleasant. It wasn't the hard, sought-after jugular romp that he had seen done in countless movies. But she had bitten him. She drank his blood and it felt like her tongue was messaging him all the way down the canal of the acoustic organ to his brain.

He breathed heavy, his chest heaving up and down as Z fed from him, stroking his cock through his jeans. His hands caressed her, knowingly finding erogenous zones that Z hadn't had played with in a really long time. It felt like she had fully penetrated him. Like she was farther inside of him than just a mere dangling pulp of flesh would permit. Their two bodies writhed together, dry humping on the floor in a heated embrace. Pushing and pulling against the alien fabric of clothes to find the salvation of flesh, and pay the toll of ravenous appetite. Before everything got X-rated however, Z pulled away and the Jadaraa Soo receded back to its regular shape. To Ryan, the veins pulling out of his ear sounded like the automatic cord return on a vacuum.

He lay under her, panting for a spell. Z kissed his Adam's apple and the hard, wet aching bulge in his pants before she stood. She was a bit lightheaded and woozy and it took a minute for her to climb down from her arousal. She offered him a hand up, looking down at his gorgeous masculinity, throbbing with life, as wonderful mischief carved across her face. Ryan took her hand and rose. Just as he was about to make some prosaic comment, Z placed a finger to his lips, shutting him up.

"Don't," she said. "You'll ruin it."

PART FOUR:

Dream of You

When all desires that cling to the heart are surrendered,
then a mortal becomes immortal.
When all the ties that bind the heart are unloosened,
then a mortal becomes immortal.

-The Upanishads

March 23, 1930.

Plumes of dust spiraled up from the wheels of the stolen triple nickel as it raced along the country road toward the Ohio/Indiana state line. Bullet holes riddled the reinforced, soft-shell top of the deluxe roadster shattering glass with little round spickets of disaster. The cops had been on them since Dayton. Simon Ray Boyd floored the tiny, round metal gas pedal pushing its pistons as fast as the racer would go. The road was rough and he and his wife, Zia Jean Boyd, bounced on the taut leather, spiral coiled seat. This made firing Simon's gun difficult.

Zia reloaded and grabbed a handful of Wanted Posters, of their earlier exploits in Arkansas in 1928 and Missouri in 1929, from a satchel on the seat between them. She kicked at the bank bags of cash at her feet and flipped around just as a bullet zinged past her pretty, little head and slammed into the dirty windshield almost messing up the curls of her millinery and aerating the thoughts from her right temple.

"You son-of-a…" The rascally robber barked as she turned about, poking her head out the passenger side window releasing the leaflets into the screaming wind.

Paper mixed with the hard swelled pools of dirt and flew through the air landing on the grimy windshield of a trailing black and white Ford coupe. Only two Coppers pursued them now. The Black and Whites were falling off like flies under the excessive chase Simon Ray led them on. He and Zia had worked out the escape route just in case they ran into any trouble. And boy had they! No sooner than they'd left Winter's Bank in Dayton did five police vehicles set them upon with voracious tenacity. It was like they were ready for 'em. Waiting for the Boyds' to exit the bank.

But these last two. They stuck to the roadster with the fierce appetite of a dog with a meaty bone. Simon Ray took a solid turn in the tough road exposing the broadside of the Model A as their wanted posters obscured the driver's vision behind them. Zia aimed for the dusty, orange license plate and squeezed the trigger. She didn't pull. Simon Ray taught her not to pull. It loused the shot and Zia had to shoot straight. The Coppers were pitchin' them a hellfire of lead and she didn't know how much more they could take. Instantly, the radiator of the closest Black and White exploded in a cloud of hot steam and the trailing coupe rolled into a farmer's field as its engine sputtered and spat its last gasp.

Before Zia could shout with glee two bullets pierced the side of the roadster from the last Cop Car giving chase and she ducked back inside.

Simon Ray was hunched low over the steering wheel as stinging metal whipped passed his head and destroyed his side-view mirror.

"Christ!" Simon shouted. "You gotta do something 'bout this!"

But Zia didn't hear him as her index finger quick pulled the trigger emptying the revolver out of the emaciated rear window thundering into both of their spoiled ears. She swung around and began reloading as more biting lead hit the speeding two-seater. Zia laughed as her nimble fingers worked the bullets into the hallow chambers.

"Baby, I gotta tell ya. You sure know how to show a gal a good time."

"You don't say?" Simon Ray retorted. His wife had an odd sense of humor.

"If it don't mean a thing," the haphazard starlet sang. "It ain't got that swing. Do-wop Do-wop Do waa…"

Zia couldn't help but laugh at the irony of their situation as she jammed the small, snub-nosed bullets into Simon Ray's revolver. Her husband was a bang dead shot. He'd have cleared these Coppers off the road miles back. Instead, he was crouched over the wheel, locked into a sucker's position waiting it out, doing his best not to get shot. He wasn't even supposed to be driving. But they scrambled into the car when the police descended upon them opening fire in the street. It mixed up their getaway and they had to improvise.

"Next time," she shouted over the din of the chase, batting her honey brown eyes up at him. "I drive."

Sloppily, she kissed him and raised the gun into the air blindly directing a loose shot before she moved into position out of the passenger side window. She aimed for a front tire of the police's Model A and fired, but as the terrain was bumpy, it was like two pigs in a sack fighting over an ear of corn. Two round specks splintered the front windshield of the pursuing black & white. *Aw Shit!* They still kept coming. Through the dirt-fog the roadster kicked up she could see the eyes of the pot-bellied Pig who spit hot lead at her. They were filled with hate – *he had a hankering for our hides.* Zia steeled herself against another hail of his bullet glory and carefully sighted the tread on the tire closest to her. She relaxed the way Simon showed her and gently eased the trigger, one shot after the other. She wasn't gonna give in. *No cop was baggin' the Boyds today!* Luck sat on her shoulder as one of the shots landed on target, killing the inflated wheel, causing the cops to career off the road and into a tree.

Zia hollered long and prideful turning around in her seat. She immediately went to plant a wet one on her lover, but Simon Ray was breathing heavy. He had been hit in the left shoulder during that last volley. Blood poured down his arm and pooled on the floorboards.

"'Bout time," he joked, noticing his wife staring at him in stilled awe. "I was beginning to think you were just playing with 'em."

Zia hated seeing that lean throughout his torso and ordered him to pull over. Simon Ray protested, claiming he was all right, that it was superficial; nothing to worry her pretty little head about. She wasn't buying it. The pain and sweat on his brow told her it was more serious than he was letting on.

"At least let me drive," she cajoled.

He nodded, agreeing to that.

Once the triple nickel cleared the Ohio/Indiana border, she traded places with her husband climbing over the gooseneck gearshift. As she took the wheel, a long shiver rode the length of her spine, stiffening her face at the sight of Simon's blood, *his life fluid*, which had soaked through the tweed coat he was wearing. Sitting down, her hand found something moist. She looked at it and it was red.

"Go on now," Simon Ray urged. "Should be a straight shot to the rendezvous. I'll be fine. Just gonna mend it up a bit 'til we get there."

Zia's strained eyes did all the complaining that he cared to hear about. He eased himself out of his jacket and she pulled back onto the road. He knew she was concerned, but they weren't that far from where he'd stashed the sports coupe and Indianapolis was just a few hours away. He could control the bleeding until then. Zia was gonna have to dig another bullet out of him, that much was for sure. This one was deep and it smarted worse than anything he'd ever felt before, but he knew she could do it. She wasn't the squirmy, all-girly type when it came to wounded flesh and blood. *No sir!* They had seen their fair share of scrapes, especially down in Jacksonville. This wasn't the worst of it by far. They were gonna be all right. Everything was gonna be all right.

Ryan Silva couldn't get the girl off his mind. Her huck-a-buck smile drifted across his closed lids as he imagined what she must have been like robbing banks and running from the law. Her bite to his ear pulsed in longing pangs and he wanted more. As he lay in bed thinking about her his hand traveled under the soft band of his underwear and he began pulling on his hardening member.

That sharp pierce and silent pop of flesh yielding to her teeth. The way her hair smelled of honey and almonds. The soft press of her breasts crushed against his chest as she pinned him to the wall. The way her tender hand moved from the side of his ribcage to the bulge in his pants as the other trailed up his arm and stroked the coarse fibers of hair along his throat while she sucked his flesh, lapping his vital juices with a velvety tongue.

The woman was damnable. Each stroke he made of his cock rebuilt her body to the scaffolding of his musculature. He burned in a white fire of desire for the vampire in such a way that he never dreamed possible. He had to be with her again. He needed to be with her again. His breath broke his rhythm. His body spasmed, but still he grew harder, more sensitive. He tightened his grip and gritted his teeth as he imagined her legs wrapped around his: her tender, smooth skin along her inner thighs squeezing vehemently about his waist, pulling him into the luscious folds of her wet fury.

His back arched and he kicked the thin bed sheet off. He imagined her arms coiling over his back pulling the nape of his neck to her hungry mouth. His chest heaved against her bare round bosom as her fangs bit down on his throat and she entered him just as deeply as he penetrated her. Ryan quaked and exploded in galvanizing convulsions. The sticky, hot fluid released along his belly and chest, weaving into his dark walnut hairs. He panted. His grand mal shuddered lightly in the lonely afterglow.

He wanted to be with her. He needed to see her again. Ryan Silva thought of the girl and rolled onto his side. Outside, it was daylight. Outside, people gathered under the sun-baked brilliance and toiled among their daily lives. Ryan waited for the sun to drop. Nighttime was his lady's gift. He imagined her lying next to him, her head resting on the pillow as he stroked her dyed red hair. And he closed his eyes.

March 23, 1930.

Zia Jean Bell was born on December 12th 1904. She was the first and only daughter of John and Sara Bell. They would go on to raise two boys after Sara recovered from a miscarriage and traumatic hemorrhage that nearly cost her, her life. It would be a fixed moment in young Zia's mind as to why she would never want to bear children. The memory of her mother lying gaunt and pale in bed in a pool of her own blood would be a calcifying factor and continual reminder of the precarious nature of her sex.

Zia was born in a South side tenant in Detroit, Michigan. A midwife neighbor and the inebriated doctor gently assisted the Bells in the living room of their small, one bedroom apartment. The birth was relatively easy compared to those that Sara would suffer through later in life. A light snow fell and John heated pots of water on a small wood burning cast iron stove that he'd installed the year before. He repaid both his neighbor and the alcoholic doctor with seven pounds of meat that he'd taken from work at the packaging factory. For the doctor's services he also added a bottle of bourbon and an opened pack of Lucky Strikes to the payment of meat, and that concluded the deal that brought his daughter into his life.

French-born magazine editor and socialite Baron Nicolas de Gunzburg was also born on this day. Zia would never read any of his magazines or even know that he was alive, though she would move in a circle of people that did. On this day, workers on the East Boston Tunnel prepared for its opening at the end of the month. In New York City, commuters marveled at traveling along the 9.1 miles of track that had recently opened, and which was the beginning of the city's massive subway system. In Times Square city officials, event planners, and marketers prepared for the first New Year's Eve celebration. Writer James Joyce was settling into his newly blossomed romance with his muse, Nora Barnacle. President Roosevelt had put his election victory behind him as he read an updated report on the expelled families that had lost their homes and livelihood in the Great Baltimore Fire on February seventh. Bids on the harbor city's reconstruction were still coming in to Baltimore's relocated City Hall and the White House. The costs of damages to Washington's sister city taxed Teddy's year-end economic plan.

Astronomer Charles Dillon Perrine still poured over his telescope and notes after just finding Jupiter's irregular satellite, *Himalia*, and members of Pi Kappa Phi relaxed into their newly founded fraternity leaving some with hangovers that lasted beyond Zia Bell's arrival. Far to the South, the infant Pablo Neruda suckled at his mother's tit in Parral, Chile while across the seas Claude Monet applied the finishing stroke to his masterpiece, *Water Lillies*; and actors at the Duke of York's Theater in London prepared for the gala premiere of *Peter Pan, or The Boy Who Wouldn't Grow Up*.

In some regards, Zia Jean would not grow up either. She would not act in the kinds of ways that others thought was responsible or sensible for a normal adult to conduct one's life and she would die before ever reaching a domestic level of maturity. She was reckless and carefree much in the same way that Barrie imagined his Lost Boys, but without that attractive veil of innocence. Zia never found an appreciation for fine art or theater, and though she shared the same birth year as surrealist painter Salvador Dali and the famous Dr. Seuss she was never aware of it. Dali's work particularly cut to the core of her, so she avoided it emphatically. She also ignored the work of Theodor Geisel as it pertained to children, and as mentioned above, Zia avoided all things that pertained to having, birthing, and caring for children, except, of course, for sex. Sex was something she enjoyed. Ironically though, Zia would grow to enjoy watching *How The Grinch Stole Christmas* every year around her birthday more than she liked having sex. Also ironic was that for as much as Zia avoided the world of art she would spend many long years of her life collecting art from famous and obscure artists with a woman who fancied it. Occasionally, this woman would notice Zia peeking out of the corners of her eyes to Dali's strange imaginings. But they never spoke of it. Because, Zia never called attention to the fear that gnawed in her gut when she spied the surreal paintings.

In 1904, California's population neared 1.4 million, 14% of the homes in the United Sates had bathtubs and the total number of automobiles only clocked in at less than 8,000. Henry Ford opened his first factory in the Highlands of Detroit, and in the spring following Zia's birth her father would go to work for Mr. Ford. It was a decision he always regretted, lamenting the impersonal conditions of the factory line. The Missouri Kid had finally been captured after an exhaustive manhunt had tracked him to Kansas: it was a failed bank robbery in Cleveland that ultimately led to his arrest. Since the Kid's daring escape less than a year earlier, the flow of thousands of dollars spent on man hours for surveillance and the ongoing investigation, abruptly came to an end. As a result, many government officials were reassigned. The Russo-Japanese War blazed through the headlines on newspaper stands. Russia had just suffered a crushing loss to Japanese forces taking the 203 Meter Hill. Many injured survivors from the brutal attack of the Port Arthur Harbor, which followed, died as Sara Bell screamed and gritted her teeth in labor.

Earlier that year, the St. Louis World's Fair introduced to the world the wonders of the ice cream cone, iced tea, tea bags, and the invention of the modern day 'Hot Dog', where one placed a popularized sausage between a bun. The tomb of Queen Nefertari was discovered. America took over the construction of the Panama Canal as the country adopted the US dollar as its currency. Anton Pavlovich Chekhov died of tuberculosis at the tender age of forty-four and the Nez Perce Chief Joseph died of a broken heart. Later in life, Zia would attribute Chief Joseph's passing to her birth, claiming that she was born under a bad sign. But there were no bad signs on December 12, 1904. There were no hints or pretense that the child born on this day in the Southside Detroit tenant would become a cold, vicious killer. On the contrary, the world was changing. Progress and industry were on the tips of the peoples' tongues. By year's end the Wright Brothers would have flown for five whole minutes. The world, indeed, was changing.

Zia Jean Bell was nothing short of a normal baby. She cried when the doctor slapped her wrinkled, purple rear. Her miniature mouth screamed for her mother's milk and the tiny digits of her delicate hands grasped for this new, vibrant world around her. Much in the same way that Zia Jean screamed now as her husband thrust himself inside of her and her hands grasped the copious piles of money that covered the hotel bed on which they made love. She rode Simon Ray like a rodeo rider. The worry of hurting his bandaged shoulder had fled from her endorphin-addled mind. She wanted him, deeply implanted, all of the way inside of her. The dark hole that tore at the insides of her belly howled to be filled by the manliness that penetrated between her thighs.

The hunger she had for him capitulated in the loss she almost bore. She had him now, whole and hardy, and she wasn't going to ever let him go. The money from the bank robbery was just a kicker. A cheap thrill that the Boyds reveled in. It was the glory of the heist and of the getaway. On looking back, in the few short days that they had left together, they both would remember how the hardbound stacks of cash dug uncomfortably into their bare backs, buttocks, and knees. They would smile about it and kiss, savoring one another. Zia would physically recall the heat and presence of Simon between her legs from that night in the Indianapolis hotel for many years to come. It was a fixed point in her mind. Though, in this bristling, sweaty moment, neither Simon nor Zia realized that this night was the last time they would ever make love.

1775. Crossing the Atlantic.

"What are the eight principles for transporting Kindred and Kind cargo along transatlantic and transpacific routes?" asked Linnet.

Despite her condition, the woman paced back and forth with relative ease, having become accustomed to the see-saw motion of the ship. Laurel was slow in answering her even though they had been going over passenger and trade routes for several days now. Since the health of both young ladies had improved over the past weeks after leaving Tangiers, Linnet had taken it upon herself to educate Laurel on all of her Mistress's commercial and civic occupations. It was Linnet's hope that once they reached the shores of Brazil, the young maid might take over her duties, handling Dominique's affairs during the immediate recovery after giving birth to Nsia's baby.

"Always use designated shipping and trade routes as defined by the Tien Däm Mu J'in Charter," the understudy finally answered. "Never deviate from accepted lanes of passage. Assign an authorized captain familiar with coven shipping procedures." She paused, thinking. "In lieu of an authorized captain approach the assigned dignitary of the receiving country to recruit from their naval officers. Manifests are always encoded, as well as accompanied by a decoy manifest in case of boarding. If the ship's captain happens to be a naval officer from a receiving country then the manifest is defined as letters of state in the common language of that country." Laurel raised her thumb on the other hand and furled her brow, thinking before she concluded. "Armed escorts maintain a low alert status so as not to arouse the suspicions of second and third class crew."

"Why?" interjected Linnet's stern voice.

"Because the Transacting Officer of the route defines the order of operations?" Laurel, unsure, looked to her mentor to see if she was correct.

Linnet scrunched up her face and wiggled her hand. "In part."

"Suspicion leads to curiosity," the homely girl hedged with some enthusiasm.

"Continue."

"Curiosity leads to questions. Questions about the trade or travelling emissaries from either clan or coven is greatly discouraged to ensure the secrecy of operations."

"And that leads to number six…"

Laurel looked down at her fingers. She was sure she was on number seven. "Refresh all non-familiar personnel and crew at every port." She folded her off-counting hands in her lap. "Kindred emissaries are always accompanied by armed escort, unless otherwise detailed. Coven kind are to be accompanied by a minimum of one familiar physician per voyage, unless flight from port is mandatory."

The understudy was sure she had listed all eight, but the look on Linnet's face was not convincing. She ran the list again in her head and became even more confident. The last answer she knew for certain as she personally booked the passage for Doctor Rohmer. He had accompanied Dominique on two previous voyages, caring for her during the daylight hours and testifying about her very rare and incurable disease. Nothing allayed the worrisome, fear-soaked talk of salty sea dogs more than rumors of incurable diseases.

Overall, learning the operation principles was not so easy. Laurel could not write anything down. And those items which she was permitted to put to paper were only allowed to exist for a twenty-four hour period total before incineration. The care for Mistress De'Paul's affairs was most complicated, and it was proving difficult for Laurel to put to memory.

"How and when are a Transacting Officer's orders of route overridden?" Linnet asked, feeling tired that the young girl had not completed the list.

"Oh, sorry. Ah..." Laurel snapped out of her mental daze, "only from a document signed by the traveling clan's J'in Ankh. Without that the Transacting Officer's orders are standing?"

Laurel was hesitant, thinking that there was more to the answer that she was forgetting. She watched Linnet as she sat. The dark haired woman was getting big, and had begun wearing the maternity gowns that Dominique had bought. Her belly poked through the curtain of the dress, covered in soft cotton. Dominique had procured fresh attire for Laurel too, but the girl did not see any need to unpack it until they reached the house in São Paulo.

"When was the last time Dominique arranged passage for an Omjadda?" she asked.

"Sixteen nintey-seven." Linnet eased into her seat, balancing herself against the waves knocking against the hull.

Laurel scoffed. "We could be gone from this earth by the time any of this would even matter?"

Linnet just looked at the girl, dazed at the ignorance of the comment. She felt fatigued and for the past week had been growing tired more rapidly. The pregnancy was taking its toll. "If you truly believe that, then why are you here?"

Laurel looked up, realizing the foolishness of her statement. "You know why I am here."

She rose as Linnet sighed heavily, stretching her back out, and placed a hand to her forehead. They both knew that Dominique held sway over the hands of time. They did not speak outright about their personal desires for the dark gift, but their mutual interest was understood.

"You should rest." Laurel coached, crossing to a basket of fruit and cheese. "We can continue the lessons another time."

She grabbed a pitcher and poured her teacher a drink in the cleanest glass she could find, which meant that it was still a little dirty. Linnet's eyes bore holes in her adopted sister's back. Sitting firm against the rollicking sway of the frigate made Linnet queasy and she was sure Laurel wanted to abandon her studies. The pregnant woman huffed and stood as her pupil returned with the repast.

"How does passenger shipping differ from common commercial shipping?"

"Transportation of kindred and kind dignitaries," Laurel explained, setting the food items on the table between them, "is governed by set rules and procedures to ensure safe passage in secrecy, whereas commercial routes are governed by the same maritime regulations and laws as other countries."

"And why is this?" snapped Linnet.

Laurel thought on it, but did not have an answer. She steadied the cup on the table and looked up at the woman who hovered over her. "I, ah…I do not know."

"Because," Linnet informed, placing a hand to the table to steady herself. "The voyage of 1697 was beset by pirates. All hands and cargo were lost, including the Omjadda emissaries that were our Lady's charge. A Kindred body washed upon the African shore weeks after the attack. Rumors of the strange beast found on the beach reached the ears of its clan and it befell Dominique to make amends for her error in judgment."

"But they were pirates." Laurel interjected. "How could they hold her responsible for…"

"Because, it was her duty. Her responsibility," Linnet breathed out, holding her belly. The weight of her person felt enormous and every shifting move the boat made as she stood still bore down on her. "Even one mistake in an otherwise careful plan can have the most dire repercussions."

Linnet began to pace.

"What did she do?"

"She burned the village that had found the body, killing every man, woman, and child that might have seen it and returned the corpse to its clan."

"The whole village?"

Linnet shook her head, a grim face counting her steps. "They demanded retribution. Either their heads or hers." She stopped at the table and picked up a plum. "This is why it is important to minimize the possibility of unwanted incidents."

Linnet bit into the plum and raised her eyebrows, accentuating her point. The small fruit's juice moistened her lips and wet her chin. The expression on Laurel's face was what she had expected. The tale was repulsive and difficult to place in one's mind.

"Did she...do it herself?"

"No. She hired the same pirates that attacked her fleet to raze the village and then dispatched them when they came to collect their final payment."

"It's all so..." muttered Laurel as she sat, her words vanishing into the imagined horror. She picked up Linnet's cup of water and drank from it, staring blankly at the planking of the floorboards.

"And on land, this differs how?" interjected Linnet as a belch lingered on the top of her stomach just inching its way to her teeth. She set the masticated plum down.

"Ah..." Laurel lifted her head from the cobwebs of thoughts. "Because, clan alliance dictates the travel of commercial and passenger routes mostly through subterranean railways regulated by Omjadda affiliates."

Linnet waited for the rest of the answer, but Laurel appeared impassive to her staring. She took pity on the girl and informed her as to how the Tien Däm Mu J'in managed cross clan contingencies while their mistress only controlled the seafaring ports. The latter was mostly due to the simple fact that Dominique De'Paul owned an armada of fourteen vessels. That made the freed Vam Pỷr an ideal candidate to regulate both commercial and passenger sea routes for the ancient race. It also did not hurt that the one-time slave of the ancient clan was their defacto J'in Ankh. That meant that, to some degree, she held some power and influence among the other J'ins.

As Laurel was learning, Dominique possessed a fierce network of business relations in both the secular human realm and Omjadda clans. She was a key figure in the social reform between the newly freed Vam and the Omjadda after the Eras of Slavery had ended. Dominique possessed strong ties throughout the emerging hybrid covens that had begun to take root within this century, and there were many that called Dominique the mother of their race. She had earned the freedom and the right – by trial and error - to define for herself how her businesses operated, and in so doing, she had taken root among many hostile forces.

Linnet tried to make it easy for Laurel. She did not anticipate being away from her obligations for too long once they reached São Paulo. For her it always came down to practical economics. It was something she had picked up from watching her father manage the King's commerce. Those that wished to partake of Madame De'Paul's goods and services – of which there were many – followed her rules and regulations lest they starve or worse yet, came under attack by the armies of men that were so easy to control, because men were ruled by money.

It gave Linnet no end of amusement that the one-time slave of the ancient race was now a master who walked among them, dictating terms for them to abide. She prided herself on the accomplishments of her Lady. Though, in light of the shocking lesson of 1697, Linnet chose to keep her notions to herself. Imparting the scope of Dominique's operations to Laurel were proving difficult enough.

In a family way, Linnet felt shaky. Instructing her pupil to continue her studies of the Blouchard Code and the Portuguese and Omjadda languages, she journeyed to the upper deck of the ship to get some air.

Topside, the radiant fire of the sun was extinguishing into the vast spectacle of the sea and the men of the crew were gathering below to dine. Those sailors still on deck watched the eighth daughter of the House of Pevensey as she sauntered the metered length of the full rigged ship. The tang of the ocean was thick in the air and even after all this time onboard Linnet still continued to overhear the staunch barnacle-talk about the ill effects of women on a ship. The banal intellect of superstitious men amazed the unwed woman. None of the ocean faring lads liked the combination of females and sickly looking passengers that hid below the decks, only to reveal themselves under the light of stars. It put a crawl in their tunics. Though, for the pay they received they followed the Captain's orders whether they liked them or not. *The desires of men were universal: coin, grog, and tail.* Dispelling evil intentions among this superstitious lot was simple, and easily affordable by the gracious women whom they mocked.

The velvet press of Nsia's voice and crush of his breath on the back of her neck swirled in longing memory by the wind's touch. Her hand circled her growing womb, feeling him inside of her. The dense aroma of the sea held with it their last goodbye. No matter how far she pushed across the Atlantic, the scent and vigor of the salty waves were a constant reminder of the day he boarded the ship that took him home. His eyes were browbeaten and downcast, hurt that she would not go with him. They said very little to each other on that day.

She, standing on the docks as if nailed to the planks: their parting was brief. He did not linger. Even after Linnet had told him that she would be accompanying the Vam Pŷr to Brazil he did not stay with her in Nicé. He booked his passage and left. Holding her on the docks, he simply kissed her cheek, and turned away. Linnet felt outside of herself, watching events play out, crying. He boarded the small vessel and tossed back a look. The sadness in his eyes was a constant reminder, the cradle of the vast sea. He wanted her to go with him.

The hard looks from the sailors ducking below deck made Linnet feel guilty. It touched her spine. The way one of them crossed himself in a Christian way, cursing under his breath in French, though just loud enough for her to hear how unhappy he was with her presence aboard ship, stapled verse from the good book to her mind. *And she said to her father, Let it not displease my lord that I cannot rise up before thee; for the custom of women is upon me.* Linnet followed him with her eyes until he disappeared. *Bastard.*

Nsia was the only man she knew that had a backbone of moral character. He did not wear a pretense to his stature and never once dismissed Linnet because of her sex. The pregnant lass sighed and cracked an ache in her back. His loving hands were across the ocean. Dominique's hands were kept to herself. Only loneliness touched Linnet's skin of late. She curled her arms about herself thinking of how her shoulders folded under Nsia's sinewy arms like wings tucking her in. Sea spray caressed her face, dotting it like Nsia's Nembo. She did not bother to wipe it off, recalling the time that she had asked him about it.

Linnet lay on top of him, naked and spent. Their breathing had calmed and they bristled with heat, cocooned in the warmth of his bed. She traced a finger over the hard, scarred skin that decorated his cheeks.

"When did you get these?"

"Twelve," he uttered.

"So young. Do all of your people have them?"

"No, it is not for everyone. I chose the Nembo to show my laahidi buuñaa; how do you say, dedication…honor. Each dot represents one day that I fasted for my Jinoo Kuntun, ah, spirit-walk. The lines represent my first kill…"

"You were twelve when you killed your first Omjadda?" Linnet leaned back surprised.

"No," he grinned. "Fifteen. I have only killed two." He drew his fingers across both of the puffy lines that marked his face for the kills and noticed the query forming behind Linnet's eyes. He answered her before she spoke. "I was not as agile as my other siblings. Weaker when I was a boy, and picked on for my height. Taking the Nembo was a way of proving my worth to my tribe."

"Sounds so brutal," Linnet noted, rolling onto her side.

"It is not. Many cultures use scarification and tattoo as a way of honoring the path, or journey, one must walk. I feel no remorse. I wear them proudly."

Linnet felt as if she had injured him by her banter. Watching him, she leaned in and kissed the rugged lines thinking of what it must have been like for him as a child to grow up in a world that chased demons from the night. He stared at her strangely as she pulled back, smiled, and shook his head. So much distance lay between the universe of their lives. Linnet felt the button of her sex unsnap and was pleased when he kissed her.

Neptune's kisses were the only favor the poor girl had these days. The expectant mother had thought that once they had put out to sea that she and Dominique would regain their usual roles. More than three weeks now and barely a conversation outside of the average duty had passed between them. The room of the galleon, from port to stern, was vast in Dominique's consummate absence, who chose to remain secluded with Doctor Rohmer. And he guarded his patient as if her ailments were real. It bothered Linnet that without Dominique's presence time wore on slowly, a malcontent mechanism of collected seconds stretched to a heartless infinity. *Were it not for you, my love, I would never have loved Nsia.*

The Vam Pŷr's ardent test of Linnet's mettle was cast with a very different hue than when she had gleaned the epiphany of ages all those months ago. Loving them both was perverse and unkind. Her body was becoming alien and she counted the days like a prisoner, etching the cycles into the stone cavern of her head. The wind wiped Linnet's long, black hair about her face and the gravid lass took a bit of solace in the knowledge that by month's end they would reach Trinidad and the crew would be swapped out. She was sick of the men's jeers and of the looks that lingered longer than she felt comfortable. With a new crew Linnet could hide in fresh faces.

She felt grotesque. The gift of pregnancy was cruel in Linnet's mind and filled with too many nasty occasions of burping, farting, and spewing one's food overboard. She would be thankful when the bastard child was out of her and she could resume her duties for her Mistress, unencumbered. *Was all of it just to see what choice I would make?*

"The Captain tells me that you have been below deck most of the day. I do hope that you were resting."

Linnet hated the fact that her heart fluttered at the perfect lilt of her Lady's voice. The enceinte consort was but a caged bird in the garden of the sea. Turning on the bow of the boat, she had not heard Dominique approach. Normally, she was used to the Vam Pŷr's silent entrances and exits, but lately with the tumbling churn of the waves and the stench of the deck and pounding swell of the sea it was hard to hear the movements of a ghost.

"There is no need for you to push your lessons with Laurel. Try to enjoy the voyage."

The pale woman strode silently past her paramour. A pocket of cool air swirled around her person as she came to rest at the nose of the ship. Overlooking the waters breaking against the gambol vessel, the matron of night looked regal facing the dying light. A cool rim of red danced on the sea, salting the hem of her dress with wet spray. It stretched across the smoky horizon as a canopy of stars that had begun to light the compass of the Captain's way.

"She has a common intellect," Linnet defined. "I will be lucky if she can manage at all."

"As you see fit," the elder woman stated, not turning around, watching the last apologies of daylight shudder in the distance. "But do please govern your pace," she said turning around. "You are not working alone this time and your health is of deep concern to me."

Linnet looked away. The sea rose and fell, a paper dragon on two wooden wheels set at the ends of the earth, and she wondered who pulled the gears that made the world spin. Too long now, months in fact, since anything other than common manners had passed between them. Crossing the distance, Dominique placed a bleached-colored hand to Linnet's protruding belly. The woman turned to her mistress as the Jadaraa Soo thrummed and wiggled, spurred by the scent of green blood and the soft palpitations of two beating hearts.

"I miss our conversations," Dominique said.

"I…" but the words choked in Linnet's throat.

The gravity of the hand on her belly was a magnet, pulling Linnet's emotions to the surface. All of the vastness of the sea disappeared into the rich allure of Dominique's tender gaze. There was only the two of them, in the whole of the world, just the two of them, vanishing and reappearing in time. The heavens were a sandcastle of bright suppuration, falling. Linnet felt a sharp pang to dive, unabashedly, into the woman's arms and enveloped herself in Dominique's rose scent and superior mysteries. *But what good am I if I can not temper the passions of my heart?* The symbiont's own wisdom steeled Linnet and she remained fixed, like the forward masthead of the ship. A roaring gale leapt off the sighing ocean and blew their hair, tussling the hems of their dresses toward one another.

"Did you tell him before you left that you were with child?"

"No."

Dominique's jaw firmly set. *He did not know that Linnet carried his heir.* That his bloodline flowed through the house of the hybrid species, so the symbiont did not know what kind of message he would take back to his people. In her haste for a union between the two mortals Dominique had not thought out every detail. His presence and her arousal were not anticipated. Too much had been left to chance. So much was happening during the days before they set sail and Nsia had left without speaking with her. Fear of straining the poor girl further had stalled Dominique in any earlier inquiries and now it seemed that things were unhinged and could go either way. There were no guarantees or grand promises shuttling ease at her back like she had made with Musa.

"And how did you leave things?"

"I am here if that matters any."

"Of course, it matters child. I am flattered by your love and devoted to you utterly."

She pressed her hand to the girl's cheek and caught a tear as it streamed down Linnet's cold face. "Have no doubt of my affection." Her eyes searched the young maid.

"Well, it had seemed otherwise."

Dominique did not argue with her, instead she kissed her. As the bow of the ship rose to meet a wave, she firmly cemented her intentions on Linnet's lips. The kiss was long and passionate. It carried eons of wanting and release. It held the promise of tomorrow and the knowledge that everything was going to be all right.

The sea seemed to breathe after the kiss and the night was awake. Dominique grabbed Linnet's cold hands and urged her to go back inside where it was warm. She protested, desiring to listen to the water slap against the full rigged ship and look upon the naked splendor of the stars. Dominique told her that she had to return to her cabin or else raise suspicion of her character. Linnet did not try to sway her to stay. She squeezed mother night's hand and bid her good morrow.

Dominique left her at the bow of the sea-faring vessel with the moon cutting its path through the sky. Glancing back, she found the thoughts that plagued her hard to bare, but now was not the time to uncork them and seek immediate answers. Now was a game of patience. Both she and the Tribe were well accustomed to weathering the cadence of days. Lie in wait for the prey to step into the trap. It was the way of the hunter. And Dominique felt her quiver of arrows drenched in her consort's blood.

After the pains of childbirth had passed and the suckling infant nestled against her warm heart, will she crave me then? What are the odds that Linnet will willingly abandon her child to the sea and the arms of its father? A war between the races, however imminent, had to be prevented at all costs. Dominique could not allow Nsia to seek reprisal against her Children of Evensong because Linnet had broken his heart. *She walked too closely with my past.* Dominique hated it, but it was true. Twice her Omjadda captors had forced her to breed before they made her take the dark drink of their blood and twice they stole her offspring from her before she could ever become anything close to a mother to the infants.

Cruelty in shades, all those years ago, and Dominique never knew what had happened to them. Did they live? Die? Were they put to some other unknown purpose? She had grown out of that horrible loss and did not relish the thought that soon she, like the beasts that had bred her as if she were nothing more than cattle, would be taking away Linnet's child. A war between the races had to be prevented. *Linnet's pregnancy could still be of use.*

As she dipped below the low hanging jam of the doorframe going into her cabin, Dominique was already composing the letter that she intended to send to Nsia. It would calm any frustrations that he may have taken with him when he left unannounced. Now only one thing remained, *would Linnet be able to let her child go?*

March 24, 1930.

Simon Ray held the single molded plastic handle to his face and clicked the receiver a few times for the operator. He gave the sterile female voice the telephone number that he'd been given before the robbery and waited for the call to go through. Zia watched him from a seat in the hotel lobby while sucking on a lollipop. Someone had left the tousled remains of the Indianapolis Star next to her, so she picked them up. Flipping through the fresh inked pages, she scoured for any report on the bank job in Dayton.

"Anything?" Simon asked as he approached.

"Nah," she responded, folding the paper in half. "Just some little Indian man causing a ruckus for Britain by marching to the sea to make salt and they're naming some planet Pluto, or something like that."

She moved to set the paper down.

"Bring it," he said, extending his hand to her.

As she took it and rose, Simon Ray cased the lobby for signs of anything suspicious. Simon Ray was never one to relax on his laurels. He didn't like to stay in any one place for too long. He always claimed that it made one weak and easy, susceptible to getting caught. Simon wasn't about to let himself and Zia get caught now. Not when they were this close to everything he ever wanted.

The Boyds crossed the street to a quaint diner and ordered breakfast: two black coffees, three eggs – one scrambled, two over easy – bacon, sausage, toast with jam, and a stack of hot cakes. The total cost came to 38 cents. Simon Ray would leave a nickel tip when he ushered Zia out the door in a calm, panicked hurry.

Zia stirred her coffee with her lollipop as she waited for the food to arrive. Simon poured over the paper. She wasn't entirely comfortable with Simon Ray's plans. She tried to speak with him about it last night, as they lay together after their copious wrangling of the flesh. Ten thousand dollars was a helluva a lot of money. A lot of money that they both barely survived acquiring. It was nearly all of the take and he wanted to give it to some mob flunky in Chicago to buy his way into Capone's gang. It didn't make a whole lot of sense to her. They'd been doing all right so far.

"I gotta prove to them that I can earn," he had said, laying his head against Zia's sweaty bare breasts. "We can't keep goin' on like we have. Eventually, we're gonna get nicked. The odds are against us. It's just a matter of time." He rose up to look at her honey browns, face to face. "This way we'll be protected. Part of an organization." He riffled a cigarette out of the ruffled pack and searched for the matches amid the loose lying bills. "You see where this country's goin'. It's goin' to shit." He lit up, took a drag, and handed the tobacco stick to his bride. "People got no work, they can't eat. Federal Government's musclin' in on big business and enterprise. States got no rights anymore. It's just gonna get worse. We gotta claim what's ours now, before we lose it."

She handed the cancer stick back to her husband. "And how's givin' over half our loot to a bunch of Wops gonna help?"

"'Cause, baby," he chimed, nestling back into the space of her curves. "Chicago's got it all. All the big action. All the big players. It's organized, right down to City Hall. We've got the freedom to operate."

"Yeah, under some crazy boss who just got outta the joint," she interrupted, taking the cigarette back from him. "What about going south? Mexico, maybe? Or Cuba even. You know, someplace where I'd look good in a bathing suit."

Simon Ray leered at his wife. He definitely liked the way she cut a one piece.

"We could live down there like royalty on what we got." She urged the point, pressing her fingers into the lovely cash that still covered the bed.

He thought about it for a minute and for a minute Zia Boyd thought she had her husband convinced.

"Right," Simon Ray chuckled eventually. "I can see you now in a little ol' dress picking fruit at the market." He took the cigarette back from her. "How long do you think that's really gonna last before you start missin' the bustle of a city and the smell of a Speakeasy?" He looked up at his wife. She knew he was right and turned away. "Besides," he said sucking in the smoke and breathing it out again like a dragon, "maybe we could get a house. Settle down. Raise a few…"

Zia quickly moved out of the bed, knocking Simon's head onto the dented mattress and spilling loot onto the wooden floor. "I told you Ray, I ain't havin' no baby." She grabbed her dress and headed for the bathroom. "So you just get that thought outchyour gaddamn head."

The bathroom door slammed behind her and Simon Ray eased back on his pillow, smiling. "Just as long as we keep fuckin' for a time, that's fine with me," he shouted through the closed door.

His wife didn't respond. This wasn't the first time she got all agitated discussing kids. *Probably wouldn't be the last.* She'd definitely come around. It was just a matter of time. For women, it was biological. So he didn't pay too much mind to her huff and gruff. He lay there listening to the bath water sing, breathing curls of smoke that mixed with his dreams of hitting it big in the Chicago Outfit.

The waitress slid Simon's plate of eggs and bacon near the newspaper he was reading and refilled their coffee cups. Zia had buttered her hot cakes and doused the fluffed, round patties with maple syrup and was cutting 'em up into even morsels when he found what he was looking for.

"Here it is. Back of the paper. Page seven." He showed her the article over the cluttered table as she took her first bite. "Eye witnesses inside," Simon read, "reported the robbers as a lone man and woman, who narrowly escaped under an exchange of police gunfire outside Winter's Bank early in the morning of blah, blah, blah…" He skimmed over the write up. "Police followed chase of the two derelict robbers to the outskirts of town where the alleged assailants engaged pursuing officers in even more gunfire before finally escaping across the Ohio State border." Simon let the top of the page fall so he could gloat with his wife. But his jeering smile was taken quick. "Looky here," he chimed, returning to the coarse Courier print. "Federal agents have been called in to examine the robbery." He slapped the paper with a pop. "What'd I tell ya? Federals movin' in on everything. Huh? Huh?"

He waited for an answer out of his wife, skimming the short article, but Zia only shrugged her shoulders unsure what to say and gobbled another fluffed maple square.

"At this time," he said, continuing to read the Star, " no more information has been brought forth or the names of the would-be assailants." Simon Ray set the paper down and stabbed the yellow eye of his egg with a stiff stick of bacon. "What I tell ya? Federals! Got their damn fingers in everything."

"Yeah. But they ain't got nothin'."

"That ain't the point, is it?" he shouted. "Damn Federal Government's been superceding State decisions for years now. Look what good they did with Prohibition. It's a mess I tell you."

Simon Ray stopped short, noticing a few strange looks from some of the diner's clientele. His hardened gaze swept their meek glances, and they turned away, except for the slack jawed cook. He kept beading him, like he knew something.

"Whatchyou lookin' at?!"

The cook went back to work as Zia turned to see whom Simon Ray was barking at.

"C'mon now," he said. "Finish up. Best we get movin'."

Zia turned right way round. Simon Ray was hunched over his plate like a turtle shoveling it in with gusto. He still hounded a meal like he was in the pen. Zia Jean pulled the lollipop stick out of her coffee and licked the drop off the paper rod that was teetering to fall back into the murky pool. Then she drained the cup. The hardened candy had melted, leaving a sweet aftertaste.

"What did Little Jimmy have to say?" she asked to ease his tension and get the know.

Behind her the bells on the diner door jangled and the look on Simon's face dropped as he sat up. *Whoever just entered couldn't be good.*

"C'mon now," he quietly said in a deep, serious whisper. "Time to go."

Zia set her empty cup down as Simon wiped the corners of his mouth with his napkin. The hard-soled steps on the floor told Zia that two beat cops had just come in to dine. They passed the booth the Boyds were sitting in on their way to the counter. One of the Officers offered Mrs. Boyd a gentlemanly greeting. Zia smiled playfully and nodded politely, flirting with the cop with her eyes.

"Say Arlene," the other cop asked their waitress as he set his hat on the countertop beside him, "Patty working today?"

"Naw, 'fraid not," Arlene answered as she poured coffee into two white cups. "She's on tomorrow, though. Now, what can I get for the both of you?"

Simon tossed his tip on the booth's table as the police ordered breakfast. He and Zia exited the diner to the hotel across the street. He chided his wife along the way for flirting with the cop. He didn't think it was too bright to be calling a whole lot of attention to themselves, considering the fact that they were wanted fugitives from justice and all. Zia always considered Simon Ray a bit uptight and too superstitious, but they hadn't gotten caught so far. She couldn't buck his intuition all that much. It'd been a handy radar. Zia apologized and waited for his temper to cool off.

In the hotel, they quickly packed, paid up, and left for Chicago. Zia wanted to protest, thinking that it was a mistake to go to the Windy City, but she kept her lip zipped. Simon Ray had already packed a satchel containing ten thousand dollars of their hard earned money to give to Little Jimmy so he could buy his way into The Outfit. His mind was set on it. So, Zia decided that it was just best to keep quiet and enjoy the ride.

Along the way it started to rain and the ruts in the dirt road got messy and they suffered a flat. Simon Ray tore the stitching out of the bullet wound in his shoulder while changing the tire. With the late start and unplanned obstacles, the Boyds decided to stay in a little motel along US-421 just a half days' ride south of the city.

That night, Zia changed Simon's bandage, mended the torn stitches, applied more ointment and some fresh Planter Leaves. The herbal remedy was something she had learned from her Momma. Zia stayed awake most of that night drinking shots of whiskey, listening to the rain as it hit the motel's tin roof, and flipping cards in a one-handed game of Blackjack as Simon Ray slept.

Outside, the sun raped the eyes and shoulders of the human cattle as they went about their oblique little lives. Ryan Silva watched the daily hustle through a pair of dark sunglasses, eating a hot dog. Mustard dropped onto the pavement of the sidewalk where ants gathered around the yellow pool and fed the larva of the colony for weeks to come.

Across the street, fitted into the architectural shoulders of urban construction rose a building. It was built almost a half century ago and the owner of the building still lived within it. On the top floor. In a spacious penthouse where sun shields blocked healthy cosmic radiation. Ryan Silva watched the building. He studied the average edifice. There was nothing unique about the erection except what was on the inside. *The building was a huge mask. A shell.* It was a carefully constructed illusion and Ryan Silva was sure that he'd notice something extraordinary today, something that would get him closer to the woman who had barricaded herself inside the illusion against the sun.

People pooled in the average edifice. People pooled out. The reality of ordinary was set in motion through the detailed mechanics of little, everyday lives. *Human cattle shuffled in, shuffled out.* There was a rhythm to the building that defined the space, which defined this point in time. The building had its own heartbeat. Ryan Silva had noticed that much.

Under the street, fitted into the bowels of the building that Ryan Silva watched, in the parking garage, on the bottom floor, tucked away in a large, angular space, under bad fluorescent lighting, rested a beat-up 1963 baby blue Cadillac. Its hood was raised. Hunkered in the corner was a cloth tarp that had been used to cover the classic automobile. The whirl click of a ratchet spun and locked, tugged and pulled on its own guided tempo as Lin replaced the engine's spark plugs. The work was quiet. The work was calming. Nobody parked down here except Lin and Z. The bowels of the building looped and stacked like entrails. It was a catacomb of silent metal, dank concrete and sewage lines. Lin had been working on the Caddy longer than Ryan had been watching her building. Each found soothing solace in their tasks. A grounding element that quelled the fire within their bellies, that pacified the agitation of their minds.

The tune-up was a ritual more than a mechanical necessity. It was a flagrant sign of acceptance. The path had been set. The course laid. The journey had begun. Not in the act of leaving physically, that came later, but in the act of preparation, where one leads the mind past the realm of readiness to leaving and the body soon follows. The tune-up was a ritual. Before any long journey Lin always made it a point to inspect and even spend time with her mode of transportation.

It started with horses when she was just a little girl. Before a ride, she would comb the animal and feed them an apple or some oats. She would talk to them and inspect the saddle, set the gauge of the strap. It helped her to allay her fears of travel. Before a long sea voyage she would visit the ship, inspect the rigging and watch the men work. She would oversee the stowing away of all luggage and gear. She would dine with the Captain.

Lin had little preparations with trains. Something about their huge, exhaustive measures and constant schedules never presented her the opportunity to imbibe their mechanics. Perhaps that was why she never liked traveling by rail. Even after she had wed the night and horses bucked at her cold touch she preferred a long horse drawn carriage ride to the fake comforts of a luxury boxcar. But then again, during those long nights, necessity and requirement proved more cumbersome than her ideals favored. The security of travel outweighed the ritual of custom, time and time again.

But cars! Cars afforded Lin with a bright, new excuse to get her hands dirty. Here was a machine not only useful in its design, but one she could love with the fascination of the horse. It was personal and isolated, with all of its little components packaged and self-contained. It was an invention in which she could unfurl the pathology of youthful days. Learning the mechanics of the combustion engine was not difficult, merely time consuming. And Lin definitely had the time.

As she slid into the driver's seat and turned the key that she had placed in the ignition earlier the torque of the engine roared to life. Lin depressed the gas pedal and the yellow, smiley face icon on the end of her key chain dangled in an awkward dance. She listened to the rotation of the engine. It had been close to nine years since she last heard the familiar voice of this vehicle. It labored in spots, sucking up the fresh lubricants, gas, and oil like a sponge. *The pussycat machine still had its purr.* Though despite the idling of the once elegant car, her work was far from done.

An undistinguished slab of concrete embraced Lin's vision in the rearview mirror. She lifted the pendant from around her neck and hung it on the stick that supported the small looking glass. The tiny silver ornament was her compass. It shivered with the purr of the Caddy and it would lead her to that all too familiar spot in the desert. She opened the locket and stared at the picture inside. The face in the black and white photograph had been placed to memory decades ago, but Lin never stopped looking at it. The set of the woman's eyes pulled at her soul with enticing power. She smiled pleasantly, probably thinking about some boy. She wore a laced dress, a broach, and had her hair done up. Ever since Lin had pulled the locket out of the stiffened hand of a corpse, she was drawn to the image of the stranger in the two-tone, gelatin print. Her face was the wind in the sails, the steam in the engine, the apple for the horse.

Lin caressed the soft edges of the worn photo tenderly. A bitter remorse weld up, but her ceremony was still incomplete. There was much that needed tending. The angst in her heart required coaxing or it'd consume her entirely. She closed the locket and squeezed until the dull ache of pain in her palm bit back the memories. She needed the ritual. It balanced her out. Its motions soothed her restless spirit. It kept the bad memories at bay. It gave her purpose where only death bloomed.

March 25, 1930.

They both slept late and did not hit the road until well after noon. The rains from yesterday had caused flowers to bloom and leaves to poke their green tinted heads from their buds. The first scent of spring was in the air. Zia rode with the window down and her eyes closed behind a pair of dark sunglasses. The wind blew through her hair and massaged the dull thud drumming inside her skull. She barely ate anything for breakfast and the thought of food just made her queasy.

When they stopped for gas she took a stroll through the little store and bought two soda pops. As the day waned to the lull of crickets Zia drank her soda on the front porch of the store and watched a young local family of four pull up, shuffle out, pick up some groceries, and talk with the clerk. The young mother was about Zia's age and she held in her arms a quiet, little baby just a few months old. Their eldest was a polite toddler who helped his Daddy pump the gas and load the truck up with groceries. The whole scene was decent and quaint and it made Zia think on having children with Simon Ray.

She knew he wanted a family. He came from a big one, the eldest of five. There was no getting around it. It was something she was going to have to deal with sooner or later. As she spied on the quiet, gentle love the young couple had she wondered if she and Simon would ever be as simple as that? Their life was always thrilling on the wrong side of the law. They were constantly on the move. How would they ever be able to grow roots? Especially in Chicago, that place was a powder keg of vice.

As Simon Ray hung the pump handle up, bringing the grand total for a full tank of gas to one dollar and ten cents, Zia slid her arms around his backside and hugged him. He turned to face his wife and they kissed to the dismay of an elderly man who was sitting on the storefront porch. He considered their public display of affection discourteous and sinful.

"I love you," Zia told Simon as she pulled back from the kiss.

"My aren't you sweet all of a sudden," he teased as she handed him his pop.

Zia watched Simon Ray walk toward the little shanty store feeling flush from the memory of their most recent lovemaking. With a warm smile on her lips and a hot feeling in her belly she strolled to the passenger side of the car. And just as Simon was about to disappear behind the wooden screen door of the shack Zia shouted to him.

"You know this is your last chance to shoot for Mexico."

Simon Ray laughed quietly. He gripped his bottle of pop tighter and entered the store to pay for the gas. Zia was in the car and ready to go when he climbed into the driver's seat of the sports coupe. He turned to his wife and grabbed her hand.

"Z?" He said, leaning into her. "You know I love you."

Her smile grew flat and wide and he kissed her. She heard the leaves rustling and a frog croaking in the woods. Crickets made beautiful music. Then he fired up the 'lil sports coupe as Zia Jean Boyd eased back into the leather seat. She placed her hands across her belly and imagined what it might be like to one day have a little bundle of joy inside. This was the first and only time she would ever consider having a baby. It was also the first time that her husband, her lover, the man who she raised hell with, had ever called her Z. The short abbreviation of her name was cute and Zia liked it.

It was dark when they arrived in Chicago and still had about an hour to kill before they were supposed to meet Little Jimmy, so they took a spin around The Loop, gawking at the people and the architecture. The bright lights, hustle, and thrashing life of the city pulsed. The Boyds could feel it running through their veins. Chicago was exciting for sure. It had an air of possibility and danger that soothed their black hearts, and by the time they were on their way to rendezvous with Simon Ray's gangster friend they both were under the spell the city had placed over them.

Little Jimmy told Simon Ray to meet him at the old Grande Hotel near Rosehill Cemetery. The once spectacular structure had been closed for almost a decade after a fire raged through the upper floors. It was never rebuilt. After lawsuits and liens the bank foreclosed, and the derelict property was only recently purchased by a dummy corporation set up by one of Capone's accountants. The city paid bi-annual fees to the dummy Corp for urban reconstruction, even though no work had ever been done. A majority of the subsidized funds went to upgrade the accountant's lifestyle while the rest was used as kickbacks to key personnel on the city's Planning Board. On paper it put all of the blame on city officials and the fictitious corporation, giving the Chicago Outfit leverage with the Planning Board and the Mayor.

A large chain link fence surrounded the illicit compound. The Boyds arrived late having gotten lost a few times. They could see Jimmy's car in the yard and the chain on the gate was unlocked. They entered and parked next to Jimmy's '29 DeSoto, paying very little attention to the erroneous zoning signs posted on the fence. Simon Ray got out of the car and stretched casually, casing the dump. The place was dank and quiet. Dirty bits of the dilapidated roof littered the ground as charred black sticks poked upwards out of the fourth story to heaven. There didn't appear to be a soul about. Zia unpacked from the passenger seat and they both walked to the rear of the car. Opening the trunk, Simon Ray took the revolver from out of his jacket pocket and handed it to his wife.

"Just in case," he said without a smile and winked.

Zia looked at the gun and the dark windows of the dead hotel and tucked it into the soft band of her dress along the small of her back, hiding it under her coat. An eastern wind carried a frigid chill over the headstones of the neighboring cemetery. The burial ground's solid peeks were illuminated by the celestial night.

Simon retrieved another revolver from the trunk and placed it in his jacket pocket. He grabbed the satchel of money under the heavy weight of Zia's downcast eyes and closed the trunk with a sharp thud that echoed across the paved streets to the deadlands, causing a flock of frightened birds to take flight. Nothing else rustled. It was all too quiet. Zia stopped him as he started to pass her by, gently placing her hand on her husband's stomach. She looked up to him. Her honey browns were furled and knotted. She wanted to tell him that they should go, that she had a bad feeling about this. But she didn't. Instead, she just lightly kissed him and got out of his way.

The door to the Grande Hotel was open, creaking in the wind. A clutter of leaves and litter filled the eerie entrance and beyond the darkness the gritty innards of the hotel were illumed by earth's satellite. Simon Ray pushed on the time-weathered door making it wide enough for the both of them to enter and stepped inside. Instantly, Little Jimmy's cheap cologne smacked them in the face.

"Jimmy?" he shouted into the cavernous gloom. "Yo, Jimmy we're here."

Stark silence ate their ears.

"C'mon man, no muckin' about."

They heard a noise off to the right, lodged in the heart of the pitch, and moved into the room up ahead. Simon nervously gripped the leather handle of the small satchel, flexing and releasing. He was uncomfortable with the set up and wouldn't be too surprised if Little Jimmy suddenly jumped out of a shadow at them with a brazen shout. He was a jokester. This was definitely the kind of moment he'd take advantage of. As they entered the registration room of the old lobby, Simon Ray thought he saw a figure moving in the shadows.

"Jimmy, whatchyu tryin' to do? Give us a heart attack or sumptin?"

The shadows remained silent and Zia nestled in close behind her husband, scanning the dark recesses of the abandoned room to the rear. She couldn't make heads or tails of the place. It smelt odd and old, dusty and rotting. Suddenly, the darkness cracked.

"Oh, I'm sorry," came the demure voice of a woman, "was he a friend of yours?"

The hollow disembodied voice moved into a bluish beam of moonlight that cut across the musty room. It definitely wasn't Jimmy. The woman was gaunt and pale. Her long black hair was put up and disheveled. She was dirty and smelled earthen. A viscous, dark red liquid stained her jaw and neck, running down the front of the old-styled evening dress that she wore. Her eyes lingered on them childishly then moved slowly to the body on the floor.

The Boyds followed her sweeping gaze to the stripped, pleated pants and scuffed polished shoes of Little Jimmy. He lay on the floor quiet and still, sticking half way out of a shadow. Simon Ray stiffened with anger and he began to breathe heavier.

"Yeah," he spat. "He's a friend of mine."

"Oh, I don't think so," she challenged in the soft lilt of her velvety voice.

"You don't know what you're talking about."

"I think he was going to kill you." The mysterious woman popped her eyes, accentuating the point and dipped below the shadow line, rising up again like a blooming, black moth. "He had a gun."

The oblique wraith held Little Jimmy's gun daintily by the handle with two fingers and tilted her head to the side, staring at them like a China Doll. Simon Ray pulled the revolver out of his pocket and thrust its barrel at the gaunt wench.

"I have a gun too," he announced through his teeth. "Now, what the hell did you do to Jimmy?"

"How nice." The ghoul smiled, dropping Little Jimmy's pistol, leaving her arm extended and limp in mid air. "Are you a bad man too?

Her grin widened. Her teeth were yellow, misshapen, and crude. She slowly started to circle the young couple.

"Just stay right where you are and tell me what you did to Jimmy," commanded Simon Ray.

"Well…" she shrugged a single shoulder, looking tiny and innocent, speaking slowly and with deliberation. "Let's just say…he wasn't all that bad…"

The vile harlot laughed. Shivers raced up the spines of the Boyds as she licked the top of her lip and started humming. Simon Ray breathed like a train starting up and pressed the cold metal of the gun tighter against his sweaty palm. He was getting upset. He needed to know, but didn't dare take his eyes off the crazy broad to see what had befallen his childhood friend.

Zia peered down at Little Jimmy's lifeless corpse, feeling like she had walked into the center of a spiraling doom. Thick black oozed from out of the side of his neck and Zia realized that the stains on the woman's outmoded dress and the sticky muck dripping off her jaw, smeared all over her fingers, was Little Jimmy's blood.

"…Isn't that right, Benjamin?" The wench said, floating on her grin.

"Absolutely, Emily. You are most correct."

A baritone voice erupted from directly behind them. Both Simon Ray and Zia jumped with a start. Simon spun the gun around ready to shoot whoever it was that had snuck up behind them, but the newcomer just gently moved his hand, sending the gun flying through the air. Zia watched it happening as if time had slowed. The clank of the small weapon hitting a wall somewhere in the dark recess of the hotel caused Simon Ray to turn his head just as the stranger pushed him back. He balanced himself, struggling, and dropped the satchel of money, falling into the waiting arms of the bloodstained woman.

Zia's eyes met those of the stranger and she was sure that she saw several veins twitching within them. Her breath held fast in the cargo-hold of her throat as she remembered Simon Ray's gun in the soft band of her dress. But before she could move to get the iron out, or turn to see what had happened to her husband, the statuesque stranger turned toward Zia, snapped the heels of his boots together with a loud click, and presented himself with a slight bow.

"Benjamin Douglas Raines, Ma'am. Please to make your acquaintance."

His courtly introduction threw Zia for a loop. He appeared refined, had a military air about him, and easily towered over them both. He was broad shouldered and casually dressed. The threads of his jacket were worn thin in more than a few spots. The poor look of his attire belied his courteous, almost polished demeanor. He, too, like the specter of the woman, was blanched and ghostly, and Zia noticed dark burgundy veins writhing under the surface of his exposed skin.

"I suggest you both sit tight," he enjoined to the angry man's frightened female companion, and then turning toward Simon Ray he offered a simple warning. "Especially you."

Simon struggled to free his arms from the tenacious grip of the grotesque lady, glaring at the brute with chiseled hate. He moved his head in violent spasms each time the ghoulish female teased the soft flesh at the nape of his neck. Breathing on him, rank and foul, and lightly stroking his skin above his collar with the tip of her tongue caused Simon Ray's shoulders to bunch.

"Get her off me."

"Emily?" The polite revenant interjected, indicating with his eyes, and she let Simon Ray go.

He cast off from her, like a boat, and nearly tripped over Little Jimmy's Italian leather shoes. Looking down at the corpse he could see that the front of the gangster's throat had been torn out. Simon Ray gagged at the sight.

"Would you be so kind as to retrieve Mr. Cross?" Benjamin's deep voice filled the room.

The black clad shade twittered a high pitched chortling in the back of her throat and exited the room. Simon Ray asked again what they had done to his friend even though it was pretty obvious. Benjamin Douglas Raines merely suggested that they wait patiently, and quietly, for Mr. Cross. Zia slowly eased over to her husband and put her arms around his waist. Simon Ray told her that it was going to be all right. He told her not to worry and kissed the wrinkles in her forehead, trying to smooth them out.

The big man just glared at them like a mountain and after a time it became unsettlingly clear to Zia that he either wasn't breathing or that his inhalations were so shallow that it didn't cause his chest to move up and down. Her stomach was sinking. She tried to control her own breath – *to remain calm.* The gun pressing against the small of her back told her that it wasn't over yet. They still had options.

A rapid stomp of approaching footfall bleated down the dead wooden halls of the Grande Hotel. It seemed to take forever for the perpetrator of their folly to reach them. Simon's eyes volleyed from the satchel of stolen cash to the pallid man to Little Jimmy's corpse and the darkened interior of the burned hotel. *These motherfuckers are gonna pay for what they'd done!*

"It appears we have an active night," the brisk man uttered when he entered the room, crossing quickly to the Boyds. "How unfortunate. Two more guests wanting to check into the hotel and here we are overbooked." He had a Southern twang and sized up the intruders.

"I regret to inform you that service has declined somewhat of late, despite our constant attraction." The man waited patiently for a second or two for either one of his newly found guests to offer a charming chuckle or whimsical smile to his clever repertoire. He gawked and toyed with his tongue on the sharp tip of a fang. "Have you met my associates..." crossing to them, "Mr. Raines and the lovely dapper Emily Rosenthal?" He held the gaunt woman's hand and she curtsied.

"Yes," answered Simon Ray. "We've had the..."

"Allow me to introduce myself," the vibrant, ashen man purposely interrupted. "I am Lieutenant Franklin Cross, formerly of the glorious South under General Turner Ashby and the fighting Virginia 7th." He nodded with a courteous bow.

The man's words broke over the Boyds with easy interpretation. He even wore the faded gray uniform jacket of the office he purported to support. Nothing else about the way he spoke or what he said seemed real to them however. The effects of the Great War still held sway over the nation and it had been well over a decade and some change since the Treaty of Versailles. But this brash rascal laid claim to another war. To a battle between the states! To a time long before a man of his youthful complexion could have partaken. Even with such a sickly appearance this man could not have fought for the South.

Simon Ray had enlisted in the Great War, the War To End All Wars, in 1917 when he was just sixteen years old. He had fought in the trenches and seen the madness that had overcome men. He could understand the demented illusions that this poor bastard must have suffered under from the effects of such terrible warfare. Simon Ray could not even begin to propose that what the man said to him was common and right.

"Look," he offered. "I don't know what angle ya'all have goin' here but we don't need to be any part of it. We ain't seen nothin' or heard nothin'. We're just passin' through to Mexico and can be easily on our way."

Mr. Cross smiled and pulled at the dollop of hair on his chin. "How appeasing," he turned to his cronies. "I do appreciate a man of integrity. But, I am afraid you will be checking out tonight."

While all the focus and attention was being paid forward to the verbose Mr. Cross, Zia took it upon herself to slowly and gently pull Simon Ray's revolver out of the soft band of her dress. The tension in the room was darkening as her fingers traversed the cold metal handle to the small whole with the trigger in it. The weapon fell into the palm of her hand as plainly as the nefarious intentions of the strangers were revealed. Zia raised the gun from the folds of her overcoat and shot Franklin Cross right between the eyes.

The few seconds that squeezing the trigger had bought them quickly vanished when the enigmatic, Southern-fried Lieutenant did not buckle to the floor in a piling heap of his own dead flesh. Instead, after the thundering pop and snapping back of his head, a deep born chuckle rambled in the man's throat. He tilted his leaning head back to an erect position as Mr. Raines grabbed the arms of Simon Ray.

"My…" Cross drew out with delicious delight. "You're a feisty one." His smile widened like grease, full and pleasing, as the Boyds watched in horror as a hundred tiny red veins squirmed under the skin of the cadaverous man and began to weave together in a fine, healing mesh inside of the hole that Zia had just made. The monster laughed. "I like that."

The man was practically aroused seeding a lecherous gaze at his would-be killer. He took a few steps closer to the other man's bride and Zia steeled her spine against his advance.

"Look," Simon Ray pleaded. "You don't have to do this. We can pay you…"

"Shhhh," said Cross, pressing a finger rudely over the man's mouth. "Don't ruin it."

Zia leveled Simon Ray's revolver to Cross's forehead again. This time she pressed the butt of the weapon against his sickly looking skin and the two powerful creatures of death faced off. The Lieutenant gloriously giggled, giddy with her stink of fear, exhilarated by her lust for violence to protect her life and that of her lover. He waited patiently for the woman's heaving breasts to hiccup and signal to him that she intended to squeeze the trigger again and uselessly put another bullet into his brain.

His stare drilled into her honey brown eyes, hypnotically challenging her, vying her to dance toe to toe with him as his rival and she did not back down. She rose to his vigorous call and met him on the field of battle as an equal. Their warring energy bristled like a crackling fire around them that only the creatures of this dark night could sense and feel. It was palpable. Taut, like a mule skin drum. Even time suspended its very subtle nature. And just as Zia began to ease the trigger back, the eager vampire snatched the gun from her perky, little hands and gently dropped it to the floor.

Franklin Cross had expected a sigh of defeat and a waning of the body from them both. But it only came from her male companion. When he took the gun the man had given up. He knew the score, the futility of all the minutes that were left for him. Ignorantly, tangled in the cords of his own mortal coil, Simon Ray didn't see the thrushing life and raging anger of his wife still defiant, still challenging the undead soldier. He was blind to her, falling down the staircase of his fear. Even in the sheer, certain face of death this woman had *not* given up. The Civil War Vet pulled at the scruff of his jowl and peered down at the floor as he drew along side the warm, fleshy killer.

"I tell you what…" the man whispered in Zia's ear, offering her a chance to dance. "You know you both aren't going to get out of here alive. By now, I am sure you've figured that out. I'm also sure that you've concluded that your little pea-shoota' isn't going to do you any good. But would you like to see how you could use it?"

Zia's eyes flicked hard at the cold Lieutenant and darted again to her husband. She didn't want to give that man a single inch. He toyed at the tufts of her chestnut hair, trying to entice a response as her rapid breath enveloped them both in a pocket of lukewarm oxygen.

"Here's what we're going to do." He snickered and it sent terrifying ripples cascading down Zia's spine. "I want you to pick up your side arm and shoot your man in the head."

Zia gulped, her breath stymied in her chest.

"Do this…" he rounded to the front of her, "and I'll let *you* live."

    He's a madman. Her breath hiccuped, choking back tears. She tried to keep her focus on Simon Ray, but his face wrinkled into a deft plea. She had to look away or else she'd crack. *That bastard!* Rage contorted her face and she balled her fists to keep herself from shaking. Franklin glared at her, stepping back. He raised his hands to the cleft of his chin, holding them like he was praying as he watched his little dare take root in the wanton woman. Zia slowly turned her head from side to side, affirming that she wasn't going to play his little game. But eventually, she looked down at the cold steel barrel of the gun lying on the grimy floor. *It's unthinkable.* Zia's mind raced like a turbulent river. The earth was off kilter, these people were freaks, and she didn't want to die in this god-forsaken hellhole of Chicago. She gritted her teeth, looked at Simon Ray who was telling her no, and knelt down.

    Her hand enveloped her husband's revolver and she rose with the heavy iron weapon grounding her to the spot. Simon Ray's eyes panicked. His breathing was erratic. He wanted to barter for his life with her and with the crazy cracker in the gray uniform, but he didn't know how. Everything was happening so fast. Words felt like glue on his tongue. Zia rushed over to him and kissed him sloppily. She told him that she was sorry and pushed herself away.

    He looked into the red, teary eyes of the woman he loved and the stark, endless mouth of his gun. He finally thought of something to say, but it was too late. Mrs. Boyd gently squeezed the trigger, just like he had taught her. Zia didn't pull. She eased it back. The gun boomed in the mineral, vacant lodging. It's muzzle flashed in an infinitely finite burst of blinding light that sparkled in the windshield of their car outside and the body of Simon Ray Boyd fell to the floor in a massive heap of dead, human flesh.

    Zia stood there with the gun still raised, unaware of the smoke trailing out of the end of the barrel. Her breath spasmed in short, controlled bursts and her eyes remained fixed to the point in space where her husband once stood. She did not look down. Benjamin Douglas Raines peeled Simon Ray's brains off his face and shoulder, pulling matter out of his hair as Franklin Cross gently removed the gun from the widow's firm grip.

"There you go," he gently cooed with pleasure. "There you go."

    He took Zia by the shoulders and turned her around to leave the

Grande Hotel. The stink of death permeated the air. She allowed the indecent man to lead her a few steps away until she stopped. Cross did not force her. He tested her spirit; curious to see how she would react. Zia turned and crossed to the satchel that still lay on the dirty floor. She picked it up. The leather creaked and she allowed her eyes to drift to her husband's lifeless form.

His eyes were still open and the hole in his forehead seemed too small, short on blood, to have caused that kind of harm to such a strong man. The vampires watched her, hanging on the fringes of the room. Zia was only vaguely aware of their presence. They were distant shadows of painful intrusion. There was only her and Simon Ray...*and well*...Simon Ray really wasn't there anymore. He would never hold her again or kiss her or make love to her or tell her that he loved her. He was gone. And she had made him leave.

The magnitude of this moment was too great and powerful for the widowed Mrs. Boyd to comprehend. Over the days and weeks that followed, though, she would pull it all into sharp focus. And in the days and weeks that followed she would easily go into her own death with the clairvoyance that unlike her late husband she would not suffer the ravages of empty decay. Death was not always so finite an end.

She would be reborn into the womb of night; spit back from the spawns of hell to claim whatever and whomever she desired with the malfeasant tenacity of timelessness. To save herself from a life of petty crimes and prostitution little Zia Jean Bell became Zia Jean Boyd – bank robber, gambler, and wife. Yet, that wasn't enough. That wasn't the total price she had to pay to find purity. To truly save herself, she had to damn her soul until death do they part. And even then...the tide of timelessness and cruel nature ate the purity of her new birth and she become something altogether unforgivable. She became an abbreviation of her former life, a shade in the darkness, a bell still screaming for something real and true to hold onto!

The pain was excruciating. Her hand was seized into a gnarled ball of twisted fingers. The muscles in her forearm were yanked into a tight knot. There was nothing she could do about it, except wait for the dark red veins of the parasite to stop convulsing. This wasn't the first time that this had happened, but this was by far the longest and most painful seizure Z had ever endured.

She sat on the couch breathing heavily, trying to flex her hand, but it would not move. She had no control over her own sinew, bone, and muscle. She gripped her arm at the elbow with her other hand and squeezed as the pain raced through her joints. She had fed earlier so that couldn't be the reason why the little bugger inside was cramping. It came and went, always unexpectedly. Though it usually ended by now. *Jesus? Fuck! Why was this happening?!*

Z heard the clanking of the door and prayed that Lin would not find her like this. That she would go anywhere else in the house except where she was. *Dammit! Didn't it just beat all that the first place she goes into was the very same room!* Lin carried a medium-sized box.

"Do you want these things? If not, I'm just gonna toss 'em."

"What's that?" Z tried to hide the pain and her dead arm.

"These tapes and CDs?" Lin stared into the box at the unkempt mess. "They're all over the place."

"Yeah," Z gritted through her teeth as spittle flew from her mouth.

Then just as suddenly as the pain came it popped and she had movement again. Z flexed her fingers, opened her hand, and bolted off the couch as if it where the fine leathered upholstery that had kept her prisoner.

"The whole back seat of the Caddy is cluttered with your junk," Lin added as Z walked up to her, cheating to her left side, lest the girl notice anything untoward.

"Hey!" exclaimed Z, digging in the box and pulling out a ratty old VHS Tape that had the date 07/19/93 scrawled in pen on its side. "I was wonderin' where this had gotten off to."

"In the Caddy. Right where you left it." Lin set the box down. "If you want this junk, take it, but make sure you clean the rest of it out of the back seat. I don't want a bunch of crap in there when we hit the road."

Z was barely listening. She followed the box to the floor and began rummaging through it like a kid in a candy store, pulling out armfuls of large flat wound videotapes. Each had different dates and notes written on them that spanned from the 1980's well past the burgeoning fears of Y2K. Then it dawned on her and she looked up. Lin had left the room.

"What road trip?" shouted Z across the expanse of the penthouse as she stood. "Lin? What road trip?"

"You know."

It was the only response that flittered back to her waiting question. Z stood there a minute making an account of time. The hardest thing for any symbiont to do was keep track of time. Somehow over the breadth of existence the concerns of the clock fell away with each passing season, melding into one dark permanence. The churn of regular hours did not add up when one hid from the light of the sun.

"Oh no," the time tough rogue uttered as her shoulders drooped. "No! No!" She thrust one of the black plastic videotapes through the air in Lin's general direction. "I'm not traipsing across the desert with you again. Oh, hell no."

The pile in her arms shifted and several tapes fell onto the floor as Z stomped away from the tattered box. She tossed the stuff on the couch. A nasty twang pulled her right arm again and Z thought it was going to cramp. Angrily, she began pumping her right hand, messaging the long extremity. "Why the hell you gotta go traipsing through the gaddamn desert again?"

"Because," the soft shining voice of Lin oozed from the entranceway, "it's time."

"Ah, that's bullshit and you know it."

Just then the call buzzer squeaked and Lin held her tongue.

Z turned to her. "Well, I ain't going."

Z expected an argument, but none came. Only the brash buzzer sounded again as they looked at each other. Lin broke the gaze when her eyes trailed to the panel by the door.

"Ok," Lin breathed, turned, and left the room.

The buzzer ignited for a third time and filled the hollow space where Lin stood with rancor. Z stormed to the panel and hit a rectangular shaped button.

"What?!" she screamed as the miniature TV screen warmed up.

"Ahhh...I'm looking for Z. Is Z there?"

The black and white features of Ryan Silva pulled into focus from the camera above his head and Z looked into the chiseled face of the guy from the other night. *Fucking timing.* All she could think about was that god-awful trip across country. She shook her head from side to side and spied the mess of videotapes. A smile cracked her mood. *The trips weren't all bad.*

"Hello? Is this the right pl…"

"Yeah, this is Z. Whaddya want?" she burst in, watching the strange, uncomfortable confusion wash over Ryan in the grainy, little monitor.

"Ah, you," he said poignantly. "I want to see you."

His frank response snapped the bruising punk out of her sandy funk. She smirked and traced his features on the thick glass with her finger. "You want me to come out and play?" She sang like a cartoon.

"Yeah," he smiled.

His taste and cocky bravado played across Z's interior theater. Her fangs ached. The horny little devil inside her bones wanted his joyride until she remembered that soulful voice of his. He was a melodious instrument. She was a careless horror. Regret etched its way into Z's skin.

"Sorry. Busy. Come back later."

The answer was quick and flat, cold despite the warm feelings that she had buried under so much muck and clutter. She turned off the audio on the com-panel and watched him. Z knew that she couldn't handle a debate. She'd lose, pants around her ankles, and sooner or later someone was going to get hurt. Silently, Ryan kicked the marble floor and Z bit down a sudden urgency to invite him up. She exhaled her want as Ryan attempted to sway her, speaking into the little box as if all his words would reach her ears. His melodious instrument and hardened tool floated through the channels of her mind as each vocal attempt he made was returned with stunted silence.

The hush succumbed to more muted nothingness until the young man became frustrated and eventually left. Devilishly, Z enjoyed spying on him. *He had passion.* Her curiosity was peaked and he had that voice, that delicious voice. She could imagine listening to it for a thousand years and then again felt that she would only hurt it. He wanted to see her again. *How quaint!* It was all so normal like an episode of Ozzie and Harriet.

Lazily, Zia turned off the monitor and sauntered over to the coffee table and picked up a remote control. She depressed a little blue button, next to a DEI logo, and the far wall split open. It folded away revealing a huge flat screen television and a rack of electronics. She slid the flat videotape into the machine and grabbed its remote. As she walked back to the couch and moved the mess of tapes out of her way so she could sit, muted static filled the TV set. Z hit the rewind button until a group of black and white images ran backwards on the garbled screen. She sat, pumped the volume, and hit play.

On the huge flat screen television the angle switched every 30 seconds from one camera to another. Rows of items and coolers of stocked beverages in a convenience store flicked from angle to angle. A clerk was behind the counter and a customer was in the far back of the store as two women entered. They cased the joint and followed the lone customer up to the counter. Suddenly, the taller of the two women grabbed the lone customer and slammed his head against the hard counter as the other woman attacked the register jockey.

"Ah, nice one." Z laughed.

The taller woman threw the man to the floor, but he landed in a turnstile of junk food items. He and the packaged goods went sprawling across the black and white checkered floor in silent action, like it was done in the days before Talkies.

"That's right," she smiled maliciously easing forward in her seat. "Come to Momma." The tall woman on the TV screen gloated in suspenseful soundlessness over the fallen customer, for just a few seconds, before she pounced on him and drove her roaring mouth into the nape of his helpless neck. Z yelled with glee and shot a fist into the air. "Lin, ya gotta see this." She shouted to her partner in the other room. "There you go, there you go. Awwww, yeah!"

She rumbled as if watching a football game, reveling in the glory of seeing herself and Lin attack and kill the customer and store clerk. There was poetry to it that only she witnessed. *A Haiku, cause the damn thing ended too soon.* Eagerly, Z grabbed up the next security tape and popped it in. *Yeah. The trips weren't all bad. They had their little perks.*

She wasn't going this time around, though. That's what she told herself, remembering her curt invocation when they returned last time. *All that way across the desert and back just to go visit some ruins, crying over some dead girl in a locket.* Z never saw any reason for it. Though now, as she laughed and hollered at the evidence of destruction that these two had caused the only thought that bloomed in her demented mind, besides Ryan Silva, was that she wished she could eat popcorn.

Z wanted a tub of hot, buttery popping corn, just like she used to get at the old picture shows. *But the little parasitic fucker didn't like it.* Something about that strain of corn made it stiffen, causing it to feel suffocated, and Z had had enough of that crap. She put the seizures out of her mind, but the urge for the popcorn remained, resounding as if striking a bell. The habit of living years slowly dwindled like the erosion of a mountain. Longing was consistent and not easily appeased. As Z spooled through the piles of videotapes that she and Lin had collected over the years, she was reminded of another, more distracting thought. *Lin said there were more in the Caddy. What joy!* Z could barricade herself behind the silent violence of more than a dozen or so murders. The buzzer signaled again as Lin entered the room and Z popped in another security tape.

"You're a fucking maniac." She exclaimed enthusiastically. "Gaddamned rock-n-roll stars. Yes, we are!"

Z hit the buttons on the VCR's remote as the call box lit up again with noise. Lin went to look and see who it was making all of the clatter. "It's that Ryan guy from the other night."

Z ignored her and fell into the couch, jostling a few tapes to the floor. "Ya gotta check this out."

With a slow, deliberate flick of her thumb, that only minutes ago Z did not even have enough control to move, the large, flat screen TV came to life. More stark images of convenience store death filled her eyes. Lin stood silently behind Z, watching herself commit murder, in grainy black and white, as the raunchy symbiont commented and giggled at their barbarous antics. Forty-seven floors below them, Ryan Silva grew angry again, dejected by the cold reception that he'd received, once more, from the sterile little box.

Behind him the city buzzed. Human cattle shuffled in and out along their little, preordained lives. Like clockwork, the sun went down. Evening dropped her dress and fell to her knees as the powder blue dusk engulfed the burning groin of Rah in its cold, dark mouth. Ryan boiled with an urgency to see the vampire again. To feel the crush of the vibrant punk and know the full weight of her teeth on the currency of his flesh. One way or another, he would see her again. One way or another, she would succumb to his desire and they would be together. *It was preordained. Destined.*

Ryan Silva never had a problem getting a woman to do anything he wanted. That was never Ryan's problem. *This rascally vamp was no mere woman, though.* That was for sure. But she was a woman, after all. And even though the grieving death of Z's parasite clung to her figure like a latex cloak, Ryan knew with dire certainty that she quaked for him as only a woman could. *One way or another...It was only a matter of time.*

PART FIVE:

Obsession, My Name Be

There is the path of wisdom and the path of ignorance.
They are far apart and lead to different ends...
Abiding in the midst of ignorance, thinking
themselves wise and learned, fools go
aimlessly hither and thither, like blind led by blind.

-The Upanishads

1775. São Paulo, Brazil.

The carriage driver wouldn't take them all the way. He said there were bad things about that place of which he didn't want any part. On the docks, an African slave loaded up their luggage and Linnet's eyes kept falling on his back. Sweat beaded his neck. He kept his eyes down, away from them, tying their bags to the rack. The crème-colored jacket he wore was frayed and soiled. The rest of their things would come along after with Dominique, who was stowed below deck with her doctor, avoiding the brilliance of the day. Linnet and Laurel were going ahead to check on the house and make ready for their mistress to arrive. Casa del Rio Dulce was only a few hours up river, and the carriage driver had heard of the place alright. He was surprised that such beautiful and young ladies would have anything to do with it, especially when one of 'em was carrying a child.

The way he put it, the place was evil. Downright stupid for going there. Bad things occurred in the woods. He warned the girls from going to their chosen destination, saying "if you valued your lives you'd turn 'round and get back onboard that ship and return to where you came from."

Linnet had to help Laurel through most of his tirade. Translating his dialect and local Portuguese slang was a bit trying at times, but she muddled through. Both girls were put out by the fearful reception they'd received. It had been over two years since Isabela's last letter, just prior to Laurel joining Dominique's entourage. It was sent from Rio de Jeneiro and there was nothing in the letter that alluded to such dire goings-on at Dominique's estates in São Paulo. Before they left Europe the three women had speculated on what could have happened to Isabela that would have caused her correspondence to lapse, but they arrived at nothing solid.

The excessive responsibilities of running Dominique's South American businesses were vast. She held hope, for a time that her former protégé was merely bogged down. The last time that she, herself, was on this particular hemisphere was the early part of the Eighteenth Century. She was pulled away by rumors of the Dalam Kha'Shiya J'in restarting the blood slave trade in the Habsburg province. She always planned on returning. Dominique knew that she had been away for far too long, caught up in the glorious confusion of living abroad with her two consorts. There was nothing in all of the women's assumptions and conversations, though, that had prepared Linnet and Laurel for the news they received when securing land bound passage to their mistress's Brazilian home.

The carriage driver said that people had gone missing, sometimes in the town too, especially young men and children. None of 'em were ever heard from or seen again. And the place was known to run through slaves, worse than any other plantation in the land. The grisly, bearded fellow speculated that a Bruxsa roamed those parts at night and was killin' 'em after they'd tended to the fields. As Linnet pressed the old bugger to tell her more she learned that things had been relatively quiet up at the Casa over these past few years. The plantation's Overseers had taken over the place and were producing a fair amount of raw goods, but the rumors and legend of the Bruxsa persisted.

That's why he wouldn't take the girls any farther than to the entrance of the long road that led to the plantation. It didn't matter one bit that Linnet was pregnant and that she'd have to walk the rest of the way to the house. The old man saw to dumping their luggage with some haste and tore out of there, lest the wilds of his imagination and haunts of past years would rip him from the root of God's green earth. Linnet and Laurel watched the rickety carriage disappear into the distance, a banging clatter of wood, creaking leather, and horse hooves. Slowly, the caterpillar growl of the jungle surrounded them and the sticky heat of the lands eked perspiration from their pores. The girls were on dry land again and the blue-gray sky looked like it was going to rain soon.

Neither one of them passed a single word as they collected what they could carry and started walking. Strange sounds assaulted their ears and their eyes cased the thick canopy of the green woods. Pressing onward, encumbered by hatboxes, perfume satchels, and a small trunk they struggled up the primitive rut-worn dirt road. Linnet kept the pace slow, laboring under the additional weight of her belly and on a few occasions they stopped to rest. A sickly stench began to permeate through the jungle and the girls spied a column of thick, black smoke rising up through the treetops.

The humidity was unbearable and they were sweating profusely. The English gowns they wore were not designed by people who had ever visited a climate like this one. Laurel had to unfasten her stomacher, so she could breathe, and it became just one more thing that she had to lug along with her. Nearing the end of the path the sandy, earthen walls of the big house came into view. Closer inspection revealed cracks in the plaster and creeping vines that had taken over the place. One of the massive, hand-carved Brazilian wood doors was open and the front landing was a mess of forest clutter and chickens milling out of the house. All of the shutters on the front facing windows were either busted or missing and Linnet thought for sure that she saw a slender young tree poking out of one of the windows from the inside.

The house was in shambles. Abandoned to the elements, like no one had lived in it for years. Dragging the small trunk behind her, Laurel thought she had heard the clamor of men and machinery in the unseen distance, but nearing the house it had grown quiet and the buzz of the forest heightened to a steady chirp. She let the trunk handle go and the Paris purchased case fell to the ground with a dull thump.

"Not quite how Dominique describe it, huh?"

"It could be worse," added Linnet, imaging what horrors lay within.

Turning around to survey the yard of the derelict domicile, the English broads noticed, with a due portion of fearful trepidation, that they were being watched.

Ryan slid the knife's blade across his forearm slowly, back and forth, in a repetitive seesaw motion. His teeth gritted as thin ribbons of red bloomed on his flesh in two-inch long lines. His brow was heavy and bent. His aura darkening, he was in a melancholy mood. It had been over a week since he last saw the redheaded hellcat and she suckled his blood and fondled him heatedly. He'd gone by the building where they partied and to the club where he first saw her almost every day or night. But he hadn't heard a damned thing or seen her out and about anywhere. The phone rang again. And again, Ryan let the answering machine get it.

"Hey Ryan, its Carol. Give me a call, Ok."

It'd been like that for days. He used to get a thrill from the amount of pussy that called his house. Seeing the little red light on his answering machine flash, telling him he had messages. It used to mean something. He would listen to who had called him that day, sometimes waiting until the week's end to bunch it all up, standing in front of the little archaic machine as if he was in line at a smorgasbord. He had his pick: Blondes. Brunettes. Dyed jobs. Redheads. Shaved. Unshaven. Tattooed. Pierced. Pristine. And the very rare occasion, virginal.

Since tangling with the vampire, Ryan hadn't been interested in anyone else. She was a cut above prime, high art, and apart from her, his whole world was 2-D. Flat, like in the days before Columbus. And flavorless. Bland, like his mother's cooking. Since The Letter cut into Ryan Silva's life he hadn't been able to think of anything but her.

The phone rang again.

"Look you asshole if don't want to hook up that's cool. Or if you're too busy or whatever. But you don't have to fucking ignore my fucking phone calls. Just…Fuck!" The frustrated voice on the other end exhaled a long, bitter sigh. "Call me back, Douch! It's Lacey."

She hung up nosily and it took several drawn out seconds for the line to disconnect and the signal to beep. Ryan cut another thin red line on his forearm as a cool breeze danced through the opened windows. *Perhaps I should write her a letter?* It just dawned on him. *She was all old and shit. People used to write one another back then. Maybe she isn't into all this modern tech? Maybe that's why I haven't been able to connect with her.* Ryan looked at the blood pooling on his arm, its jagged design, and got an idea. Though manifesting it turned out to be harder than he thought.

First, he had to find a blank piece of paper. Searching the apartment, he eventually found one in a collection of magazines and bills, dripping blood onto the floor. Then, he blotted the streaks of red goo onto the clean, white sheet. *What better calling card to leave a vampire than this!* Though, just to be sure, Ryan signed his blood letter and wrote his phone number at the bottom of the page. After that, he went in search of an envelope, which wound up being an altogether more arduous task.

Ryan wasn't the pen and paper kind O' guy. He paid all his bills online and communicated mostly through emails and his cell phone. The antique messenger device trilling in the background of his apartment was something he searched for in pawnshops and thrift stores a couple of years back. He still held pride over the fact that he had figured out a way to route his voicemail to the chichi yard-sale find. His was a different world than what the one hundred year-old symbiont came from. He had to remember that. Z came from a time before the automobile, the man on the moon, digital phones, Imax, and birth control pills. He couldn't expect her to play by his rules of engagement.

Suddenly, Ryan felt better as if a sheet had been lifted off of him. It made sense. *It had too.* She wasn't from his age. The bloodsucker was forged before all of the things that he regularly took for granted. As he tore apart his desk drawers and cupboards, looking for an envelope, he knew that he was on to something good. The phone rang again. And again, he ignored it.

"Ryan? Theresa. Mindy asked me to call. We're over Mickey's. Mindy said to get your ass over here." Mindy's voice chimed in with some blurred quip and the two bubbleheads started laughing. Theresa cut it short by simply saying, "Later."

The phone clicked.

After the beep, the synthetic voice on the microchip recording informed him that the tape was full. Ryan finally found an envelope from some letter he received sometime ago, and decided to reuse it. Walking over to the blinking light on the decades old answering machine, he stuffed his blood letter into the paper folds. He stared down at the tiny, flashing light – his menu to the buffet of women, and felt nothing for the possibility of a late night hook-up. The Letter had cut him deep and he wanted her. So, Ryan hit the delete button and the computerized voice informed him that he had no new messages.

1775. São Paulo, Brazil.

Through a space in the woods, rutted by travel and rain, past the barn and broken livestock fence, stood about a dozen half-dressed men staring at them. Their dark skins glistened with sweat. Thin and muscular, they stood around another man. A portly fellow, who was fully attired in muddy boots, dirty breeches, a sweat-soaked shirt, vest, wearing a straw fedora. He was unshaven and his scraggly black hair was tied into a loose ponytail. Both girls noticed the whip he carried in his left hand. He eyed them with peculiar intent, slowly gnawing on a strip of sugarcane. He spit the sweet brown liquid onto the ground and yelled at the slaves to get back to work.

Laurel jumped at the sudden boom of his voice and the strange atmosphere of the woods surrounding them pressed at her back. Her question sprang more out of fear than a need to know. "What happened to the woman who lived here?"

The man just rolled his eyes over her, chewing his cud, and Linnet spied lash scars across several backs of the brown men as they returned to their labors. Some were recent. Some weren't. A sudden heat rose within her.

"She gone," the man informed in a lazy Portuguese. "No one left 'cept Inácio and Rui."

He walked toward them, biting the end of a cut stalk.

"Do you know where…" Laurel fuddled her translation, "Where we could find her?"

She looked at Linnet for support, but her attention seemed elsewhere. This grimy stranger was coming over to them and her only companion was lollygaging in the jungle heat. Laurel nervously held onto her stomacher. The strings of the decorative corset trailed to the ground, and as the large man got closer, she felt stupid for carrying it. So, she set it on top of the small trunk and braced herself against his intrusion.

"Why you come here?"

He noticed the baggage they carried and Linnet finally acknowledged his presence with a hard countenance, having found it difficult to peel her eyes off of the abuse of the men. With such a quick observation it looked to her as if the taller, darker skinned males were whipped more than the shorter, light-skinned ones.

"Who are you?" Linnet shot back.

"Inácio Braga. I run this plantation with my cousin. Who are…"

"Did you work under Isabela da Nóbrega?"

The man just glared at the pregnant lass and she repeated the question.

"I think you in the wrong place. No one here by that name." He spit the sweet brown liquid onto the ground near Linnet's shoe. She didn't flinch or look down. "Best if you kept moving. Maybe you find her in a different place."

Linnet reached down and lifted the satchel she was carrying earlier trying with some effort not to look as impeded as she was by the bulge along her mid-section. "We have some trunks at the entrance of the road. Would you be so kind as to send a few men down to carry them up to the house?"

Linnet turned and started walking away, dismissing the man. Laurel stood still, awestruck at the woman's stalwart approach.

"And who are you to think I should send my men to carry your things?" He wiped a corner of his bearded mouth with his sleeve.

Linnet stopped and turned. "Why Mr. Braga, I am Linnet Albee and this is Laurel Davenport and we're wards of Dominique De'Paul. And I haven't decided whether or not if you're trespassing on our property."

The pot-bellied man laughed, rolled up his whip, and hooked it onto his belt. He removed his hat to fan himself. The top of his head was balding. Laurel felt increasingly uncomfortable near him and grabbing her trunk, moved closer toward Linnet.

"This place," he rolled through his mirth, "is not goin' to work for you."

"And why is that Mr. Braga?"

"No man with you. Out here in the jungle. Women got no way of workin' the land." He placed the straw hat back onto his brow. "So many things gonna go wrong for you."

"We have a deed signed by His Most Faithful Majesty. I think things will go along just fine."

The mirth cut from the man's face and he tossed the gnawed bit of cane to the ground and glared at the two female upstarts. Without warning the sky released its water. Heavy drops hit the earth, patting the short space between them.

"If you don't mind," Linnet bid. "The trunks, Mr. Braga…the trunks?"

She turned around and headed toward the dilapidated house, quietly fuming at the indignity of his not so small threat. The rain was warm against her skin, unlike her English weather. It felt good and despite Linnet's repulsion at having to enter the casa she felt a powerful need to rid herself of the sight of Inácio Braga.

Inside, the animals that had escaped from the stables had used the place profusely. It stunk. Laurel chased two goats outside and shooed chickens off the dining room table. Mildewed straw matted the corners and rain fell through the roof in a couple of spots. The entire structure needed to be redone. It was a daunting task that neither girl cared too much to put their backs to, but they had little choice. Dominique would be arriving tonight and if any one of them cared to have a hot meal later on then they had best start in the kitchen.

The stone hearth was in good condition. Linnet found a rusty trivet covered in cobwebs and leaves, but it appeared that all of the cookery had long ago gone missing. They'd have to wait for their trunks to be brought up. One stroke of luck was that the huge storage bins still housed dry coal and wood. She and Laurel could build a fire if they wanted, but they could not rustle up any hot grub.

"Has Dominique truly a deed with King Joseph's signature upon it?" Laurel asked, reverting to their native tongue, once they had started cleaning the main hall. Her attention constantly fell out of the windows to the fields in the distance and the backs of the slaves who were working.

"Ney," Linnet responded. "It was signed by his grandfather, John IV."

"Oh, for pity's sake." She flipped a rag furiously, dusting off a shelf. "Do you think these men will really care about the warrants from a gaggle of women?"

Her inquiry went unanswered as Linnet spied two of the shorter, light-skinned slaves walking up the long path. The rain was ceasing, a short spell over the land, when Inácio and another man burst into view. Linnet took this newcomer to be Inácio's cousin. They were arguing. Inácio tugged at his arm, holding the skinny man back, who was yelling, visibly upset. Linnet knew that it concerned them, but she could not make out what they said at this distance. Frequent nappy heads poked out of the nearby sugarcane field, looking fearfully at the two men. Linnet laid the shoddy twig broom aside as she strode to the front entrance of the house.

"We will soon see."

Laurel caught her moving out of the corner of an eye and fell in behind her, wondering what was happening now. Outside, the two men were heading toward the house. Linnet met them on the landing and the chickens pecking about ran off at Rui's hasty approach.

"Tell me your business with our claim. I heard it from him, now I want to here it from you."

Linnet lifted her chin. "Our business is our Lady's affair. We have no claim other than her command."

"So what is it, then?" The man was as dirty as Inácio and up close he had that burnt sickly sweet stench about him that they had smelled coming up the path. "What is to become of this place?"

"When Dominique arrives she will tell you herself."

The hard, thin man grimaced. His temper a boil "I will not be run off from the harvest I worked."

"She'll…"

"I'll not be run off by the likes of you."

"Our Mistress is fair." Laurel interjected. "We have no need to quarrel."

"Rui?" Inácio urged. "Rui, save it. We wait for her."

"Ah," the hard man scoffed, angry and undecided.

From atop the landing, Linnet looked down at them both, a shiver bracing her flesh. The portly man's cousin was itching to unsheathe his blade, but could not decide the extent of the trouble rash action would cause. Her and Laurel's throats would go easy against the cold metal of his dagger, but the thick stink of the English crown on the two women would most likely fall heaviest on him if he settled the issue now. Linnet waited for him to back off, standing erect and proper like a good Christian woman.

"Rui?" Inácio called again, and he eventually stepped away cursing the ground he walked.

The two slaves that Linnet had spied earlier lugged the abandoned trunks down the long path and the heavens above were ever so blue. The forest around them was thick and noisy, oppressively green, and Linnet felt corrupt by the ordeal of her devotion, waiting on the Vam Pŷr to settle the dispute of the ruins. *Could have stayed with Nsia.* Linnet sucked a gulp of air inward, filling her lungs with the crisp breath of the jungle and the putrid stink of the Engenho, vowing to never again look back on what might have been. She was here, liking the place or not. She was grounded. The boat had come ashore. And it had nearly been two months since she had last put her eyes upon her African lover.

Laurel charged the slaves to set the sodden luggage in the main hall of the house where they had been cleaning. The rectangular boxes were soaked by rain and filthy with mud. Linnet approached the two men, noticing their slick black hair; different than that of the traditional indentured African. Each had faded blue tattoo bands that decorated their arms.

"What is that?" She asked, indicating the tattoos.

The little man looked fearful at her strange words, turning to his friend, she tried again in Portuguese. He didn't have a word in the invader's tongue to explain to her that it was the mark of his people, so he asked his companion how to answer her. They spoke a strange language together, one that Linnet had never heard before. Fast with click, odd pops, it bounced in their mouths, fluid and easy. He told her in Portuguese that it was just a picture.

Linnet put her hand to her chest, "Linnet." She repeated her name, "Linnet."

The odd, little man crossed eyes with his friend, unsure how to answer. No person from the main house had ever spoken to him before, let alone tried to learn his name. It did not bode well, becoming too familiar with the white ladies, especially when Inácio and Rui were arguing over them!

"Guajajara," he said and smiled, a bright row of yellow teeth.

The other man pointed at his bare chest and said, "Vaz."

"Do you know of the woman that used to live here?" Linnet asked them both. "Did you work the land then?"

Both men nodded and told her that they worked the fields, cutting the cane sugar and carrying bales to the boiling house. She asked them again about Isabela, but they only restated that they worked the land for Inácio and Rui. They moved toward the door, as they spoke, nervous to be in the house for so long. They didn't want to get into any trouble. As they left, Linnet's mind was churning and Laurel noticed. She followed the Indios slaves past the door, watching them as they rejoined their group beyond the swell of vines and trees.

"This does not bode well," she said, heavy in her chest.

"How is that?" Laurel asked.

"I believe they were Guarani natives."

"Working the fields?"

"Slaves," Linnet uttered with a finality to the word that sunk to the root of their bellies.

They knew full well the stories that Dominique had weaved for them in the long hours of the night about her home in the Southern Hemisphere and her days as a blood slave under the savage rule of the Omjadda. She had love for this land and its natural people and a raw hate for her imprisoned days. Dominique's heart, sometimes it seemed, was still tied to the feelings of far away places. Now, here among the jungle scenery of the Portuguese colony the illusion that she weaved about Casa del Rio Dulce was shattered, and Linnet felt a gloom overcoming her.

"Dominique is not going to like this," she said, staring off into the distance. "She is not going to like this one single bit."

    The club was packed. Carnal bodies shook the currency of their souls to the pulsating rhythms. The air was stinky and hot. Ryan scanned all of the faces, searching for just one. *Just one face. On one girl.* Dancing somewhere among the assemblage. *Was she waiting for me? Was she here?* He glowered as he looked about the club, shaking his leg out of time with the beat of the song, a vehement hop and shutter that amped him up more than it relieved his tensions.

    Eventually, he got up and hunted, crashing into people as he cut through the throng. The jostled fools barked and spat curses at his departing back. Ryan didn't care. One face. One girl. *She had to be here. Had to be!* Ryan walked toward the bar and a hand reached out and landed on his shoulder. He stopped. *Could it be?*

Upon turning, he was greatly disappointed.

"What the fuck, Silva!" The girl shouted. "So, now you pretend not to even see me?"

    Lacey Chaney was a lewd, opinionated brunette who was too intelligent for her own good. She had a thin, raspy face, a sharp nose pierced with a Celtic loop, and a row of braided, black hair that hung across her face. She wore rich cherry lipstick, a beat up leather coat over a green muscle T-shirt, motorcycle boots, jeans, and a Harley-Davidson belt buckle. The word *Bitch* was tattooed to the left side of her neck in a beautiful cursive script.

    Lacey was an artist: painter, photographer, model. Her works were on display in several key galleries in L.A., Chicago, and New York. It kept her checkbook fat. The day before Lacey ran into Ryan at the club, a black and white photo that she took of Ryan's penis sold for $3,200 to a wealthy sixty-three year old widow, who took care of her late husbands Mastiff Hounds.

"Naw," he persuaded. "I'm just…busy. You know." He shook his head, unable to lie to her. He didn't really have shit going on.

"I've been calling you for a fucking week, man. So what? You don't return my calls now. What's up?"

He scrunched his face, pushed his shoulders up, and ran a hand through his dirty blond hair. He didn't really have anything real that he could tell her and he wasn't in a sociable mood. "Just goin' through some stuff right now. I didn't mean to let you slip…"

"What's this?" she barked grabbing his wrist, and pulling his sleeve back, revealed bloodstained bandages that covered the cuts on his arm.

"You cutting again?" Her eyes pleaded with him for it not to be so.

Ryan yanked his wrist out of her hand and pulled his shirt's sleeve back over the wrappings. He scanned the crowd to see if anyone else had noticed.

"Jesus, Ryan. What the fuck?!"

Lacey wasn't sure what she was more pissed off at. The fact that she had missed the photo opportunity to shoot him cutting or the fact that he'd been dodging her or the fact that he'd gone and cut himself up after he promised her that he wouldn't ever do it again. She grabbed him by the hand and ordered him to come with her and started walking in the opposite direction from where he was going.

She was more of a bulldozer than he was, cutting a jagged course through the overflowing dance floor. She not only pushed people out of her way, she also verbally assaulted them, picking on their hair, their dates, their attire, and their bad dancing. She said absolutely anything to disrupt them from their little ego bubble and get them the hell out of her way, so she and Ryan could be alone in some space quiet enough to talk.

Basically, she threw cutting boy up against the wall in the ladies room and ordered the other girls to shut the hell up or she'd rearrange their makeup in the style of Picasso. She stared at him, waiting with her arms crossed. He knew what she wanted. But how could he tell her? He would sound like a complete idiot! *I cut myself and sent the blood in a letter to a vampire.*

Even he didn't believe that vampires existed at first, and it was right there staring him in the face all night long before he finally came around. And even then, he wasn't completely sold that what he thought, was really…

what he thought. There just had to be more to the whole undead-bleed-your-neighbor-dry-bunk than he learned about from watching movies, but he hadn't had another opportunity to discover it.

Since that first night with the punk Ryan hadn't been able to think about much else, other than Z. It was just like the spell he saw Bela Lugosi place on Lucy in that old black and white version of Dracula: he felt hooked. He needed to see her like a fix. He wanted her to bite him again. Just thinking about it got him excited.

"C'mon Silva, spill." Lacey was getting agitated.

"Just..." he grimaced and sighed. "Some girl."

She pulled the long sleeve back again and tore a hole in the bandage wrap until the dark red lines glared out from under the medical tape.

"You did *this* over a girl? And after you told me you were done with this kinda shit."

Her shock and disapproval were evident on her face. Her rough manhandling of his arm had opened the fresh scabs and several cuts began bleeding.

"I mean, what the fuck, Silva?" She let go of his arm. "She got a silver lined snatch? Ain't no chick worth all this bullshit. I thought you knew that."

He laughed at her eloquent point. But nothing about it was funny to the artist. She was serious. He had wounded her. Each cut on his arm pierced her delicate soul.

"You lied to me."

She looked up at him now, silent and still, and he saw the hurt scrawled across her meringue face. From somewhere deep inside of himself he felt sorry. It was a small, inconspicuous voice. A tiny whisper. He had lied. *Yeah.* And he avoided calling her back because he knew it. Now, she knew it too.

"I've just been in my own head about it, you know?" he started sincerely. "Been feeling like I'm getting nowhere. And it's...not just *the girl*. It's everything. I just feel..." he balled his hands into fists and lifted them to his chest. "I don't know. Frustrated."

He released his curled fingers with the word. Yet the glare from

Lacey's crystalline blue eyes made him feel small. Made him feel like being frustrated wasn't good enough. Made him think that she knew he wasn't totally being honest with her.

"Who are you?" she asked as a blond girl exited the far stall smoothing the rear of her lavender colored dress. The flush of the toilet boomed in the expectant moment between Lacey's question and Ryan watching the young woman exit the restroom without washing her hands, meekly spying on the two of them. "Who are you?"

He didn't have an answer and he was tired of being grilled. "I don't know." He started to leave and she pushed him back up against the wall.

"You're Ryan Fuckin' Silva, that's who!" She bopped him in the shoulder with her fist. "You could have any girl you want. You don't need this bitch. You could walk out there now and take home your pick. You *own* this place! That's who you are." She sized him up with her eyes. "You remember him?"

"Yeah." He meekly lied.

"But what?" She saw it on his face.

"There's just gotta be more out there to life than this. That's all." He tried to convince her and failed. "I'm just tired of it, you know. Want something different for a change."

"My…" She cooed. "She's really got you spun around her finger, don't she?"

Ryan felt tense under her microscopic glaze. "It ain't like that."

"Who is this bitch?"

"Nobody you know."

"If I did I'd kick her scrawny little ass."

She doesn't get it. Lacey can't understand that there is more out there to life than just the same ole, same old. Despite her stunning analysis I do need the woman. She makes the mundane possible. When will I see her again? All this talk made Ryan yearn for Z more. He and Lacey were old news.

She was there at a time in his life when the curve was good and the money was gravy and he helped her out: gave her a place to stay, food, and time enough for her to get her art together. It was the launching pad she needed to propel her to be the woman that she was today. He knew it. She knew it. Sure, they slept together back then and pretended to be a couple, but it didn't work out. She sprouted her own wings and went her own separate way. They had their arguments. They had their tender dream moments. Heck, Lacey even met his Mom and no other girl had ever done that. But that was yesterday. Z was today.

Ryan was grateful for their friendship and how they always stayed in touched. Lacey was the closest person he knew. And sure, they hooked up every now and again because the sex had always been good. But she was rarely in his world now. She slipped past his radar into God knows what the fuck. She was gone. It was all how it was meant to be. Lacey had moved on to bigger and better things, while he stayed behind, stuck in LA, doing the same old shit that he'd always done, and he was plum tired of it. *How could she even begin to understand?*

Lacey pulled him into a quiet stall and shut the door.

"Tomorrow," she said, unbuckling his belt. "You come by the studio. We'll talk, have some wine, take some pictures, maybe fool around…" she smirked. "And get you outta this funk that you seem so content to be in." She dipped her hands into his pants, under the elastic ban of his underwear, and grabbed the muscle around the bone of his hips.

He wanted to protest her advances, but Lacey Chaney had made up her mind. She was all fired up, gliding on clueless.

"You don't need her Ryan." She earnestly tried to lock his eyes. "You may think you do, but you don't."

He exhaled slowly and stared at her, feeling the cold metal stall against his back. There was a long moment between them before she said, "I'm gonna take care of you. Just like you did for me."

Lacy eased Ryan's pants off his waist as she slid down the length of him, gathering the well-worn denim around his ankles. She took him into her mouth and worked him as if her bold, feeble efforts could ever make him forget the vampire. He felt nothing for the artist anymore. Her wet, toothy orifice felt distant like a lighthouse in the fog. He knew what he wanted and this wasn't it. Though he didn't have the heart to tell Lacey that she was wrong about what he needed and that her wild tongue was just wasting its time. Against yesterday and today, back to the wall and a girl at his groin, Ryan closed his eyes and focused on cumming – *just to could get it over with*. And he hoped that she would never know the difference.

1775. São Paulo, Brazil.

"How can you prepare for a problem when you do not know what it is going to be?" replied Dominique rhetorically to Laurel's complaints when she arrived last night. "If those two men are the sum total of our worries then you can consider us lucky."

The young maid was not moved by the Vam Pŷr's indomitable reasoning. Her first day on the plantation had been trying, burdened with strangers and filth, surviving on little more than a shared wedge of cheese, a collection of nuts and berries, a carafe of wine, and a tin of salted meats that she had taken from the ship. Linnet was nothing more than an instigator with the Portuguese men and Laurel was quite sure that they would return in the morning seeking their heads to retain their claim on Dominique's land.

"Yes, and we'll be lucky indeed if these savages don't string us up during the night."

"Expecting trouble and anticipating disaster will not avail you to the hardships ahead," instructed her mistress as she inspected a small wooden door with a skeleton key that neither she nor Linnet had been able to open all day. "Nor will it allow you to accept and meet the challenges that will surely need overcoming."

Laurel growled behind her teeth, angered by the level-headedness of her Dark Mistress. Her disposition was quickly displaced by surprise, however, when Dominique disappeared behind the door. Both ladies crossed to the opened portal, having thought earlier that it was nothing more than a small closet of sorts. Before them was a set of descending stairs and the dark hollow of pitch black. Dominique had vanished into the gloom.

"Most of the supports are intact," came her voice. "Root damage and the plaster needs to be redone, but it appears in a better state than I thought. Can you fetch me a candle?"

Curiosity spurred the heels of both women as they scurried to the unpacked trunks for the waxen light. Igniting their wicks, each woman headed downstairs. The smell was musty and stale and the stairs were remarkably strong, braced by cut earth. A large curving tunnel stretched out from the steps, wide enough for two men. As Dominique had mentioned, the plaster coating the walls was severely cracked. Roots had busted through in several places and there was evidence of previous water damage. Inlaid stone fitted the walkway and in the burning light insects and spiders scurried out of the way.

The tunnel wound to a wooden door with a metal latch. It was partly opened. Upon entering, the orange light fell onto a large round room and Dominique standing in its center. The space was partly furnished. The Vam Pŷr took a candle and crossed the room, alighting wax stubs mounted in a freestanding candelabra. Both young maids were struck by the hidden beauty of the cellar. Recessed shelving cut into the walls and the stone tiled floor wound in a decorative fashion to a colossal four post bed that was missing its canopy and bedding. Sheets covered two bookshelves and there were three armoires along the far wall. Linnet pulled one of the sheets from off a tier and dust filled the air.

Dominique pulled out another key from the chain that she wore around her neck and began opening the armoires. Though not all of them were locked. Inspecting what sparse contents remained in the cabinets, she did not find what she was ultimately looking for. Linnet noticed many empty spaces on the bookshelves, and what books were still there could greatly benefit from a bit of polish and fresh air. Dominique pulled out from the old wooden credenzas, leaving their doors wide. She was not at all pleased by the shape of things.

"Nothing," she exhaled. "Not a single word. And it could take months trying to track her down in Rio de Jeneiro. If she is still even there." She turned to her consorts. "Was there nothing else said about this place from the cabmen that might elude to Isabela's murder?"

Linnet shook her head. "No. He gave me the impression that things had grown quiet on their own, without incident or provocation."

Dominique pursed her lips, thinking for a short spell, and then lifted her eyes to Laurel. "Now we begin to see the scope of the problem we face and as such can apply the right ointment." She lit from the room, heading back upstairs, followed by her maids. "Isabela is gone and has left no detail of her whereabouts. So, we must assume that she has abandoned all activities that were in her charge. An accounting with the local magistrate will verify the severity of loss to my holdings here and in Minas Gerais. Though, some documents in my care will not hold up to the judgement of today's standards. We will need to learn who in the province are the best men to bribe.

As to the squatters, tell them that I will meet with them tomorrow evening. I have no intention of attributing a deficit to their coffers, but I will not tolerate this plantation housing slaves under the conditions that you have described. We can procure the necessary hardware and household goods we'll readily require within the township and that will suffice for our immediate needs. It will take us a considerable amount of time to mend Casa del Rio Dulce to its former glory. And we will need the backs of many strong and able-bodied men. The ones already living here on the plantation will do for now, but we must correctly ascertain whom of this lot, if any, were under bondage while the Countess lived here."

"Might I suggest that we not so hastily alter the conditions of the slaves just yet," advised Linnet. "It is the custom of this country to employ The Trade as its chief labor source."

Dominique stopped in the main hall and turned to her paramour, resolute. "I'll not stain my hands with it. Damn King. Damn country. We make our own way."

Dominique continued onward to her trunks and Linnet sighed. They had too many obstacles to tackle at once. Grinding against local customs would only seek to undermine their achievements.

"I only meant to infer that we maintain appearances until we have achieved some measure of security."

The Vam Pŷr did not respond and busied herself with unpacking and preparing her chambers below the house. Linnet left the matter, knowing full well the tender subject of her mistress's captivity. There was so much still yet to do to make the house livable and the girls had been working all day. Laurel crossed to the front door and opening it, listened to the sounds of the night. Off in the distance specks of firelight from where Laurel guessed the slaves were quartered dotted the darkened landscape. The small candles that they had burning in the house felt insignificant against the unknown forest and deep pitch that stared back at her. This was a strange and savage land and she had never seen anything like it before in her whole life.

She wondered what would become of the three of them, mere women in a man's world attempting to steer the oar of their own lives. The tasks ahead seemed daunting and she had neither Dominique's determined will or Linnet's courage, but she trusted the Vam Pŷr. Ever since they had met on that cold wintry night in London, Laurel had seen many strange and wonderful things while in her company. Often it terrified her, but she had learned one thing about being in the presence of the odd woman. Dominique was formidable. She bent the stubborn wills of kings and queens to her purpose. If she felt that they could carve a home out for themselves in this god-forsaken jungle, than all she need do was trust her mistress.

The day broke early at Casa del Rio Dulce with a rooster crowing at the sun. Dominique remained below, until at least they could repair the shutters on the windows and the girls went to work preparing the kitchen for daily use. And though Laurel wanted to silence the bird that sang to her under her window that morning she rustled up two hens instead, snapping their necks, and hung them on hooks above the meat table, bleeding them for Dominique, determined to feast on a substantial meal today.

It wasn't long before Inácio and Rui came looking for the Lady of the Casa Grande and they were not pleased to hear that she would not meet with them until nightfall. Nor did either man like the claims that the pregnant woman made on the use of their slaves. They had bought each and every one of them, outright, they affirmed. None were left over from when Isabela ruled the Engenho. Though Linnet tried to parley with them, they did not seem too eager to discuss the warrants of the land. Dominique heard everything in her subterranean abode, finding no pleasantries in the raised voices of the men. They were common thugs, looking to advance their station at the dereliction of the Countess's duty, and though she could not be sure without looking them in the eye, she too felt that they knew more about what had transpired at Casa del Rio Dulce than what they were letting on.

The day passed quickly with their individual tasks and Linnet made it her goal to get out of the house and survey the grounds. She inspected the stables, staying away from the senzalas, sugarcane fields, mill, and boiling house. She did not want any trouble from Mr. Braga or his cousin. The barn seemed to be in a well enough condition to house animals and it still possessed a stock of tools and harnesses. She made a mental note to have Laurel purchase some horses and a wagon when she went to town.

Beyond the southern slope of the house was a long grove of Orange trees. The fruit had not been picked for at least a season. Most of it was dead on the vine or had fallen to the ground and rotted. But the trees were still lovely to stroll through. Placing her hands to her protruding belly, Linnet considered, for the first time, what she might call the child that grew within her. If it were going to be a girl she thought to name her Audrey, after her mother, or Charlotte, after Mrs. Lennox who was her favorite living author and poet. If it were to be a boy then she thought of calling him after his father or her father, but neither, Nsia or Emerson, seemed appropriate for the child she carried. It was only fancy, after all, and she had too much work that needed to get done to be sauntering through the grove.

Returning to the house, Linnet stopped among a thicket of green to empty her bladder and found a small trench beneath some vines and leaves that was part of the property's aqueducts. She followed it until it disappeared underground and happened to locate one of the centrifugal pumps. Curious to see if time had clogged it with rust, she noticed the saturated ground and concluded that Laurel must have managed the manual labor of its mechanics earlier when she was walking through the grove. Having this task supplanted, she fetched a hatchet from the barn, one that she had seen earlier, deciding to rid them of the nuisance of a small tree that was growing up through the floor in the livingroom.

Dusk was thickening across the land when the men returned with four riders on horseback. They called the woman out and Dominique met them in the yard. A cold shiver raced through the hot blood of the thoroughbreds at the scent of the symbiont and they became uneasy under their riders. Dominique's pale features did not offend the hard men and it was obvious to her by the way they sat in their saddles that they were, or had been, at one time, soldiers.

Linnet and Laurel joined their mistress outside, watching from the vantage of the landing. They did not like the men on horseback. Their clothes were soiled, their countenances mean. Linnet wished that she had loaded a musket before evening overtook them.

"These lands are cursed and hard to manage," mentioned Rui. "What need would you have of 'em?"

"They have been in my family for generations," affirmed Dominique. "Since the first settlers crossed the sea."

"And abandoned they were to the likes of a Bruxsa and a heathen woman." Shouted one of the men on horseback.

He had a narrow face, a thin mustache, and sat up in his saddle when he spoke.

"I know nothing of this or what happened to the caretaker I left installed." Dominique slowly walked closer to them, unsettling the horses.

"I will pay you handsomely for the fields worked and time spent; and perhaps if we can find an accord on the bevy of slaves housed on my land I will keep you on to tend to the functions of the Engenho."

"We deserve more," stated Rui.

Dominique turned to him with a calm voice. "That is all I am willing to offer."

Inácio stepped up. "São Paula has changed much since your ancestors were last on this shore."

"Oh, I do not think so." Dominique breathed, observing the threatening posture of the men.

"We do not take kindly to strangers taking what is rightfully ours," said the curtly, moustache gentleman in the saddle.

Dominique passively folded her hands against her waist and straightened her back. "Then we will settle this in the magistrate's office."

Rui broke the seal on his knife. "We gonna settle this tonight."

Dominique barely caught it out of the corner of her eye: *Inácio's whip trailing through the air toward her.* She grabbed the thin leather end, winding it around her forearm and pulled. Inàcio fell, face first, into the grass and dirt. The horses bucked at the sudden movements of the strange smelling thing as Dominique swung her arm around, over her head, and slammed the hard grip of the whip against Rui's temple as he advanced. The man dropped his knife and fell to his knees, grabbing his head. Dominique released the hold that she had had on her Jadaraa Soo. Her sentient veins flushed to the roof of her skin, maddened by her rage, thirsty for blood, and frightened the horses. They reared back, neighing wildly and kicking their front hooves at the retched woman. One of the riders fell to the ground as the other three got control of their beasts and rode off back down the long road from which they came.

The fallen stranger stood and drew his sword as Dominique called the master's end of the whip to herself. His eyes looked to Rui and Inàcio, aching from the lashes that they had received at the hands of a simple woman. *A woman?* He heard the thundering ground of his stead and retreating companions and knew it wasn't worth it. Murdering these women so the Bragas could keep the plantation. *She offered to pay them well enough. They needed to take what they could get and soothe their licks.* The former soldier sheathed his sword, turned, and walked away wanting nothing more to do with any of it. Down the lane, he found his horse picking at some leaves.

Dominique gathered Inacio's whip into her hand, curling it slowly as she strolled over to Rui. Linnet and Laurel were panting, awestruck at the quick and violent turn of affairs. They had barely breached the seal of the house before the wickedness was already done. They stood aghast at their Dark Mistress, surveying the yard, having never seen her handle herself in quite this way before.

"I have made a fair offer and you tried to take it by force." She stepped on Rui's knife as he reached for it, flicking his eyes up to the woman with hate. "Now, tell me of the one that used to govern this estate."

Rui grinned, a devilish smile, and huffed to himself. "I don't know what you're talkin' about."

Dominique kicked him and Laurel gasped. She stepped on his neck as Inàcio rose.

"She take us on," the Overseer said.

"Shut up!" Rui shouted at his cousin.

"Before she left; she hired us. To work the Engenho. She said we could have the land, but had to kill you to own it."

Dominique stepped off Rui's neck, feeling as if her stomach was falling off a cliff. She could barely hold her parasite down from revealing itself to the men. *Isabela had told them to murder me.* "When?" It was all she could muster.

"A couple seasons ago. But we make the land our own. We turned the factory 'round. She was no good. We have been good to the land and the land has been good to us."

Dominique slightly shook her head, a conflux of thoughts bustling, and walked away from them both. She couldn't believe it. She looked up at the worried expressions painted on her consorts and stiffened. She couldn't let them see any weakness in her. *Not now!* She stopped and glared at the Bragas over her shoulder.

"My offer still stands. I will pay you for the fields you worked and the bevy of slaves. But I never want to see either of you again. Or the local magistrate will be the lest of your troubles." Dominique walked off, avoiding the eyes of her paramour and her servant. "Linnet will see to the transaction of payment."

The Vam Pŷr entered the house with Inàcio's whip and the four strangers looked from one to the other, uneasy. The darkened forest smelled sweaty and lush, and was lively with its nightly buzz. Linnet and Rui affixed a price to the Braga's service that she was not ultimately pleased with, believing that the men deserved nothing for their treachery. For the life of her, she could not fathom why Dominique would pay them off and it was something that she planned on ferreting out after business had been conducted. The Overseers hesitated at signing the document that she had prepared earlier, but signed their mark regardless upon seeing the small sacks of gold that Laurel had brought from the house.

Inside, Dominique paced about her cellar. Though upon seeing the girls returning, she stopped and informed them both that she would not be taking blood this evening and that she mainly wanted to be left alone. Linnet tried to sway her to her company, but the Persian woman would not concede. The night ended quiet and lonely for everybody, leaving a brand of questions fluttering through their heads where no answers lingered in the savage folds of this untamed place.

"This is Ryan." The recorded message played. "You know what to do."

Beeeeeep!

A breathy moan broke the seal on Ryan's empty apartment and quivered. "I'm thinking of you," and she squealed, in the back of her throat. Mouth open and wanting. "Shit, Silva, you need to get over here. I'm *so* wet."

The voice spasmed a shaky breath and then, click!

"You have six new messages." The antique answering machine reported, soaking up the silence around it. Its flashing red digital number blinked up at the sterile eyes of the ceiling. Looking down, a crème-colored gaze, the number looked like a nine and headlights from a passing car moved across its flat expanse, lighting briefly the darkened bulb behind the tinted glass housing of the ceiling light.

1775. São Paulo, Brazil.

In the weeks spent fixing the house Laurel became a presence in the township and Dominique took to wandering the fields and groves of the plantation alone at night. A mood had taken over her of which she would not speak, and often she was spotted by the slaves on her nightly sojourns. Rumors sprouted amongst them about her vestige. Her blanched form like a ghost, walking through the trees, spying on them: it was reminiscent of the previous Lady of the House, and they were afraid. Those few indentured men that still lived from those old days remembered the wickedness of Isabela da Nóbrega. How she enslaved them after the ghostly form of this woman had left the Engenho and how many men and women that used to be among them were taken to the big house and never seen again. The older ones spread fear that soon they too would become missing, swallowed into the belly of the Casa Grande. None of the younger, newer purchased slaves believed their odd prattling. It was just nonsense from decrepit men who still believed in their superstitions from the Motherland. To the virile slaves their backs had been spared from Inácio's whip by the intrusion of the women. They didn't toil in the heat of the Boiling House anymore and the work at the Mill had all but ceased. To them, these new landlords were revered, though held in speculation, as all those of the white race were.

In the release of her normal duties, Linnet began to occupy herself with the state of her dark mistress. The young mother-to-be found it hard to sit silently by as the enigmatic woman pulled farther away from her. She visited the freed blood slave in her subterranean chambers, but was often turned away. Living was cut into pieces. The three of them, nestled in the project of the big house, rarely speaking, moving around one another like dejected pieces on a chessboard. Something was going to snap and everyone could feel it.

Slaves worked on the roof, plastered the walls, carved new shutters, and installed newfangled glass that Laurel had purchased while in town. Slaves repaired the fence around the barn as Laurel stocked the stables with animals and wagons. Linnet was surround by a flurry of activity from men that reminder her of her dark skinned lover. The solace that Linnet had once sought when she came ashore to this distant marl was now alien to her. Unwanted. She felt isolated and alone enveloped by a hundred eyes. So in her bland absence of duty, pushed away from the loom of Dominique's arms, Linnet took to overseeing the cleaning of the orange groves.

Bushels of dried, rotten fruit plucked from limbs and lifted off the ground were hauled to a pile in a clearing that was set ablaze with other matter and construction materials. The fire released a sweet, effervescent stench as it burned down to ash. Many slaves came out from the Senzalas to watch the pile burn. An old woman sang a dirge. Linnet watched her and Dominique stood on the flat roof of the main house watching over them all.

Through consummate study, Linnet had devised an irrigation system to bring water to the orange trees from the Tietê River. She was seeing to its installation when Laurel returned from the township bringing even more terrifying news of the history of the house than she had on previous occasions. The locals often met the young maid's forays into town with trepidation. Rumors were abound about the new owners of Casa del Rio Dulce. Many wondered if they were of the same ilk as the previous caretaker. Laurel brought back tales of locals finding bloodless corpses of the plantation's slaves washed up on the riverbanks or found loosely buried in large pits near the plantation's borders. It seemed that Isabela da Nóbrega had left a furious reputation in her wake. Speculation was thick as to the nature of her soul held in the bosom of the Darkest One. During her hold on the land none from the township dared cross her for fear of going missing.

Dominique had told Linnet and Laurel that Isabela was a self-absorbed, self-serving Spanish courtesan before she was resurrected in the blood and surmised that in her absence the woman had become more like her old self: egomaniacal and a hedonist fond of sensuous delights who took pleasure in feeding on human beings until the last beat of their hearts shuddered. Dominique's holdings in the Portugal paradise were in shambles and her plantation was reputedly damned. Her claims to her mines at Minas Gerais were steadily being forestalled by the Magistrate. And though the object of the coin moved those of the regal and the cloth the same as the commoner, Laurel was unsuccessful at finding a bid that would move the Magistrate's interests along a course of action that would appease the Vam Pŷr. Tensions mounted between them and the locals with each new discovery as to the conditions of their affairs

While in town, an old woman approached Laurel and told her about her son. He was only seventeen, a good boy; murdered some time back. His death was attributed to a Bruxsa that was known to roam the forests near Casa del Rio Dulce. The aged hag inferred that the nightly ghoul was none other than the whore, da Nóbrega, herself, though it was never proven. The woman held her head low, leaning into Laurel as she spoke so that her views would travel no further than to the quaint breasts of the English lady.

She told Laurel that the body of her son was found in a glade one morning after he had been missing for nearly a week. He was drained of all his fluids, pale and sickly, and was buried in the cemetery of their church that same day. The next night his grave was found empty. At first, it was thought to have been robbed, but that was dispelled when the young man began to be seen in the township. He attacked and killed a girl from the village, scared others, and was eventually hunted down by a militia that found him eating the remains of a boy that the young man had known well in the days of his youth. The specter of her son was captured and burned along with the bodies of his victims, lest they too rise from their graves to murder and feast on the blood of innocents.

"Since then she said that she has been marred socially," explained Laurel, "and told me to mind myself well here."

The look on Dominique's face was not good. *These tales within the township were devastating.* She sat. *Isabela had taken things too far.* Her maids watched her and she noticed them waiting.

"The blood of Ornn Däm Mu becomes anew when it is taken within the body. Your fluids, your own blood feeds it and by so doing forms the Jadaraa Soo. It is no longer the blood of an Omjadda that flows through your veins nor is it your own blood that flows either. The Jadaraa Soo is a new life, a new being, created by the amalgamation of the two of you. I have explained this to you both previously, but what you have now told me makes me think that Isabela tried to change this young man into one like herself by her own accord." She stood and began to walk slowly around her consorts.

"I did not leave any of Ornn's blood with her in my stead. Nor do I intend to leave it with you once you've gone through the transformation. That duty has yet to fall on any that I have chosen to resurrect. I want to be clear in this matter. Not all can handle or should be purified in the blood. It is a burden that I know not yet how to delegate. I trust in time that a solution will present itself, though for the time being, adding to my fold is my charge. Isabela knew this. And yet she went against my wishes and tried to turn a man using the blood of her Jadaraa Soo." She shook her head, thinking about the damage that had been done in the eyes of the town. "I caution you both," she paused for effect, "you will only birth an abomination if you attempt to resurrect someone with the blood of your Jadaraa Soo. They will no longer be the person that you knew them to be. If resurrected they will be consumed by the thirst to feed, having no control until it destroys them."

"Even to become so damned as to feast like a cannibal upon another soul?"

asked Laurel.

"Yes." The confirmation sunk like lead into their guts. "The hunger of the Jadaraa Soo is strong. Only by tasting the original source can one be assured of the outcome. It takes a strong intellect to master the melding nature of this gift. I urge you now, while you are still considering the path of your desire, think on the vicissitudes of time and companionship and set your heart to my judgement."

"Yes Mistress."

Linnet, silent through the tale and the explanation, hand massaging the child in her belly, rose from the couch and crossed the floor to leave.

"Have you no say in what we have discussed?" Dominique asked.

Linnet stopped and turned. "No, Mistress."

"Then you agree that it is for the best, to avoid tainting our waters with impure blood?"

"As you deem fit."

Linnet turned and exited the room. Dominique sighed, but before she could follow after her dark haired muse Laurel beset her with papers from the bank. Duty overshadowed all aspects of their lives in the colony. It was the wind in their sails. The fire that burned in the hearth at night. The model of their daily keep. The women were encumbered, carving a staple yield from the thick jungle site.

The next evening Linnet woke to find the Vam Pŷr standing in the dark interior of her room watching her sleep. She cut a black figure, silent and unapproachable, near the foot of her bed. Linnet woke with a start, feeling the woman's presence in her room.

"What are you doing?" She rubbed the sleep from her eyes. Dominique said nothing, standing there, a mass hovering in the silent gloom. "Come now, you woke me, speak. What is it that you require?"

"I heard him," she softly uttered in the language of her second home.

"He is gone." Linnet answered, having the gorgeous African on her mind from dreams. "We saw to that ourselves. Come now, join me."

Linnet pulled the covers back on the bed and scooted aside to make room for her, but the woman remained still, a sullen presence in the room.

Linnet lay her head back down and patted the emptiness in her bed.

"I was below in my chambers and I heard him…"

This time Linnet awoke fully. The tone in her mistress's voice was unsettling. She sat up in the bed. "Whom did you hear, Dominique?"

The Vam Pŷr shook her head softly, and raising a finger on her hand told the girl to shush. "Can you not hear it?" She stepped closer to Linnet. The pregnant woman shook her head, no. "He is so strong," uttered the symbiont, sitting on the edge of the bed.

The look on Dominique's face as she passed a tether of moonlight, falling on the floor, was one of amazement. Stilled wonder. Linnet did not know what Dominique was babbling about and was quickly becoming unnerved.

"Of whom do you speak? Come now, it is too late for this, tell me…"

The glazed expression across Dominique's face birthed a horrible idea in Linnet's bonnet. Separated as they were, over these collected days, the young woman imagined the blood of her symbiont paramour turning bad, causing her to gnaw on Linnet's flesh and bones like the young man in Laurel's gossip from town.

"Your child, Linnet," spoke the apparition after a time, washing away the woman's aroused fears. "The beating of his heart. I can hear it."

Linnet leaned back and placing her hands to her protruding belly peered into her round form as if it were a crystal ball. "You hear the beating of his heart?"

Dominique nodded. "He rousted me and I had been listening for a time before you woke."

"Huh?" Linnet found it odd. "What does it sound like?"

"Oh…he is strong."

"It is a boy then?"

Dominique smirked, "it sounds like a boy."

Something about that sent a shiver racing across the landscape of Linnet's piqued flesh. A breeze pushed aside the curtains and the call of a rooster announced the dawn. The Vam Pŷr left the engorged woman alone in her big bed tied to her fears and the intrusion of her pregnancy. Linnet could not fall back asleep. The beating of her unborn son's heart occupied the corridors of her mind.

Giving birth to a daughter had mostly consumed the prospect of the child. Linnet knew now that she had secretly wanted the babe to be female. Dominique's claims that the gestating infant possessed male sex had uncovered hidden motivations and made her lie of omission to Nsia all the more harrowing to bear. She withheld a son from his father, an heir from the lineage of his people. For days after this awkward interchange, Linnet felt that she was robbing Nsia of the fortune of a son. Guilt banged on the shores of her being.

Nsia had talked so often of his family when they were together. The pride of his people had made him strong. It was a strength she loved and missed. He had no child at home. His bloodline was fruitless. Linnet was the sole receptacle of the next generation of his long family tree. Somehow knowing the sex of the unborn child tugged at the chords of Linnet's soul in a manner that she had not thought possible. So, she began to write Nsia a letter. To inform him that she was soon to bear him a son.

However, each handwritten confession to the man seemed worse than the last. Linnet crumpled her efforts into paper balls and tossed them away into the burning hearths of the big house, her frail utterances of language were becoming nothing more than smoke and ash. She felt an increasing urge to confide her sins and fears into the bosom of her dark mistress, but found, with steady frequency, that the languishing grace that the two had once shared abroad before coming to this savage place was hampered by obligation and silent retreats. Frustration rode the edges of the English woman's skin. The mettle of the Vam Pŷr's mood was causing a definite stir within their quiet household and it rapidly reached a boiling point with an explosion of fire!

Linnet was asleep at her writing desk again, having nodded off while composing a letter to Nsia. She woke to the sounds of neighing horses, the scurry of slaves, and the smell of sickly-sweet smoke. Moving as quickly as she could for a woman in her condition, Linnet threw a robe on over her nightclothes and headed downstairs. The hem of her gown ignited in a fluttering whisper as she descended the opened stairway. Fearful eyes from the house servants watched her as she pushed open the Casa Grande's large carved redwood doors. Her fingers scraped across the rough polish of the wood, saw it, and gasped.

Above the tree line, where the mill and boiling house were, a glowing orange mass brimmed. It illuminated dark wooden spires that poked the sky and filled the night with thick chasms of sugary smoke. Servants ran from the house, slaves ran from the Senzalas toward the blaze with maddened haste and buckets of water. Linnet's eyes searched for Dominique and Laurel, but only found their stable hand, Guajajara, talking with what appeared to be the portly vestige of the former Overseer, Inácio Braga. She slowed her pace, staring. But as soon as he spied Linnet he ran into a thicket of bush behind the barn, leaving the lone eyes of the native peering coldly at her. The half-sized man led a mare back into the livery stables and Linnet continued onward in the direction of the chaos.

What was he up to? Linnet feared the worst and by the time she reached the mill it was falling into itself like a matchstick construction, a cascade of burning hate assaulting her lungs. A fortune in Hogheads of raw sugar and palates of Palena were being destroyed in the raging flames. *Inácio had returned for revenge.* The fire danced, brightly and hot, crackling with thunderous salvo. Even the stones of the decimated boiling house were burning.

Linnet looked about. Neither Laurel nor Dominique were anywhere to be seen. *What had Inácio done with them?* The black skins of the African slaves glistened, pasty moist, dotted with sweat in the furious light as they too fearfully watched the engine of the factory burn to the ground. In an odd way, beside herself like a book on the nightstand table, the heaving perspiration on the male slaves reminded her of how candlelight had lit the sweat on Nsia's chest after they had made love. The thought was distracting, misplaced in this vile setting, and Linnet felt bared in the brutal light. Something was not quite right. It only took the pregnant lass a moment to notice what it was.

Buckets of water lay strewn everywhere – *over turned, some broken.* The hefted liquid still filled many hollow shells and it was obvious that some receptacles had had their wet bounty emptied onto the grass. The yard around the massive fire glistened with moisture. Not a drop, it seemed, appeared to have made it to the hungry flames.

"Why weren't the buckets used or the hoses and pumps from the river?" She asked angrily to those standing about.

The gravid mistress had seen many slaves carrying buckets toward the flames on her way up. She thought their intention was to squelch the blistering furnace! Instead, their efforts seemed wasted. *Were they conniving with the Overseer to destroy our land?* Linnet spied a slave holding his right arm with blood trickling down to his pink palms. She asked him directly, but he did not understand her. He did not speak Portuguese. The language of his tongue was still tied to the African Savannah. Linnet asked another and another, switching from English, French, and Portuguese, until finally someone told her what she needed to know.

"The Missus she gone crazy," a young black woman told her in her best, broken efforts. "She would not let us put out da fire. She whip us as we near." The frightened slave pressed her hand to the gash in the man's arm, pleading. "We couldah saved the boilin' house, but she stop us. She stop us."

Linnet took stock again of the watery carnage and saw now that most of those gathered around the blaze bore signs that they've recently felt the sharp sting of a lash. The slave continued to press to Linnet that they did their best to try and save the refinery houses but were not allowed. She did not want to be punished for the destruction that they witnessed.

Linnet interrupted, asking where she had last seen Dominique and another, hardened slave pointed to the North field. Linnet turned, looking across the road. A small light flickered behind a patch of golden and pink Ipê trees. The North field was beginning to burn.

The extra weight that Linnet carried as she crossed the expanse of the plantation was not as difficult to bear as the thought that Dominique was destroying their home. She huffed and puffed as she followed the dirt road to the furthest sugarcane field. Confusion swirled in the air around her. Servants and slaves still ran about trying to beat back the tide of flames, unaware of the vicious intentions of their overlord. Natural instincts had risen in the madness plaguing them and they, like Linnet, had sought to save the Engenho, despite the fact that its very existence was the sole reason they were enslaved. The irony was not lost on Linnet as she made her way north and fell into a group of men trying to douse the flames before it got out of control and destroyed the valuable crop.

Their efforts were met by a ferrous will. An ardent heart! In the fray, at the edge of the field, backlit by an inferno cataract, stood Dominique! Her arms were raised shouting at the mule headed thrall cracking Inácio Braga's whip to keep them at bay.

"Fools!" she screamed in vivid anger, "Such ignorant fools! You rush to save the very thing that enslaves you. Where is your courage? Where is your spirit? Let it burn!"

Linnet was awestruck! She had never seen her mistress in such an aggravated state. The pallid beauty roared over the mouth of the flames until the thrall shrank back, just as they had done at the boiling house and mill. Linnet knew that Dominique had not been happy with the use of African and native slaves as the chief workforce of her mines and fields in Brazil. But it was the staple of the country. It was the way of the land. There was nothing out of place by it. By all practical senses, after hours of debate, Dominique did reason to maintain the status quo on the plantation until the matter with Isabela could reach some form of resolution. The three of them had agreed to stop production and shift all labor to the necessary tending of the house and livery. Linnet was sure that Laurel had confirmed that Dominique had agreed to this. But this razing of the factory to ash was not the path of practical senses. It was madness!

"Dominique!" Linnet shouted. "Come away. You have made your point. Let's leave before you scare the Bateys."

The Vam Pŷr was richer in color than normal. The veins that usually mapped her eyes were engorged to a thick, ruddy black. *She had overly feed*. Fear ripped across Linnet's skin, cold and uncomfortable in the hot light of the burning field. She knew this look on the dark mistress and wondered who the poor devils were that had crossed her and passed under her teeth. The pregnant maid only hoped that their bodies were, at least, engulfed in the raging flames that illuminated the night sky. For if not, their discovery would inspire more rumors within the township and ignite the buried fears of the captives. Linnet reasoned: there was only the three of them against the rising sins of the past and the unfocused might of all those around her. She knew they were isolated from any real source of protection. Watching Dominique now, a torrent of rage, scaring the good hearts of her inhabitants, she felt death closing in.

"Dominique, please…before it is too late."

"Back to the house with you! I am far from finished." There was frenzy in her eye!

"This is enough Dominique," the young maid urged. "You are scaring them."

The freed Vam Pŷr, flushed with ridden anger, stepped to the insubordinate lady. "Go back to the house." She gritted her teeth and her elongated canines sparkled devilishly in the razor light.

"The hell I will," spat the consort.

The corners of Dominique's mouth curled. Fear edged to the tops of Linnet's bones and rode her English flesh like a river rapid, but she stood her ground. Quietly, Dominique's dark, engorged eyes bore into the young woman, a seething tempest of black blood. Linnet's heart pounded in her chest, audible above the rage of flame. *Is this how it is to end?* Linnet placed a hand to her belly and a tear ran down her cheek.

Though instead of murder, the millennia old woman thrust her torch in Linnet's hand, saying, "In that case, the South field needs to be razed."

Linnet stared up at her, motionless in the cocoon of chaos that surrounded them. Her fear dissipated to billowing guilt. She had doubted her Dark Mistress to the most degree. Sorrow flitted down her spine.

"I will not leave a single one of them to suffer the yoke of my land any longer." Dominique tightened her grip around Inácio's leathery whip. "I'd soon burn the whole country to the ground than bear this indignity one more day."

Dominique placed her hand to Linnet's shoulder and squeezed. It had been weeks since they had last touched. The young maid felt her knees buckle under the weight of the wanted embrace. Tears flushed from her eyes and Linnet finally felt that she understood the predicament that her Lady had been strained under. She shook her head in agreement unable to find words to parlay.

"All of it," the freed woman added before turning away. "Not a single stalk standing. And tell them, tell them all…" Fire glinted in her eyes. "I will kill any one that attempts to harvest the sugar from the ash."

Dominique walked back to the edge of the field of fire. She was a radiant Phoenix against the bright cackle and chalky smoke that lifted into the iridescent sky. The vessels of flames were her children, and they screamed at Mother Night! Linnet sympathized as much as she could. For nearly three hundred years the woman toiled under the yoke and lash of the Omjadda, buried in the deepest pits without hope or chance of escape. The scars from her ordeals were deep rooted. A new and more terrifying level of sympathy arose in Linnet and her insignificant twenty-one years of age paled in comparison to the raging beauty. It eclipsed her own selfish pain that being near the Vam Pŷr had caused over the past few weeks by being held at arms length from her wrath.

Linnet stepped back from the clearing and turned to several slaves standing behind her. Invigorated, she ordered them to pick up a torch or branch of flame and follow her. *If thy eye offends thee, pluck it out,* she recalled from Scripture. Three slaves followed her as she marched to the Southern field. They were of mixed descent: Tupi, Guarani, and African. Indentured servants sold at auction for the profit of vile production. Inácio and Rui had bought these men to line their pockets with gold and silver. Now, they followed the expectant mother and by her orders set the crop alight.

They basked in the purification of the orange glow. Silent. Each slave wondered what would come in the rush of morning. How would they keep their beds at a farm with no fields to tend? What would become of them? These women destroyed their own fields and factory. Would they be sold at the next auction? These foreigners were puzzling, secretive, and had brought many strange possessions with them. The slaves did not know what would come next from the newcomers. Their lives were built on shifting sands. All around them the plantation burned. It burned in deafening brilliance and looked as if dawn had come early and cracked the night.

"Araci?" the Tupi man said, "Araci?"

It took Linnet a minute to figure out that he was calling her. He spoke to her in his native tongue, but she did not understand the words spoken. She, Laurel, and Dominique had only just arrived and were busy with too many things to focus and learn another language. Portuguese had been easy enough for her, but teaching it to Laurel had been a chore. Languages were always easy for Linnet. Even during her sessions at home her tutor praised her often for her gilded tongue. She knew eventually that she would get around to discerning the native speech, but presently time did not permit an opportunity to absorb them. The two native slaves talked amongst themselves and the Guarani man interpreted for her.

"He said that you brought forth the dawn. He called you Araci. Goddess of the morning light." Her eyes darted to the man, no bigger in height than she was. The beauty of their spoken dialects was quick and bright. "He wants to know if we are to leave now. To go work another farm. He asks because the last masters still have his wife and child."

A quiver chipped at Linnet's spine, tingling uncomfortably. Staring into the soft eyes of the Tupi man, she understood fully why the plantation needed to be razed and felt foolish that it had come to this great extreme to make her witness just how callous she had become to those around her. Embroiled in her affairs, she had been blind to the suffering taking place within her own reach. She was not just the last daughter of her father's estate anymore. She was a benefactor of men. She was soon to be a mother, and she was the heiress to a history of the symbiont race. Shame filled the spaces between her flesh where her pride had hid so thick before. Their endeavors on this distant shore were not just the repair of Dominique's business, though, that may have been the impetus of their arrival. Linnet realized now in the blazing shadows of the fire's light that she needed to make a home of this place, a real home in the way that she had always dreamed. Or else she would build another England here, complete with all its walls and distracting manners.

"You are not being sold." Linnet shook her head and reached out to the slave. "No one is, ever again. Your home is here."

Linnet found Laurel as the prickly fingers of dawn revealed the black smiles and ashen teeth of the charred fields and ruins of commerce. It seemed that she had been working most of the night to quell the slaves from putting out the eastern fields. Smoke still rose from the embers of production and the misty morning smelled of burnt sickly-sweet. Linnet crunched sooty earth beneath her feet as they went from shanty to shanty to inform the inhabitants of the plantation that no one was to harvest any sugar from the ash. Dominique wanted everything untouched and Laurel urged the African slaves to flee the Engenho.

Linnet was taken aback. She was not aware that Dominique had cause to rid the land of the high valued occupants. She had been too embroiled in her own musings of late to remain intact to the daily going-ons with the Magistrate over the deal for the indentured men. Laurel informed her, on their walk back to the Casa Grande, that it was looking as if they were going to have to return a portion of the men to Inácio and Rui. Dominique thought it best for them to flee into the jungles and find whatever quilombos that would take them in.

Linnet saw worry lines digging into Laurel's brow. The events of these past trying weeks had not been kind to her. The young girl had been thrust into a position that she was not well suited to take. Linnet felt responsible, and reaching out to her, pulled her close. Both girls were dirty and bore charcoal and ash marks from the evening.

"Do you ever," Laurel began with a hesitant voice, "ever think to not take the drink?"

Linnet smirked. "Of course. I would be foolish if I did not question my motives from time to time."

Laurel lifted her head from off Linnet's shoulder. "Then do you not question them now?"

Linnet noticed Laurel's eyes trail to her belly and she stopped in mid stride. The field smoldered around them, hazing the vision of the distant house.

"No. I do not." She smiled. "For a time I did, but not any longer. As much as I feared this place I've come to realize the value of us being here." Linnet saw the question form on Laurel's face before she even asked it and knelt. "Being with Dominique is like this field." She pulled a shriveled, black stalk of sugarcane from the ground. "It is masked in misery and yet there is a beauty to it that is unmistakable. Just like this burnt stalk is bitter, life with her can often be scary." Linnet peeled the husk of the plant back to reveal the melted sugary pulp. "But deep within, if you are strong enough and patient, you will find a hidden treasure that is sweet." She rose and sucked the cane and licked her lips. Handing it to Laurel she said, "What you and I are asking of her demands a certain amount of forbearance in our insufficient judgements. We simply cannot measure the want of this desire or hold her to standards that we know are faulty."

Laurel licked the sugary vein and it tasted good. Encased in the charred, raging anger of the freed blood slave life still tasted sweet. They enveloped one another again, clinging to the aftermath of the fires, two small rafts afloat in a sea of smoking ash and walked back to the big house.

"Do you think this was the worst of it?" Laurel asked as she licked the sticky cane.

"We can only hope."

Laurel sighed. "This would go great with a cup of Earl Grey and crumpets."

"With honey-butter," Linnet added.

"And jam. Oh!" She turned to her adopted sister. "Orange Marmalade." She pinched her eyes, pining for the delicious treat. "But we finished the last tin of it aboard ship."

"Next year," Linnet urged, pulling her close. "We will have our own. After tending to the groves this season, we'll can as much as you want."

"I've spotted some cashew trees on the north side. We could churn the nuts into butter."

"That would be nice."

They laughed together in the misty twilight, making plans as the day lifted around them. For the time being their fears and worries drifted away with the smoldering fumes of the past. The plantation was subdued. There was no turning back. Linnet placed a free hand to her belly and felt the baby turn and kick.

"This is Ryan." The recorded message relayed. "You know what to do."

Beeeeeep!

"Whazzup Playa! Saffron's baaack. In LA fo' a 'lil biznest aaaanndd…I thought we could hook up over the weekend. Right now, I got a photo shoot and a party tonight at the director's house, but then…me and my best buddy Milo are hittin' up this cool Afro-Cuban joint. You know the one on The Strip. Gonna git our groove on with some mad Salsa. Mpphf! Maybe I'll see ya there? Don't disappoint. Kisses!"

Click!

"You have eight new messages," the machine reported as Ryan exited the building that was across the street from where Z lived.

He had searched the highrise thoroughly. None of the Lobby elevators would take him up to the Penthouse without an authorization code entered into the access panel inside the lift, and the stairs only went as far as the top floor. He called the suite again from outside the building, but the little square box continued to give him cold static. The top floor of the building was inconveniently secure, cut off from the penthouse. There wasn't a ladder or door to the roof anywhere, like the place had been purposefully blocked off. Ryan was sure there had to be an alternate way to reach the top suite. *There just had to be.*

Leaving the building he needed perspective and decided to cross the street. That's when he saw the garage entrance from one of the stairwell windows, when he was inside the neighboring building, and thought he'd give that a try. Walking passed the arm of the mechanical gate, Ryan thought about it. *If I were a vampire which way would I park?*

This was assuming, of course, that vampires drove. He turned left and started heading down the sloping structure toward the lower levels. He spiraled down and around the parking garage until he came to what looked like the bottom. Rows and rows of parked cars. Ryan exhaled an air of defeat. The only way now was up. He scuffed the tar worn concrete with his shoes and looked to the sterile conduit snaking across the low-lying ceiling connecting the bland, buzzing lights. He was depleted. Every turn, in every direction, met with obstacles. Wherever opportunity resided it avoided him with consummate clairvoyance.

As he cleared the pick-up bed of a silver toned F-150 he saw another lever gate with its own electronic keypad, and it led to an even lower level. Ryan smiled. The concrete earth had just opened up for him. He walked around the striped wooden arm and followed the spiral down until the dank musk of oil, dust, and axle grease greeted him.

A Blue 1989 Harley-Davidson Sportster with a fatboy tank was the first vehicle Ryan spotted. A matching sidecar rested under an old brown tarp and the bike looked as if it hadn't been used in a while. At the flat planed bottom level resting in quiet slumber was a row of cars: a1958 aquamarine Chevy Impala with exquisite tail fins and elegant chrome that was now faded and buried under decades of dust. Its whitewall tires were cracked and the chrome was tarnished. A 1946 Austin 10 was virtually black by the amount of time that had piled on top of the classic transport. The tires on a gray 1963 Buick Riviera were flat and the vinyl roof on the American Motors pony car, a '69 Javelin SST, was splintered, chipped, and flaking away to nothingness. Ryan walked around a custom built '71 forest green Gran Torino Cobra and peered into dust covered tinted windows. Its fat, slick cheaters were stopped with wooden wedges and the front end of the vintage muscle car was up on two concrete blocks. It looked as if someone had been recently working on it. The scoop hood was off and it rested against the concrete wall of the basement level. The 351 small block engine had been bored and stoked. It had full racing cams and roller rockers. The carburetor was completely stripped, and its parts neatly arranged on a tarp-covered table near the earthy Gran Torino. A filthy, oil stained rag draped over the primered front panel and a handprint was visible in the dust on the driver's side window. *Signs of life.*

The tenacious stalker leveled himself with the small, five-fingered impression, eyeballing greasy faint fingerprints. He wondered if they belonged to his beloved Z. He raised his hand to the tinted glass fossil. The evacuated five-fingered grime piqued his desire to continue onward.

A single cylinder British thumper was ravaged to the frame, a skeleton of its former self. The motorcycle had definitely seen better days. Its innards were scattered and strewn haphazardly around like a junkyard centerpiece; obviously it was a project that had been shelved. Though similar to the Gran Torino, a 1974 Moto Guzzi Eldorado was up on blocks like someone was tending to its care and restoration. The V-7 Sport drum brake was nearly fixed. Unlike the Torino though, the bike was not covered in dust. It had tasted tarmac more recently than the muscle car.

Under a dried, cracked hood was a 1957 Cadillac Eldorado Brougham. The two door, brushed stainless steel car was in mint condition. But its covering crumbled under Ryan's touch. He cursed at his curiosity as it fell away onto the prefab floor. On the far wall, at the base of the long spiral arm of hardened cement, a large, heavy duty toolbox was chained to the concrete wall with thick, massive bolts. Ryan tugged at a few of the drawers. It was locked. The whole lower level resembled an auto garage more than a place to park.

A large tarp rested in a heap behind a beautiful 1963 baby blue, hard top Cadillac. The rings of its white wall tires sparkled, having just been washed and waxed. The bulbs in the two-set, dual headlights had just been replaced, and some one had spit polished the chrome grill. Ryan ran his fingertips along one of the small fins trailing off the back. The license plate on the one time luxury sedan read: ETRNL BTCH. Ryan chuckled at the owner's ironic sense of humor. This car, like the others, was a vintage classic, but unlike most of the other vehicles stored down here decaying into rust this one was ready for the road.

As Ryan walked around the Caddy, noticing the clutter of videotapes, clothes, and CDs littering the back seat, he spied a gray painted door next to an elevator portal. He quickly crossed from the car to the accesses. He tried the door first. It was locked. It had a ball shaped doorknob and he reasoned that he could pry it open with a crow bar if he needed too.

He depressed the call button for the elevator and the sliding doors immediately opened. Ryan smiled optimistically feeling like he was finally getting somewhere. He stepped into the small steel box. The elevator was colorless and bland except for two earmarks of spray painted graffiti. One was the Anarchy symbol and the other was a DK Logo that Z had done in '78 that stood for the Dead Kennedys. There was only one operation button on the panel by the door. *Things couldn't be any simpler.* Ryan hit it and the elevator doors immediately shut.

After a few seconds the carriage did not move. He hit the button again and the doors opened. He was still in the basement of the parking garage. He tried it again. And, again. But the same thing always happened. He remained fixed to the spot! It was a road to nowhere. He exited the lazy mechanical device pondering what to do next.

Ryan crossed to the long, junkyard row and searched through the smattering of engine parts, buckets, and coverings trying to find something – *anything* - that he could use to pry the gray painted door open. Nothing presented itself as useful. He scanned the empty parking spaces, polished Cadillac, dusty bikes, bolted toolbox, crumpled tarps, parts, and automobile relics one last time unaware that high above his head was a camera watching him. It rotated on its precise rhythm recording his presence and actions, and displayed it on a little, dust covered monitor, in a tiny room that hardly anybody visited.

Ryan left the lower level of the parking garage set to return with a crow bar all his own and gain entrance to the Penthouse. One way or another he was going to reach his prize. He was going to see Z again. Ryan Silva knew what he wanted and he wasn't going to stop until he got it.

"This is Ryan." The recorded message relayed. "You know what to do."

Beeeeeep!

"Listen Bitch." The deep whine of a feminine voice raged. "Don't know what the fuck you think you're up to but it ain't gonna work this time. Lacey's with me now and we don't need your weak dick interfering again. So, just back off! She's got serious people interested in her and she don't need you coming back into her life with your macho bully bullshit messin' her head up. If I hear that you were with her again, or if you try to call her I'm gonna personally kick your skinny white ass into the Pacific! Do you get me?! Just back off."

Click!

"You have nine new messages." The machine reported to nobody.

1775. São Paulo, Brazil.

The air was solid and muggy. A breeze entered through three six-inch slats near the ceiling on the wall where the tub sat and was pulled through two opened windows. It carried the mixed scents of the jungle and distant rain. The bath water was cooling and Linnet rubbed it over her protruding belly. She was getting close. The way she stuck out of the murky bath reminded her of an island poking out of the sea. She was the Isle of Nsia.

The fetus had become more active since the fire. It unnerved her when he moved, pushing her bladder into her spleen. Placing a hand to where the little tike somersaulted, Linnet tried to figure out which appendage was poking her insides now. *Pregnancy was an odd sort.* She'd become a gas factory and was eating all the time.

Thinking of names, Linnet liked Frances, George, and Albert. Though nothing seemed so right as William. The idea of giving the brother whom she never met a face was pleasing. It brought an ounce of solace to her soul. Growing up she labored under the shadow of William's death. To resurrect his spirit and wash away those painful years with the birth of her son, proudly christened, Linnet imagined that it would gratify her parents, heal the rift that her mother took to the grave, and settle the debt that her father bore with raising a house of women.

She ignored the more obvious facts of her parturient nature: An African father, an unchaste and unwed daughter. Deep down she knew this gift of a child, named William or not, from her spoiled womb would have devastated them both. They were too saintly in their moral upbringings, strict in their devotion to the King and Protestant church. Her father would have wanted Pastor Gruebl to preside over her wedding, just as he had for all seven of her sisters. Linnet sighed, grateful for the vast distance of the Atlantic between her and her family. She was the Isle of Nsia and the bride of twilight. She could not even begin to imagine the horrors that her father and sisters would endure if they knew of her life with the Vam Pŷr.

To some degree, Linnet felt that she deserved the admonishments that had become a staple of her visits into town. Following the days after the fire news had spread quickly and the women of Casa del Rio Dulce had become the talk of every social circle. Now, it wasn't just rumors of bygone haunts that surrounded them. The dismissal of the Overseers, razing their fields and mill, and the escape of the African slaves had become fodder for local gossip. Linnet moved and the water gurgled, sucking in around her expanding form, and the island sank.

Earlier that morning, while procuring supplies with Laurel, Linnet overheard a gaggle of Portuguese ladies talking about her. Their dresses were fine silk, imported from Spain. They wore gloves that matched their outfits, covered their heads in quaint little bonnets, and held their parasols as high as their noses. Their fashion was seasons behind the French gowns that hung in her closets. She heard them talking about the recently widowed Mrs. Duvergé until she passed the ladies in the thoroughfare. Then their attentions shifted to Linnet's round form, wearing visible indignation of her gravid state. She clenched her fist, digging her nails into her palm as she overheard one of the socialites call her unborn son a bastard. Her blood boiled, but Linnet kept an aloof air about her and simply bid them a good day with a polite smile and nod.

She was better than they were and she knew it. She swallowed her hate and turned it to sympathy. They were just bored housewives whose husbands were more devoted to their military office, businesses, and boy's club than to tending to their shriveled chaste gardens. They had nothing else to do in their pathetic little lives than to occupy themselves with the affairs of others. It was sad really and by the time Linnet had crossed the muddy street she was in a better cheer. William was not a bastard. His father was a warrior and an educated man whose family heritage stretched back to the beginning of Man. Linnet doubted that a single one of those highfalutin' whores of stature could even trace their lineage back ten generations.

Upon exiting the store, she made it a point to properly introduce herself and Laurel and offered to assist with the funding of the upcoming church social that she had heard about while in the store. Leaving them in the market square like that, Linnet could only imagine the looks of awe that wrinkled their faces. She was resolute to keep her head held high and not steal any glances, though she desperately wanted to see them stewing in their own bitter chatter. She would have spied on them from the carriage as they left had not Laurel decided to stay within the town, urging Linnet to return to the Casa without her. There were matters that she needed to attend to that were best suited to her going on alone.

It had unnerved Linnet to ponder what attractions the young maid kept so secretively. Worse than the stiff humidity that this day had bore, the whole affair with the pompous hens, and Laurel's insistent tone had made her feel icky. The mild Lavender in the herb soap she caressed over her form was soothing. The water had passed tepid and was now cooling rapidly. Birdsong flittered through the windows and it occurred to Linnet just how tranquil their home had become since Dominique had purged the sickness from the factory. A new mill and boiling house was already being constructed. The ash on the fields had been plowed under, churned into the ground to make the soil more fertile, and there was talk of razing the existing Senzalas to build more efficient housing for the workers.

Dominique's plan to give the field hands and house servants a percentage of the crops they worked was bold. *Wait until they get wind of that up their dresses. Then they'll have something to talk about!* Linnet chuckled and hefted her gate out of the bath.

Getting dressed, she caught her misshapen reflection in the stone polished mirror. She cradled her womb and passed gas, and sighed.

Pregnancy was an odd sort. She wondered what Nsia would think of her naked form now. She was getting close. Soon she would bear his child and she still had not completed the letter that she had started over a month ago. She was the Isle of Nsia and all she wanted to do was go downstairs and curl up in Dominique's bed. She held her enlarged breasts and thought about the last time the Vam Pŷr had bitten her, suckled her rich fluid. They were in England then and life was different. In the soft toned sheen of the mirror Nsia's evidence of passage was bountiful.

Linnet missed her Dark Mistress's embrace and could only count the days until she was rid of this burden in her belly, and once again, able to lavish in the bloom of night with her lady.

"This is Ryan." The recorded message played. "You know what to do."

Beeeeeep!

"Hi. Hey, this is Carol, again. Hellooo. I guess you're out of town or something. That's cool. Just...need to talk with you when you get back. It's about that little, well..." She nervously laughed. "Not little. You were great, in fact. But! There's this thing...that I need to talk with you about. And I just thought you should know. Nothing major...yet." There was a long silence. "Oh God, that didn't sound so good, did it? Look. I'm not trying to freak you out or anything. Really, I'm not. I take full responsibility. I just need to talk with you, Ok? So...when you get back to town, or whatever, just gimme a call. Ok? Well...I'll talk with you then. Bye."

Click.

"You have twelve new messages," asserted the synthetic voice.

1775. São Paulo, Brazil.

Dominique was in the solarium. Since the completion of the house she had taken to spending her nights there among the stars and open air. A new moon was invisible in the sky. Macaws and monkey howls drilled through the steady chirp of crickets. Laurel still had not returned from the day's duties and Dominique felt lively.

"Good," she said upon seeing Linnet. "I was going to send for you."

Linnet crossed to the edge of the terrace, smiling that her mistress wanted her company. The solarium was a large space, comprising the whole roof of the main house. On one side it was buttressed with the wall to the second story and a bell tower, which unfortunately held no bell. The young, pregnant maid peered into the ubiquitous night as her mistress spoke and her wet hair dried in the hot southern air.

"I feel it would be best if you took leave to have the baby." Dominique's words stung Linnet's ears painfully. "Spend time away from all of the bustle which our arrival has stirred and enjoy the local flavor during your last term." Dominique paused, expecting an argument. But none came. "I took the liberty of employing a mid-wife this week whom Laurel tells me is favored among the locals with a mastery of care and infant survival. She would be accompanying you."

Linnet stood up straight, aligning her posture. "And where am I to go?"

"Laurel is procuring a small villa in the port city of Santos. I think the ocean breezes would do you some good when the time comes."

"Will you not be attending then?"

Dominique strolled to Linnet's side. "You know I can not."

"I know you will not."

Dominique lowered her head and turning, said, "Why do you choose to look at it in those terms. I have…"

"You can not even look at me." Linnet spread her arms out, revealing her expanding form as the Vam Pŷr turned to her. "Am I so grotesque to look upon that you shun me continuously?"

"No," Dominique uttered, crossing to her consort, "not ever. It is that I…" she held Linnet by the arms. "It is the parasite within me that keeps me away." The look on her paramour's face was as distant and vacant as her touch had been over these past months. *I am losing her.* Dominique lowered her head, dejectedly ashamed. "The scent of you is overpowering. I fear…I fear that if I…"

Linnet leaned in and lightly kissed Dominique on the lips. The Vam Pŷr sucked in a breath and stiffened. A shiver rippled her entire form. The blood parasite, quivering with the luscious flavor of the girl, plumb and ripe for the plucking, distorted Dominique's mind with violent images of hunting and feasting from the primordial days of the Omjadda. Her blood was hot. The girl was intoxicating.

"You do not understand." Dominique stepped back. "There are things about the Jadaraa Soo that I would not have you know."

Linnet scrunched her face. "But yet, you would have me drink of Ornn's blood?"

Dominique shot her a look that revealed the suffering she endured, her composure broken like a vase thrown to the floor.

Linnet stepped toward her. "Do you really think that I do not know the cravings within you? I have felt its touch just as strongly as I have felt yours, and you still doubt that my love for you will carry me through the charade that you find your own countenance monstrous. How foolish you are to think such a thing?"

Linnet shook her head from side to side. Her eyes were penetrating like daggers as she pulled the tufts of her eyebrows down. Dominique felt small under the weight of the young woman's truth. "The only thing you have achieved by hiding your nature is that you have kept yourself away from arms that love you."

The millennia old woman bit her lower lip to keep it from shaking. The cold shiver that had been traveling through her broke like a wave upon her pale shore and a single red tear fell from her eye, staining her cheek. She felt the tendril fingers of her Jadaraa Soo slither over her shoulders and arms, wind across her ribs, climb under her breasts and embrace her. Quickly, she crossed the flat tiled roof to her most precious gift, placing a hand to the woman's round belly.

"My foremost concern has been you and the baby."

"I know."

Dominique's body sighed. The thirst for the woman's green blood, so pungent and fresh, feeding the fetus, still clanged within as loudly as banging on a kettle pot. Her mind was a torrent of parasite fed visions. She could not wait for Laurel to return so that she could feast on her maid and satiate the passion for Linnet's blood that coiled within.

"When would you like for this to happen?" asked the girl, laying her hand atop Dominique's.

The Vam Pŷr looked up. "Tomorrow. First light.

There is something else. Linnet saw it deep within Dominique's eyes as the lively chirp of crickets ceased and a horse in the stables neighed.

"You will travel with a full accompaniment of servants and meet…" The words halted in Dominique's mouth as her ears pricked. Her hand shot away as the flowerpot besides them exploded in a violent clank of dirt and plaster.

She stepped back and her eyes went wide, hearing the zing as the small lead ball flew past her ear and tore through the strands of Linnet's dark, raven hair. "Stay here!" she shouted, pulling Linnet down and rushed from the high vantage of the solarium to the deadly ground below.

Linnet was shocked. It was an abrupt and untimely end to their dialogue. Confusion wrinkled her face until she turned and saw a fire brewing in the stables. As the glow wildly grew more fervent, fearful snorts and neighs erupted from the trapped animals inside. Below, she heard Dominique shouting orders and she witnessed one of the servant boys take from the house toward the burning livery. He did not make it far. No sooner had the young knave reached the breadth of the yard did a musket shot ring out. The servant boy quickly fell dead.

Linnet stood and gasped, having seen the powder burst from the muzzleloader in a patch of thick growth and the tumble of the boy as he fell to the ground. Another flash exploded and sparked. A crack of thunder! The potted fern in the old Kiva that stood next to her shattered in a silent rupture of heat. Fear gripped her ribs as she jumped back as more gunfire hit the Villa. All of a sudden she remembered seeing Guajajara and Inácio Braga talking the night that Dominique had set the fields and mill ablaze. *How could I be so dumb?!* As the angry maid rushed from the top of the main house she spied another group of men closing in on them to the rear of the Casa Grande.

"Thirteen of them," the pregnant lass shouted as she descended the flight of steps rather spryly for a woman in her condition. "Around the back. They have flintlocks and torches."

"They're going to burn us out," stated Dominique as she handed a servant a musket.

The native man just looked at it like the alien contraption that it was. Obviously, he had never fired a gun before in his life. The hardened Vam Pŷr rushed about, ordering the other servants to prepare water as more muzzle-loaded lead tore holes through the plaster and adobe walls. Linnet took the rifle from the native man and began loading it. The unskilled native was in his late forties. He was petite like many of his people. He was nervous and shaking, terrified. Linnet was frightened too, but for some reason she remained calmed in the chaos of the attack. As Dominique headed for the carved redwood doors, ready to meet her attackers face to face, Linnet grabbed her by the arm.

"I should have mentioned it sooner," she hesitated sheepishly. "I saw Guajajara discussing something with Inácio Braga the night of the fire. With everything going on I...forgot."

Dominique placed a cold, ashen hand over Linnet's and told her to remain hidden and safe. She wanted to kiss the gravid woman amid the bustle of servants and the hail of pellet rain. She wanted to hold her and tell her that it was all right and not to worry. Dominique wanted a lot of things. She yearned to make up for the distance that she had placed between them, but at this pressing moment the intrusive chaos beckoned with haste.

The freed blood slave of the People to the East threw open the decorative doors of the Casa Grande and entered the muggy night. Linnet raced after her, stopping at the huge redwood doors, recalling how the servant boy had crumbled like a piece of paper in the yard. Musket fire erupted in a barrage of powdery smoke. It tore through Dominique, scrapping chunks of flesh from out of her person, but she plodded on as if the stinging balls of lead were nothing but mere hardened fumes. Linnet's mouth hung agape as she watched her lover disappear into the darkened woods.

She had to snap out of it and shut the doors. They were vulnerable to attack. Violent screams shattered the visceral dark beyond the yard, ungodly and raw. Those within the house turned toward the eerie shrieks, and panic set in.

Linnet strode to the thick mass of servants and finished packing the muzzleloader. Giving orders, she gave each a task to do and commanded the old, native man and a teenaged boy to come with her. She opened the wooden shutters on a window in the rear of the house half expecting to mount the musket and take aim, but was awkwardly surprised at the wild-eyed stare of one of her attackers already so close to the Casa-Grande. Hastily, Linnet raised the long rifle and shot the intruder in the face. He went down in a salvo of blue powdery, acrid smoke and another man grabbed the bad end of the emptied weapon, trying to pull it out of Linnet's firm grip.

The frightened servant, whom Linnet had taken the musket from earlier, began pounding on the stranger's face and shoulders with his small, angry fists. The dirty man quickly let go of Linnet's musket and she fell on her ass. Though before she had time to rise, the interloper shot the middle-aged servant dead with a pistol. Outraged, Linnet clobbered him over the head with the butt of the stock weapon, breaking his nose as blood spewed all over the sill.

Shutters crashed in, followed by torches. Tapestries, rugs, and drapes began to burn. Linnet reloaded her rifle, trying not to look at the dead man at her feet, as servants worked to quell the rush of flames with the limited amount of water they had stored in the kitchen. It was not enough. Sooner or later they were going to be forced to flee the house and gain access to the pumps and fresh air. *That is when they will open fire on us!* Another torch flew into the room and crashed against the wall near the painting of Linnet that Sir Joshua Reynolds had done. Hot, red sparks splintered across the floor as the torch landed in a corner amid several clay pots of flowers. Stinging smoke started to fill the room and billow out of the windows as the flames grew hotter and more intense, clogging the air with bitterness.

Linnet raised her musket again and rested it on the plaster jamb of the window. The invaders were falling back to take up positions in the growth of the forest. She sighted her musket and saw Inácio Braga leading them to their murderous hovels behind a row of Cajá trees. Hate flared in the parturient woman. She fired at the portly bastard, but missed. She turned to the young servant that was still with her and handed him the musket to reload. The young native was barely twenty; still a boy in his facial features and shape. He was shaking and crying, looking down at the fallen native who had given his life to save Araci. In the haste of the firefight Linnet had not realized. The man whom the interloper had shot and killed was his father.

"Yabi?" Linnet asked, making sure that she had his name right. The young boy shook his head. "We will avenge your father here, this night. I promise you that. But right now, I need you to load that weapon. Can you do that?!"

"Yes, Missus."

Linnet took the wooden handle of the front loading pistol from him, cocked the lever back, and placed a percussion clip over the hammer nipple. "Stay behind me and keep your head down."

Linnet crossed to another window to take aim. The young boy was concordat to her orders, keeping his head low as he reloaded the barrel of the muzzleloader. Linnet sighted a poorly hidden fellow and fired, igniting retribution. He fell dead in a clomp of trees. Yabi jolted at the blast of the single shot, sucked in a breath through trembling lips, and tried to act brave. Returning musket fodder exploded around them and the hurling sounds of hot lead balls whizzed past their ears. Yabi cowered behind Linnet's fleshy barricade, just as she had told him, working as fast as he could to load the long rifle like he had seen her do before.

The fire was getting more invasive. Smoke stung Linnet's eyes. Around her, servants were coughing as they fought the blaze. She took the long rifle from Yabi, aimed, and fired into the thick clump of Cajá trees. Then, she grabbed the boy's shirt and led him to the front doors of the Villa. They didn't have any other choice. All Linnet could do was pray. She did not know what she would find once she flung the large doors open – *a hail of flintlocks or a quiet retreat?* Luckily for them it was the latter. Blistering screams pierced the darkened canopy and Linnet feared for her Dark Mistress.

Outside, she quickly rallied the remaining servants to fetch water and squelch the flames before the main house met the same fate as their stables. She was driven to save as much of their home as she could. Though even more pressing, in this ruined night, than saving the elegant structure, was Linnet's flustered need to distract her people from stumbling upon Dominique's nocturnal fury. Hearing the blistering screams of dying men erupt all around them in the absolute dark was bad enough! It would not bode well if the retainers uncovered Dominique tearing the attackers' flesh and drinking their blood. Once things were steadily underway to fight the flames, Linnet checked the powder of her weaponry, and went to find her lady.

No sooner had she reached the edge of the trees, to the side of the Villa, did she encounter the first body. It was Rui. His arms were torn from the sockets of his shoulders. A chill ran through the young maid's spine and she felt sick. Rui's face was contorted and twisted in fear. His throat had been torn out from where Dominique had bitten him. It was a horrific reminder of how vicious the Vam Pŷr's embrace could be.

Linnet stepped lightly into the darkened wood, having no knowledge of what dangers truly existed. A scream exploded to her right and then she heard running. Linnet barely had enough time to raise the barrel of the muzzleloader before a fleeing intruder, escaping in her direction, overtook her. Linnet pulled the trigger and was spun around by the kick of the blast. The stranger folded in half like a reed and tumbled to the ground right where she had been standing.

The Portuguese man grabbed his gut and moaned in pain, yelling, "Bruxsa! Bruxsa!"

Again that word struck Linnet's ears and she had not learned what it meant. She needed to find Dominique. She needed to know if her Lady was all right. With the musket in hand, spent of its shot, Linnet left the groaning man alone to die. To bleed out on the jungle floor as he made his peace with God. Further on she found more shredded corpses. The carnage was terrible. She was right to hide it from her servants.

In the splintered light from the burning Casa, toward the back of the house, she finally found her dark mistress and the tear-streaked face of Inácio Braga kneeling before her. His hands were up and balled. He was praying for her forgiveness, but Dominique was not in a giving mood. Linnet approached, calling her name. She wanted to interrogate the Overseer, find out all of the players who were involved in this catastrophic evening, but Dominique did not heed her consort's cries. Her Jadaraa Soo hummed too loudly in her head to even notice Linnet approaching.

Linnet gasped as she watched her strange paramour lift Inácio with one hand, by the bulk of his black hair, off the ground. His pathetic whining chilled the muggy air. Dominique was covered in a visceral bath of blood and gore from head to toe – *the root of all this strewn carnage.* Like a beast, like a wild, unbridled animal of the forest, the symbiont reared her head back, hissed and exposed the tendril points of her sharp fangs. She tore into the weeping man's throat. It was horrible. It was the same mouth that had kissed her, passionately and gentle, so many times, yet now in the terrible glow of the flames it was used in retaliation and murder. It was fearful and grotesque, like a lioness tearing into prey. The viciousness of Dominique's mastication was sickening, but Linnet could not look away. Braga's legs quivered and twitched, convulsing as they dangled in the air until slowly, they jittered and then stopped.

Dominique dropped the man, dead to the ground. He landed with an awful thud. Mother Night's chest heaved exuberant pants from the exhilaration of the kill. Musket ball holes and powder burns stained her body and clothing from where they had drilled through her deadening flesh. She was a mess. It was ghoulish. And still, Linnet could not look away.

She approached and the Vam Pŷr wiped Inácio's blood from off her chin with the back of her hand as the Jadaraa Soo began to absorb the vital fluid through the pores of the skin. A twig snapped and the creature turned quickly, ready to pounce. Dominique saw her maid and relaxed her posture. As Linnet neared, she noticed that Dominique's eyes were completely black. The veins of the parasite were flat and ruddy, engorged from the feast it had eaten. The sublime lady of Persia appeared rosy and demonic and Linnet did not know what to say. She heard Yabi shouting for her. She turned and saw the young servant boy ready to enter the woods near them.

"Do not let him see me like this," urged Dominique in a soft whisper.

"I won't," Linnet pledged.

She called out to him and told him to wait for her by the side of the house, near the edge of the Cajá trees. She was coming out of the thick. When Linnet had caught up with the young lad he told her that he had seen two men run off the plantation, along the carriage road, and that the surviving servants had beaten back the flames. He asked if she had found Dominique and Linnet lied, telling him that she was following the fleeing men.

The excessive thrall of events made Linnet's head swoon and she encouraged Yabi to lead her back to the rest of the group. She handed the young man her musket and took his free arm for support. As he led her back to the front of the main house, Linnet peered into the darkening tumble of the forest. She knew Dominique was in there, watching them through a veil of black death. The plantation felt as if it were the center of a spiraling doom. She could feel her lover's dangerous, blood-filled eyes boring into her, and could not shake the vision of Dominique's gaunt, pale extremities splattered with viscous red butchery as she tore into Inácio Braga.

The nurturing side of Linnet that had been swelling with her belly over these past months told her that the way Dominique dispatched the former Overlord was cruel. Inhuman. Even though he had it coming and would have easily killed her had he had the chance, Linnet could not stop feeling haunted by it. The carnage that littered the forest floor was brutal and only hidden by the dark abyss of the night. If only two men escaped the Engenho lands on this gruesome eve then they could count themselves lucky.

The echoes of the intruder's screams as Dominique tore them apart and gorged on their mortified bodies rattled through Linnet's cerebral carriage taking shape to the sights that she had unwontedly witnessed. It did not bode well – *all this killing!* There would surely be stories once the scared men reached the township. Linnet felt queasy just thinking about it.

Perhaps Dominique would follow them? Perhaps if they made it to town they would just leave them alone now. Perhaps this was the storm that had been brewing since their arrival? Perhaps they had learned all too well the horrors that awaited them at Casa del Rio Dulce!

Perhaps, Linnet pondered, *perhaps*? These vile men had found it not so easy to dispatch a couple of foreign women. *The fairer sex was not so weak as one assumed!* At the front of the house Linnet consolidated the servant's efforts into a more efficient line to quell the final remnants of fire that still consumed a few homey corners. The stables and livestock were lost. All the animals Laurel had purchased were dead, tortured in their last moments. Hate flared in Linnet, thinking about the indignity of Rui and Inácio's attempt to usurp their land. *They deserved what they got!*

The consort swept her gaze across the smoking embers and recalled how a shower of musket balls had not slowed Dominique down. An electrified impulse titillated her excited mind – *She was invincible.* The mere thought that one day she might become like Dominique, that she may be reborn in her mistress's image. *Well…*after witnessing such guttural, animalistic savagery Linnet was more terrified at the prospect than ever *and yet…*seduced by the idea as well. That one day she could become a woman so powerful that she could lift a stout and portly man up to her jowls with one hand like he was nothing and wade through a cannonade of musket fire! The thought was dizzying. The strength of the Vam Pŷr was frightening and thrilling at the same time. The young, pregnant maid was both appalled and attracted to the mysteries of unending night.

In the darkened wood, Dominique, ashamed at the gruesome tally of her quarry, set about burying the unwanted dead.

Mindy's face was buried in the pillow. She moaned a high soprano, like the whine on a squeaky awning, clutching the tussled bed sheet with white knuckles poking behind silver rings. She panted heavily. Ryan grabbed her with both hands, around her bottom, in the crease of her folded hip, and pulled her to him repeatedly, spearing her hard; ass up, on her knees, slapping her fleshy seat with the flat sting of his hip. It was unmerciful. Rapid. Pounding…pounding. It drove her crazy. Her lips quivered. She could not speak.

Finally, numb drunk and sweating he pulled out of her and she collapsed on the bed shaking as little aftershock orgasms riveted up her spine. They were on fire. Fervid. The air was sultry and stank with the vivid mingling of their sexes. He glared down at her like an animal, hungry for the raw sensation of flesh. He imagined that he fucked another girl, a girl with dyed, red hair and a painful overbite. He pulled at the spry legs of the sexy vixen. Mindy tried to catch her breath, but her fingers were tingly.

He lifted one of her legs and she opened for him like scissors, cutting a garden in spring. He climbed into the wet seat, placed his hand onto the small of her back, and pulled her to him. She clawed at his arms and chest. Finally grabbing him before he could penetrate her again, she pulled him to her mouth, too weak and glowing to move. She kissed him hard, willfully, jutting her tongue inside of his mouth and scraped her nails across his back, tearing red streaks along his sweating flesh.

Her squeal of utter pleasure exploded in his room as he entered her again. Closing her mascara stained eyes, the lids pressed so tightly that they shattered the composure of her brow, she whined in heaving palpitations. Her body went rigid with enjoyment, her flower exploded with dew.

Ryan lifted her up, out of the crosscut position, so that their coupling was face to face. He dreamed of the vampire. He imagined Z. His orgasm was building vehemently, but he held it back. He wanted that special something that only The Letter could provide. Mindy began to swivel her hips, gyrating in a licentious circle and the quickening sensation in his groin was maddening.

"Bite Me." Ryan asked as his breath began to crumble to the feeling. "Bite me."

Mindy moaned miles away from his urgent words cocooned in unrestrained lust. He asked her again more vehemently, inching toward a climax. He placed his hands to her head, so close to the nape of his willing and eager neck. He practically begged, and she bit him.

Her teeth were soft, round victuals, flat, deadened bumps! He urged her to bite him harder, and harder, pressing her delicate shoulders with more vigor and force so that the chomp would resemble the women whom he longed for. His commands broke their gyrating rhythm and woke the girl from her delirium of delight. He begged her now. It was obscene. And with each unsuccessful clamp of Mindy's teeth to the salty, hot flesh of his neck his growing exhalation waned and dire frustration crept in.

"Harder!" he plied, rigid with the desire to be fulfilled.

"If I bite you any harder I'll draw blood," the not so timid girl explained, halting at the precipice of his need.

A violent shudder rippled through his skin and he tossed her off his lap.

"No, wait. I can do it." She wanted to please him.

He was crestfallen, smacked with this unreasonable desire! Mindy sat up, in the throws of their dying passion, and asked him again to let her try. She felt desperate to make him happy. To please him as hard as he had been pleasing her. And she looked so cute with her white, piqued skin flushed from their union, sincerity clamping the tufts of her eyebrows down, and the petite diamond encrusted crucifix that Ryan had stolen from the red-headed hellcat and given to Mindy to display around her neck. Adorable! But Ryan moved to get dressed never noticing how beautiful and compassionate a lover she truly was.

"Just forget it," he grumbled as Mindy reached out to touched him. He turned hard, accidentally pushing her off the bed. "I said forget it!"

Mindy tumbled backwards and landed on her naked, well-plied bottom. She was shocked and gasped, "You Son-of-bitch! What the fuck?" Ryan got up and walked toward the bedroom door. Mindy grabbed the closest thing to her and threw it at him. "You Asshole!"

The item she threw just so happened to be her tangled jeans resting by the foot of the bed. The faded blue denim struck Ryan lazily in the back and fell limply to the floor.

"Don't you think it's about time you left?"

He exited the room and walked dejectedly into the kitchen and poured himself a glass of water. Mindy pitched a hell-storm of adjectives, curse words, and personal defects at him while she got dressed. She was livid and tore out of the room of coition embittered and enraged. He mocked her righteous anger by forming his hand into the mouth of a puppet and slapped his finger-lips together to indicate that she was just yammering on. Ryan desperately tried to tune her out, agreeing with almost everything she said, and indicated the beautiful release of the front door.

His phone began to ring.

The constant ringing and Mindy's mile long bitch-capade wore on the thin fabric of his nerves. He needed a few seconds of decent quiet and calm. Yet, he was awarded with the shrill slamming of his door and the incessant clatter of the phone!

Beeeeeep!

"Hey, Silva. Lacey. Look, I got the pictures developed and I thought we could go over them with drinks. I'm free tomorrow night 'bout seven. I know Angie called you the other evening. Shit. Sorry 'bout that. But I wanted to let you know that..."

Ryan didn't want to know. The perpetual noise just needed to stop! He grabbed the decade old answering machine, one that he specifically searched for a month and a half to find at garage sales and yard sales and retro shops online. He tore the cables and cords out of the wall and threw it with unkempt malice, smashing it to little bits that scattered like plastic razor-plane bombs all over the livingroom.

Once Ryan's breathing had eventually calmed, it was quiet.

Song

PART SIX:

Fertile Soil

What lies beyond life shines not to those who
are childish, or careless, or deluded by wealth.
'This is the only world: there is no other,' they say:
and thus they go from death to death.

-The Upanishads

1776. São Paulo, Brazil.

By spring, whispered rumors had reached a fervid point in the township and the humid subtropical winter that had just passed brought with it an outbreak of cholera. The epidemic had laid siege to the coastal ports of Santos and worked its way through the frightened streets of São Paulo, and a Bruxsa was to blame.

The two men that had escaped the Engenho last year had not tempered their tongues about their crimes or what had befallen them on that horrible night at Casa del Rio Dulce. Linnet and Laurel did their best to squash the notions that a bloodsucking demon witch, known as a Bruxsa, prowled the lands of the plantation. But it was of little good. For years before their arrival the fears of the town folk had swelled with the bloated corpses, emptied graves, and missing persons that had become a hallmark of the landscape under Isabela da Nóbrega's care. Linnet and Laurel's open witness to the lies they assayed could not avert the fertile soil of fear teeming in the people's hearts.

Because the two lucky escapees did not guard their tongues meant that they were easily found by authorities. Each man was charged with murder, conspiracy to murder, and the destruction of private property. Summarily, the two men were hung by the neck until dead on a rainy August morning. Their wickedness had been done and this righteous justice simply added to the terrible legacy of the De'Paul estates. The women of Casa del Rio Dulce were now infamous!

Ten days after the murderers felt the taught pull at the gallows pole, Linnet gave birth to a mulatto boy in the city of Santos. William was seven pounds, eight ounces and cried for his Momma's tit with clenched fists and closed eyes. The Midwife had kept Linnet in bed for two weeks after giving birth so she could regain her strength. By fall, Linnet returned to the Engenho and a newly constructed Casa Grande.

The joy of her arrival was moderated by the bruising gossip that swirled around them. Regardless of what they did, stories grew. In town, people regarded them strangely. Looks lingered, veiled comments followed, and prejudices set in. It was not enough that people were shocked and outraged that they had burned their own fields to ash, freed their slaves, and fired the Overseers that were ensconced in the sugar industry. No. Now, the women were consorts of evil. Dark hearted harlots who had wed Satan. Even Linnet's nine-month-old son was thought to be the devil's spawn. It was for all senses and purposes, outrageous!

But the Vam Pŷr and her consorts were shrewd women. They used the public's base fears for their profit, which chiefly worked for their benefit in the courts. The validity of Dominique's claims to her mines at Minas Gerais was a long and drawn out legal affair. One that was often written about in the local tabloid. The prejudices arrayed against them were cited many times as reasons that usurpers tried to steal the Lady De'Paul's deeded wealth and property. The proponents of mercantilism were many, but the supporters of a woman's rights were very few. Coupled with the Portuguese crown finally affirming Dominique's claims, it was still a touchy, bureaucratic matter that moved slowly along. It was Linnet's idea to use the witch hunt against them in their court proceedings to curry legal sympathy in their favor.

As an accord to appear normal, Linnet and Laurel, usually accompanied by several Indios servants, regularly attended church services. They became involved in public functions, parades, and market fairs. They did not shrink from ridicule and rumors. They embraced them and became more civic. William was baptized in the church and Linnet Albee sponsored a lavish celebration in her son's honor that was opened to the entire community.

The more they were accused, the more they embraced. It could be said, and it was argued in court, that Miss Albee, Miss Davenport, and the Lady De'Paul were perfect examples of good, Christian women. They gave, they minded their own business, they attend church services regularly, they handsomely tithed, and they simply wanted to raise their heir like any other in the colony.

The shrewd women went so far as to craft intricate stories about William's father, Winifred Albee, when they took conversations in public. Linnet and Dominique spent many a night in their odd embrace, laughing, as they arrived upon tales to spin about the imaginary gentleman. As they told it, he was a captain in the Royal British Navy and had died at sea defending the crown from a galleon of cutthroat pirates. These lies, of course, curried public sympathy to a point, but the haunt of a Bruxsa was ingrained in the local lore and there was little more they could do to forestall the tide that would soon overtake them.

When necessary Dominique dispatched a ringleader or two who was stirring up too much trouble. This quelled the potential for violent uprisings somewhat, but it also backlashed, spreading even more rumors of an unearthly fiend that prowled the shadowed streets and deepest jungles of São Paulo.

It was a tug of war.

As grief over lost loved ones mounted with the spread of the disease, a Bruxsa was imputed to be responsible. The nerves of the Butantã populace had been chipped away for too many years. Moods were thin and passions ardent. There was only one place notorious enough that deserved the full might of the township's ire.

So, the attack came late at night.

Escorted by the former slave and stable hand, Guajajara, five Portuguese men armed with cutlasses, pistols, and knives navigated the plantation stealthily and entered the main house. A middle-aged Guarani woman accompanied them and it was assumed that all the servants were asleep in their quarters and the nefarious ladies of the estate were nestled tightly in their beds.

Laurel had just placed William back into his crib when they accosted her in the upstairs hall. The infant had woken up earlier that night and roused Laurel from her bed. She took the young Albee heir to his nursemaid, who fed him instead of Linnet. The favored consort was at the root of the house with Dominique, and Laurel did not see any need to bother them with a little nighttime feeding.

The young woman had become accustomed to caring for the infant since his birth as Linnet and Dominique re-ignited their passionate affair. Soon after Linnet had returned to Casa del Rio Dulce her dark mistress took her to her bed and feasted from the vein that ran up her thigh as they collided time and again in their untamed lovemaking.

Laurel did not scream as the blade slid across her throat, though she did try. Her death was quiet and callous. Grubby hands with stubby fingers clasped over Laurel's mouth from behind her as she felt the blade's sting. She bled out on the rustic wood and tiled floor, eyes wide and staring.

The Indios woman quickly moved into William's room, and wrapping him in a blanket ferried the young master from the estate. It was a cool night out and the child slept unaware, in the arms of a stranger, that he had just been kidnapped.

Guajajara led the rest of the men to where the servants slept, and one by one they were all murdered with their dreams. Among them was the orphaned teen, Yabi, who had taken a shine to Miss Albee the night that he had lost his father to the banditos. A balding man, who was in his late thirties and held the post of Sergeant At Arms of the Royal Portuguese Navy, plunged his knife deeply into the boy's chest. He had the charge of carrying out the awful deed of ridding the land of the Bruxsa and her brood.

It was true, the Sergeant had no malice in his heart for the foreign women. He followed orders, recruited because his heart was filled with pain. Sergeant Francisco da Sillva was a loyal man, a proud man, admired by his peers and underlings, who had recently lost his three year-old son, Jacobi, in the cholera epidemic. The man was broken up about it and now his wife was in bed with the disease. She too would soon pass. Francisco's world was fleeting by, faster through his aging fingers than he could scarcely fathom. Nothing was there for him anymore except his aching anger and duty. His grievous loss was the perfect breeding ground for his superior, Captain Miguel Simões, to exploit.

Captain Simões was a man with malice in his heart. He had lost a rich revenue stream when the Lady De'Paul and her entourage returned to São Paulo and asserted their rightful claims. He was slated to lose even more wealth from pocketed bribes if the women continued to reign successful in the local courts and the full operation of Dominique's mines at Minas Gerais were returned to her. He couldn't let that happen.

The Captain was outraged by the crown's support of this sickly female intruder. He represented the King and Queen of his dear Portugal home in the far colony of Brazil. The Captain was a man of consummate duty, even though he sometimes bent the rules in his favor. The way he saw it, if the House of Bragança did not see the evil of Dominique De'Paul then it rested upon his broad shoulders to do the right thing. It was an easy decision for him to make, one that allowed him to rest peacefully at night knowing that for the honor of His Most Faithful Majesty, El Captain Miguel Simões, would protect the crown – *even against itself*.

Sure, he bent the rules every now and again, dipped his hand into the till. He had to. Brazil was still very much a savage land, wrought with peril. The French were constantly trying to muscle their way onto His Majesty's shores and steal the riches of the Amazon. Miguel Simões placed his very life on the line for his most honored sovereign lord. Miguel held a stressful position of government. He was here, taming this uncivilized land, while his monarchs languished in the luxury of Lisbon. He wet his whistle on good Godly conscious because it helped to keep the merchants and tradesmen, the Bandeirantes and the French, the common folk, slaves, and natives all working together in a tempestuous, easy alliance. It was a hard harmony and he was the wheel that made everything flow. And he was poised to take the credit for eliminating São Paulo of its nasty Bruxsa.

Dominique watched Linnet sleep. In the five hundred and twenty-seven years that she had been a symbiont she had not slept once. The lack of a need for sleep was considered a benefit to the Omjadda in that they could work their slaves continuously without fear of death or exhaustion. A sacrifice of blood every now and again from the human cattle they herded or from the livestock that was tended was all that was required to maintain a stock of Vam in any given keep, and the workload of any one man or woman was greatly doubled. It was an efficient system for awhile and during Dominique's nearly three hundred years of bondage she never thought that she would ever walk free again. *Surprising, the turn of one's life.*

She was happy with the young woman from Abingdon. Happier than she had ever been and it appeared that all of Dominique's dark beauty and sickly disposition did not stay her consort's feelings. They had traversed the open intimacy of the enigmatic African and suffered the barren quietude of the maiden's pregnancy and returned to the other side of the world to find each other again, waiting. Linnet was open to her in body and soul. She loved the Vam Pŷr. And for that, Linnet was an extraordinary person. She was the sun that never touched Dominique's cheek and the fullness of life that had been robbed from her. Simply put, in a heart that beat to the strings of a veiny puppet master, Linnet was a precious gift.

Dominique began humming a little tune that she remembered her father singing to her on nights out in the desert. It was the only thing she had from those times. The Omjadda had taken everything else. On many nights, when she was harbored away in distant lands, made to endure harsh treatment by the cannibal angels, many years before she undertook the ritual of the black blood, she would hum this tune to calm her nerves and make her fall asleep. She did not remember the set of the face or the gauge of the eyes of her parents anymore. That had been lost eons ago. Dominique only knew this song and as she hummed the little ditty she tried again to pull from the locked vaults of consciousness the images of her mother or father or brothers. She even tried to recall the last time that she actually could remember what they had looked and felt like, but even that proved impossible. Her mind, like her distant home and memories, were a valley of dust.

Dominique hummed her tune by the soft glow of candlelight, spying the voluptuous curves of her paramour in delicate slumber, and hoped that she would cherish the beautiful gift before her for another five hundred and twenty-seven years. That one day, far into the unforeseeable future, she would not have to wonder what the young woman looked like, or smelled like, or even tasted like. That she would still be with her naked in her bed, but the odd, unfamiliar creaks on the flooring above Dominique's head suspiciously tingled up her spine that even her lofty dreaming hopes were in jeopardy.

"Linnet?" The blissful shade gently whispered, pressing at her shoulders. "Wake up. Someone is in the house."

Linnet shook the sleep from her head, and rushing out of bed her thoughts turned immediately to William. Dominique went to the door as her companion dressed. She paused and listened for movement on the opposite side, but heard none. Quietly, she opened the wooden barrier and stepped lightly into the hall. Rounding a turn in the earthen corridor beneath the main house, the deathly woman found them as the blade of a cutlass swooshed past her face. She pushed her attacker back with both hands, narrowly removing them before another sword came crashing toward her. She turned again to avoid a jab at her middle and a shot rang out. The musket ball caught Dominique, hard in the shoulder.

The explosive report of the pistol boomed in the corridor and Linnet jumped. She looked around for some form of protection, anything that she could use to beat off the invaders, but nothing appeared so readily available in Dominique's chambers. She ran toward the door, her mind colliding with panic about her son and her lover. Though no sooner did she enter the long hall did she have to double back. Two men, carrying swords, had broken through Dominique's defenses and were barreling down the hall towards her. Still sleepy, the raven haired beauty nearly fell as she slammed the door shut to barricade herself within the round, windowless room.

Linnet was trapped. The sudden rush of adrenaline from being hurtled into the middle of yet another intense plight so soon after waking made everything seem like some impossible dream. Her mind reeled, trying to pull the cobwebs from her thinking but the feeding with Dominique earlier that night had been intense and left the poor girl exhausted from the loss of blood. Startled and dazed, Linnet grabbed an iron candelabra and tried to bar the door with its wide base, decorative handle, and long stem. The lit candles jostled in their holds as she moved it and they fell onto the floor, splashing hot wax across her hands. It stung, but Linnet ignored it.

Barely had she put the candelabra in place did the men reach the door. They tried the lever, but it would not open. So they beat against the door with their shoulders and a curt scream bellowed from the other end of the hall where Sergeant da Sillva, Guajajara, and two others tangled with the Bruxsa. Linnet knocked the flaming wax off the other candelabra and swung it around just as the men broke through the thin blockade. She did not hesitate or think about what to do. Her son needed her. Dominique needed her. She was driven by the most primal urge of her core, that of a frightened mother to protect her young.

Swinging the solid candlestick set with both hands, using all her might, Linnet bashed the first man that entered the room – smack upside the head! The sharp, decorative iron tore huge gashes along the left side of his rugged face. His portside eye was crushed and his jaw was severely knocked out of place. He went down in a pool of his own blood, crying in agony. The second man rushed her. Linnet tried to place the iron shield between them, but he grabbed the spires on the patterned end and pushed the base into her belly.

Linnet stumbled backwards. Even if she had not been weakened from a lack of blood pumping through her system, she would not have been able to match the strength of the intruder. Her footing gave and she fell. The candelabra clanged on the stone tiles as Linnet's assailant raised his sword, high above his head.

Dominique twisted the head of the man that had lunged at her, snapping his neck at the base of the skull. His yelp was shorter than his thrust. The eyes of the two men in front of her followed their fallen comrade to the ground and behind them Dominique spied Guajajara. *The vile, little native remained in the rear flanks while others did the dirty work for him!* An intense hatred boiled in the pit of the Vam Pŷr's abdomen for his Indios blood. She cursed him and Sergeant da Sillva shot her dead in the chest with a single pistol round. He quickly dropped the spent weapon to the floor and grabbed another from his thick leather belt. He fired again. This time he hit her in the pit of her hate.

She should have gone down with the first shot, thought the Sergeant At Arms. Despite what he had been told about the Bruxsa he still expected some kind of reaction other than her defiantly standing on her own two feet fighting. It was amazing and horrific at the same time and as da Sillva's last shot punctured the beast's belly his man moved in for the kill.

The frightened fool slashed wildly, screaming in the heat of battle, and hacked Dominique's right arm completely off. The cut was clean and the limb fell to the ground next to their dead comrade. The veiny blood parasite wrangled its mutilated form out of the severed limb, seeking to reattach itself. But the sliced arm fell to the ground much too quickly as Dominique cried out.

To the frightened men, hardened by battle among normal, regular soldiers, what they witnessed appeared unearthly and unnatural: terrifying, dark red tentacles clawed the air from the stub of the Bruxsa's shoulder and the cut end of the arm lying on the stone tiles. Neither man had ever seen anything like it in their lives. What rumors they had been told had not prepared them for such horror. Having no basis for understanding, the men stared with wild eyes, seeing the devil incarnate, evil inhabiting the shell of a woman. Everything they ever thought about life eroded in a few measly seconds and gave pause to their fight.

Dominique, ignoring the pain chuckled, a chortling laugh deep in the burrow of her throat. She bared her fangs and the former stableman ran from the basement and out of the house screaming in terror. Sergeant Francisco da Sillva and his companion crossed themselves and prayed to the Mother of Jesus. Dominique bent down, and picking up her fallen limb, reattached it to her body. The thirsty veins of the Jadaraa Soo intertwined around themselves like old lovers, greeting after some fashion, and the Vam Pŷr wiggled her fingers on the severed limb. She flexed them into a fist, ready to fight!

Linnet kicked her assailant in the balls. The man's face twisted up like a lemon and he fell to his knees. Linnet scrambled to her feet and the discomforted attacker swung his cutlass aimlessly. The tip of the crudely sharp blade cut her nightdress and drew a thin, red line across her abdomen. Instead of running from the room like she should have, Linnet swung her small feminine fists at the man. The brute was not so incapacitated as he was pissed off at being kicked in the family jewels. He grabbed Linnet by her wrists and flung her to the floor. She landed hard like an armload of logs. He rose with the hurt in his belly, cursing her, and kicked her in the ribs.

It quieted her down all right! As he continued to curse her he punched her in the face, splitting her lip, bruising her cheeks, and blackening an eye. Then he picked up the beaten woman and threw her onto the bed. He told her she wasn't going to enjoy any of what was to follow, making it a point to tell her that he was going to like it, though. That he would enjoy abusing her wretched flower so much that soon she would beg him to kill her. He promised her that. He promised Linnet that she would beg him to kill her to end her misery.

The vile man tore Linnet's nightdress off in two, long violent tugs, ripping the flimsy garment away from her scared, naked flesh. He slapped her several times, letting the sting sink in, as she screamed, "No!"

Laughing at her yelps, he unbuckled his belt.

Dominique did not want her attackers to see how vulnerable the limb was, so she played to their fear and it gave her strength. The man who had just lobbed the limb from off her body slowly backed away. She was a demon witch! She was a Bruxsa, a spawn from Hell! What he witnessed had to be palpably false. *Nothing on God's green Earth could ever be like this! It had to be the work of the Devil! Had to be!* Prayers broke upon his lips as the cutlass in his hand seemed nothing more than a mere useless toy. How were they supposed to defeat a thing that could not be killed by powder and steel?

As the man shrank back with his growing fear, he stepped into the Sergeant, who also was at a loss at how to destroy the beast, even though he had been instructed. He was told to hack her to pieces. *To keep cutting until all that remained was a sluggish stack of goo. Do not relent! Keep hacking away!* That and fire were the only means they knew about that would slay the beast and rid São Paulo of the ghoul's grip. Da Sillva pushed the frightened man forward. He yelled at him to keep cutting, but his fear got the best of him and he fell into the capable hands of the Bruxsa! Dominique made quick work of the man, tearing into the nape of his neck like a lioness. His blood felt good pouring over her jaws and the Jadaraa Soo sang as warm, coppery wetness splattered across the walls and the dumbstruck Sergeant.

The man's screams raised the hairs on the back of Francisco's neck and it was the first time in years that he felt like he wanted to live. To truly live! The death of his son and stricken illness of his wife were far from his mind now. His own mortality and beating heart pressed upon the bone bars of his ribcage to flee. And that was precisely what the Sergeant At Arms did. As Dominique drank the visceral fluids of the intruder, Sergeant Francisco da Sillva fled. He ran from the house, a coward, praying to God to save him, praying that he would be able to escape the nightmare of the demon of Casa del Rio Dulce.

The Ravager's pants fell down around his ankles as he climbed atop Linnet. He stunk of Cachaça and sweat, poking his unshaven face to her motherly breasts. He grabbed Linnet's still screaming face and stared into her terrified eyes.

"Devil's Whore!" He said and spat in her face as he grabbed her by the wrists, pushing her legs apart.

He thrust his fleshy sword into her womanly grove rudely, defiling her! She had only known the intimacy of one man, and he had been gentle and kind. Nsia was a prodigious lover. No one had ever tried to force himself on Linnet before. It was harsh and cruel. She felt dirty like she would never be clean again. And no sooner had the man wrecked havoc in Linnet's pudendum did Dominique grab the insolent bastard by the scruff of his neck and toss him against the far wall of her bedchambers. He landed hard on his back and fell to the floor. Dominique did not hesitate.

She lunged at him with a fury and hate so reviled that it shook the rafters of the Casa Grande with blood curdling screams!

Dominique spat the man's grotesque flesh out of her mouth as he tried to hold back the crimson tide pouring forth from the holes in his muscles, veins, windpipe, and esophagus. He died slowly, grating a bubbling wheeze from an opened mouth, mystified at the vibrant color of his own hands. He considered how impotent he was to stop the bleeding. All he could think about was his promise. How he was going to make that cunt rue the day with his brutish manhood. How he was going to make her beg for him to kill her. He had promised her that; and like the compassionate person that he knew himself to be, he would have obliged her mournful petitions by whatever painful manner of death he could devise at the time. *It was strange. She was supposed to be the one who begged. Not me!* Her cries were supposed to ring in his ears like church bells. Now, he could not even utter a single syllable. Death gasped at his heels and it was funny. *Funny, the course of one's life?*

Linnet was shaken.

Dominique lifted her off the bed and asked about William. She had no time to feel defiled or disgusted. Her attacker was bleeding out on the floor and her son needed her. William needed her now! They quickly ran to the upper rooms of the house. Linnet threw on a simple, one-piece garb as her bare feet pounded the stairs. Dominique followed closely behind her scanning the rooms and shadows as they went along. Linnet tore down the hall, but there sprawled by the door to William's room was Laurel's lifeless body. It was a very bad omen.

Linnet began to cry, imaging that same fate being committed against her newborn. As much as she wanted to fall down by Laurel's side and release her anguish over her death she could not. She had to know. She had to see for herself if the child that she and Nsia had brought into the world was so quickly and unexpectedly torn from it. Linnet had to view for herself William's lifeless corpse.

Slowly, the new mother went into the boy's room and ran to his crib as Dominique attended to her fallen consort. By the sudden, shrill shriek inside of the room one would have expected to find William's small, expired body held tightly in Linnet's arms. But as the Vam Pŷr stepped delicately into the darkened chamber it was much worse than she had thought. The crib was empty. William was gone.

"They've taken my son!" Linnet screamed to the greedy night as tears streamed down her face. "They've taken William!"

Dominique watched her lover, her precious gift, writhing in anguish like it was in slow motion. She was helpless as to how to console the grieving woman, besieged by her own reluctant memories and fervent rage of when an Omjadda female had twice taken her newborn sons from her. Dominique had fought each time to retrieve her child then, but that was only until a guard had rendered her unconscious, crowning her upside the head with the butt of his staff. And she woke with the baby stolen from her cell.

Death bloomed around her, a funeral bouquet, and those long ago feelings of being betrayed by the ancient beasts for the indignity of simply being human capitalized upon her senses in a pent-up fury. It was worse than anything else that she had endured in captivity. Having reached maturity, the Omjadda forced her to pair with a man – *a stranger* – and bear his seed, being nothing more than a flesh machine. Cattle. A human factory. Few things had ever matched the callousness and cruelty of being used in such a vile, careless way. It prepared her for the barbaric oppression of being a blood slave. Though truly nothing compared, except this night. This vicious, indecent night!

Mirroring each theft of her child killed what little hope remained. Buried deep inside, past the months of rape, swelling with the infants, and laboring through the pains to bring the unwanted children into the world, the young slave only briefly possessed motherhood's joy while the little bundle was in her arms, suckling from her teat. It stabbed her to see Linnet going through that now. The symmetry of time was crashing in on them through the thick jungle, leagues and eons away from where and when she was held prisoner.

Dominique had fought hard to bury her past with her true name, but there was no escaping fate. Its tendril fingers slithered up the backside, strangled hope. It folded time around them like a blanket. For all of the Vam Pŷr's extraordinary power, the wounded child of the Omjadda felt paralyzed and weak standing in the boy's room. One could not break free from the abuse that living gave. Her glorious gift seethed with that same awful suffering that she had once faced. Dominique had failed to change anything real in her life or in the lives of the ones who she loved. Laurel was dead. Linnet grieved, visibly and raw, shrieking into the murderous night. William was gone.

The Vam Pŷr tightened her fists, drawing down the points of her eyebrows. No. Not like this. Her head rocked a tight cage, gnashing misshapen teeth, and swore an oath that unlike her children, William would be returned to his weeping mother. He would come home again.

Linnet Albee raged against his empty crib. Her screams splintered the violent night with horrible loss and a hideous not knowing. She cried so loudly and vividly that it woke the field hands in their huts and roused them out of their straw beds. One by one, they made their way through the dreadful dawn to the big house and found the doors wide open and their world torn asunder.

Music chortled and giggled. *An old Red Snapper song.* The DJ was dipping back. Ryan scanned the dance floor. There wasn't any smoking allowed in the club, but he puffed hard from the cancer stick like a deluxe gangster in a Guy Ritchie film, feeling raw like bruised felt wrapped around an army surplus can of peaches.

He didn't really smoke. That's what he told himself. Only when he was stressed out; he hated the taste. It was like licking dry asphalt. His breathing was an engine as the little rings and streams of tiny suicide fanned past his face. He was a cartoon reflection of a Marlboro Ad gleaming in the high shine of the dance floor. No sooner had he stomped the cigarette out did a hulking bouncer in a black muscle tee two sizes too small – *it could've fit my sister* – told him to watch his step, that he was keeping his eyes on him.

The warning was as pathetic as it was futile and Ryan pretended to act as if he didn't know what the steroid homo was talking about, covering the squished butt with his foot. *Fucking bastard!* Ryan went to the bar and ordered a beer, watching the sloping curves of the Bartender's backside: Brunette. Green eyes. Long legs. Subtle mouth.

The cold, effervescent hops squashed the dry asphalt taste in his mouth and he wondered why nobody had ever put out beer-flavored toothpaste. *For the morning after the night you wanna forget.* He was starting to feel better than he had in weeks. A bit of his old self was creeping back into his Levi's, stepping into his bones. He was beginning to feel the hard-honed edges of that confident gigolo he hadn't seen in a while. *Where's Lacey Chaney now when she wants to bust my balls in the Ladies Room!* He sucked the cool, tingly liquid from the small round port of the glass bottle and wiped a bit of foam from his lips with his tongue. The dance floor was stained with a bushel of contested losers. The lights were offensively bright, quirky with the kick drum and bass. Everyone was a shadow. Without warning somebody slapped the beer from his hand, sending it crashing to the floor. He quickly turned.

"You fucking asshole!" Theresa shouted at him as she pushed and punched him. "I always knew you were scum. I fucking told her you were a piece of shit and now you've gone and proved it. Nice job." She threw the diamond-encrusted crucifix that he'd stolen from Z and gave to Mindy, in his face. It hit him on the lips and stung sharply. "Dick!"

She stormed off.

People were looking at him. Scowls the size of zip-guns twisted their faces, judging him for the dramatic ridicule. *You're no better than me.* The music chuckled, bouncing its exuberant rhythm. He touched a finger to his mouth and pulled it away with a smatter of blood on it. She'd cut his bottom lip with the cross. He wiped the sprayed hops off his mid-section and picked the unwanted, stolen gift off the floor. He shook his head. He was an asshole. He knew it. Mindy was a sweet girl, one he actually liked. *Fuck it.*

Ryan stepped over to the bar again and ordered another beer. This time he ignored the bartender's billboard curves and fleshy roadside attractions. He dabbed his split lip with a napkin and then...saw *her.* She was cutting a path through the club with that dark-haired chick from the penthouse. *Ling? Lynn? Lori? Fuck it.* Hastily, Ryan dried the blood from the edge of his mouth, tossed the napkin, and went in search of the slender back, sexy vampire that he'd been dying to see. He stuffed the jeweled loot in a pocket along the way and his beer arrived with nobody to claim it, except a stranger.

When he caught up with the punk she was on the floor, dancing, nearly hidden in the throng. A beacon of incandescent red hair, Z was his favorite flavor among the shadowed lights and he approached her slowly telling himself to *be cool.* The cuts on his forearm tingled. Z saw him and smiled. *She smiled.*

"Hey stranger. Where you been keeping yourself?"

One of her arms languidly hung across the shoulder of the dark haired chick. They were slowly moving. Out of time, out of step. They danced to their own meter. Lin just stared at him, a penetrating gaze that took the mettle out of his moment. Ryan chuckled to himself.

"Oh. I've been around. You get my letter?"

The vampire laughed and dipped her head. Lin whispered something in Z's ear and both of them chortled. Ryan began to grow uncomfortable. *It wasn't supposed to go like this. It just wasn't.*

"What's so funny?"

"My friend called you an eager beaver," informed Z. Lin's eyes just penetrated. "You like to chew wood?"

Before Ryan could answer the misguided question Z bopped him lightly in the crotch, laughing. They were having a go at him. Ryan chewed the inside of his bottom lip and felt foolish and it occurred to him, in this odd, play-school moment, that he was the only one on the dance floor who wasn't dancing.

"Care to dance?" He offered the wry woman his hand.

"How gentlemanly." And she obliged.

Lin's eyes lingered on him longer than he cared for. It was like she was dissecting his soul, trying to discern some hidden confidence and reason out of him that he had no clue about. She scared him. He saw real danger in her glare. Death seemed possible in her kiss.

Ryan thought it best to say nothing and just dance with the vampire. He had yearned for this, thought about it almost every waking moment since she'd pierced his flesh and suckled his blood. Z lifted a finger and touched his lip where her studded cross had cut him. She pulled the pallid digit away and looked at the droplet of blood on her ashen fingertip. The small, red dot popped.

It must have started bleeding again. The vampire stuck her finger in her mouth and sucked. He could have sworn she purred, but the music was way too loud to be sure.

"Mmmm, poetry," said Z in reference to the letter that he had asked her about a minute ago.

Ryan felt a need to explain the cut, but didn't. Z placed her pale hands to his hips and started bending and twisting like an 'S' in front of him. His sigh slipped past his lips as he grew hard watching her and he finally broke. "I've been thinking about you."

"Of course you have."

"No really. I haven't been able to get you off my mind."

She bobbed her head and flung her hair. "So, I've noticed." She crossed her arms, displayed them wide, thrusting her chest outward.

"I want you to bite me again. I want you to feed from me."

"You're all aflutter." She flicked her eyes at him. "You should relax."

Ryan couldn't relax. He'd sought her out in vain and she'd been vacant like his mother. The vampire wasn't getting it. He grabbed her by the wrists and stopped dancing.

"I'm serious," he urged, raising his voice. "I want you to bite me. I'm telling you, I'm yours."

Z stopped and glared at him. He was making a scene. "Maybe I don't want you."

A raw, hidden anger flashed. It had been building for weeks, welling up from the soles of Ryan's shoes to his shoulders. "What kind of fucking vampire are you?" he shouted, pissed.

Lin heard him and curiously turned, moving around to get more than her friend's back. She saw Z stiffen and pulled her hands out of his.

"You need to slow down, cowboy."

He got in her face. "I tell you, you can have me. That I want you and you toss me away like some fucking idiot? Ignore my calls and wonder where *I've* been? Who do you think you are!"

"You *are* being a fucking idiot," Z calmly informed.

"Well, fuck you!" he yelled, "What gives you the gaddam right to be so high and mighty! Huh?"

Everyone in the immediate vicinity stopped dancing and turned to the arguing couple. An unwelcomed feeling dropped in Lin's gut. Z was getting angry. She wanted to reach out and snap the little fucker's neck.

"You need to stop this." She warned through gritted teeth. "Stop it now."

"I said I want you to take me…"

"You don't want that." Z shook her head in a tight cage, side to side.

"Yes, I do," he urged, ignorant of the vampire's true meaning, arguing a point that was never in question or should've been raised on the dance floor. "Yes, I do!"

"Oh, no you don't…"

Though, before either of them could continue to rant, two muscle bound bouncers stepped from behind Ryan.

"I told you I was watchin'," said the guy from earlier. "Take it outside."

"What? No." Ryan tried to explain.

The other bouncer placed a hand to Ryan's shoulder.

"Get your fucking hands off me you pig son-of-a-bitch."

He turned around violently and tried to push the hulking man aside. That was a mistake. The bouncers secured Ryan in their grips without breaking a sweat and began escorting him to the door. He bucked like a bronco, but it was no good. They simply dragged him through the crowd, off the dance floor as he shouted at Z.

"You're a fucking vampire! It's what you do. What's fucking wrong with you?"

Ryan's crazed shouts curried comments from the jilted mob:

"I'm a vampire, too."

"Hey buddy, suck this!"

"I got yer vampire right here."

Z was a nettled wall. Maddened in the spotlight. If it weren't for the fact that this little escapade had brought massive attention to the truth of her and Z, Lin would have laughed at the absurd nature of it all. Z, on the other hand, wasn't finding any of it funny. She quietly fumed; the cosmic shit machine, spinning. Lin huffed and turned away. She couldn't console her just now. Nor did she want to. Z had made a right well mess of things with Ryan. It was her debacle to clean up, but that didn't mean she didn't have any say in the matter. Quietly, while all the fascination was paid forward, Lin slipped out the back of the club.

The two beefy bouncers tossed Ryan to the curb and told him to go home. He fumed outside and kicked the lip of the concrete. Everything had just gone so horribly wrong so quickly. *What the fuck had happened?*

Finally, after almost a month, he had a chance to be with the woman again and he blew it. He fuckin' blew it! *Pathetic amateur!* Ryan punched the air a few times and wandered into the alley to cool off. He felt like such a schmuck. The place stunk of trash. He buried his face in his hands for a moment, lamenting the fact that he'd opened his mouth. He punched the brick wall of the club. It stung blissfully, harder than air. He cursed, and slowly rational calm began to settle back into the cobwebs of his stupidity, but it was short lived.

Lin found him there in the alley with his back to her. She spun him around and tossed his ass against the solid red brick and mortar wall, knocking some empty boxes and crates to the fetid, beveled alley bottom. She jabbed her arm against his neck, pinning him to the brick.

"What's wrong with you?" she asked. "You got a death wish or what? Do you have any idea what you've done?"

Ryan's ocean blues stared into the soulless, drab eyes of Z's dark haired companion. Her sharp canines flared as she spoke and he was unable to budge from the vampire's vice-like hold.

"I'm sorry." He spat through a half-crushed windpipe. "I just lost it."

"Lost it?" She tilted her head with the question scrunching her face. Lin stepped back and he fell to his feet. "You nearly got your neck snapped."

Ryan coughed and spat up phlegm. "I didn't mean to..." he looked at Lin. "I just wanted to be with her again, that's all. I just tried to tell her that and..." He looked pitiable, rubbing a hand through his wavy locks. "I don't know, things just got outta hand."

Lin's mouth hung open by the sheer ignorance and audacity of the man. Then, she shook her raven's nest awake and stepped to him again. "You're stupider than shit. I should kill you myself."

Ryan raised his hands up and begged for his life. "No, no, no, wait! Please wait! I love her. I only wanted to be with her. I swear. That's it, that's it!"

Lin stopped short, a breath away from ending him. He was close to tears. She couldn't believe what she saw or what she was hearing. She poked him in the flat meat of his shoulder. It felt like he'd been jabbed by a rod of lead.

"You need to wise up. That's not how you treat a person who you claim to love." She stepped in close. "We have rules to follow. There are things about us you don't understand." Her eyes swept him like a broom.

"Teach me," he implored. "I want to learn."

Lin couldn't decide if it was worth all the trouble or not. Willing meat wasn't something someone like her came across every Sunday afternoon at the local buffet. She knew from her years as Dominique's consort just how precious, and useful, a willing soul could be.

"Do you know what we call people like you?"

Ryan shook his head, "No."

"Kulak." She rolled the word off her tongue like just uttering it denoted its revolting, lowly station.

"You wanna be my little Kulak Bitch?" she asked Ryan with the full authority of a vampire, centuries old.

"I want Z," he started with an indignant tone.

Lin poked him. "There ya go. You're doing it again."

He started to protest and Lin quickly grabbed him around the throat and slammed him up against the wall again. This time he couldn't breathe and she dug her pointy nails into his skin in the back of his neck.

"You don't know what you want," she whispered through her long teeth, an inch from the ear that Z had suckled, "or how to get it."

"Hey Ryan!"

The two heard a shout and Lin, turning, released her hold. Ryan Silva gasped for breath and coughed through the welcomed air.

"What was that shit?" asked a grinning friend, lightly, as he wandered down the alley with two other blokes. "You goin' mental on us or what?"

Lin turned to Ryan, eyes blazing, seething like a stamp. She didn't utter another word and left. If he hadn't gotten it by now, then there was little she could do for him. As she sauntered toward the mouth of the alley, crossing paths with the three young men all of their eyes were drawn to her voluptuous curves and shapely shoulders.

"Damn," another friend reported, feeling a pang of jealousy, desire, and awe for the curvaceous quality of the vampire. "No sooner you get your sorry ass tossed out the club do we find you out here scammin' another chick. Damn, you certainly roll. Gimme what you're huffin'!"

The local boys goofed it up and Ryan tried to play it off as they misread it. Though, behind the mask and manly chatter, he knew he was lucky to be alive. That if they had not decided to exit the club and come looking for him that he'd be nothing more than a rack for a sheet in a cold, metal room.

1776. São Paulo, Brazil.

Galloping horses chewed holes in the earth with their thudding feet. The path into the jungle was narrow. Fat, broadside leaves and hidden branches whipped the stern bodies of the beasts and the soft faces of Linnet and the three field hands that accompanied her. She was hardened to the switches that flogged her skin. After the beating she'd received from the rapist the heavy leaves felt like nothing more than mere drops of rain.

She was driven, pressed onward by a single, isolated thought to find William, find her son. It wasn't so much that she wanted the little tike back because she missed him. That was there, it was a part of her. Missing the child had set in after the initial shock and drama of discovering him gone, but Linnet felt so detached. Callous. Selfish even. So consumed by the loss that it terrified her. William was the only thing that had made Linnet feel even remotely human and connected over the past year. Her time with the Vam Pŷr was aloft the earthly tether. As cold as it may sound, she wasn't ready to give that up.

The men were hard pressed to maintain her pace as the jungle thickened. Two of them shared a steed and had never ridden a horse before today. All they could do was hope that they did not lose sight of Araci; forged to their mistress they were by the murders of their kith.

Behind Linnet and her companions the sun held its morning zenith in the sky, clear and shining. Golden, crystalline droplets of dew wet the combed fur of the domestic beasts as they plowed through the lush growth. Macaws reported their approach. Snakes stayed coiled around branches. Monkeys swung from tree to tree, some following them, others fleeing. Whole flocks of birds refused to nest until the wild crashing below had passed. Still, the path got narrower.

Linnet brought her mare to a halt and dismounted. Lush earth, cramming with the damp animal scent assaulted her flaring nostrils as she grabbed the reigns and tied the horse to a tree. *Plenty of green to keep her busy.* Linnet tucked the muzzleloader pistol into the hardened band of her leather belt and grabbed the machete from its sheath on her saddle as the field hands arrived.

Thiago was the first to dismount. He was a tall Guarani man

who had spent most of his life among the Portuguese and been harshly mistreated by them. He was competent on the spotted stallion he rode and Lin was sure she could trust him to hold his own if things got messy. Vaz and Jabajara on the other hand were not adept on the horse. They rode the animal bareback. They were highly knowledgeable about the jungle in this region and the native settlements that hid beneath its fervent canopy. Linnet's Tupi wasn't the best. She was still learning the language. With a clash of dialects and pigeon languages growing from the influx of run-a-way African slaves she felt she might need them both to translate for her if they were forced to search among the hidden Quilombos that darkened the mountainous jungle for Guajajara.

When the farmhands had been awakened by Linnet's shrill screams and the sudden wreckage of dawn rumbled from the Casa Grande, they wearily traversed the sodden grounds to discover the savagely butchered bodies of Laurel and all the house servants. They were horrified and shocked. It was too gruesome for words. Many wept. But when they learned that the young master had been stolen from his bed by one of their own they were even more mortified by the crimes. Somehow, the murderers and thieves had taken their hope, too, when they ferried the young child away.

To the Indios workers that lived and toiled on the plantation, they had come to love and respect the women who ran the house. They found them to be good people who treated them not as slaves, heathens, or property, but paid them a decent wage. The old Senzala was razed and better living quarters were built. They were allowed to live with their families on the lands they farmed and raise their young. They could pursue their own religions and customs, and for the most part, they lived their own lives. Many found Casa del Rio Dulce a haven from the bonds of slavery that permeated other plantations and the ever-expanding lands of the greedy Portuguese. These acts of murder, that ripped them all from their quiet little dream, only amounted to further hardening their hearts to the already loathed monarchy that bled their homeland.

Many of the workers had never seen the pale, ashen complexion of Dominique up close, and while shuffling through the house regarded her with odd fascination. Over the year that she had been with them they had begun to call her Jaci – for the moon, the mother of night. They said she looked over them every evening. From the portico atop the main house, where Dominique spent most of her nights, she did in fact look just like the moon. Her pale, luminescent skin shone down over the cane fields, orange groves, and bungalows like the all-present watcher in the sky. Though on this night, this torrid, dreadful night, even Jaci could not hold back the tide of what was to come.

Linnet did little to shield her mistress from the curious throng, as she normally would have. She was walled into her own nightmare, ebbing against the stone façade of loss and seething hate. Entering William's room where Linnet hid, Dominique held the arm that had once been severed. The wound glowed red against her pallid flesh as the parasite worked to heal its host. She did her best to shield the wound from view. Dominique knew she needed to feed for it to repair properly. The symbiote panged for blood in a repetitive wave of pain and ancient imagery, but despite its calls the Vam Pŷr concentrated heavily to retract the thrushing barnacle veins from the visibility of her skin. Her blood splattered clothing and whiten hue drew too many fearful eyes as it was. She worried about scaring the workers further.

"I will go after them and find William," said the moon.

"No." Lin dropped like a stone, red faced, teary-eyed, worry cutting her brow. "I will go."

And just as Jaci was about to disagree with her consort, a young field hand named Cimi entered the room carrying an aromatic sweet, nut-brown mash on a banana leaf. She approached Dominique and held it out to her. Dominique looked at the penitent girl, but did not understand a word she said.

"Tell her I do not want to eat," the cagey revenant told Linnet.

"It is for your arm," informed the consort rising and crossing to them.

The grieving mother thanked Cimi and took the flat leaf with the Bacuri seed paste from her. Dominique watched as the young indigenous girl made a circle around her face and shoulders while talking with Linnet in her native tongue. The Englishwoman shook her head understandably as Cimi's eyes flicked from Dominique back to her. Finally, the young girl left and Linnet dabbed a handful of paste onto her fingers and applied it to the cut on Dominique's arm.

"Well?" The anxious moon inquired hotly. "What did she say?"

"She said you are too pale," Linnet smirked. "She thinks you need to rest and eat more meat. That you've lost too much blood from your cut."

"Huh," huffed Dominique quietly.

The salve was warm on her cold flesh and the symbiont turned and looked through the opened doorway where the young girl had exited. The gesture of medicine was simple and kind and it touched Dominique in a most sincere way.

"You know this isn't necessary," she offered without looking, head still turned, gazing at the echo of the girl.

"Yes," Linnet agreed, continuing to apply the Bacuri paste. "But it will ease their fears a bit."

Dominique shook her head in agreement and watched her distraught Linnet administer the ointment.

"You need to wrap this in a wet cloth," she told Jaci, handing her the banana leaf. "Stay below. I'll return later."

The moon watched her lover go, but called out to her as she reached the door. "Lin?"

The raven haired woman stopped and turned. Neither woman could put the turmoil of feelings into the havoc crash of words. Their eyes locked, penetrating the isolated wall of fleshy clique, and there was nothing more to say.

Linnet strode to her room and threw on a common dress that she used for gardening over the one-piece garb that she had taken from Dominique's room after the rapist had torn off her nightdress. She put on a pair of leather work boots and grabbed a buccaneer's belt that hung behind the door.

As she stormed through the blood stained house, she ordered Vaz to run to the stables and procure three of their best horses, saddle them, and bring them to the yard. The half naked native, clothed only in a long pair of shorts, ran from the house to the stables as fast as he could. She sent Jabajara to the field house to get machetes as she primed two muskets and a pistol.

With extra powder and balls she met them in the front yard. Vaz had placed a single saddle on the mare. Linnet set the gauge of the strap and stowed her gear in the rear pouch. She looked at the two natives and innately knew they wouldn't be enough.

Thiago was among the movers of the dead, taking them from their rooms to the front yard of the house, when Linnet told him to come with her. As she mounted the mare Dominique approached with leather skins of water. Linnet reigned her horse in before she could buck. The animal did not like being so close to the bloodsucker. As she passed the flasks to the men and her maid she told them, "Guajajara was with them."

Gasps and talk erupted from those that had overheard this horrible news. Many knew Guajajara from when he worked the plantation, back when the Overlords ran the lands and when they first attacked to reclaim the Casa. There had been rumors that he had started the fire, which destroyed the original barns and stables. And now, he was instrumental in this atrocity? It was a harsh blow, indeed! Linnet pulled hard on the reigns, driving the metal bit further into the horse's mouth. Her face twisted with a hardening scowl as she said, "Now, I know where to start."

The young woman had never forgiven herself for forgetting that she had spied the native talking with Inácio Braga that night Dominique set the fields and mill ablaze. Now, it looked as if she continued to suffer under that same small infraction. It, returning again and again, like a bad penny. As the four of them rode from the Engenho the first rays of dawn began to splash across the river. Its bright eye blinked into the canopy of trees and through its thickened mesh Dominique saw the glimmer of the approaching dawn. It had been so long since she had seen the rise of the sun. Her heart longed to stay with the field hands and view it now. She needed a ray of light piercing the belly of her consummate darkness.

All around her the workers looked at her oddly, carrying dead bodies and blood soaked bedding from the house. The entire scene was melancholy and she could not remember the last time that she was ever so vulnerable and surrounded by so many unfamiliars without the aid of a consort. Her gaze swept the long line of corpses lying on the ground. Laurel was among them. The men that bore the dead from the house had folded the murdered servants' hands across their chests so that they looked peaceful. It was a silent and reverent gesture. It echoed the gravitas hanging in their hearts.

Dominique wiped a loose strand of blood-clotted hair from Laurel's colorless cheek, feeling more alone than ever. The stench of putrid and drying blood assaulted the parasite hard and it shuddered ever loudly in her ears to be satiated. Jaci reflected on the flavor of the girl and her companionship. She was robust and fruitful, a delightful bouquet that would surely be missed. In honor of her fallen maid she ordered the men to dig graves along the north side of the cashew trees. It had always been Laurel's favorite spot. Now, she could rest there forever. Never alone, never waiting, kept in the bosom of the earth.

Dominique stood among the dead. The burning orb rose higher in its palace of the sky and the darkened morning brightened. The mournful symbiont took her leave to the bottom of the Casa to wait with each anxious moment for her consort to return. *That is, if she was going to return?* Life was never so uncertain than when one thought they had it all figured out. She spied Cimi hanging by the entrance to the house as she entered and did her best to thank the young girl in her native Tupi. Dominique even went so far as to offer her a gentle smile with the points of her fangs covered up by the whitened curve of sickly lips, but inside…inside the parasite raged for the young girl's blood and Dominique felt monstrous.

The Casa Grande stank of death. The violation was obvious and Jaci subdued an urge to raze the big house with flame. In her chambers, she could hear the clatter of steady footfall above her head. It informed her what was going on and where they were throughout the house. Even the smell of smoke, from where they burned the bedding and sheets outside, found its way to her nostrils.

Desperately, she wanted to be among her field hands, helping them to bury the dead. Duty tore at the shoulders of her dress. She wanted to feel the coarse earth between her fingers and be as free as they were in both the shadow and the light. But she could not! She was a blood slave, stuck in the earthen chamber below the house, restless and heated. The parasite hungered and roared inside of her head, thrumming like a bad hangover.

There was no escape. She could not dare expose herself to the men and women that worked the fields, who now cleaned up after the horrific deeds of cowardly men. It would surely spell destruction for her as plainly as her feet padded a tense path in her chambers. She could not wait in this pit forever for Linnet to return. Morning had only broke and already the moon prayed for the coming night. Never in all of Dominique's long existence had she ever felt so much a captive to her misfortune than she did in this very moment.

Linnet waited impatiently as Jabajara and Vaz drank from their leather satchels. She armed Thiago and Jabajara with muskets and extra ammunition and headed into the bush. An anxious Jabajara handed his weapon to Vaz. He had never fired a rifle before and he didn't think to start. Besides, a musket was only a one shot item. A machete, on the other hand, never needed reloading

The information Linnet had on Guajajara's whereabouts was a month old. She wasn't sure if he would still be there, but like she had told Dominique, it was a place to start. A while back she hired a tracker to find their ex-stableman. For the longest time there wasn't any news from him and Linnet figured that the tracker either died or ran off with half the money. But then suddenly, he resurfaced and told her that he'd found the native rat among one of the maroons a few clicks south of the Guaira Waterfalls.

Linnet wasn't sure why she sat on the information. *Another mistake.* She could have easily sent a group of men into the jungle to kill him. Men like that were always easy to find. The raw side of the country spat them out like watermelon seeds. But she hadn't. She'd allowed herself to get carried away in her little bubble with her son and Dominique and life on the plantation. Now Laurel was dead, William was missing, and fourteen good and trusted people were never coming back. She rent her anger by cutting the huge fan leaves that got in her way with her machete.

No sooner had they entered the thick fauna did the morning sky open and shower them with warm rain. Above their heads and the risen canopy the big, blue giant stayed effervescent and clear as the water fell from the sky. Not a cloud lingered in sight. The downpour was condensed and it cooled the air briefly. Drops fell from leaf to leaf, cascading in syncopated rhythms, a choir of wet percussion. They reached the cascading cataracts of the descending falls and Linnet and her party took a moment to rest before the climb down.

Overlooking the great canyon from the jut in the Paraná River, feeling the rush of unending water roar down the mystical stairs worn into the hard fabric of the earth, the raven haired woman felt a quiet peace. For as far as her eye could see, trailing into the mists that rose from the crash of the falls to float above a landscape of trees, was nothing but soft green. Birds flitted over the timber-ocean, and far off to the right tiny puffs of black smoke rose from a group of campfires on the forest floor giving position to their destination.

When they had reached the encampment Linnet ordered Thiago to sneak around to the opposite side. She and the others would enter from the path. As they waited for Thiago to get into position she spied a few of their former African slaves living here. A group of Indios women chatted away while weaving baskets from Tucumã fibers as others tended to the fires, fixing breakfast. An ex-slave breast fed her young and a small group of kids ran around huts chasing one another. There was no sign of Guajajara or William.

Behind a thickening bush, Linnet had waited long enough. Thiago was either in position or near enough to it. The brazen woman walked into camp with the natives following. Vaz held his musket at his side, like it was nothing more than a flat stick. In her hand and Jabajara's were the sharply angled blades of their machetes. Heads turned toward the three visitors. Linnet's face was stern. Her darkened, tired eyes met with the people that looked in their direction. A tense hush fell upon the makeshift village as people rose silently, wondering what to expect from the armed party. A group of men to the right and back of them, behind a row of huts, began following them to the center of camp. Three others copied them to the left, weaving out from behind the small shelters to be more visible. Children ran to their mothers.

Linnet stopped near the middle of the encampment. Her gaze washed over all of the faces that stared at her. And she saw it. It was a simple thing. A human gesture, a quirk of silent reason. The eyes of an elderly woman shifted to a hut two doors down from where they stood. She turned to the men tailing her and cocked her head slightly to one side. They knew who she was. They knew why she was here. They said nothing. They did nothing, but make their presence known. It was more than enough to tell her all she needed to know.

Slowly, Linnet walked to the hut, silently pulled the flap back, and stepped inside. Guajajara was asleep from his nocturnal ravaging with a thin, sinewy arm around a woman. Linnet raised the tip of her machete to the conspirator's nose and booted him with her foot. He jolted awake. His eyes popped open and he saw the flush tip of the machete's blade point. It smelled of sap from cut leaves. His gaze followed the flat side of the metal to the handle and the woman who held the deathly instrument over him.

He gasped in fear and shrank back uttering something about how Linnet was a demon's whore. Guajajara's woman woke and moved with a flash of anger toward Linnet. Vaz stuck the muzzleloader in her face. She immediately froze. The native man told her to move back and the woman shrank to Guajajara's side in rigid terror.

"Bring him outside," Linnet ordered and exited the hut.

Jabajara and Vaz obeyed, dragging the poor man outside by both arms. The disheveled woman cried for her lover and followed them. Guajajara ranted and protested. He cursed them and called Dominique a Bruxsa, extolling how she was going to bring death and doom to them all. Linnet seethed quietly, listening to the filth erupting from his teeth.

"Still your lies or so help me I will cut off your tongue!" Linnet shouted in a pigeon-hole-Guarani and rose the machete to his mouth.

The ex-stableman reluctantly fell silent and his eyes pleaded with his native brothers to heed him and pity him or else they and their children would befall an unthinkable death at the hands of a demon-witch. But they knew nothing of Jaci being a demon or a witch, as he professed. She was the moon that had looked over them in their darkest hours. She had set the lot of them free. She was known for her kindness on her lands and provided a home to the Indios where others sought to shackle them in chains. Casa del Rio Dulce was a haven from the foreign men that struggled to enslave them in perpetual servitude. To their ears, Guajajara sounded like a raving fool.

Thiago uncovered himself from the bush and walked up to his group, surprising a few of the locals that had not seen him at their rear. He knew Guajajara. They had worked together under the Braga yoke for many years. He had no particular like or dislike for the man. He did not consider him a liar, nor did he think he could be trusted. Though, in all the years that Thiago had known him he would have never expected the betrayal of which he witnessed and was made to carry from the house to the yard. Men and women, some his own people, murdered in their sleep! A lady of the house butchered like an animal! Linnet's son stolen! The corpses of Portuguese men lead a trail to Guajajara. That was guilt enough for Thiago. So, as he entered the crowd he pulled back the hammer on the musket, rose the butt into the hunch of his shoulder, and aimed the opened end at the man's face. Guajajara's silent pleading and guttural rants were stowed as he glared into the dark abyss of the fire stick.

The traitor's woman cried out for the life of her lover, pulling on her nest of tangled hair in anguished tufts. Several women of the village came to comfort her and pulled her away to the side of the action. Her sobs and steady pleading rent a shrill air to the late morning.

"Where is my son?" Linnet asked.

The murderer said nothing.

She stepped closer to Guajajara and jabbed the machete into the ground and crouched behind it staring him hard in the eye and asked again. But his only response was to curse Dominique as a demon and a witch.

"There is no Bruxsa!" Linnet shouted, more to the crowd than to Guajajara. "Where is my son?"

Jabajara implored him to answer Linnet. He had heard the stories from those that were there that night when the Lady of the House had burned her own fields; had fought off attackers while with child. He knew how she had freed the African slaves under harsh criticism and local protest. He had seen the white woman go toe-to-toe with merchants and docksmen without the faintest glimmer of fear or trepidation in her stance. The young field hand didn't want to see what she would do if Guajajara didn't answer her. He feared the worst, so he implored his native brother to do the right thing.

Linnet rose and looked at Jabajara and enlivened his fears. "Tell him, that if he doesn't tell me who took William and where he is in the next ten seconds I will kill that woman."

As she spoke a fire burned in her eyes and she raised the sharp tip of the machete's blade and pointed it at Guajajara's lover. The young field hand relayed the message to the arm-bound man in their native Tupi. The ex-stableman did not need Jabajara to tell him what Linnet had said, however. He understood her well enough, and he knew enough about the demon's consort to know that she wasn't bluffing!

The native began breathing hard and his brow knotted. Linnet had had enough. She walked over to the innocent woman and Guajajara began weeping. Linnet looked into the tear-streaked face of the Tupi woman. She felt nothing. She stood in front of her and raised the machete high above her head, just as her raping attacker had done earlier that morning. Guajajara cracked.

"Sergeant Francisco da Sillva!" he shouted in huge weeping sobs. "Sergeant da Sillva."

Linnet knew him, not greatly, but she knew who he was. They had met on occasion. She looked again into the face of the native woman she nearly murdered...and still, there in her deadened heart, felt nothing. She lowered the machete and walked back to Guajajara. Thiago watched the Lady of the House intently. Her ploy made him uncomfortable, that much was obvious. Linnet caught his stare and wondered if he would have let her kill that poor woman. She wondered if he would have turned the musket on her and shot her in the back. In the few steps it took for her to stand in front of the man who had led murderers and kidnappers through her door, Linnet Albee wondered a great many things, like, why Francisco? Why now? And who was really pulling the strings?

"Where have they taken him?"

"I do not know." He wept.

"Where have they taken him?" Linnet repeated slowly lifting his chin with her machete so his eyes could see the truth of the situation.

"He would not tell me," pleaded Guajajara. "They had a Guarani woman with them. She did not tell me her name or where she came from."

The man crumbled like wet tissue in the arms of Jabajara and Vaz. Linnet nodded to them both and they let go of his arms. The former stableman fell on all fours crying. Linnet exhaled heavily. Turning her back toward him, she took a few steps in the direction of the villagers. She looked the lot over. They weren't happy with what was going on. Solemn faces swept in a crooked line, but for the most part, it wasn't really their business. She knew that the fear of Bandeirantes and Soldiers descending upon them stayed their hands. They dared not kill a white woman in their quilombo or they'd forfeit their own lives.

"You have to believe me," started Guajajara again, rising to his knees, tears staining his tanned cheeks. "I saw it with my own eyes. A Brux-"

Linnet warned him that if he started speaking that crap again that she was going to cut his tongue off. She just neglected to tell him that it would still be attached to his head. The raven haired woman's actions were swift and unexpected in the calm loll. It was a single, clean stroke that separated the native man in two. As Guajajara's head tumbled through the air, end over end, his opened eyes saw his body spurt blood into the air and spasm and fall over. His head landed with a hollow thud and rolled toward the woman that had loved him. She shrieked and rent her hair, pulling out globs of the thick, black tresses. The villagers stood shocked, in stunned silence, at the killing.

Vaz quickly raised his musket toward the villagers. Thiago turned, in the heat of the moment, ready for anybody to make any sudden moves, but nobody did anything. Guajajara's body bled out and Linnet cut a path through the crowd from whence she came and didn't say a word to anybody else. Inside, a single thought rattled around her head. *Sergeant Francisco da Sillva.* His name became a constant drumming, a beacon of light.

Sergeant Francisco da Sillva. At least she had a name. *Sergeant Francisco da Sillva.* And she knew the face that fit the name. Though more importantly… she knew where to find him.

With a pair of old binoculars from the building across the street

Ryan watched the sun shields rise from the penthouse windows and glass portico doors. He spied into the opened portals, but didn't see anyone. After awhile Lin crossed his path. A shiver raced up his spine, looking at her. He tried to cheat the angle so he could see into the room she entered, but his view was limited. A minute later, the sable haired vampire walked onto the balcony terrace and spread her arms wide along the sun-baked railing, peering down on the city below. Ryan watched as she breathed in the night air. After being contained behind concrete all day, sucking in, expelling out, refueling the roots of her Jadaraa Soo with city soaked, heaven-puke was soothing and calm.

The air was balmy and the sky held a touch of rain in its lungs. The scary bitch was clothed in a faded pair of jeans. She wore boots and a black vest decoratively embroidered with silver colored thread. The locket that usually adorned her neckline was missing. After a few cigarettes, she went back into the penthouse, out of Ryan's sight.

A few minutes later, Z entered through the front entrance carrying what looked like a bundle of mail. Ryan wondered. Hoped. She stepped out of frame and returned a few seconds later carrying a manila envelope with his writing on it. He watched as the object of his desire opened the large envelope and took out the piece of paper he'd placed inside. She looked at it and stood very still for the longest time. Then, she moved to crumple it like it was nothing more than trash. A flash of anger ripped through Ryan's cells until Z stopped short and smoothed it out.

Under the long sleeve of the shirt he wore, on his other arm, were fresh, thin slashes and the bandages that covered them. This time he got more creative with the design of the blood and actually went to an art store for a piece of acetone paper, used for water coloring. Instead of just blotting the cuts like he had before, he made a pattern, cutting himself until he had just the right shade of color, tone, and texture. He first thought of making a flower or a heart, but both of those ideas sucked. Too cliché and corny. So, he stayed abstract, and he was pleased with it, forming red rorschach wings. On the bottom of the page he simply wrote, *I'm Sorry.*

As Z stood there looking at his creation, Lin entered his view again saying something to her. She interfaced with the control panel near by. *The vampire talked with somebody. That meant there had to be somebody downstairs at the main entrance of the building.*

Ryan moved the binoculars to see what he could see, but the angle was off. The hard edge of stone eclipsed his view. The entrance was on the other side of the building. When he shifted the tiny figure eight back toward the penthouse they were both gone. Distant thunder rolled overhead, sounding like his eardrums were stuck under a carpet. A few moments later, Lin came in through the front door carrying a small, soft-shell cooler. She went in the direction of the kitchen. Ryan tried to cheat the angle on the other side, but the kitchen was completely out of sight. The sky cracked, bellowed, and rumbled like it wanted to do something. As he moved around, searching for a way to peer into the sterile room, he spied Lin's reflection in a small circular mirror set in a golden-like sun mounted high on the wall.

In the mirror, Ryan spied the scary vampire punching in the code on their stainless steel refrigerator. She opened the behemoth utility and unpacked clear packets of blood from the soft-shell cooler, hanging them up on a rack, rotating them by date. Ryan huffed at the average domestic simplicity of it and what Z had told him about feeding where she lived finally clicked. Why would she risk feeding in her lair on the purchase of strangers when she had the red-ready-mix available in easy six-packs and two-liter for sale items?

Speak of the devil. Just then, Z entered, talking to Lin. She handed her his letter. Lin turned to face the tattooed obsession and all Ryan got was the flat nothing of the vampire's back and the black silk of the vest she wore. He cursed and exhaled a tense sigh. The sky was quiet. He was edgy and wasn't at all sure why. They were talking about him. He wished he could hear what they said.

Eventually, the vampire fell into view again and it was obvious she was shouting at Z, all wide mouthed and animated, throwing her silent tirade into the other room where Z hung out of sight. Finally, a short excursion into domestic bliss and the crazy vampire threw her hands up and exited out of frame. Ryan remained locked onto the passage of the portico doors, searching for a shot of his divine love, truly wishing he had a bug, or something like the people in spy movies used, so that he could hear what they were fighting about.

He searched for Z – a confused collection of close up forms crashing through the sideways figure eight, but he couldn't find her, and for the longest time there was no visible movement in the house. Dead empty and the sky about to rain, heavy with that pacific scent, the heavens held it back like a greedy lover, and Ryan metered out each excruciating breath vacillating on whether or not he should go and raise her on the com-panel. Finally, the tall, lanky curves of his object of desire wandered into the livingroom and sat down on the couch. *Must've been another room that looped around.*

Ryan could see her clearly if he cheated the angle diagonally. Shortly after that, Lin walked out onto the balcony and smoked a couple cigarettes, flicking the butts into the Santa Ana air, onto the street below.

The sky overhead thundered, and lightning crackled between clouds like a railcar, igniting short bursts of orange rimmed plumes. Ryan toggled between the two of them; each isolated in the luxurious tomb. Z sat on the couch. The back of her head was motionless. Lin watched the stratospheric storms. Envious, Ryan watched them both, and in due time, the dark haired woman went back inside and crossed to Z. Folding her bare arms across her chest, Lin paced while she talked, barely looking at her companion. The sky rumbled like a bully. *I wish I had a bug.*

"You don't want to go with me this time, that's fine," spoke the elder vamp to the dyed red punk. "To be honest with you, I could use the break."

Lin took a long pause, pacing behind the couch. To Ryan's infinite-looped view she kept falling in and out of frame, her face a scowl, a crash of worry. Z remained motionless on the couch. He pined to know what they were talking about!

"We're drifting," she continued. "Have been for some time now. It's normal. It happens to our kind. We've had a good, long run of it though." Lin smiled. "So, perhaps its best if we both just went our separate ways before one of us said or did something we regretted for the next century or so. I've had my fill of that nonsense, as you already know; and there's nothing worse than one of us with a stick stuck up our ass, carrying a grudge generation after generation." The vampire reflected. "I mean, just look at how Dominique has treated you over the years."

Lin paused, expecting one of Z's usual retorts about the Vam Pŷr, but none came. She looked at the back of Z's head, thinking that the girl was listening to her. Lin stopped pacing. "We've lived a lifetime together, you and I. You've always been there for me. I will never forget that. You came along at just the right time and I know I don't always tell you everything or share everything with you that you want me to. It gets harder the more you go on to remain open and even interested. Everything loses its flavor. Everything fades. But I want you to know, if it wasn't for you I don't think I would have lasted as long as I have."

Lin started to slowly walk around to the front of the couch. "It's important to find someone who can help you connect with a given age. We're so disconnected all of the time. Stuck in our little bubbles. We become numb to even the simplest pleasures. Maybe this Ryan guy isn't the right one, or maybe he is. I don't know." Lin stared down at the floor, thinking. "I know it's not the answer you wanna hear, but I do know this…

268

if there's a chance, even remotely, that he could be a rock for you in this age then you should at least give him a try. He seems interested enough to learn, anyhow."

Lin looked to her partner of nearly three-quarters of a century. Z's eyes were open and slightly downcast. It appeared to her that the vampire reflected on what she was talking about. Ryan focused his lens, cheating the angle to get a better view. "And if he is the right one for you in this age," concluded the raven haired beauty. "I'll talk with Dominique to consent to have him turned. Only if it's what you want though."

Lin's gaze remained locked on Z. The vampire hadn't moved or twitched an inch. She was silent as the grave. It wasn't like her exuberant friend. Lin waited. "Did you hear me?" She snapped, a sharp bite to her words. "I said I'd talk to Dominique…"

Nothing! Z still remained fixed, like a statue, lounging on the couch with her legs spread out in front of her, her head tilted downward and her eyes staring at her feet like she was pondering. Lin took a few angry steps toward the symbiont and then stopped suddenly, and gasped.

"Z?" Lin called emphatically. "Z!"

Lin's face became a wash of awe and she couldn't believe it. Z was asleep! A bitter rock sank to the pit of Lin's stomach and she brought a hand to her face and took a few steps toward her friend, but stopped again. *Oh, my God. She slept.*

Lin needed some air. She felt dizzy. Her head felt light. The room swam and suddenly felt claustrophobic. Stunned, she took a step backwards and a word crashed her reason.

"What?" Z asked suddenly with a biting tone that hinted of their argument earlier.

Lin turned and looked in astonishment at her dying companion.

"Do you want something?" Z's voice softened a little. The strange glare on Lin's face juxtaposed her anger. "You're just staring at me. What is it? I got something on my face?"

The vampire searched with her hands, but couldn't detect anything out of place. Ears. Eyes. And nose. *All there.*

"No," Lin meekly retorted. "Nothing…sorry. Sorry."

Ryan couldn't make out all of the action that took place in the living room, but he could sure tell that something had upset that crazy vampire bitch. She tore out of the livingroom in a hurry. The demented dame entered the balcony terrace again, panting heavily. She acted exasperated. Her eyes were wild and she kept grabbing her head and shaking it no. *Crazy Bitch.*

Ryan yearned to know what had just happened inside of the penthouse. Because whatever it was, it had shaken the resilient killer up. The whole thing was like watching one's favorite soap opera with the volume turned down. The drama gnawing at you to discover what intricate plot line had just untangled from the mesh of callow lives.

After a few minutes of frantic pacing about, Lin finally walked over to one of the lawn chairs that the girls kept on the roof and sat. She pulled her legs tightly to her chest and remained there, almost a gaddamn statue. Occasionally, she smoked a cigarette or two until dawn poked its weary fingers through the bleak morning clouds. Z only wandered outside once and they didn't speak to each other. The sky bowled strikes that seemed to lead farther and farther away, out into the oceanic distance.

Ryan's first foray as a Peeping Tom had left him anxious and fluxed. He fell asleep just before dawn with his binoculars around his neck. A light morning rain misted his face, waking him to find a cold gray light and the sun shields on the penthouse tightly drawn.

1776. São Paulo, Brazil.

By the time they reached the horses it was late afternoon. It was a long, silent walk back. Linnet knew they were thinking about it. She was thinking about it. What Guajajara said about Dominique could not be unsaid. It was out there. All Linnet could do at the moment was hope that it did not spread any further. She liked these men. The thought of killing any one of them or having them killed did not bode well with the Lady of Casa del Rio Dulce. *But if worse came to worse…*Linnet knew she would do what she had to do to protect what was hers.

Vaz and Thiago both knew Guajajara from their vassalage under the Bragas. Time like that bonded people, yet they had stood by her in her moment of need. Linnet and Laurel had met the dead native and Vaz on their first day in São Paulo. All of that seemed so far away now. The capitulation of events distorted her perception of time. It felt impossible, recalling Laurel's cold, gaunt face in the upstairs hall. Never again to hear her smile, talk with her during the day. She was the only one, besides Linnet, who knew their mistress's secret. And now she stood on the precipice of everyone learning it. The dense press of the jungle was huge as they rode their horses, quiet and slower. The active sounds tangled within the thicket felt oppressive. The air was uncomfortably dry. Their days of the little summer were nearing. And each moment felt stranger than the last.

Dusk bristled smoky lavender and night had dropped her dress by the time they reached the center of the township of São Paulo. A foul wind blew, kicking up dust devils and foretold of a storm brewing in the heavens. A single candle lit the interior of the Sergeant At Arms abode. The door was unlocked.

Linnet's back was sore and her legs were tired from riding. Her men looked beat. They all stank from the heat of the day – it had been long, hard, and it wasn't over yet. None of them had really eaten anything either. The Indios men did pick some fruit on their walk back and Thiago still chewed on a strip of Anona root to keep his strength up, but Linnet had not eaten a thing. She'd been too anxious to even think about food, let alone pass it across her gums.

The door creaked opened. Thiago entered first, musket raised, eyes casing the layout of the house, peering into deep shadows. He was followed by Linnet. Jabajara and Vaz brought up the rear. The raven haired woman did not expect to find the Sergeant at home, but there he was, sitting next to his wife, holding her hand, as she lay in their bed dying of cholera.

"I tried to run," he quietly said upon hearing them, "I knew you'd come for me. But I could not leave her. I just could not."

Out of the corner of the desperate man's eyes he saw Thiago with the musket raised high and the blood stained machete in Linnet's hands.

"I won't fight," the Sergeant yielded. "But not here." He turned and looked Linnet dead in the eye. "Not here."

Slowly, she shook her head in agreement. Linnet owed him nothing, but she didn't want to be cruel – *to kill the dying woman's husband over her deathbed.* The frazzled maid still had some dignity intact. Sergeant Francisco da Sillva rose from the chair. It creaked loudly. He bent over the bed and lay a moist cloth atop the forehead of his withering wife. He towered them all in height, had broad shoulders, was muscular, and if he truly had the heart for it he could have probably succeeded in avoiding his capture.

The Sergeant stared down at the woman whom he had loved since his academy days. He was quiet and still, the mood was somber. He did not want to leave her side, but inevitable ruin invited him elsewhere.

"Come on then," Linnet gently urged.

The Sergeant kissed his wife goodbye and left their bedroom. In the outer room, Linnet motioned for them to go outside. The Sergeant flashed a worried look and crinkled his brow, but he followed. Outside, he looked around, his face knotted in stark and evident fear.

"Is she here?" he asked the devil's consort with a trembling voice.

"No," Linnet informed.

The Sergeant At Arms immediately crossed himself in the name of Christ and thanked the Virgin Mary. Then, he gulped, "Are you taking me to her?"

"Not if I don't have to."

Linnet let the thought sink in. Whatever Dominique had done to the poor man he was truly frightened of her. She could use that fear to her advantage to get her son back. All eyes were on her to make a decision, to point a direction. They could not just stand in the street all night. The strange companionship and armaments would eventually draw attention.

"Over there," she pointed up the block, "La Cantina."

The Sergeant started walking followed by the four horsemen of *his* apocalypse. Overhead, the sky rumbled, distantly angered, behind a billow of murky, burgeoning clouds. At the entrance of the alehouse they halted to stow their cutlery. The Rojas Lunas was a cesspool of social depravity. It stank of raw meat, vomit, and brewing hops. Mud-coated straw matted the dirt floor and a gaggle of off-duty men from the Royal Portuguese Navy made a ruckus in the back of the tavern. They were well on their way to three sheets in the wind.

Linnet whispered to the Sergeant not to try anything and assured him that if he did his neck would be the first to feel the sting of her metal. The Bar Maid, a roily pound cake of a woman, greeted the Sergeant by name and quite rudely told Linnet how they didn't serve natives in her fine drinking establishment.

"We are not here to drink," Linnet checked. "All we need is a quiet room in the back for about an hour or so. We'll be out of your way."

"It ain't no bother if you drink or not," the ruckus wench countered. "But we still don't allow those types in here. So, shoo 'em out or ya best be on your way."

"You know who I am?" asked Linnet as if it mattered.

"Aye, I do an' I don't care too much for ya. Just so ya know." She cocked her hand to her hip and brandished her eyebrows.

"I can pay you well for your troubles."

"Don't want your money, Miss," the Bar Maid scoffed, not budging an inch.

"Célia," the Sergeant interjected. "I have business with this woman and these men and I don't want to tarry too long from Ema. She's not doing well today. So, if you had a room where we could conduct our business privately…"

At the mere mention of the Sergeant At Arms' dying wife the husky bar woman changed her tune and became rather accommodating. The room was small and dank. A table with a chair was offset in the corner. An oil lamp rested on top of it. The round, rutty table was crammed amid stacks of crates, barrels of mead, and bottles of Cachaça. As the barkeep lit the oil lamp Linnet ordered some food for her men. The bigoted woman begrudgingly agreed and stormed off in a furious waddle.

Linnet drew the machete from her belt and laid it on the table as Thiago locked the door. She handed Jabajara her pistol and placed the old wooden chair in the center of the room and invited the Sergeant to have a seat. Linnet needed to clear the air.

"Just because you are known and liked here does not mean I won't kill you." She paused for effect. "So, do not think for an instant that the favor you curry absolves you from even one single drop of blood from my servants and Laurel whom you murdered, or the fact that you stole my son away from me."

The Sergeant stood. "Of course not. It would be rude to think otherwise. But know this Miss Albee…I do not know where your son is and even if I did, I would not tell you."

The arrogant man slowly sat, nonchalant and unwavering. The childless mother seethed and he could see it on her face. It was pleasing.

"I think you do know where William is and you *are* going to tell me."

"That is unfortunate for us both," the Sergeant pronounced. "Because, I have no reason to lie to you. We both know you're going to kill me anyway so why don't you just get to it and get it over with."

"You'd like that, wouldn't you Francisco?" Linnet countered, taking a seat on a wooden crate. "It would save you the trouble of having to bury your wife next to your child."

"You brought this plague among us!" the officer yelled, flushed with anger. "And the sole cause is within the walls of *your* house!"

"Sergeant." Linnet sighed. "Dominique is many things, but she is not the cause of this epidemic or the reason why your wife now lies dying or that your son was prematurely placed in the ground…"

"She is unnatural and an abomination against God!"

Linnet stared at him. Things were skirting the edge. She did not want a repeat of the Guajajara incident.

"Maybe so," she said, switching to English so her companions would not be able to follow the conversation. "She is not like you or I." The consort rose from off her perch on the crate and crossed the expanse between them. "She has been alive for a millennia. She helped to build this entire town from across the sea. She's a part of a world behind this one that you, and most people, know nothing about. Your ignorance is paramount in this situation Sergeant, and believe me when I say…the only abomination that either one of us has seen that is against God, as you put it, is the murdering of innocent people. Laurel was a good woman. She did not deserve what you did to her. So, I implore you Francisco do not try to protect some self righteous moral ideal here, which you falsely hide behind."

Linnet stood over him now, awash in quiet anger. He looked up at her in stunned silence. "Tell me who the Guarani woman is and where I can find my son," she paused. "I don't want to kill you, Francisco. Worse yet, I don't want to have to send one of them to go fetch Dominique. Because, believe me Sergeant, whatever it was that you think you saw or you think you know…you have *no idea* what she truly is or is capable of doing. There *are* some things that are worse than death."

Linnet wandered back to her perch, sat, and looked at the man chewing on her words.

"God will save me," the Sergeant eventually professed in English.

Linnet shook her head. "Not this time."

There was a knock at the door and the Indios men weren't sure what they should do. Linnet nodded and Thiago unlocked it. The blustery Bar Maid entered with several plates of stew and a slew of profanity at the indignity of serving natives her fine pulled pork.

Even with the aroma of cooked meat, vegetables, and broth so close by Linnet she still hadn't the stomach for eating. The Sergeant too was not in the mood to consume the tavern's morsels, but at least Linnet's men finally had a chance at a meal. They helped themselves and satiated their ravenous hunger.

"If you do not know where William is," continued Linnet once the wench had left, "then you at least know who does."

"I do," the Sergeant professed. "And it is a name I will gladly take with me to the grave."

Linnet sighed. "Then, you leave me no choice." The crippled mother rose and turned to Jabajara, who was stuffing his face with a piece of stew-soaked bread. "Go to the house and ask the Mistress to meet me here."

Sergeant Francisco da Sillva began reciting the Jesus Prayer in his native Portuguese and breathing heavier as the fear of revisiting the Bruxsa gripped him. When the young native had fled the room to complete his lady's commands Linnet sidled up close to the Sergeant and spoke again to him in her native English tongue so only he would understand.

"Pray you tell me who has my son before Dominique arrives or you will see what hell truly looks like. I assure you, Francisco, I will implore my Lady to not be kind with you. To show you wickedness that few have ever witnessed and none have ever lived to tell. Yes, Sergeant, there are things worse in this world than dying, and I promise you that if you keep me waiting much longer you'll have a personal glimpse into what those terrors be."

"The Lord is my shepherd," da Sillva recited, trying to avoid thinking about Linnet's warning. "I shall not want. He maketh me to lie down in green pastures, and though I walk through the shadow of the valley of death I will fear no evil for thou art with me…"

Vaz and Thiago grew uncomfortable as the military man continued to loop his prayers unceasingly. It dragged the atmosphere in the room down to a stagnant level that belied an eminent panic hovering just over their shoulders. The natives did not fully understand what was really going on, but they had heard the prayer before from the Missionaries.

Linnet sauntered back to her perch. She was pissed that it had come to this, pissed that she had to send for the Vam Pŷr to rescue her son, that, yet again, she was unable to resolve a problem without the aid and assistance of Dominique. Vexed that she forgot to inform her lover of what she had witnessed that night of the fire. Irritated that it kept coming back to haunt her. Furious that her son was now in peril because of her stupid mistakes.

All day long she had been tracking the breadcrumbs, following a broken trail to William. Somewhere, he was out there. He could already be dead. He could be alive and well. Linnet did not know. That was the worst part. In the hollow shell of her shoulders, as she listened to the Sergeant steel himself with the words from a book, a book that she considered daft and inaccurate, all Linnet Albee really knew was that she still had to pull the chain, one link at a time, to find a child that she desperately knew in her heart she never truly wanted in the first place.

She craved Nsia's love. She yearned for his passion and their embrace. He made her feel full in ways that Dominique had never done, but he was not what she truly wanted. His seed may have reached her belly, but it did not fully penetrate her heart. Linnet felt unnatural, knowing too well that she did not really want the pregnancy or the child it bore. *Yet...finding him gone like that, ripped from his home like a copper pot!* Linnet wrinkled her brow. Guilt was the nourishment that kept her going.

As the Lady of Casa del Rio Dulce watched the Sergeant At Arms recite his prayers, she knew he had it all wrong. Dominique was not the abomination against God that he should fear. She was. Her heart was black and unsettling. She knew that she did not posses the kind of love that any mother would naturally have for a child that they had just passed through their body. She was the abnormal one. She was a harbinger of death that would eventually reap his soul.

"That's right, Francisco...pray," the pitiless, hard-hearted woman pressed. "Pray for us all while you're at it. Come the dawn we will all need a little forgiveness and consolation. So, pray Francisco, pray."

of the

PART SEVEN:

Affair of the Necklace

Behold the universe in the glory of God:
and all that lives and moves on earth.
Leaving the transient, find joy in the eternal:
set not your heart on another's possession.

-The Upanishads

Two Hours Ago.

Lin sat behind the wheel of her Cadillac ready to go. She put her hand to the key in the throttle of the steering column and couldn't turn it. Something didn't feel right. Something was off. All she could think about was the fact that Z was dying. That the blood parasite that fueled her fabulously long life had entered its final stage of living. She had exhibited what Dominique called Réveiller Sommeil, the waking sleep.

She was so young. Too young! Zia had barely crowned a century. Somehow, it didn't seem fair. Dominique was nearly eight hundred years old. Lin was pushing three hundred, a couple more decades and she'd be finishing her back tattoo. She knew other symbionts who were older than she was. Yet, what was fair in this world? They consumed the blood of others to stay afloat and cheat the reaper of a death that should have rightfully been his when they imbibed the Omjadda blood. They murdered people on whims and acted as gods over the lives of others. *What was fair? What was right? Nothing these days seemed to make any sense anymore.* The growing disconnection that Lin felt tugging at her well-worn bones was now the only thing that saved her from going completely mad!

There was a time in her life when she loved Zia Jean Bell. Not like she had loved Dominique or even Nsia, but she loved being with her and she loved the way that the crazy vampire made her feel. So free! So alive! If there was anybody who encapsulated life, it was Z. Now she was dying. The light of her Jadaraa Soo was extinguishing.

Linnet's eyes bent to the silver locket hanging on the rearview mirror. The face in the photograph was still inside of its decorative wings. The bloodstained memories in which she acquired the necklace still churned in her mind's corridors and she still felt the pull of destiny pushing on her shoulders. It *was* time! But Linnet could not just drive away from Z like she had intended. Something about that seemed so callous and wrong now. The aging symbiont stared off into the gray existence of her after-life and the drab surroundings of the garage.

Now.

Lin lay on her bed sliding the silver locket across the chain about her neck, thinking. Waiting. Afraid to approach her companion. Afraid to leave her alone.

A Half Hour Ago.

Lin made the call. She ordered herself a warm meal from The

Service. Someone whom she thought they both might enjoy feeding upon.

Now.

While ruminating on her decision to share Belmont with her dying friend another idea popped into her little dark haired head. Ryan Silva ached for Z's teeth. He professed to love her. He claimed to want to learn what it was like to be a part of their world, but his desire was obsession and it had already proved disastrous once. *Could the man be tamed to respect and follow our ways?*

Lin knew he could. The allure of the immortal kiss had its way of stabilizing even the most ardent passions with tempered promiscuity. Even if he didn't work out Lin knew Z would enjoying draining the man dry. They could bend the rules just this once. They didn't have to wait for the thrall of his beating heart to cease outside of their city borders. *No, if Z chose she could feed on him and educate him to be her consort. Or, if she chose she could kill him and drain him just how she liked. We could dispose of the body together so that it would never resurface to create a stir.* Time and practice had a way of training a killer to cover her tracks.

The locket zipped quietly across its silver chain. *Z always had a darker heart*, thought Lin, ignoring her own black vessel. *She loved the thrill of violence.* It excited her in a way that Lin never really came to embrace. Not that she didn't try. *What's the point of living a long life if you don't mix it up, take chances or try new things?* Though ultimately, Lin found out that it was something she could do with *or* without. Violence as a recreational vehicle just wasn't her thing. It didn't get her off the way it stoked Z. She didn't abhor it. It had its place. She just didn't care one way or another. As long as the humans minded their own messy business, and left her alone, she didn't really give two cents whom did what to whom.

The bell chimed. Lin crossed to the panel near the door and buzzed Belmont up. A minute later, the handsome, hulking man was standing in their foyer. Z wandered up to see what was going on. When she saw Belmont standing there an ire of jealousy sparked.

"Didn't you order me anything?"

Lin took a second to think about it and reported. "Sorry. This dish is mine."

Belmont smiled at the small tug of war. He liked it when the Immortals fought over him. It made him feel all the more special.

"What am I supposed to do?" the vampire asked rhetorically, more as an affluence of annoyance.

"Well…" Lin said, drawing the word out in prodigious play. Placing her finger to her temple she mimicked The Thinker. "Don'tchya have that cute little boy toy that's been fawning all over you?" She placed her hand to Belmont's arm, smiled, and shrugged. "Why not give him a call and see if he can wet your appetite."

Lin led her muscle-bound meal to her chambers. Belmont turned to the excluded vampire and said, "See ya later Z. Maybe next time."

Fuming, Z stood alone in the foyer for a minute before she rattled the preposterous idea out of her head. *Call Ryan! That sum-a-bitch screamed in a room full of people that I was a fucking vampire. He couldn't be trusted. What was Lin playing at?* Z knew Lin long enough to know that she was up to something, that she knew something that Z didn't and this was her manipulative little way to make her understand. *Damn it!* Z hated when Lin did this.

The vampire crossed to the house telephone. She picked it up, ready to dial The Service for her own repast, but in a defiant huff the miffed punk slammed the receiver hard into its base. Lin wanted her to call *him*!

Why? Z turned in the direction of where Lin's bedchambers were. She had half a mind to burst in on them and demand that she tell her why she wanted her to hook up with Ryan, especially after what he had just done. *That little shit ousted me in public!* The indignity of it was still fresh and vibrant in Z like a pop tune that wouldn't die. She stood at the precipice of a rude moment, but she didn't barge in on her flatmate. Instead, Z resigned herself to forget Lin and to forget Ryan.

She retrieved a packet of cold blood from the refrigerator. She didn't need a warm body to snuggle against as she fed. She didn't need a live, thrushing heart pumping ounces of smooth, gorgeous blood into her mouth, nourishing the Jadaraa Soo. She was stronger than all of that! She didn't need any of those convenient luxuries like Lin did. *The bitch is too pampered!* Z could take care of herself, and had been doing so for over a century. She didn't need Lin's machinations leading her like a mouse in a damn labyrinth with cheese.

As Z poured the red hued contents from a clear plastic packet into a glass and passed the chilled beverage over her gums, she cursed the wily vampire under her breath. Lin's idea stuck in Z's crawl like a wedge, but the resilient punk wouldn't budge. She wouldn't give either one of them, Ryan or Lin, the blissful satisfaction of being coerced into any action in which she didn't want to fully partake. The symbiont scraped a fang against her bottom row of teeth mauling the whole thing over like a rancid merry-go-round. She shook her head, sneered, and scoffed at Lin's feeble attempts to make her react. Taking another swig of the brisk, thick wine, Z began to think that it tasted better already!

She crossed to the livingroom and slid Fear's, The Record, out of its jacket and placed it on the turntable. The rascally punk cranked the volume so that it would shake the roof as the arm electronically lifted the needle onto the black, grooved plastic disc. The worn vinyl sizzled and the first track, *Let's Have a War*, pounded through the speakers. Z bobbed her head in time to the frantic pace of Fear and grabbed another VHS Tape from out of the box that still darkened the carpet. She popped it into the player and sat back with her ruby drink, watching the security camera footage of the dynamic duo of destruction ransacking another convenience store, killing all of the people inside before setting the place on fire.

Z remembered that trip fondly. They burned through three shops, taking what they wanted as they crossed the Southwest to visit those damn adobe ruins. Z never got the big deal of why Lin had to go all of that way to New Mexico and back again to stare at some patch of desert. Z never complained about it though. The stops along the way were fun. Definitely a way to get her ya-yas out. They shared a laugh then. It was in stark contrast to the bitter pill she swallowed and the distance that now separated the two of them.

1776. São Paulo, Brazil.

The hours raged on with no word from Jabajara or Dominique, and the Rojas Lunas closed for the night. Before Linnet would allow Célia to boot them back to the Sergeant's domicile she requested a piece of paper and writing utensils. The roily maid was furious. She regretted granting access to the woman and her company. It had been one thing after another all night long, claimed Célia, complaining as she went to fetch the writing items.

In the space between, Vaz asked Thiago, in his native Tupi, how much longer he thought this was all going to take. He was bored and getting sleepy. Thiago told him to be quiet. The barkeep returned and planted the utensils and a sheet of paper rudely down on the rutty table and told them they had fifteen minutes to clear out, and then that was it. She waddled from the room in disgust. The Sergeant looked at the clean sheet of paper and to Linnet. Her expression mirrored the paper, impassive and blank, staring back at him, waiting.

"You'd best hurry Sergeant. You now have less than fifteen minutes to write your confession."

Francisco's eyes went wide and he chuckled to himself. "I do not think so."

The raven haired wench crossed to her perch on the crate, grabbed her machete, and sat. She looked at Thiago and he caught the message, raising his musket and taking aim at the Sergeant. His dislike for the Portuguese, and thusly, the Portuguese man, fueled his actions. Linnet was reposed. The Sergeant At Arms just wasn't getting it, and though a tempest brewed beneath Araci's dirty, tired skin, she did not show it.

"You either confess your crimes on paper or we will kill your lovely barkeep and put her out of her retched misery, and that will be another death weighing on your conscious for which you will have to atone in hell for."

The method had worked with Guajajara. So, in her lonely agitation at not hearing anything from the Vam Pŷr or her servant, Linnet felt a need to do something. Dawn bristled behind the gates of the Rojas Lunas only a few hours away. The sun's course was plodded, turning on the axis of the galaxy, set in motion by the gods when the universe was spun into play. There was nothing the young, crippled mother could do about it. The calm fury of its approach was assured, and so far, the military man had been true to his word: he told Linnet nothing.

"You now have ten minutes, Sergeant."

The man glared hot at Linnet for a terse moment before he wet the tip of the quill in ink and wrote a few sentences confessing to the murders and abduction at Casa del Rio Dulce. He expected them to kill him now, but they didn't. Instead, they crossed the short expanse from the tavern to the Sergeant's home - *there and back again*. The earlier winds had died down, stars poked lazily through cloud tufts, and it was evident that while they had been holed up in the back room of the cantina, it had rained.

"I guess your Bruxsa had other duties to attend to this evening than coming to your aid." The Sergeant gloated as he walked in front of them, leading the way to his imperfect little home where death waited in his marriage bed.

Thiago saw anger flash across Linnet's face and that was all he needed. He struck the belligerent man in the soft spot behind his knees with the flat end of the muzzleloader – *Smack!* A bright lightning of pain riveted up his spine. He immediately crumbled to the stone cobble street, breathing in the wet earthen stink through flaring nostrils. Linnet was taken aback by the native's assistance. She had not expected such a sign of devotion. It pleased her.

"I would mind my own business if I were you," spoke Linnet, standing over him. "Perhaps if you had, none of us would be here right now embroiled in this unnecessary situation."

Linnet walked on, leaving the Sergeant to pull himself up. By the time he caught up with her, she was at his door holding it open, a reversal of edict that belied their true positions of power.

"Hurry Sergeant," she glibly commented, "I'm sure your wife has missed you so."

Francisco's hate boiled as he crossed the threshold of his home. The meekness and weak-minded attitude that they had found him with earlier that evening was now wearing thin. It was being replaced by an explicit desire to kill Linnet and her party. To finish the job, so to speak! Now that there was no Bruxsa, or the threat of a Bruxsa to scare him, to temper his hand, the Sergeant grew in confidence that he had to wipe this evil woman from off the face of the Earth!

Belmont caught the orange that Lin threw to him. He was naked in her bed. He always preferred being naked when an Immortal fed from him. It left his clothing clean and free from spills and allowed the bloodsucker to tap a vein from any place on his body that they wished. On occasion, it also led to sex.

Sex with an Immortal was something altogether different. For Belmont it was an exquisite cherry on the top of his favorite ice cream, the coup de grâce of his evening, season tickets to the biggest game, Shangri-La, and a ride through Disney World while tripping acid. It was beyond his form of words. It wasn't like fucking a regular girl. Vamps were different. Unique. It lent a new meaning to the term, *strange*.

He enjoyed it when they fed from him, that's why he was a Sanglant, and sometimes that, in and of itself, was sexual. Though, when he and a symbiont were combined in the frenzied, passionate, cold, steely grip of union, it was...*well*...one would simply have to have had experienced it to fully understand. It was beyond the comprehension of mere mortals to imagine.

On the other hand, some Immortals did not like Belmont with his clothes off. Instead, they liked to play hunting games. The Service would give Belmont the general vicinity to be in and told him the basic scenario. The vampire would track him and he would have to act afraid and run for his life. Games were fun. Sometimes, he would go alone. Other times, he would be paired with another Sanglant or they would go out in small groups to entertain larger parties. Then it was simply a sport of cat and mouse with the purchase of blood at the end if it.

The Prêteur de Sangs were given a code to indicate the sort of chase and defense that they could expect from a Game. Belmont's considerable size and muscular build aided him on Red Level Games, and he was often requested. He practiced Muay Thai and was known to hit hard and not hold back. Some Immortals liked that, preferring a good, hard run with a bit of struggle before the feeding. It lent a reality to the game that the symbiont craved when a Sanglant fought back with all of his or her might. Other Immortals just played games for laughs. It truly all depended on the client.

On occasion, a Sanglant would be killed during Red Level Games. It was infrequent, a highly unlikely probability, but it did happen. When the unfortunate did occur, the client was usually socially marred within their community or worse. Loosing oneself in the thrill of the hunt to where they drained their Sanglant dry, following that thrushing pulse of their heart to that last solemn beat, was a stigmata that most symbionts wished to avoid.

Sometimes, Sanglants inadvertently got themselves killed. The muscular bound man had heard tale that during one Red Level Game a young girl, while fleeing onto some tracks from her pursuers was hit by a subway car. For the most part the games were relatively safe. A few nicks and cuts; a little scrape here and there and some bruising, but that was par for the course.

Extinguishing the light of a Sanglant had dire repercussions: banishment from The Service for a considerable length of time and being penalized with a hefty fine. There were rules to follow. One could not just do as they pleased with them. Murdering their most prized possessions was not the sort of thing that The Council took lightly. Everyone knew murder happened, that every now and then one of the bloodsuckers plucked an average nobody from off the streets to satiate the urge of the Jadaraa Soo. It wasn't supposed to happen, but it did. It wasn't talked about in social circles. Nobody addressed it openly. But killing Sanglants? That was strictly forbidden.

There was talk of one vampire, a while back, that had been blacklisted from The Service for abusing his Sanglants, so he took to hunting regular folk. There were always rumors like that and such tales floating around the herd. How one person heard it from so-and so, but no one ever knew about it directly. This tale, however, was supposed to have been the real deal, written about in all of the papers because the symbiont amassed a body count. The local authorities had intervened before The Council could clean it up and the whole thing turned into a hot mess. This was long before Belmont's time, of course, and from what he heard, The Council ordered the death of that Immortal and he fried in the sun.

Extermination by sunlight, Belmont learned, when he first became a blood lender, wasn't like it was portrayed in the movies. Immortals did not just burst into flame at the mere sight of the sun. It was a long and slow process that lasted almost the entire day. It was known to be agonizing and extremely painful. The Jadaraa Soo did wither and die by the sun's touch. It dehydrated slowly, becoming brittle and hard. It would alight to fire only after it had dried, burning the unlucky vampire from the inside out. Of course, this usually happened after blindness and paralysis had rendered the creature incapacitated and immobile, so that its slow death was assured. It was rumored that the Immortal was still conscious as he or she burned from the inside out and that its agony would not cease until its head was severed from the body.

Belmont didn't know if any of these stories were true. He'd never seen an Immortal executed and the symbionts weren't too gregarious with the how and why of their world. If you followed the rules, played along, and if they liked you, you advanced. If not? Well…let's just say the rate that Sanglants became Immortals was incredibly lower than the rate at which humans became Sanglants. It was a highly competitive field and the opened positions among the hybrid ranks were desperately coveted. Some Covens even went so far as to sponsor competitions with their Kulaks that awarded the sole survivors with membership into their brood. Different regions and countries had different ways to promote blood lenders to Immortals. The Council governed each and every one of them. So, no one became a vampire now-a-days unless it was sanctioned.

"You know, you're the only one who gives me oranges," Belmont said as he peeled the bright, round victual.

The vampire sat on the bed next to the naked man. "How else are you to regain your strength after?"

He smiled. "It's sweet."

The beautiful, hulking man took a bite from the fruit. Lin watched as juice sprayed into the air and rolled down his lip to the cliff of his chin. She wiped the sticky liquid from his jaw-line with her finger before he could reach it. Lin smiled and then licked the small bit of juice off of her own digits.

"I used to tend an orange grove in Brazil," Lin told him. "I'd take my son on walks among the trees. We'd listen to the pickers sing, share the fruit, and William would ride the carts." She smiled, remembering him laughing.

She had that faraway look about her and began fidgeting with her locket again. Belmont knew better than to ask personal questions, so he continued to eat his orange, letting the Immortal's memory take her to a place that only she could visit. This was commonplace among the breed. Their memories were often the nest that carried their attentions away. A lot of the Immortals opened up to him during his visits. Some didn't. Belmont just figured that it had to get awfully lonely sometimes, living a life that never ended. He wondered how he would handle it.

Lin Pevensey was a regular of his. He knew a little bit about her. Though, it wasn't much really. Lin was never that talkative and they had never had sex during a feeding. Unlike her flatmate, Z, who liked to ride him as if he were a bucking bronco while she tapped his veins, Lin was strictly business. Belmont couldn't help but notice how she was built for speed. He excited her and though Lin never specifically asked for him to be clothed or unclothed during their sessions he could tell that she didn't mind his nakedness. He found her eyes wandering now and again to his junk, but it never led anywhere. During one feeding a few years back, she let her hand fall between his legs. She fondled him lightly, but nothing else happened. Nor had anything like it ever happened again, even though Belmont often wished it would.

Lin Pevensey was a missionary feeder. She liked it from the nape of the neck in the curve from the shoulder. Her puncture marks stung a little, as bites always do, but the vampire had not taken that much blood from him this time. It was obvious to Belmont that their time together would be longer and the feeding would be spread throughout the day. He liked that.

It was easier to handle and Lin always made him feel comfortable, unlike other Immortals sometimes did.

"You were Dominique's consort, weren't you?" he asked after a spell. It was a safe question.

Lin nodded that she was, just as the stereo in the other room blasted back to life. This time it was the Dead Kennedy's Plastic Surgery Disasters. Belmont chuckled. It was obvious to them both that Z was still a little pissed at being left out and she was getting back at them with loud music. It was childish really. Neither one of them minded the machine gun tunes all that much. The sound proofing in the penthouse was very good.

"Do you mind if I ask why you never took a seat on The Council?"

Lin shook her head, indicating that she did not mind and thought about his inquiry even though the answer was readily available. "While Dominique and Ramielle were busy forming The Council I was in South America funding military coups and guerilla resistance to the Brazilian slave trade."

"Wow," the man piped, raising his eyebrows. He hadn't known that, and took a bite from his fruit.

"I'd been fighting continuously for decades really. So, when I was asked the only thing I wanted at that point in time was to enjoy a little peace and quiet. Becoming a council member didn't sound like it was going to be all that quiet. So, I went to Asia." She chuckled, thinking about it. "I had always wanted to go to China, but Dominique was too afraid that the Emperor was going to chop off her head like he had promised."

"Do you think he would have done it?"

"Oh yeah, without a doubt," Linnet answered riotously laughing.

The vampire played with her necklace and Belmont watched her suspiciously. "Isn't that silver?"

"Yeah," Lin nodded.

"May I see it?" He sat up and swallowed the last orange wedge. He licked his fingers clean before picking up the necklace. He opened the locket. "I thought silver was poisonous to your kind."

He stared at the picture. The photograph was a black and white portrait of a beautiful woman. Her hair was done up in a Victorian style and she looked of Spanish decent, but the clothing of her neckline suggested American tailoring. Belmont's eyes did not detect these details. He simply noticed how pretty the girl in the photo was, and said so.

"Silver is poisonous if gets under the skin," Lin added as he closed the decorative wings and handed it back to her. "See how they run from it?" She indicated with her eyes how her veiny blood parasite retreated from her fingers when she touched the silver locket.

"That's completely wicked," noted Belmont, watching the ever-present veins of the Jadaraa Soo dive deeper into the vampire's body.

"My skin protects me from the silver."

"But? What if…"

"It's not pretty," she pointed out, catching his gist. "Silver poisoning is fatal. Even the smallest amount in our blood can be quite devastating."

"If that's the case, then why wear it?" He looked up at the dauntless hybrid. "Aren't you afraid that the silver might seep through your skin?"

A flash of memory tore through Lin's vivid mindscape: *The bloody, dead hand of a woman hung out from a pile of mangled corpses. The chain of the necklace was twisted around the dead girl's lifeless fingers. The locket lay in her blood-covered palm. The thick stench of death and sand stung her nostrils as her ears vibrated with the manic cackling of Jordan and Prophet. The eyes of Ramielle Eirinhas bore through her ragged soul and bits of flesh were stuck between her teeth.*

"Enough with all this talk," Lin said, rising up and pushing against Belmont's broad chest so that he would lie back on her bed. "Don't we have more banal matters to contend ourselves with?"

Lin straddled the naked man and sat upon his mid-section.

"That we do," agreed the meat wagon, "that we do."

Belmont stretched his throat for her so that she might more easily attack her first bite at the base of his neck, but the vampire chose to excite a different mark. Trailing her fingers across his muscular chest, Lin's tongue fondled the tip of a fang, and Belmont knew that he was in for something different from the missionary immortal. In anticipation of Lin Pevensey's bite his handsome member grew hard and Lin felt it poking her beneath her jeans, pressing upon her dormant sex.

She looked down at the beautiful man and picked a place to plant her teeth on his golden tanned chest. From the other room, the Dead Kennedy's song, *Bleed For Me*, ironically rocked through the soundproofed walls. The volume on the stereo had to be deafening for it to reach Lin's room. The mechanical physics of waveforms and density were not the foremost thoughts ebbing across Lin's cerebral cortex. She heard the clatter of wind, the banging shutters holding tightly in a sandstorm. She inhaled Belmont's musk. Right now, she needed the distraction from the nightmare of her memory and the Sanglant was tantalizing. Lin wanted to forget. She wanted to forget her past and forget that Z was dying. Lin fixed a spot just above his left nipple and dug in. Her silver locket fell gently across Belmont's palpitating abdomen.

Lin's teeth were sharp and painful in a delightful way. The Prêteur de Sang sucked a cool breath through his teeth as Lin sucked his blood. He enjoyed the change of pace from this regular client. It held promise. As the veins that comprised her teeth unwove itself from its shape and snaked through Belmont's delicious brawn his manhood pulsated steadily against the rigid seam of her denim pants, knocking to get in.

1776. São Paulo, Brazil.

Sergeant Francisco da Sillva sat holding his wife's hand. Her breathing was growing shallow. She would not last the night. Linnet had been waiting in the military man's small, rented domicile with Vaz and Thiago for nearly an hour now and still there was no sign or word from Jabajara or Dominique.

Vaz had fallen asleep. Thiago was holding it together but it was clear that the man wanted nothing more than to curl up in his own straw bed. Even Linnet felt the tug of sleep pull at her arm, but she was too restless and agitated, vexed at the slow pace at which her inquisition plodded. Just when she was about to give in and resort to violence as a means of extracting the information that she wanted from the Sergeant, there was a knock at the door.

Now.

Ryan answered the door and Lacey stood behind the busted screen wearing her favorite leather coat over a white blouse, a plaid school skirt, black socks pulled up to her knees, a pair of rugged Docksiders, and worry falling off her face like a leper.

Thirty Seven Minutes Ago.

Ryan dug in the trunk of his car looking for his crowbar only to find that he didn't have one. Upon pressing his neighbor, whom Ryan had only met once, if he could borrow his crowbar, the best the neighbor could offer was a four socket tire iron. If Ryan were actually trying to fix a flat then the tire iron would have been incredibly handy, but since Ryan intended to pry open a gray painted metal door at the bottom of a parking garage, the iron would not work.

So, after a quick trip to Walmart and a jaunt through the automotive aisle, Ryan had in his possession a new and usable crowbar. As he stood in line waiting for the woman with two screaming kids to hurry it up and forget about price checking the slacks that looked three sizes too small for her very prodigiously round hips and bottom, he wondered why it was called a crowbar. It didn't look anything like the soulless, black bird. One end had a socket, bent at an angle, to loosen or tighten the nuts on one's car wheels and the other end was filed down to a sharp wedge. There was nothing crow-like about it!

Now.

Ryan opened the busted screen door to let Lacey in. His apartment wasn't what she was expecting. What appeared to be his telephone and answering machine was scattered in tiny bits all across the floor and it was hard to avoid crunching the little pieces of plastic with every step she took further inside. Dishes filled the sink. The garbage needed taking out. In a jagged pile on the kitchen counter was a stack of unpaid bills, which hadn't even been opened yet.

Lacey sighed. Ryan didn't look that good either. He was thinner than usual, like he hadn't been eating, needed a bath, and dark circles surrounded his eyes like a tired raccoon.

"Can't say I like what you've done with the place. But now I know why you haven't returned any of my calls."

"Yeah, well...I had to fire the maid. Caught her snorting coke and banging the chauffeur on the veranda near the pool."

She looked at him with a wrinkled brow. "Its good to see you haven't lost your sense of humor."

He returned her stare. "What are you doing here?"

"I wanted to show you these."

Lacey held up a standard manila envelope, indicating the pictures inside. It was similar to the envelope that he had sent to Z with his most recent blood letter. The artist soon became distracted by a tip of white bandaging poking out from behind the sleeve of Ryan's shirt. Lacey sighed again knowing full well that he'd gone and cut up his other arm. She regarded his thin frame and worn features finally understanding the gravity of her friend's downward spiral. Her face twisted into an even more pathetic clump of worry than when he'd found her at the door.

"Don't," Ryan preemptively uttered. "I'm not in the mood to hear it today."

"Jesus, Silva," the artist declared. "What's going on with you? Have you looked in a mirror lately? Talk to me!"

Genuine concern scrunched Lacey's brow and she felt close to tears.

"Thanks for the pictures," he commented curtly. "But, perhaps you should just leave."

Ryan's stalwart obstinance floored Lacey. He was the only person that she thought she really knew. He had always been there for her and she for him and she thought he'd be the one that would never shut her out. They talked about moments like this when they were together and promised each other to always let the other person in, even if it wasn't what they said they wanted at the time. But his door was closed. Bolted. Locked. He had walled himself away from the world. The normally lewd, opinionated brunette opened her burgundy painted lips, but there was nothing that launched off her tongue. So, for a long, tense minute she just stared at him and he just reflected an angry, impassive wall.

"Really," he added to break the awkward silence. "You should go. I've got things to do."

A tear parachuted from Lacey's eye as she crossed the plastic, shrapnel floor to her ignorant friend. She pressed the envelope of pictures against his bony chest, holding them there, and peered into his deadlocked eyes, standing in his oxygen, breaking apart.

"Don't shut me out," his one-time lover pleaded. "I know you can't see it right now, but you need me. You need somebody to drag you back from this black hole you've got yourself in. Your fallin' baby, you can't see it, but you are...and I'm afraid you ain't gonna come back this time. I'm really afraid you..."

Ryan grabbed the manila envelope and stepped back, breaking the circle. "Thanks. I'll look at these. I'm sure they're great." He shook his head in a tight cage.

Lacey couldn't move. She was floored and staring at Ryan's ghost. He had already checked out. The room swam, the garbage stank, and he was standing at the far end of a tunnel. She wiped the tears from her cheeks smearing her eyeliner.

"What you..." she started.

Ryan immediately cut her off. "*Really*. I've got things I gotta take care of."

He avoided her gaze and walked to the opened inside door. Lacey stayed planted for a minute. She breathed heavy looking at him. Sadness filled her hollow vessel like the rising waters on a sinking ship. Eventually, she slowly headed toward the door. She didn't know what else to do.

When she reached him she turned, leveling herself to his gait and in the softest, most gentle voice that Ryan had ever heard come out of the battered filth wagon that was Lacey Chaney's crude mouth, she invited him to attend her art opening this coming weekend, pressing upon him how much she really wanted him there. Ryan said that he would come, a polite service. But Lacey knew he was lying.

She opened the busted screen door, it creaking in the late afternoon sun, and left Ryan's apartment feeling like the parting tore away flesh from the innocent child of her creative being. She sniffled and wiped her eyes again, smearing black make-up, and the flimsy busted door hammered in its frame and rocked to a close.

1776. São Paulo, Brazil.

Thiago was closest to the door so he answered it. With him standing in the way, Linnet could not see if her pale mistress was at the threshold. All the anxious woman saw was the muscular back of the larger than average native. After what seemed like an eternity of waiting, Thiago moved aside so Jabajara could enter. Dominique was nowhere in sight.

Linnet was livid. Her face flushed red and the Tupi servant shrank back for fear of a violent reprimand. Meekly, he told her that Dominique wasn't anywhere to be found at Casa del Rio Dulce, but Linnet did not want to hear it. She had wasted enough time already. Francisco needed to talk, whether he wanted to or not!

The angry charge stormed into the Sergeant's bedroom telling him that she had had enough. The scene was not what she expected and it caused her to pause. Francisco da Sillva was strewn prostrate across his wife's belly, weeping. In her fury and huff she barely noticed that Ema, the Sergeant's wife, was dead. He looked up at her, seething hatred so focused that it boiled through the coarse red-streaked retinas of his eyes, and the man was on her instantly with both hands clamped around her throat, squeezing the life out of her.

They crashed through the opened doorway and Vaz woke with a sudden start. Jumping up, he knocked the pistol off his lap. It landed on the floor and the firing cap fell off, rolling under the chair from which he sprang. Thiago quickly raised his musket, but the Sergeant turned, lifting Linnet off her feet to obscure his line of fire. The Lady of Casa del Rio Dulce was turning blue. She feebly attacked Francisco's firm grip, but her punches were getting weaker. Jabajara ran to Linnet's aid and the impassioned Sergeant backhanded him across the mouth. He dropped to the creaking floor, spitting up blood.

Linnet tried to speak. She tried to breathe. Raspy, guttural noises erupted from her mouth as the light in her eyes started to dim. Linnet was fading fast. Her body went limp, her vision blurred, and the last gasp gurgled from her split lip just as Thiago clocked Francisco da Sillva upside of the head with the butt of the long rifle.

The Sergeant let go of the dying matron as his knees buckled. He folded like a flag without wind, coming to rest beside the woman he was just trying to kill. Jabajara rushed to his mistress's aid just as Vaz found the firing cap and placed it back where it belonged on the hammer clip. The native turned the gun to where the action was, ready to fire the weapon too late.

Air rushed into the exhausted lungs of Araci and she coughed and spat up her life, rolling onto her hands and knees. After a minute or two, Thiago and Jabajara helped her to stand as she caught her breath. She rubbed her bruised and sore throat as she told them, with a weak and sandpapery voice, to find some rope and tie Francisco up.

Once the Sergeant was sufficiently bound with a rope that Thiago had found among the man's riding gear they propped him up in a rickety chair. Vaz doused him with a bucket of cold water to wake him. Roughly, the Sergeant came round. He panted, getting his bearings, and glared at the three of them with abominate rancor. His head throbbed. He felt cottony. He tried to move, but found that he was tied as if a python had coiled around his mid-section.

"Go on then," he said, the fire of his fight going out. "Do it. Get it over with."

Linnet grabbed the man unkindly by the jaw. His face was beat up just as bad as hers was now. "Not until I get my son."

"Burn in hell." He spat on her.

The spittle landed on the clothing covering her breasts. Linnet wiped it off and smeared it in the man's face, pressing her palm hard against his brow and nose.

"Who has my son?"

The Sergeant said nothing.

"Where is he?"

He shifted his eyes to look at her. "A better place."

Linnet shook her head. "Wrong answer."

She stepped out of the way and Thiago slammed the butt of the musket into the man's stomach. He grunted in pain, twisting up from the blunt force, coughing and spitting up saliva. As he sat there curled over the volcano in his gut he started laughing through the searing pain. He lifted up. Drool hung from his bottom lip and chin, snot dripped from his nose, and he laughed.

"There is nothing you can do to me." His cackles mixed with tears. "Nothing. Nothing. You will never get your son back I promise you that. I promi…"

Thiago hit him again and his promise was spat onto the rustic floor. Once the initial rivet and explosion of pain subsided to the constant dull ache of torture he laughed again. He laughed and Linnet knew he was never going to tell her who had his son and where they were keeping him. He probably never knew where William was, just as he had told her at the beginning of the night. Thiago was about to clock the belligerent,

Portuguese murderer once more, but Linnet stopped him, telling the vengeful native that he had had enough.

Dawn hid behind the door of the Sergeant's empty home and Linnet was no closer to rescuing her only child than when she set out twenty-four hours earlier to look for him. She was devastated at her failure, but was too fatigued to truly feel the full gravity that it bore. The cogs of her thinking capacity turned slowly and the only sound that registered in her ears was her own, raspy breath. The inevitability of morning killed the possibility of hope. Linnet turned to the soldier and told him to get up.

"We're going for a little walk."

The Market Square was already busy by the time they arrived with their prisoner in tow. The morning was golden and cool. For all sense and purposes, it was a beautifully fine day. Linnet and her troop looked the worse for wear. People stopped in their tracks and turned in their direction, gawking. The sight of Linnet Albee leading Sergeant Francisco da Sillva tied with a thick hemp rope and followed by three armed natives was disturbing. They were all dirty, disheveled, bruised, and bloody. Linnet held in her hands a soiled machete and a rolled piece of paper.

People followed them to the center of the square, where Ms. Albee brought a halt to her parade. She looked at them as they gossiped about what they witnessed, seething to add this little atrocity to the mounting rumors that had been spread about her. She didn't like the townsfolk of São Paulo all that much, but they were consistent. They didn't like her either. She scared them because she was independent. They stood on baited breath to catch the latest tidbit from Casa del Rio Dulce and it was their morbid curiosity with her going-ons that she hoped to curry favor in now. It was why they gathered. It was a spectacle and a show. She told Thiago to put the Sergeant down on his knees as the interest of the crowd climbed to a fever pitch.

"Two nights ago," the exhausted, brazen woman shouted. "Men, led by this man, Sergeant Francisco da Sillva, broke into my home. They murdered my aid, Laurel Davenport, and fourteen of my most valued servants, and stole my nine-month old son."

Shocked and frightened gasps erupted through the assemblage like a ripple and Linnet let them whisper about it. She allowed them the fury of their tongues to whip their gossip. Since she had arrived at São Paulo she was a common topic among many of the people that were gathered around her this morning. Her life and activities, true or not, were continual fodder for their devilish minds. Too many times it had worked against her, now she would control the flow of information. She would rile them up in a way that they had never been. She would stir the fetid cauldron of the social contract and flush the Sergeant's silent co-conspirator out from the bush in which he hid.

"Is that not what you did Sergeant?" Linnet asked loud enough so the crowd would hear.

He refused to answer until Thiago gave him an ungentle rap to the ribs with the muzzleloader.

"Yes," he grunted softly.

"Louder," Linnet urged through clenched teeth.

"Yes!" He shouted and glared at the woman with all of his hate.

At the Sergeant's admittance the crowd gasped as one giant sigh. Linnet raised her fist high above her head, tightly holding onto the rolled confession, which the condemned man had written earlier that night, his profession and plea to God. "I hold in my hand the written confession of Sergeant da Sillva," screamed Linnet. "It details his participation in these crimes and names *all* those involved who helped plot and carry out these heinous acts."

If there were any doubters among the crowd at this point they were swayed by the sight of Francisco's signed and sworn statement. The Sergeant stared up at Linnet, shocked at the blatant lie that he had listed the names of all those involved.

"I want my son!" Linnet shouted to the impassioned crowd. "They still have him and won't give him back."

The crowd booed and hissed, pulled ever so easily to Linnet's favor. A vendor threw some rotting vegetables at the Sergeant, hitting him with the limp produce.

"I want my son!" Linnet screamed again and the crowd hollered for him to return the boy to her.

It finally dawned on the Sergeant what the malicious devilkin was up to, but before he could shout out against her the crippled mother turned and stabbed him through the sternum. He felt the tug of the rope around him loosen as the machete blade slit the binds, piercing his chest. His breath caught in his throat. Linnet stared into his beady, little eyes as his death washed the complexion from his face, spilling across her hand.

She did not look away. She remained transfixed to the Sergeant's pupils, a vision of motherly anguish, until the last glimmer of life evaporated and extinguished from his eyes. Only then did she rise and remove the fresh corpse from off her blade with the flat side of her foot. The Sergeant's body fell to the cobblestone, in the center of the market, with a hollow, dull thud. The shocked and embittered crowd reacted by pelting the bound corpse with stones and fruit. Linnet and the natives left Francisco's body in the Market Square for the authorities to find.

By the time they reached Casa del Rio Dulce a small contingent of five men from the Portuguese militia were close at hand to breaching the plantation grounds. Linnet dragged her tired feet to the decorative red doors of the Casa-Grande as the thunder of horse hooves galloped up and surrounded her.

She was only a few feet away from the sanctuary of her home and the fulfillment of a bath, sheets, and a bed in which to bury her failure. She was exhausted and frayed, depleted of strength. They ordered her to stop as several of the men dismounted, ready to take her into custody. She was unarmed and alone.

The field hands had returned to their huts and their own family and friends. The sun hid behind a blanket of trees, shooting golden spires of light into the approaching dusk. The messy, raven haired murderess did not fight. She did not speak ill of them, or try to flee. They were just doing their job. She had left her machete in its pouch on the mare's saddle when Thiago took the horses to the stables, and if she had it with her now, she would not have used it. The instrument had tasted too much blood. Linnet let the men grab her by the arms. She held tightly to the sole piece of paper that would save her from the gallows. Though, before they could mount her to a steed and whisk her away from the Engenho a familiar voice broke through the air cautioning the men of service and duty.

"Let her go this instant," Dominique said from atop of the steps. "Or none of you will leave my lands alive. I can assure you of this."

The young Officer perched in his saddle, feet tightly implanted in his stirrups, did not appreciate the tone from the pale looking matron.

"We have orders to arrest this woman and bring her in for questioning concerning the murder of the Sergeant At Arms, Francisco da Sillva," he reported deftly.

"By whose authority?" The Vam Pŷr asked as she descended the steps.

"By Captain Simões, himself."

"Well, you tell Captain Simões that Dominique De'Paul would not allow you to remove the hero that captured and killed the man responsible for the murder of my consort and servants, and that perhaps he should be busying himself with finding Ms. Albee's son, William, who was absconded a fort night ago by brigandes and thieves, while *he* slept duty bound in his bed to protect; instead of arresting helpless women who need nourishment and rest."

Dominique's eyes were impassive, but the man had his orders. In the tense moment between the duty-bound officer and the freed slave of the people of the East, Linnet handed the young officer Francisco's handwritten confession. He read it and grew visibly upset by what the document reported. Their horses stammered, restless, so close to the Bruxsa. The young officer rolled the parchment back up and returned it to the greasy and grimy woman.

"I will take this under advisement with my superiors, but rest assured…" he claimed, having to reign his horse in, "I will return to straighten this matter out."

"And you will be welcomed when you do," said Dominique with a nod.

The young Officer ordered his men to leave the prisoner, fall back, and mount their steeds. The men were obviously upset by the change in events. They knew the Sergeant and couldn't believe the rumors circulating about him. They wanted to arrest this girl and charge her, see her hung by the neck until dead, for killing a man that many thought was a decent and good human being.

As they rode from the plantation, with thundering hooves and the sting and crack of leather whips, Linnet turned to the gaunt vision of loveliness who was simply garbed in a formal black gown of mourning. The need to reproach her for her earlier absence vanished. Linnet wobbled, light-headedly, breathing heavy and said, "Now, I know who has my son."

The exhausted maid crashed toward the ground, a victim of gravity and time. Every muscle of her being gave out from fatigue, lack of sleep, and no food. She landed in the soft, ashen, able arms of Dominique De'Paul.

The needle on the record player skipped statically around the faded, generic label of a Ramones' album. Lin followed the dull, trance rhythm to its source, but Z wasn't anywhere in sight. *Perhaps she called Ryan.*

Lin holstered the needle and curiously flipped through the stack of LPs piled by the player. Some of these albums hadn't been dusted off in decades. Z was being nostalgic. She needed to connect with somebody from this age. *Maybe she gave the obsessive boy a second chance.*

Stretching her spine and cracking her neck, Lin wandered to the clock. Her blood parasite purred, satiated by the blood of the Sanglant. Lin's natural, innate sense told her it was Dusk, but she wanted to be sure before she raised the blinds. *Nothing like an accidental suntan to start the evening off right!*

She picked up the apartment's remote and hit the tiny button that lowered the huge metal shields, folding the slats into each other as they fell into their closet sills. The mechanical whine and flap filled the expanse of the penthouse. It was a calming rhythm, a gentle cascade. Lin noticed the door to Zia's Hot Box was wide open. She went to investigate and found the rascally vamp sitting in a ratty old comfy chair holding Buddy Holly's guitar in her lap. She looked asleep; but then again, she looked awake when she was asleep. So, Lin didn't really know if she was truly there or not. Good thing Z spoke or Lin might have stared at her all night.

"Peepshows cost extra, you know."

Lin entered the vampire's treasure trove of curiosities, oddities, memories, stolen artifacts, and junk. "Wanna go out tonight. Some place new. Different," stated Lin in her usual, candid way, asking Z if she wanted to go.

"Got any place in mind?"

"No," she drew out, leaning against a rack of vinyl albums. "Thought we'd cruise around 'til we found trouble."

"Sounds like my kinda party," Z joined, rising and placing Buddy's guitar back on its stand. "Belmont leave?"

"He's sleeping. I taxed him pretty heavy."

"He's a big boy. He can take it." Z sized Lin up exiting her Hot Box. "You take him on a 'lil Linnet Love Boat Ride?

Lin embarrassed, laughed, and scrunched her face up with a definite, "No."

Z whistled. "He's good." She relished the words as if the man was between her thighs.

"You're crazy, you know that?"

"Absolutely," Z agreed, throwing her arm around Lin. "Without a doubt; certifiable." She cocked her eyebrows high. "And that's why you love me." She kissed Lin on the cheek and mussed up her hair.

Z bounded to her turntable, mouthing a fast paced drum rhythm. She removed the Ramones' record, jacketed it, and searched for another LP to listen to as she got dressed to go out. Lin watched her. A small smile curved her lips and a quiet peace settled in her bones. Z was alive and vivacious as ever.

"Whatdaya think?" said the colorful, hyper vamp turning to sport two albums. "Violent Femmes or Bad Brains; I Against I." She spoke the title of the last album in a low, guttural voice that sounded twisted and demonic, but before Lin could provide an answer Z shouted, "Wait! I got it."

She tossed the two choices aside, unsheathed a different album and loaded it on the turntable. A few seconds later the Stooges graced the stage.

"Belmont told me Freya's petitioning Dominique to sanction his ascension with The Council."

"Yeah! Wooha." Z responded along with Iggy, bobbing her head. "He deserves it." Then the playful vamp struck a classic Pop pose, singing, *'Down on the street where the faces shine. Floatin' around I'm a real low mind. See a pretty thing - ain't no wall. See a pretty thing - ain't no wall.'*

"Do you have something to drink?" a naked Belmont interjected over Z's musical escapades.

'No wall, no wall, no wall.'

"Isn't that what we've got you for?" Lin smirked, a devilish grin.

"Funny," the Sanglant mused, enjoying the vampire's humor.

"C'mon," the raven haired client directed, "in here."

Z shouted over the crunch of guitar to the naked beefcake walking around her penthouse. "Don'tchya think ya shoulda put on pants?"

Belmont stopped and turned to Z so as she could get a good look. "Is it bothering you?"

"Oh no," the vampire said, admiring his member. "Not at all. I love the little pony show."

Z wiggled her finger and bit her lower lip, sort-of dirty dancing to *Down on the Street,* being playful with the adored Sanglant. She neared him, and across the street in the adjacent building Ryan Silva got an eyeful, growing angry as he spied what was happening in the penthouse suite. He gripped the binoculars with an infinite fury, focusing.

"So, I hear you're about to become one of us," the rascally vampire noted, dancing around the naked man.

"Yeah," said Belmont, turning to go wet his own whistle.

"Welcome to the freak show," Z offered with her arms raised, getting back into the groove of the song.

'*Deep in the night I'm lost in love. Yeah, deep in the night I'm lost in love.*'

Through the two, tiny locking circles of the binoculars Ryan followed the naked man until he was out of sight.

'*A thousand lights look at you. A thousand lights look at you.*'

An infinity loop of rage boiled under the surface of Ryan's skin. His mind reeled at all of the possibilities that the naked man could have enjoyed during the excruciatingly long hours of the day with the sun shields drawn tight against his peeping eyes. Worry shattered his reason and his breathing hiccuped, gaining pace.

'*I'm lost, I'm lost, I'm lost — yeah!*'

1776. São Paulo, Brazil.

Though Linnet was convinced that Captain Miguel Simões was her man, Dominique was not. She rationalized that it was a perfectly obvious chain of command decision for him to have ordered those men to come and arrest her. She did, as the elder woman pointed out, just murder the Sergeant At Arms in a public forum. Linnet followed her reasoning, but something still stuck in her craw about the Captain.

Since she'd returned that night Linnet also felt a slight distance between the two of them and wasn't sure why. The timing for such an ebb and flow of this kind of chasm was not what the young maid needed from her partner right now. Instead of being with Dominique in her bed below the house, Linnet was asked to sleep in her solemn room, alone in the big house where every shadow crept like an intruder or ghost and William's crib still remained empty.

The bath that Dominique gave Linnet after she'd awakened from fainting and taken a small repast of liquid and fruit was loving and gentle. *Why couldn't each day be like that?* The Persian beauty insisted that she wash Linnet and ran the water for the bath herself instead of sending one of the field hands to do it.

The house was a lonely shell of its former self with most of its occupants dead. In the vacant repose of the dark, silent dwelling the two survivors lavished in each other's company, enduring their sudden isolation together. While her strange paramour slowly pulled the soft, damp cloth across her naked back the young woman asked her why she wasn't at home when Jabajara came looking for her.

"I was hunting," the stoic blood slave recalled. "I had to feed, lest I loose my arm to the cut."

The consort turned and looked at the night creature.

"A wild boar." Dominique answered, knowing full well the question that plagued the young woman's mind. "It gave quite a chase, I assure you. It's skin was tougher than I remembered. It seems that I've grown accustomed to the delicate palette of you and Laurel in my old age."

Linnet stroked Dominique's face lovingly, wetting her cheeks with sudsy water, remembering their fallen companion. In her rush to find William, Linnet did not have much time to mourn her fallen sister. The great big house was absent of her vibration and scuttlebutt. Its roof worn by bloodstains and stark memories, felt drained.

"I'm sorry I was gone so long," said Linnet in that way that made Dominique's dead heart ache.

"I'm only sorry that William did not return with you."

Linnet pulled her knees tighter to her wet chest as Dominique lifted her long black hair to ferret the cloth around the jewel of her neck.

"Perhaps," Linnet started slowly. "It is for the best…" The woman paused, a rigid ball in the tub, a bucket of snow in her chest as Jaci listened to the silence falling around them.

The moon's bone white fingers spread out like a smile, separating like teeth, through her paramour's coal black tresses – water squeezed through the delicate touch and fell into the murky bath. "…It has been so long since you and I have been so…alone together. Perhaps, it would be best if…"

"We will find your son, Linnet," Dominique affirmed, cutting the words out of the young girl's mouth.

The crippled mother just stared absent-mindedly at the suds and ripples in the water.

"I promise you," avowed Mother Night again. "We will find William."

There was a long silence before Linnet meekly agreed with her. "Yes. Of course we will."

The space preceding her consort's answer was disturbing to Dominique to say the least. The Vam Pŷr had never seen her maid so disheartened. It vexed her to see her lover so troubled, without hope. Linnet failed to fully impart her meaning to Dominique. She felt black and hollow inside just thinking about it. She knew they would find William. She did not know how or why she knew this, but she knew that he was still alive, and most importantly, it was like what the Sergeant had told her, he was in a better place.

Linnet wanted nothing more than to be with Dominique. She wanted her with every fiber of her being without reserve or compromise. The prospect of them being together without a crowd of production and people thrashing around them was tantalizing – *she had to admit it*. And the new mother felt wretched for feeling that way, even though it was, after all, how she felt.

When the candlelit bath had concluded, Linnet joined her dark mistress below, grabbing an orange as she passed through the kitchen unclothed. In Dominique's chambers Linnet begged to be taken, pulling the enigmatic shade into the nape of her neck and allaying her fears that her body could handle it. Dominique could smell the bloom of Linnet's sex blossom its bountiful flavor at her touch. Her bare curves and voluptuous flesh incited the bloodsucker to undress her fangs and plunge them deeply into the willing canvas of skin.

In the throes of the feeding they made love. Each, holding the other like desperate life rafts amid a turbulent sea. Each woman knew silently in their hearts that all they truly had together was this moment. In their hungry arms they were dying, cradling their evanescent dreams of tenderness. There would be no tomorrows like this one. Fear and necessity wed their passions to unclothe their guilt so they could hide in the grotto of mingling limbs.

Several days later the letter came.

It was inconspicuous looking. A thick unbleached parchment surrounded by another parchment no bigger than the size of a strong man's hand. Dominique recognized the wax seal immediately. It was a seal she used over a hundred years ago. It was the crest of Isabela da Nóbrega.

Linnet was out in the South fields when the letter arrived. Dusk faded through a patch of thickening gray clouds, orange wafted on a faint breeze, and Dominique stood on the eaves of the roof reading the contents of the letter. She was not surprised at what she learned from it. It made perfect sense when she considered it. The estranged Vam Pŷr was only perplexed by whether or not she should tell Linnet that Isabela held her son.

As Belmont dressed, he asked the vampire a delicate question, one that he knew he could ask Lin Pevensey. Other Immortals would have scoffed at his inquiry or worse yet, delighted in taking him close to the question's brink, without ever providing an answer. It was a thought that had been matriculating his interest for some time now and with his ascension soon to be granted it occurred more and more often to him.

"What is it like to drain someone?"

The query struck the raven haired beauty as a bit odd as she counted out the three thousand dollars that she'd planned on giving the blood lender for his services. This amount also included a thousand dollar tip. Payments to The Service were either made directly to active members just as Lin prepared to do this evening or on a monthly billing cycle that included both live and inert deliveries. It was all so neat and organized. Very normal and regular, an institution that Dominique, with the aide of Ramielle Eirinhas and Michele Delacriox, had set up during The Council's formation in the Nineteenth Century.

"José Onofre," spoke Lin after a long pause in which Belmont figured his question would go unanswered. "He was a greasy barrel of a man. Son of a bitch, he pissed me off." Her tongue absentmindedly toyed with the tip of a fang as she reflected. "Can't remember what he did now. But, I recall…relishing the thought of snuffing him out, like nothing else was an option. I had to do it. I *wanted* to do it." The vampire paused with that glazed look in her eye that Belmont knew so well. "But, after…" the mood of the revenant shifted and she finally looked the Sanglant square in the eyes with earnest. "I followed his heart down to its last beat. He was a bastard. A cruel man. And I wept. I didn't so much take from him everything that I could, as much as I lost some part of myself that I knew I'd never get back."

Belmont just stared at her. It was more honest than he had thought she'd give. Lin smiled and handed him his money.

"Thank you," he said more for her honesty than for the wad of cash. "When did that happen?"

"Oh," Lin reflected, "a couple of years after I was turned. 1788… No…'89." She shook her head, fact checking. "Yeah, eighty-nine."

They both headed out of the bedchambers.

"The next one was in 1835 during a slave revolt," the vampire regaled her guest as she neared the front door. "So was the third."

"Have there been many?" Belmont boldly asked.

The Immortal smirked knowingly. "Let's just say that once you loose something, something else fills the empty space."

Belmont thanked her again, opened the door, and turned to leave.

"Hey," Lin called, remembering. "There's this guy been hanging around; seems like he might fit into your line of work. Could you talk with him for me?"

"Of course," the Sanglant offered, smiling. "Anything for you. You know that."

"Thanks. I'll send him your way." Lin gave him a friendly parting kiss and he left.

The door silently kissed the frame, goodbye.

From the building across the street, Ryan noticed the dark haired bitch and the stranger's demeanor as they reached the front entrance of the Penthouse. It was obvious to him that the naked man was leaving. Ryan would have to race if was going to make it in time. His car was parked in the garage below, so he tore from his predatory surveillance perch just before Lin gave the beautifully tanned and muscular man her friendly smooch.

Ryan's Toyota Camry careened from the parking garage onto the street. He turned the corner to the front of Lin's building just in time to see the naked man dip his head into the backseat of a black Audi. Ryan sighed, easing back from the exhilaration of the hustle and followed the Audi to a bland bunker of a building. The car pulled into a guarded parking garage. Ryan cursed as he pulled his car off to the side of the street. He left the engine of the Camry running.

The building that the Audi entered looked ordinarily impassive like a government building. It was featureless and had little tiny slats for windows. None of them were alit inside. It definitely wasn't built to allow its occupants the luxury of observing the street outside or ferrying golden cosmic radiation inside. The massive block was only two stories high above the ground and Ryan theorized that it held deeper levels.

Frustrated, he waited. Ryan wanted to see if something was going to happen or if the Audi was going to reemerge. He had hoped to question the naked man, who looked just as debonair and handsome with his clothes on as he did gallivanting through the penthouse with his pecker flapping in the wind. Just when the overly eager peeping tom had tired of this jaunt to nothing-ville and was readying to quit, his limited patience was rewarded: Belmont exited the front of the building through a smaller door inset in two huge metal doors that had bolts the size of fists riveted around its border.

The Sanglant walked down the sidewalk in Ryan's direction on the opposite side of the street. Ryan watched him for half a block before he spun the Toyota around and slowly followed him in his car. He crept along for a few blocks when the hulking gigolo turned down an alley. Ryan figured that this was his chance and sped past him down the street. He took the next light and came through the mouth of the alley on the opposite side.

Belmont stepped aside for the car to pass him as glaring lights blinded his eyes. He was surprised when the vehicle stopped. Ryan hastily moved to exit his blue car, but came up short, considering the size of the man and the rippling washboard stomach and biceps he had gleaned through his binoculars. To protect himself he grabbed the newly purchased crowbar that had been sitting in the passenger seat. Ryan Silva exited the foreign sports car, leaving the headlights on to obscure the muscular man's vision. The songbird figured he needed all of the edge he could get.

"How do you know Z?" Came the question behind blaring lights.

Belmont had a hand up, blocking the harsh illumination. "Do I know you?"

"Just answer the fucking question, asshole!"

"Fuck you," replied Belmont.

He turned and started walking back the way he came. The naked man's flippant response didn't go over all that well with Ryan. He wanted answers. He needed to know what they did together all day alone in the penthouse, which didn't require clothing.

"I said, how do you know Z?" Ryan yelled as he slammed the crowbar into the stranger's broad back.

The genteel hulking man winced in pain and thrust his shoulders back into the hurt. He turned abruptly, violence gripping his face as he flared with bright red anger. "You'll be sorry you did that."

Ryan's eyes went wide as the man grabbed him and picked him up with one hand and threw him against the front end of his Camry. The automobile's grill dug into his back and the crowbar flew out of his hand, landing on the dilapidated cement with a volley of clinks and clacks. Ryan, panting from the searing pain that splintered the inside of his ribs, looked up just as the Sanglant was nearly upon him. Without thinking, Ryan reached out and retrieved the crowbar from off the soiled cement and walloped the man hard in the knee and shin.

Belmont went down yelping from the blow. His knees surrendered to the hard concrete as Ryan lifted up, already in motion, and swung the socket end of the crowbar with both hands held tightly around the iron rod. The bent mechanical instrument slammed against the Sanglant's temple, shattering his skull. Belmont fell to the alley floor dead. Ryan rose up, out of breath, and a little disoriented.

"Now, answer the fucking question, you stupid son-of-a-bitch,"

Ryan reiterated to the deceased man unaware of what he'd done. "How'd you know Z and that…" he gulped. "Other one? Whatever her name is."

The naked man, in his fine two hundred and fifty dollar suit, lying in a puddle, did not respond. Ryan looked down at him and saw a small smattering of blood wetting his dirty blond hair and running, in a single streak, over an expressionless forehead.

"Hey?" Ryan uttered, kicking him, catching his breath.

The Camry's motor hummed and Ryan's breathing slowed as his eyes drew in all of the details.

"Get up." He swallowed hard and it felt like sandpaper in his pipes.

Belmont didn't move. Ryan's shoulders slumped and the reality of what he'd done galvanized him to the spot. His mouth hung open in disbelief and his throat went the way of the Sahara. He looked at the bloodstained instrument still held tightly in his hand and then toward the mouth of the alley and the cars passing by on the street beyond the gate of unreason and shattered morality.

"Aw shit," Ryan uttered, feeling a strange numbness enter his flesh and fill his bones.

1776. São Paulo, Brazil.

By the time Linnet woke for the day Dominique was gone. She'd taken the carriage and a team of horses along with Thiago. Cimi brought Dominique's note to the young mother on her breakfast tray, but Linnet never touched the milk, fruit, bread, or cheese because the contents of the note stole her appetite.

My Darling Linnet,

I have gone to procure William. I am sorry that I did not speak with you about this before leaving. Trust me when I say that this was the only way. I know you would have talked me in to going to fetch him yourself. He is with Isabela. She has ransomed his life and safe return for my willingness to meet with her at a time and place of her choosing.

Whatever misfortune Isabela has counted against us I

know she will not harm William, just as J know J am entering a trap of some devise. Jf J am destined to not return then know that my final thoughts were with you.

Always,
D.

Linnet read the small, cut piece of paper a dozen times. She even fled through the house to the root chambers in hopes that it was not too late. Yet the finality of the dark mistress's wish was accurate and assured. She was gone. Linnet cursed herself for allowing Dominique to talk her into sleeping in her own quarters last night. If she had not listened, perhaps the woman she craved would still be here.

Cimi also could offer no other news than Dominique's request to deliver the note once Linnet had awakened. All that was left for her to do now was wait. It was a prospect that did not bode well for the addled consort. The vacant house drew in on her and its solid wood and adobe walls felt more like a tomb.

Traveling by day was risky for the Vam Pŷr. A myriad of things could go wrong. Chiefly among them, were busted carriage wheels and encounters with thieves. Yet it offered Dominique the opportunity to arrive with ample time to scout the location and ascertain the threat of the trap, *if*, as she suspected, that was what was really going on. There was always the slim chance that Isabela, as she claimed in her letter, did rescue the infant from those that had ransacked the Casa. It was a most unlikely prospect, one bordering on the fairy tale side of truth.

Isabela was smart not to leave that much of a window between the delivery of the letter and the demand to reach the rendezvous. Though Dominique knew the cunning and shrewd intellect of her protégé, she hoped she was not smart enough to figure out that Dominique would risk a daylight approach.

By the time they reached the mountainous pass near their destination, dusk was close to descending, but still bright enough that Dominique did not venture outside. Through the thick, velvety curtain that separated the brawny native from the dead Persian princess, Thiago was instructed to look about cautiously.

He returned shortly after nightfall. So silent were his soft padded feet that he would have gone completely undetected had it not been for his masculine odor. He did not reek. Dominique's olfactory senses were merely heightened. Any normal person would have never known the native was stalking them. He reported that a small military garrison, heavily armed, occupied both sides of the appointed area.

So, it was a trap after all. Isabela was as discreet as ever.

The arrogant whelp meant to box Mother Night in and be done with her. Dominique asked Thiago if he had seen William and the man reported that he had not. The Vam Pŷr closed her eyes and thought. Thiago could not help but stare at her. The sheen of her pale skin was almost luminous in the dark wood at night. Something about the woman frightened and humbled him all at the same time.

Dominique listened to his slow, steady breathing amid the jungle sounds. She needed the strong native to return William to Linnet if, for some reason, she was unable to do so. So, he had to remain with the horses and carriage. The vampire usurper would have left proper instructions for dispatching her tutor or she would have brought the child. It was clear that Isabela did not intend for Dominique to escape the ambush and it appeared to the freed slave that her choices were very limited. In the back of her mind, Dominique knew that Linnet would have had a plan by now. *She was ever so clever.*

Dominique walked to a small clearing on the back of a huge rock. It jutted out from the side of the mountain and pointed in the direction from which they came. They had passed a small village ten or so miles back. She glared down on its dimming lights. She tried to think in a manner that reminded her of how Linnet thought and an idea struck. Though, Dominique did not like it. She did not like it one bit. It was highly dangerous and most likely would fail all on its own, but it was all she could think of, and time was running short.

The appointed area, where Dominique was intended to meet Isabela, was a small opening in the trees at the top of the mountain where meadow grasses waved in synchronized dances to the open sky above. The clearing was surrounded on two sides by a ridge. A growth of shrubbery and trees flanked opposite the rock slope on the far side of the meadow so that there only appeared to be one way in or out. A light breeze fingered the leaves of the trees and the quiet rhythms of the forest filled the starry night.

Captain Miguel Simões waited with his men in the tangential piths of a ring of custard apple trees. The thick, fibrous bark of the fanning trunks produced an aromatic scent that did not mix well with the stench of gunpowder, dirty sweat, and murderous intent. The appointed time was midnight. The moon had reached its zenith and waned. His quarry was running late, but he had his orders. He was to wait all night, if need be. His mistress was confident that the ghoul would show. Isabela had taken great pride in crafting the man for the part that he now played. It was her praise and the gift of her affection that he hoped to reward himself with once the nasty business of dispatching Lady De'Paul had been conducted.

Simões's avarice and pride were the perfect breeding ground for Isabela da Nóbrega to launch her assault against the self-imposed and pretentious Vam Pŷr. Isabela was never a slave of the People to the East. She imbibed Omjadda blood at the hands of Dominique. For two years she courted the arrogant shade before she was allowed entry into the hidden realm. Tending to the woman's businesses through her own personal contacts, following her to strange and sometimes barbaric countries, to mend governmental relationships between greedy, fat, revolting men, all to win the confidence and love of the symbiont. All to wed night.

Isabela allowed the creature to feed from her, like a stuck pig, during her nocturnal visits. Admittedly, the Spanish Courtesan enjoyed those brief repasts though she now viewed them with contempt. Dominique had grown fat on her charity. She was Mother Night and the Vam Pŷr was soon to be nothing more than a fading memory. It did not matter that knowing the Persian shade gave Isabela opportunities that she never would have had elsewhere. It did not matter that becoming one of Dominique's Children of Evensong gave her an edge over the world, possessing power and influence that she relished and envied. The out-of-date fool continued to reap the benefits from Isabela's hard-earned labors while she remained locked in the Southern Hemisphere working herself away.

Isabela could not allow Dominique to bleed her any longer. The feeding had to stop! There came a point when the vampire had said enough was enough. Isabela da Nóbrega had called uncle. She had made up her mind that she would no longer support Dominique and her brood with her efforts. The plantation and mining operations in Brazil were as much hers as they were anybody else. The only hitch to that proviso was the annoying little fact that all of the deeds and decaying documents that gave Dominique legal rights were in her name and kept on her person. It was a minor technicality, one that the arrogant revenant helped Isabela to remedy by returning to São Paulo.

But she came with that dog of hers, fat with child. Linnet Albee! Linnet Pangbourn! It made no difference what she called herself. The English bitch played the part that Isabela had crafted for the Vam Pŷr over a century ago! She stole the position that was rightfully hers. *How dare Dominique shower this human whelp with such lavish affection and care! Did she not think that it would reach my ears all of the way across the ocean? Her cavorting and love affair with the girl! Did she think that it would go unnoticed?* The gall that Dominique had to brandish their affair out in the open for the entire world to witness – *It was beyond rude.* It was down right indignant!

Dominique had grown daft and lazy in her advancing years. She rested on her laurels far too often. More than any one who had amassed such wealth and power should. Dominique had taken her previous acquaintances and dearest friends for granted while abroad, treating her new folly with unearned equality. It was sad, really sad, thought Isabela as she schemed and hatched plans to snare the symbiont and take what she felt was rightfully hers. *Truly, sad.*

Of all the things that Isabela was left to deal with over the decades since Dominique's absence, she could not reconcile herself to allow her former pedagogue to turn the pathetic, English trollop into a child of night. Not when she was denied the gift to give to others. That was something she could not allow at all, and if it meant the destruction of Dominique herself…*oh well. She had a nice run of it. Longer than most. Surely, she would be missed, but not by anyone living or walking the earth now-a-days.* Isabela's alliance with the local Portuguese government and years of stuffing the right pockets paved the way for her to make such a reality truth.

She had educated her man on the symbiotic condition and how to dispatch her properly, without the omens of previous failures. Captain Miguel Simões was confident in the ability of his men. He had trained them exactly how Isabela had instructed and she had seemed pleased. There was no way Dominique De'Paul was going to slip through his fingers again. The fiasco with Sergeant da Sillva had tied his hands and created a right well mess for him to clean up in São Paulo. This new stratagem of theirs was, at least, out of his governing jurisdiction. Things could get messy all the way out here in the bush and he didn't have to worry about it. As the snap of a twig told him that his party had arrived Captain Simões intended for things to get messy. *Very messy.*

He noticed moonlight falling on the hood of Dominique's cloak first as she unfolded from the shadow and entered the clearing. He raised his musket as she neared the center of the grasses. His men had strict orders to remain absolutely silent and to fire, only after he had launched the first shot. The Bruxsa slowed, apprehensive. Captain Simões's heart thudded in his ears as she stepped near the mark. Timidly. Slowly. *Almost there.* But, before Dominique could reach the center of the meadow the rotating click of an idiot pulling the hammer back on his musket distracted her attention. She turned.

El Captain Simões did not hesitate. There could not be any mistakes. His dark mistress would not approve of any more failures. He fired and shouted the order and the once quiet meadow erupted in a hail of stinging lead, thunderous claps, and the stench of acrid blue smoke. When the volley of twenty trained guns had released their fury, the Captain immediately order the second wave.

"Baonietas!"

Two times ten men ran from the fertile, vibrant edge of Jauari palms, Anona trees, bedstraw, and wild plantains and impaled the still standing figure from all sides.

"Cutlass!" the Captain ordered, charging into the clearing with six other men.

As the long gunmen held the cloaked figure at a distance with their bayonets the Captain and his men chopped and hacked the woman to bits. It was offensive overkill and the body of Madame De'Paul lay strewn on the forest floor in little misshapen bundles of butchered, oozing flesh.

PART EIGHT:

Fearful Symmetry

One is the outcome of knowledge,
and the other is the outcome of action.
He who knows knowledge and action,
with action overcomes death and
with knowledge reaches immortality.

-The Upanishads

"Why did you want me to call Ryan?" asked Z as she saddled into the baby blue Cadillac next to her beguiling companion.

Lin loaded the smiley face key chain into the neck of the steering column and turned to her friend. "Because despite his idiocy he really likes you and I think he has what it takes to make the cut. He's from this age, and I can see it in you Z, you need someone to connect with who understands what's going on these days. This world is so big and loud. It's moving at a pace that neither one of us understands."

Z cocked her eyebrows, "Yeah. That's true."

"I don't know," Lin concluded, pumping the gas petal. "I just think you should give him a shot." She turned the key and the old engine roared to life, rocking them in the large front seat. "And besides, even if it doesn't work out, what's one less asshole in the world?"

Z chuckled, twisting around in the bucket seat and dived across the armrest, sticking her ass up in the air to ferret through the junk that cluttered the back seat and floor.

"I thought you were going to clean that up?"

The rascally vamp flipped back around with a short stack of CDs. "I am," she assured Lin, tossing the unwanted silver-backed discs into the void of the backseat region until she found something akin to the nudging mood she was feeling.

The raven haired beauty pulled out of the parking space as Z cranked the jams. They entered the lit, paved pathways of destiny and confusion; riding high on the wings of their own illusion, looking for neon light distraction, a pint of warm blood, a good DJ to dance to, and the brilliant dark underbelly of the city of lost angels.

1776. São Paulo, Brazil.

Olim Vasquez was a drunk that just so happened to be crossing the muddy street when Thiago stopped the carriage in front of the only cantina in the small village. Olim huffed and waved the well-to-doers away with the flick of his inebriated hand as he entered the Cantina de Varrão Selvagem.

Dominique peered through the curtains of the carriage window to the hand-carved sign above the doddering door that the drunkard had just entered. A painted boar's head stared back at her, taunting her brisk memory about the hunt and wild meal that she had endured the other evening. The Vam Pŷr considered this a good omen.

"Wait here. I won't be long," she told Thiago as she closed the carriage door, donning her evening cloak.

She opened the pub door, spilling hazy orange light onto the street and entered. Intruding upon the cavorting solitude of the locals, silence descended the room like leprosy, and the insular bunch stared at her ashen form and fancy foreign clothes. Dominique sallied up to the bar.

"A bottle of Cachaça," she ordered.

A gray haired barkeep, unshaven, with one good eye, the other droopy and going blind, rustled an unopened bottle from a hay-packed crate behind the bar and slammed it down in front of the woman. Dominique tendered two copper pieces for it and spied Olim Vasquez sitting alone in the back of the tavern.

The bartender bit his tin to check its worth and the normal hubbub of the evening slowly rose again as the pale stranger took her bottle and joined the lonely man. Olim finished his last drink as Dominique sat. She popped the cork on her trade and filled his glass. The man tensed his jaw as his mouth grew wet. Batting his eyes from the free liquor to the odd-looking harlot, he considered it rude to refuse a drink. So he tossed it back, down the hatch, and set the empty glass on the rutted table. He wiped the refuse from around his mouth as the stranger poured him another.

"I owe you money?" he asked, eyes down, liquor up, spilling the sugary blend past his teeth.

"No." Dominique refilled his glass.

"I dun fixed that fence I fell in, so if it were your sheep, I'll get 'em back."

He splashed more on his chin than the gaping hole in his face.

"Not my fence. Not my sheep." She turned the bottle to the empty vessel again and only filled it half way.

"Then what you want?" He looked up at her. His eyes were glassy, half closed. He sipped the Cachaça from the shot glass.

"I need someone to help me with a little work."

"Leave the bottle and I'll do it in the morning."

Dominique grinned and he set the glass down with a small tap.

"Tonight." She rose, corking the sugar brew. "And you'll be able to buy your own bottle." She tossed a gold doubloon on the table and Olim's eyes lit with fire. "There's five more of them just like it waiting for you outside."

Dominique left the cantina, taking the bottle of Cachaça with her. Olim stared at the coin between his fingers for a short time, feeling its weight. It was more money than he had made in years. Five more like it and he'd have a fortune. Olim Vasquez figured he didn't have anything to lose. What he had to lose was already lost by his calculations.

The Vam Pŷr barely got herself situated in the carriage when the local man busted from de Varrão Selvagem inquiring what she wanted of him. He asked for another drink as he took a seat across from her, claiming that he needed it for his nerves. Dominique passed Olim the bottle and let him pull from the small round end. She watched him. *The ruins of a man, drowning.* What she had in mind wasn't going to save him, but it was a heck of a lot quicker than the road he had already chosen. She took the bottle away from him, wanting him able handed and ready.

"You can have it when we're done."

"With what?" He wiped the wet stain on his lips with the back of his hand.

Dominique explained to Olim that all she needed for him to do was wear her cloak and follow the path to the top of the mountain. Olim was a drunk, but he wasn't stupid. Or so he claimed. Wearing a woman's frock wasn't any big deal. There had to be a catch he surmised. The carriage rocked them from side to side as it climbed the mountain pass. Mother Night assured him that there was no catch and stuck another gold trinket in his breast pocket. The heftiness of the coin, so close to his beating heart, made it difficult to see any other reason but hers.

As the stranger spun it, she was a clothing designer from France, here on a private commission, and would also be accompanying him up the mountain pass to the meadow. Her experiment was a simple one, though it required an assistant. Unfortunately, her regular girl was sick with the cough and she has been urgently pressed to finish the sample by morning from her wealthy client. She also explained that she had just finished this marvelous garment that she wore and needed to test the material of the outerwear and could not fully accomplish such a task by herself if she had to wear it as well. The details for this discernment were vague and mathematical, but Olim did not care. He had two gold coins in his pocket and the promise of a bottle of Cachaça at the end of it.

He'd been to the top of the mountain a few times, but that was in his youth. He knew the path and of the meadow there. It was a lovely enough place to find himself come morning after he woke up and wandered back to town with a handful of gold. People were gonna look at Olim different now that he had money. *Get a little respect.* So, Olim Vasquez donned Dominique's cloak and ventured up the mountain pass to his horrific death as the clever blood slave spied the trained and rehearsed maneuvers of Captain Simões's garrison, high above the meadow from atop the ridge. The revenant was impressed at the deft skill and fortitude with which the Captain had attacked her decoy.

Their single shot weapons exploded and echoed off the rocks of the cliff face as she dropped to the outer edge of the clearing. The Captain yelled for bayonets and the forest came alive with men, charging the slagging corpse as it wavered in its place succumbing to Newton's outlandish theory of gravity. Simões attacked and while their blades were occupied on skewering and slicing Olim Vasquez to pieces the moon crept up behind them. In their prideful moment, in the exhilaration after the kill, when the men's fears and worry had vanished to a celebratory state the Vam Pŷr attacked.

She grabbed the back of the first hapless soldier and tossed him high above her head, slamming him against the jagged and pointy rocks of the ridge. The man's spine snapped in three places. He fell to the edge of the meadow a cripple and prisoner of his own mangled flesh. Dominique then picked up the man's empty musket and walloped the two soldiers that had stood next to the unlucky bastard with the flat, broad stock of his weapon.

Dominique moved in the fashion of a Dervish, twirling like a spiritual dancer of God from her native homelands, and made quick and bloody work of Captain Simões's men. Most of them never even knew what had hit them. A flash of white. A blur of crimson smiles. Dominique tore through them with such speed and voracity that the lost and beguiled spirits of the soldiers remained rooted to this plot of earth forever, haunting the woods of this once tranquil mountain meadow.

She only spared one man. It was the man that her brilliant lover, her pride and confidant had claimed to know where William was when she first returned from her ordeal after the murderous raid. Dominique did not believe Linnet then, but standing here and now, over the cowering Captain, covered in the blood, bile, and gore of so many men, the staunch matriarch was amazed at her consort's innate grasp of the intricate plot. *Linnet's intuitive rumblings were spot on, yet again.* Dominique made a mental note, vowing to never again dismiss, so easily, her paramour's assumptions.

Convincing Captain Simões to take her to Isabela was not difficult after the decimation of his garrison. Dominique was not surprised to find out that she was closer to the ungrateful neophyte than she had hoped. The Captain led the Bruxsa to a hidden cave just a few miles from the appointed meadow. *She would have wanted the news of my death as quickly as it could travel.*

The small cave had been mined to go deeper. Tool marks decorated the narrow walls and led to a spacious cavern below. Dominique could smell water from an underground stream and the decaying rot of corpses unproperly earthed. She encouraged Captain Simões to go first into the torch lit cavern by poking him in the back with his very own cutlass. The man entered the flickering firelight and the staunch presence of Isabela da Nóbrega. The conniving countess stood and applauded. The Captain felt that her adulation of his services was most premature. He tried to say so, but Isabela ignored the military man. Instead, she turned her attention to the black hole of the tunnel and to her former mentor and partner that stood hiding in the abyss.

"Bravo," she said, clapping. "Bravo. Do not keep me waiting, Dominique. It has been so very long since I last beheld your munificence. Please, treat us to your beauty."

The Vam Pŷr stepped into the underground hall, dirty and grimy with gore, holding in her hand the Captain's blade.

"My…" spoke the pale, white figure who was dressed regally in an emerald silken gown and purloin petticoat. "You do look a dreadful mess. I hoped my emissary would have treated you better, but it appears I was wrong." The highborn vampire motioned a finger toward the Captain and ordered her guards to, "Kill him."

Two men stood at either sides of the countess's Brazilian wood chair. Their hair was black as the deepest pitch, had olive tan skins, and heavy eyes. One wore the wisps of a mustache and the other was clean-shaven. Both were tall and thin, revealing sinewy muscle under fine fitting clothes. They lurched forward at Isabela's command, drawing their swords. Dominique trailed them with her blanched, cerulean eyes. The Captain cried out for mercy to his dark mistress, begging for his life. His pleas clung to the stalagmites and the pitiless creature ignored him, staring at her long-lost counterpart. Dominique allowed Isabela's lackeys to get near the Captain before she interjected.

"Enough of this charadé, Isabela. Bring me the boy before this cavern becomes your tomb."

Her preened bodyguards stopped in mid-stride, ready to skewer the Captain just as he had skewered Olim Vasquez, and looked to their Lady for direction. Captain Miguel Simões shivered in his dirty polished boots, sweating, adding his putrid stink to the rally of corpses that lay shoddily buried somewhere within the gouged out rooms and catacombs of Isabela's subterranean retreat. With the mesh of smells Dominique was unable to detect William's scent anywhere in the vicinity.

Isabela smiled and stepped down from her dais. "What makes you think that I would have him here?"

Dominique gripped the hilt of the Captain's sword tighter. "Do not test me further…"

"Test you!?!" exploded Isabela. "You leave me here for nearly fifty years alone, living off the benefit of MY charity, and it is I that tests you?" Her eyes twitched, beady and hard, boring a hole into the Persian woman. "I have been dutiful enough and you've been too arrogant to notice that I've moved on."
Isabela straightened up and a vertebrata in her neck popped. "Did you think to return and claim what was yours? What I've worked to achieve?" She walked slowly around the kneeling Captain, playing with his sweat-laden hair.

"What you've achieved here is an abomination?" Dominique spoke softly. "The town folk fear you. I left on urgent matters with instructions for you to care for our interests and you've perverted them. "

"Look well, Captain," she spoke on sing-song lips, "here is the temptress that you've failed to relieve me of on so many occasions. Watch how she delicately cares." Isabela glared at the Vam Pŷr with wide eyes. She grabbed a large tuft of the Captain's wet hair and pulled his head back as he grunted in pain. She looked down at him. "It is all an act. She doesn't care about anything…or anybody, for that matter." She tossed his head away and he fell to the floor.

"Do get up," she commanded as she crossed to her regal chair. "At least have the dignity to stand on your own two feet and stop your pathetic sniveling."

"The child?" inquired Dominique as she stepped farther into the room.

"Yes," she spoke without turning around, giving her back to the brazen symbiont and tilted her head to the side. "Linnet's brat."

"If you've hurt him there'll be no place for you to run."

Isabela turned and the hem of her gown swooshed against the air. "See?" she appealed to the men of her crew. "See how rudely she judges me?" Isabela grabbed the sides of her gown, ready to sit. "What kind of monster do you think I am?"

The wrinkles on Isabela's brow were cavities of hurt, lined with years of insult; she played the victim to the gross apparition of Dominique standing in the room, covered in the blood of so many slain. There was no other way the pampered wench could play it; she'd been checked. Slowly, the woman sat, staring at Dominique with explicit hate. It filled the cavern like a flood.

"I rescued him." She smiled and there was nothing behind the prideful grin. "I saved him from a life of torment…"

"You sent murderers to *my* house!"

"I was rescuing him from you." Isabela smiled at the look on her former mentor's face and there were a million notions lying in wait behind her thin lips. "What do you think his life would have become under your watchful care? So, attentive and doting. Were you going to wait for him to reach manhood before you converted him into your fold, or are you choosing them younger now?" Her tongue volleyed on the tip of one of her fangs. "That girl you keep with you is so very…very young."

Dominique took a large step into the candlelit room. "I am warning you," she spoke through clenched teeth.

"Yes," she drew out with delicious delight. "You keep saying that."

She chuckled and motioned a command with the flip of her hand and one of her obedient servants exited through a hanging tapestry. Isabela leaned into the cushion of her high-back chair and raised her fingers together like a church steeple. She placed them to her mouth and considered the situation carefully.

Her man with the mustache sheathed his sword, keeping his hand on the hilt, and returned to her side on the dais. Moving closer into the makeshift hall Dominique spied familiar trunks. They were partly opened, stuffed with fabrics, dresses, and jewels. She could see gold poking out from behind various tapestries, uncured and raw, straight from her mines at Minas Gerais. Isabela was right on one thing: she had helped Dominique to build her empire. The woman deserved more attention and appreciation than what she had been previously given. But that did not alter her actions. She had tried, on many occasions, to kill Dominique and her consorts and had nearly succeeded. Laurel and fourteen of her most trusted servants were dead. Their spirits' haunted the hallways and forest of the House on the Sweet River. William was still missing and the contemptible courtesan gloated in the high-backed chair. *What is she playing at?*

As Dominique tried to decipher her former pupil, she recognized many items in the cave as belonging to her collection, which had once filled the grand expanse of Casa del Rio Dulce. She and Isabela had built the plantation together. They forged a strong alliance, and together had carved a hefty portion of property, ships, and wealth from both the Spanish and Portuguese crowns. *It made sense that she felt rejected, but her jealousy was not what had weeded into the fears of the folk of Sao Paulo!*

"Though, I am glad to see that your new bitch has inspired some spunk in you," announced Isabela with the concord of the moment. "I am interested to discover how well you will take care of such a lovely bundle of joy, all by yourself, when you return to Casa del Rio Dulce to find her neck slit and her body dangling from the highest tree."

"How dare you!" Dominique roared, charging the contemptuous courtesan.

Brandishing the Captain's sword, she rammed the broad metal point at the jeweled-laced collar that adorned Isabela da Nóbrega's vulgar neck. The Countess's fervent lapdog unsheathed his own sword and raised it to Dominique's sublime, white throat as she vaulted toward his mistress. The Vam Pŷr's force of motion caused there to be a cut. The man's blade rested in the thick skin of Dominique's neck. Black blood trickled down the sword's sharp gleaming shaft and dripped onto Isabela's pampered lap.

The ungrateful lady laughed loudly. Cackling so lusciously that her braying echoed throughout the cavern hall to the gentle sway of innocent trees surrounding the mouth of the cave. "Kill me," Isabela informed with belligerent confidence, "and you will never reach your darling Linnet in time to keep her whelp from becoming an orphan."

The repulsive neophyte smiled. A vile smile! A smile spread so wide it was a whore where her mouth should have been. Perverted lips continued to bed a deep pronged laugh that was soulless, uncaring, and insane. Dominique lowered her weapon, feeling the unbroken chain of regret fill the expanse of her being. She had made Isabela. She had wed her to night with the blood of Ornn Däm Mu. She had set her above all others and made herself vulnerable to the woman's demented machinations. Her pride for her brood was an opened, festering wound. Isabela's guard removed his sword's tip from Dominique's throat as her eyes flicked up at the mortal. He understood the cold rancor that glared at him. It dropped like lead to his belly and he stiffened his stance, defying the symbiont's efforts to mistreat his queen.

Stepping from the raised dais to the hall floor, Dominique seethed with a boiling hot anger. *Had she sent men back to the house after Linnet? Is she bluffing?* The unknown was a cruel sonnet that lit harsh verse upon Dominique's mind until Isabela's consort returned with a middle-aged Guarani woman holding William in her arms. The baby was asleep and wrapped in the same blanket that had covered him the night he was taken from the house and Laurel was killed.

"See?" Isabela said, motioning for the child. "I am no more a monster than you, my dear." The Guarani woman handed the infant to the ignoble aristocrat, sheepishly avoiding the Vam Pŷr's gaze.

It was her that led killers through my fields. Dominique's knuckles itched around the hilt of the used blade. The symbiont's shoulders bunched and she popped a crick in her neck. She wanted the woman's blood, cracked open and wasted – *full on the floor or stuffed down my jaws.* Laurel's plum-blossom laugh lingered in Dominique's cerebellum until she saw Isabela cradle the child. *Linnet's child.* Whether she liked it or not, she was held in check by the small wonder that rested in the vampire's cold, calculating arms. Dominique counted the trail of corpses that lay strewn before her feet by Isabela's schemes. *Wasted flesh having arrived to this earth a product of biological accidents ground out by the irony of human arrogance.* It had to stop somewhere. *Can I ill afford to lose all?*

William had purpose. He was meant to be a peace between her kind and the tribe of hunters. *So innocent!* Rocked from the cradle at such an early age, before he could fulfill his destiny and become the bridge that would unite two continents of peoples, two species of race, and stay the ardent arms of war. Linnet's baby was not just another child of man meant to walk the earth. *He had a purpose!*

William was the seed that Dominique had crafted between Linnet and the warrior. He was the product of careful orchestration to wed two contrary forces. He was the nucleus of peace that was to be planted in the African landscape, in the now barren lands of the Omjadda's once golden Lanz Gur Mae. Dominique knew this and felt no better than her scheming rival. They were both manipulating others to get what they wanted in this world and it all came down to this: a valley of corpses, the rape of hope, and what Dominique decided to do within the next few seconds.

Could I dare disrupt the prospect of peace for my people now when life still beats in William's little heart? Can I live with myself without the woman whom I've come to love more than existence itself? Can I damn my race to a long suffrage of war that will only end with our eventual genocide? Is simple vengeance worth it?

Dominique saw fear mounting the native woman's brow. Isabela's lapdogs eyed her every move. William was alive in the snake pits of the Countess's arms. *Perhaps my kind does not need saving?* The moon considered the tide of her actions. Here was her protégé acting out against her for her own vile greed of wealth and power. Was this not what Nsia had talked about back in England? *Is this what my children are to become? Base creatures of avarice! Bad enough to live a half-life! But to become akin to the very beasts that tortured and imprisoned me all those years…*it was maddening. That prospect alone caused Dominique to flex her bony white digits around the Captain's cutlass.

All while Isabela plotted, hatching schemes, Dominique was busy mapping out a course of peace for her kind, sacrificing her consort's heart and blood for the cause. The Vam Pŷr felt unappreciated. *My own child stands in the way.* Dominique wondered if this was a sign too, an omen that her Children of Evensong were but a blight on the face of the earth, as the tribe of hunters had assumed. *Are we but the second terror of the Omjadda to be inflicted upon the race of men? Can we not rise above our shackles or should we fall too, just as Rome fell?*

Isabela slowly stroked the infant with her long painted nails. She smirked like a python, her eyes black as her heart and Dominique felt the corners of her mouth turn down. *Perhaps, the song of my people need not be sung.* She sucked a breath through gritted teeth, not knowing what to do. Her head swirled in a conflux of reasons and ideas, propositions and outcomes. Her world and ideals had been constantly challenged since she escaped the confines of the Tien Däm Mu J'in. She thought she was building something in the world, but it was proving itself to be nothing more than the rotting stink of bodies that lined the earth of this subterranean bunker.

Dominique felt embittered and enraged – *betrayed by my own Coven!* It stung, leaving a nasty taste in her mouth like witch-pyre-ash. She wished Linnet were here. *She would know what to do. She was clever in these predicaments.*

In the muck that clashed about her soul, Dominique stood tethered to either hope or damnation, each tugging relentlessly at the worn threads of her tired reason. *Hope or Damnation?* The matron of night spied the contemptible courtesan caressing William in her alabaster hold. She flexed her grip around the cutlass and exhaled.

Damnation was looking pretty good.

The ride over to the building felt as if it never happened, walled behind a head of cotton, a minefield of drive-in spectacle that Ryan remembered watching as a boy. Parking on the bottom level, nearest to the space that the vampires used, felt as if it never happened. But it did. He floated on a cushion of air away from the vehicle with the unlike bird bar held in his hand. Looking at it reminded him of the Maltese Falcon. The earnest expression on Humphrey Bogart's face as he held Mary Astor, about ready to kissed her.

It reminded him of the look on Lacey's face just before she left his apartment and the blood trickling down the forehead of the naked man. The images were stuck to Ryan's mind like flypaper. He wished his visions could be replaced by something else. Something more simple. More pure. But when he thought of the red headed hellcat, all he saw was her dancing next to the man that he had killed. Ryan was sure that the man had tried to fuck his red headed prize, but Z had said no. He would have been forceful. Ryan was sure of that.

He imagined Lin fucking him as Z watched. He imagined them both suckling the man's cock and feasting on his warm blood. Ryan's mind was a gutter of love and every turn and tumble his gray matter took became more irrational and unpredictable. He needed to see her again. He needed to see Z. He needed to understand the unlawful chain of events. Ryan needed her to love him.

When he thought of his life before the vampire bit him, all he remembered was watching the intoxicating punk at the club. When he thought of how he had tried to reconnect with his vampire lover his thoughts stopped at the sight of the naked man dancing with her. *He deserved it*, Ryan told himself, feeling as if he never existed before the dyed red punk entered his life. *The man had gotten in our way!* If Ryan did exist before The Letter came into his life and cut him up, than he couldn't remember it. All those intrusions to his and Z's union that took place between that first bloodletting fondle and that fixed moment in the alley were simply the tampering machinations of the naked man. Now, that he was dead Ryan was sure that he'd find his love waiting for him, locked within her castle.

Ryan did not recall sitting in the Camry looking at the drab underground parking facility. All there was, was the incalculable girl, the rhythm of her touch, and the thought of bliss in her ashen arms. *There were no more barriers. All roads led to heaven.* He had the key. *The princess was in her tower.* Ryan stared straight ahead, into the mouth of the cave, floating on angels of air. The door to his night-born princess would not hamper him. She waited. He was sure of that. She wanted him. He had the key.

Ryan looked down at the bloodstained crowbar lying on the floor of the passenger side of his vehicle. His cell phone rested in the seat next to him on a Walmart receipt. He had turned his phone off a couple of days ago after he'd destroyed his answering machine. Ryan remembered a gambol of noise. Lots of loud faces, spiraling aimlessly. There had been too much noise in his life. Too many women. *Now, there was only one.* The bent metal looked heavy – *an instrument of murder and the key to bliss* – all wrapped in a single tool.

Sam Spade delivered him the artifact. *No sense loosing it now, cupcake. You're so close!*

Ryan imagined Z talking to him, spurring him on, and pressing against his shoulder blades. She wanted him. She was the white flesh prize. She sparkled. There was only one path from the confluence of unabated guilt and the annoyance of faithless friends: and that was to press onward. To claim the prize and prove them wrong. He was a knight and had merely slain the dragon that had kept his lady captive…*had kept them apart.* The princess was locked in the tower, high above, and he needed to rescue her.

The echo of his car door closing stayed with him longer than the sound had actually existed, reverberating in the concrete shell of the parking garage, but Ryan did not recall opening or closing the door. Sounds were waves around him. Crossing to the gray painted door happened as if it never did until he noticed the empty space where the '63 Cadillac belonged. Confusion filled the parking space and its wide, glaring mouth galvanized him to the spot. It awakened him a little. He was being tested again.

The princess was in her tower.

He crossed to the door and jabbed the flat wedge of the unlike bird bar between the lip of the door and the frame and pulled. *Easy.* Just like he thought it would be. Ryan opened the metal door and a small square room stared back at him. A weak light dropped down from above. The cinderblock room was empty. It went nowhere that he could see and held nothing in it to carry him to his love.

Did it exist solely to torment?

No. Ryan stood there, glaring into the great big nothing for a minute before he decided to step inside. *I've killed the dragon.* Once he entered the small, square room he looked up, and finally, the room had something of value to offer. Just above his head, a couple feet from his fingers reach was a metal ladder. And from what Ryan could tell it lead all of the way up to the penthouse suite. He smiled. *The princess was in her tower and he was going to rescue her.*

He shoved the crowbar into a belt loop and tried to jump up and grab onto the bottom wrung of the ladder, but every time he came up short: just under an inch. On his last try, though, the crowbar fell from his belt loop and noisily clanged on the cold concrete. The noise hit him in the exact way that splashing water on his face didn't and he bent down to pick the falcon up. As he rose he noticed a small metal panel in the corner on the wall that buttressed the lift. Curiously, Ryan approached it. It looked like the covering to a fuse box. Ryan pulled on the thin metal ring that it had as a handle and it quietly opened. Inside, was nothing more than a switch, a single, solitary switch!

Ryan flipped it.

He heard no change. Nothing happened. He looked around to see if it had done anything inside the little room but all the molecules of air the comprised the dense space were unaffected. Stepping outside of the box, past the gray painted door, Ryan stood in full view of the tiny rotating camera. He didn't see anything different out there either. Silence was the cultivated condition. He went back and turned the switch to the original position that he had found it. Again, there was no visible or audible change. Concrete began to lap at his heels. He flipped it up once more and again stepped out of the little box and looked around.

The elevator was a sideways smile. Curiously, he set the crowbar down on one of the tarps that were used to cover automobile parts and depressed the lift's call button. Immediately, just like before, the sliding doors parted and Ryan stepped inside. Though, this time when he pressed the single button on the elevator panel the doors did not open again like they had. Instead, he was taken up.

He heard music in his head.

Ryan's heart pounded against the interior of his breastplate. He felt butterflies flitting through the spring in his stomach. He was ascending. *The elevator worked!* When the carriage slowed its climb and the braking clamps held the lift in place and the doors parted like two pieces of sliced bread, Ryan knew that he had reached heaven. He had killed the dragon. He had used the key. He was on his way.

Ryan stepped from the small graffiti tagged vessel and headed to the door at the other end of the softly lit hall. At the inviting barrier Ryan took a minute to compose himself. He didn't want to come off too eager or rude like he had done before. There would be no more incidents like the club. He need not worry. Fear and guilt parted with the opening of lift doors. *Be humble before the princess.*

Ryan was confident. He did not have to gloat about his achievement or condemn the long separation that he had endured. It was all over now. It had been a trail of necessity. One, that had only made him stronger. Their coming together was preordained. Nothing could stop it now. It was fate. Ryan knocked on the penthouse door and waited.

He knocked again. And waited.

He turned the handle to the small barrier, half expecting it to be open for him, but it was locked. After all he had suffered, to come through the trials and tribulations, he was met again with another locked door. But unlike all the others, this one did not give him vacant answers. This time it did not daunt Ryan's heart. This time there was cold, simple reason. *The Cadillac was gone. They had merely stepped out for the night. And if it weren't for that muscular bound idiot getting in my way earlier, then I'd have been here before they took off. I would have been in the arms of my true love. She could have supped from me while we copulated amid our reunion.*

Ryan believed that the naked man had tried to deceive him. That he had tried to keep him from claiming his prize. For that, the fool had paid the ultimate price. Interference was not tolerated. He couldn't disrupt their love. *It was stronger than all of that!* No, the naked man was merely a distraction, a ruse, a dancing idiot, and a common lure. *All I have to do now is wait.* Dawn was not that far off. The vampires were bound by the limitation of the dark. The sun sat on both sides of the day and boxed the night in with its brilliance and deviled illumination.

Z would return. This tower was her castle and her tomb. Ryan did not seek to free the fair maiden from her tower, like in the stories of old. Nor did he seek to join her in the prison of her princely fate. *No.* He understood it now. Everything was finally clear. *Together they would erect new paragons of wonder, craft their own stories, build their own dreams.* He would join her in her immortality and they would be together forever. *It was his destiny.* He was to become a vampire like her.

All he had to do was simply wait. She would return. And when she did? He would be here, a symbol of valor and love. Her knight in faded, denim armor. He was her prince. She was his princess. There would be a soft afterglow from sex. The candle in his soul burned brightly with a fire for the hellcat punk. It illuminated her way to him. Happily ever after could happen to those when they believed...*truly believed*...as Ryan believed.

1776. São Paulo, Brazil.

The look on Dominique's face was damnable as she crossed to Isabela. Both of the Countess's bodyguards broke the seal of their swords from their sheathes, eyeballing the untamed Bruxsa.

"Give me the baby," Dominique said, glowering, ready to extract the child or lob off Isabela's head.

The insolent vampire flashed her eyes. "Of course. It had not crossed my mind to do otherwise." She smiled.

That vicious, lying grin!

Isabela handed the infant to Dominique. William was awake, quiet and wide-eyed, staring up at her from the folds of the blanket. His soft, round checks bowled with mirth as he looked up at the familiar pale lady. *So tiny* – the possibility of hope. In Dominique's arms she could no more slay her one-time servant and doom her lot to eons of genocide. She was compelled to have him fulfill the intentions for which he was born.

"You will leave this place," Dominique uttered. "This country...this continent. You will find no safe harbor in your country of old or from its neighbors." She watched the insolent woman's facial features become taught and hard from her words. "Pray that you have not harmed a single hair on Linnet's head. For if you have," she raised the cutlass, pointing it at her eye. "There will be no place on or under this earth that will keep me from you. Do you understand?"

Isabela glared at the Vam Pŷr, not liking the tone or the deal she meted out.

"Do you understand?" Came the query again through gritted, tense teeth.

The contemptible courtesan straightened her back and squared her shoulders, ever the product of nobility. "As you see fit to dictate, I will take what is mine and travel north then. But know this…all of those lands are mine."

Isabela propped yet another fake smile on her cold, rosy lips.

"For now," cautioned Dominique, knowing full well that the Dalam Kha'Shiya had already laid claim to the northern landscape. They would not take too kindly to the arrogant brat staking dominance in their sovereignty. The rude usurper would soon find out the penalty for crossing the Omjadda J'in. America was their domain. The petty war brewing between the Colonists and the Crown was just as much orchestrated by the Omjadda J'in as it was sought by the people of this age. Nothing enslaved men faster than the illusions of freedom. Dominique knew that all too well, having learned it firsthand from a sect of the ancient brood. But these were Isabela's problems. She would discover them soon enough. Right now, Dominique had to traverse a whole lot of ground in a very short time.

She turned to Captain Simões and simply said, "You are indebted to *me* now."

Isabela's nostrils flared and she ground her teeth as her former mentor started to storm from the cave. "This is not over Dominique." The Vam Pŷr paused neared the mouth of the entrance. "You may think you have won something here, that you can impose your will on others." Isabela stood, folding her hands against her childless abdomen. "But you will learn one day soon that the net you've cast will only ensnare yourself. I pity you."

Dominique did not know what was worse: Isabela's hate or her pity. She wanted neither. The cold atmosphere of the damp cave was clawing around her shoulders and Dominique felt a powerful need to rid herself of this place. She backed away, disappearing into the black ink of the cavern, and Isabela continued to shout, "I pity you Dominique. I pity you…"

It nagged at Jaci's harried soul. Her former protégé tormented her with some hidden truth, but she was right about one thing: *this was far from over.* As she made her way through the length of the tunnel she heard the misguided Countess order Captain Simões over to her. The violent slap across his cheek followed her down the dark expanse. Then she heard his yelps as she neared the mouth of the hovel. She knew Isabela would have her way with him for foiling her delicious dreams of empire, but she would not kill him. She needed him at his post. *Better the thorns on the roses than no garden.* Dominique had plans of her own to utilize El Captain to ferret out her courtesan's schemes. *The poor man; it would have been better if I had killed him.*

As she made her way to the carriage her memory drifted to her conversations with Nsia. *Am I like them?* He had accused her of following in the footsteps of his enemy, living like a parasite within human society. As she ran through the woods Dominique felt unsure. She had brought Isabela to Brazil and set her up at the plantation to tend to her holdings. She had delivered to the people thier Bruxsa and enlivened their deepest fears. Dominique thought she knew Isabela better than that. She thought that the once noble Spanish beauty understood what it was that she was creating. *I allowed myself to be deceived.*

Isabela had imitated the Omjadda. Dominance through fear and intimidation. She fashioned power and wealth, acting with the vile habits of men. The Vam Pŷr exhaled, pulling the tufts of her eyebrows together. Worry plagued her judgements. She did not know if her dear lover would be safe and alive when they returned to the Engenho or hanging from the yardarm of a tree. Isabela was shrewd, a cunning adversary. *I must find a way to care for my species or we are merely destined to fall as Isabela has fallen.* The Spanish countess had left her stain upon this land and Dominique knew that it was her fault. There had to be a way to govern her kind so incidents like the ones that had happened in São Paulo would never happen again.

Nsia was correct to believe that there existed members of her race that coveted the ancient being's power and position over man. Something had to be done to keep Dominique's children in check or a future of entrenched warfare and ridiculous power struggles would tear the world apart. She was sure of it. *Something had to be put in place to keep my Children of Evensong from ever becoming anything like the monsters whose blood resurrected their souls.*

It was a necessary hope that birthed within the cranium of the Vam Pŷr this night, a hope that she knew she needed to find. *Never again would the plight of one my own tempt fate so maliciously.* Dominique looked down at

William. He gazed upon her with open eyes, a steady hope that beamed up at her and the clear crystal sky of a billion stars behind her head. William was already burdened with the responsibility of peace. It weighed on Dominique's conscious that she had not formally spoken to Linnet about the intentions that she had for the boy. She feared pushing her away. She placed a finger to the boy's forehead.

"You did not ask for this burden. Yet, it is yours to bear. Know this…your parents did not willingly go into their romance with the knowledge that their seed would seal a rift and hold back a tide of war. They produced you in their frolic, in their joy and happiness. You are here because you were meant to be here. They spawned you in love."

She smiled at the child, covering her fangs with wide lips. William's creamy mocha colored cheeks blushed and he cooed. Dominique ducked under a branch and wondered if his life, his blood, would be enough! If all that they had endured would be enough. Isabela's taunts clung to her clothing, hung from the fabric of her mind, and danced in the bloom of her anxiety. Isabela had made the ancient creature feel fear.

As she wound her way down the mountain pass she made another mental note to inquire among the Tien Däm Mu about the plans of their subterranean railcars. Such hidden devices like that and mysteries of their non-fire light could greatly aid her cause in assisting the symbiont race to flourish and carve out for itself a simple way of life in the world among the gods and man. Running through the woods, in a deep hurry, was simply not the way for one to travel when other sources existed!

When Dominique's gaunt extremities unfolded from the dark abyss of the woods William was asleep. She shouted to her coachman that they had little time, that they needed to reach Casa del Rio Dulce by morning or Araci may befall some ill.

Thiago drove the horses to the fullest. Their hooves pounded for hour after hour over darkened paths, bridges, and muddy roads. The carriage rollicked uncomfortably, side to side, and Dominique did her best to hold Linnet's son in ease. He slept through the majority of the bumps and jolts well enough, but woke with a hunger in the early dawn gnawing at his tiny gut.

Dominique did her best to pacify the noise machine, letting him nurse on her finger. Though eventually, that did not soothe the infant's demand for milk. His belly ached! And the aged woman chided herself for being so ignorant in overlooking such a simple thing as to bring with her a satchel of goat's milk for the child. She was, after all, coming to rescue him! Now, her mistake was amply paid by the shrill, unceasing cries that the young master made.

By the time they reached the Casa, dawn had completely lifted her dress. The baby still cried, starving for milk, and though Dominique did try to sing to him, and comfort him with bouncing, it was obvious that the only thing that would quiet the little tike was a nipple...or, a harsh bite on the neck. Dominique shouted to Thiago through the thick, black curtains to hurry and find out if Linnet was all right.

Imprisoned in the unmoving carriage by the warden of the sun, Dominique still felt the thrushing of the road. William still felt the maw of empty nourishment and the Vam Pŷr's worry for her paramour clawed at her chest as the wailing infant ate at her nerves. Suddenly, the door to the carriage opened. Rash, unreasonable sunlight flooded into the darken conveyance and Dominique was blinded by the bright exposure.

Had the insolent wench finally played her Master Stroke?

The carriage lurched with the weight of somebody entering it. Then just as suddenly as when she was bathed in the glow of the sun the caliginous atmosphere returned. No stinging deathblow came. Dominique called out, asking who was there, helpless in the slowly subsiding sun-blindness to understand what was going on. She did not hear the reply. Her ears were still deaf by the retreating Jadaraa Soo. The parasite took its time to refill the cavities of sight and sound. The crippled matron blinked against the fervent white that clouded her vision until sluggishly the dim details of the carriage reformed into view and there was a blessed silence that had surrendered to her battered ears.

"You are all right," Dominique said to her paramour.

Linnet smiled. "Yes. I'm all right."

Dominique peered at her raven haired beauty as William nursed on his Mother's teat. Smiling, she said nothing else. The Vam Pŷr had bet on the possibility of hope and in this quiet moment was rewarded for it. She had everything she needed in the world, right here, in the close confines of this wood and leather box. Everything else – Isabela, the Mercantiles, Captain Simões, and sending William to Nsia, all of it...it could wait. What truly mattered was at hand.

Thiago banged on the side of the carriage and informed Jaci that he could not find Araci anywhere on the grounds. The tone in the native's voice was worrisome and concerned. He asked what he should do, but the only answer that came from behind the walls of the calash was laughter. The laughter of the two women of Casa del Rio Dulce.

❊❊❊❊❊

Two out of three ain't bad. At least that's what that sappy song from the Seventies said. Lin and Z had driven around the city for a spell bathing in the harsh glow of neon candy and then refueled their parasites at a familiar club that offered vampires and neophytes a place to meet. However, the two roughhousing wenches quickly decided after they'd nibbled on a few hopefuls, that the music there was shit. Now, they were in search of a good after-hour's joint so they could get their groove on.

They parked the Caddy a block away and proceeded to walk to this place that Z had heard about from Manuel. To Z, it felt just like old times, but nagging thoughts plagued Lin. She had planned on telling the vibrant punk that her parasite was dying. Except every time Lin took a cerebral turn toward telling her, it made her belly lurch. So the two spunky broads acted normal, fell into their carousel, getting along like they used to, talking about anything and everything. Being random. It was fun!

They laughed it up as they walked past the line that was waiting to enter the club. They made fun of the people, mooing at them and tossing demeaning comments about their prissy attire. Z spied a young girl talking on her cell phone and decided that she'd do it. She walked over and grabbed it out of the girl's hand.

"She'll call ya back," the vampire said to the person on the other end of the line and hung up.

"Hey!" the young, blond girl bitched. "What do you think you're doing?"

"Calling Ryan," Z answered flatly and began dialing.

The girl reached out for her iPhone, but Z kept turning so that it was just out of reach with every lunge that she made in her little, hiked dress to retrieve the palm-sized electronic device.

"Relax," coached Z. "I'll give it back."

The girl reached out for it again and Lin slapped her hand.

"She said she'd give it back." Her tone was firm and finite.

Blondie fumed. Z squinted trying to remember the last digit of Ryan's phone number and recalled the flavor of his first blood letter.

340

Instantly, the lone numerical symbol melted from the fog and clicked into place. *Perfect.*

"Shhh," Z told the frowning girl. "It's ringing."

Lin started humming the theme to the TV game show, Jeopardy, and Z chuckled. The young girl didn't even get the reference. Over a billion viewers in its twenty-five years of international adapted broadcast syndication and the girl couldn't Ring In an answer because she didn't how to phrase the question. Alex Trebek would not be amused. It was a Daily Double filled with cash prizes and there was no one to bank!

Double Jeopardy and Z clung to the line, but it just continued to ring and ring and ring. Now, Z didn't have the question because she didn't know that Ryan had pulled his answering machine out of the wall and smashed it to pieces on the floor. She didn't know that he had turned his cell phone off and that it sat in the passenger seat of his Toyota Camry in their parking garage. Z didn't even know that Ryan owned a Toyota Camry. *What's pissed off and crazy for $100, Alex?*

Number two among TV Guide's Fifty Greatest Games Shows of All Time and Z simply thought, *Oh well. Final Jeopardy! Round.* The rascally vamp tossed the phone up into the air for the young girl to catch. Blondie hustled, watching her wallet dwindle and her network of contacts flipping into oblivion. She caught her iPhone, landing the jeweled, electronic device into the flat pinks of her palms.

"Goth Bitch!" the miffed girl fired back at both game show enthusiasts.

As they neared the front of the line, Z turned around, opened her mouth, and wiggled her tongue to the cute, young thing through two outstretched fingers. The girl gasped and commented about how rude the lewd retort was, acting shocked like a pent-up Catholic. She'd never been so demeaned in all her life and complained about it to the do-nothing spectators around her, trying to curry sympathy.

Little did she know that they simply wanted her to shut up. She could have figured it out had she exited her tiny bubble long enough to read the placid looks on their faces, but as it was she was a victim. She had been yammering on that cell phone the whole time that she had been standing in line. All the people around her knew the intimate details of her conversation whether they wanted to or not. From their bored points of view, the bodacious broads had done them a favor! Now, the human cattle could shuffle along at the gracious command of the Doorman's boast and enter the wanderlust spectacle of bullshit whims, cheap booze, grand lights, and a booming bass without the incessant rants of blondie's twenty-something's up and comings.

Though, much to the chagrin of those at the head of the line, Lin and Z easily schmoozed their way into the club. They were the freaks at the peak. The vampires looked down on the waiting throng! Inside, amid the crowd – Hypnotrance's sweaty assemblage – disco lights pulsed and the stink of live flesh cavorted with the two carefree punks. Finally, the constant contestants had found their third trick of the evening – *a good DJ to dance to!*

1780. São Paulo, Brazil.

Linnet strolled through the orange grove. William ran between the trees laughing and playing peek-a-boo with his mommy. The day was hot, muggy, and stiff. The Little Summer was upon them again. Workers loaded baskets with fruit, tending to the harvest of the groves. They sang songs as they picked the bright, round capsules. Linnet usually found solace among the bristling fresh scents of the trees and songs of the native peoples, but today their bountiful cheer was far away and distant.

She cracked one of the effervescent jewels open and handed half of it to her son, wrapping the other half up in a cloth that she carried with her. She knew their days were numbered. Watching him joyfully bite into the juicy victual, she wondered how she could do it. How could she willingly give up her own flesh and blood to the sea? Turn her back on him, basically letting him think for the rest of his days that his mother was dead.

For years she knew this day would arrive. Since Dominique returned with him from Isabela's lair, Linnet knew that she would have to let him go. The matter arose during the late hours one afternoon as she changed William's diaper in his room. Dusk lingered in the sky and Dominique hung in the doorway. The child had only been back in Linnet's care for a few weeks, and though nothing was said outright about it, there had been a huge silent wall in their discussions about the future. The Vam Pŷr was sending for three new consorts to fill their home, but more than that, talks skirted certain issues. Slowly, Linnet figured it out.

"It amazes me the amount of excrement that such a small thing can make."

"He eats more than enough I assure you." Linnet folded the soiled cloth diaper and dumped it in the receptacle. "I am surprised it is not more today. He usually spills his drawers. He had a big lunch."

"Funny," Dominique said, moving into the room, "that the product of the human body is waste."

Linnet folded and pinned a fresh diaper on the lad, and lifting him up, turned. She was not getting her mistress's meaning. "It is only natural."

"Yes, that is what intrigues me," she caressed William's bare back and the infant reached out for Dominique's hand. "We eat and the waste from the parasite is life. You eat and the production is fecal matter." Her eyes flicked down at Linnet. "I would think ours a more efficient design."

"Perhaps."

Linnet moved away, carrying the child to the nightclothes she had set out.

"I thought about your idea to erect a governing council."

"And…" She playfully tucked the boy's chubby arms into the holes of his shirt.

"I like it. Though, it will take some planning. It must hold itself higher than the mere courts of Man."

"Of course."

"I shall want your aid in this endeavor."

Linnet said nothing and blew a smile into William's face. The infant gurgled and cooed, practicing his sounds as he rocked on his bum and reached out for Linnet's fingers to right himself. The thought struck her again and her smile disappeared.

"It is your intention to send William to Nsia, is it not?"

The question was finally out there, set between them like a platter of slaughtered beef. Linnet did not turn around to meet the gaze of her dark mistress. She kept her head down, her attention on her boy. Dominique did not move closer to her.

"Yes."

The aged woman watched her dark haired beauty's head nod up and down as she swallowed the simple word. She straightened herself up and lifted her son to her chest. Linnet turned and looked at the Vam Pŷr, square in the eye, before she left the room, leaving the master architect alone to stew in the truth of it. Days later, Linnet would outline the terms of which she would send him to his father, informing Dominique that she had already mailed Nsia a letter with the enclosed facts. It left little to say of the matter after that. Linnet would care for her child for the first five years of his life and his father would have him after. Dominique posted no arguments.

Linnet was shocked at the ease of her own callous selfishness, to forgo her child for the black blood and ashen arms of her night-born paramour; it was a vine that rooted around her spine. She realized that it had been there her whole life. The only time that she did not feel its delicate pull was after she agreed to send William away. Though lately, as the years moved on and William grew, she began to feel the vine growing through its normal haunts, moving across her back in the same manner that she had witnessed Dominique's Jadaraa Soo slither under the dark mistress's flesh. William was her gardener. He had pulled the vile weed out from its normal field in her soul when he was born. Linnet believed that, recalling the pains of childbirth. Having him had changed her, but it did not change her want for the Persian woman. She looked to her boy now and more and more saw Nsia staring back at her. He was growing into his father's son.

The letter to Nsia that announced William's eminent arrival had been writ. It rested now on Linnet's desk in her office. All she had to do was give it to Ana Luiza to mail. It seemed easy. Mailing a letter. Giving it to the servant girl and looking away, yet here she was with her son on a walk through the orange groves instead of completing the task that she had set for herself on this day. William's fifth birthday loomed and with it her good-byes.

Linnet looked down at her son. He picked the white strings off the fruit before he took another bite, concentrating with every strand. Her brow knotted downward as she peered across the vast orchard. The day was bright. The heavens blue. A gentle wind had suddenly picked up and eased the jungle heat.

Linnet and William made their way back to the Casa Grande. He wanted up, tired from running, so Linnet carried him up the hill that led to the big house. He played with her coal black hair and spoke of things that he saw and questions that popped into his growing mind. He was having a big day with his Mother and as they neared the portico Ana Luiza met them.

"Araci," called the Portuguese maid. "The workers say they've spotted a Çuçuarana in the north field."

"Tell Thiago to take a hunting party and capture it if he can," decreed the Lady of the House. "It will fetch a nice purse with the English. But do not to take any chances. Kill it if need be. We can always make it into a nice stew later if we have too."

The maid nodded and left to do her mistress's bidding. William made a face and asked what a Çuçuarana was, having difficulty pronouncing the hard word. Linnet told him that it was a big cat and for him to call it a Puma – *a word which he could pronounce.* She formed her hand into the large sized kitty-cat, playfully using her fingers as teeth, and tickled him. He laughed as they entered the house.

Upstairs, he went down for his nap easily and was soon fast asleep. Linnet walked to the small veranda that attached to the four year-old's room and overlooked the side yard and a clump of trees. Beyond the growth were the western sugarcane fields, a barn, and a couple of huts where a group of field hands lived. So many wonderful and interesting things surrounded her son at the Engenho. *He enjoyed living here so much.* The plantation was a village unto itself and everyone adored the Albee heir.

Word through the Senzalas was that the young master was being sent to school abroad. Only Linnet and Dominique knew the difference. If all was to unfold according to plan, Ana Luiza would soon find out that William was not going off to school as rumored, but to his father in Africa, and that she was to remain there with him as an emissary between the Vam Pŷr and the tribal hunters.

Dominique informed Linnet just the other day that Ana Luiza's lessons were progressing nicely and that she was confident in the duties that the young maid was expected to perform. The venerable moon had taken to educating the Portuguese lass about the hidden world behind the veil of this one, showing her secrets and rare histories that stretched before the dawn of Mar. William was not the only seed of peace between their two peoples: the knowledge that the Vam Pŷr imparted to Ana Luzia was also meant to mend the rift of years that Nsia had spent away from his son. The next few months were crucial and the weight of its success bore down on the matriarchs at the House on the Sweet River.

Life had been what Linnet had always dreamed it could be over these past few years. From the shores of Portugal, Ireland, and France Dominique had collected three astute and willing servants to meet her nocturnal needs and educate in the way of her grand design. She had taken to Linnet's idea to form a council and with her new aides had busied herself with its formation. Linnet had stepped up to oversee the plantation's production and delegate the workings of Dominique's mines in Minas Gerais. For years, business was running smoothly and Linnet inched more and more responsibility from her shoulders to respected men of office. It gave her the time she desired to raise her son in the manner she chose.

Linnet promoted Thiago, Jabajara, and Vaz to managerial positions on the plantation and in their native hands sugarcane production had increased. Everything was in play that the Englishwoman needed to ascend the ladder of evensong and join her mistress, once and for all, in the full embrace of the gift.

Yet she felt as if she was hanging on. Ever since that night when she was introduced to Dominique at the Opera, Linnet knew that this woman was going to forever change her life. She just had no idea as to how. The love she felt for her son grounded her and pulled her heart in contrary directions. Often, Linnet did not think she could go through with it. She toyed with the thought of prolonging the transformation for yet another year, maybe more, but deep in the belly of her reason the dark haired maid knew that if she did not part with William now, and send him to Nsia, that she never would. Youth was fading from her countenance. A few more years and she would be thirty.

Her mother was dead and buried at thirty-eight. She was already becoming an old woman. *Best to capture the glamour of youth while it still graced her features.* Linnet's selfishness to remain with her son was paramount until she closed her eyes and thought of her African lover. It had been so long since she had felt the tenderness of his kiss. All her body knew was the embrace of the Vam Pŷr. Linnet could not imagine ever knowing anything else ever again.

She recalled Nsia's stories about his homeland and remembered that she once found it exquisite and lovely. *A young boy needs his father to grow strong and capable in the world.* Linnet knew this. *William would find the Savannah just as beautiful as his Brazilian home. Nsia's family was large like it is here.* Linnet told herself that she did not have any other choice. She sighed, wishing Dominique were there to comfort her in her hesitation.

A chill wind picked up from the East and the sky began to slowly darken. It looked like a volley of rain had drifted in from the sea. That salt scent from the Atlantic and the green shores of Santos clung to the molecules of air. Linnet pulled her arms around herself thinking about the solace she had found in the ashen embrace of her dark mistress. She exited the veranda, shutting the glass doors to protect her son from the oncoming rain.

Dominique was away on business with Coralene and Deven. She was not scheduled to return until tonight, but even that seemed too far away. The letter loomed on her desk and there was no getting around it. Linnet kissed William on his sleeping brow as she left and called Ana Luiza into her office. It was time.

The young maid gracefully listened as Linnet informed her of her role to play in the scheme and handed her the letter written to Nsia. Ana Luiza was composed and stoic, claiming to understand her duty fully. She professed to feel that Dominique had groomed her for something significant. Though, at the time, she did not know what it could be. The Portuguese, chestnut haired woman was thankful for the charge and pledged to watch over William until her last breath and do all that she could to be an ambassador on their behalf. The woman's attentiveness did not ease the burden that Linnet felt.

A crushing loneliness remained in Linnet Albee's office after Ana Luzia had gone. The painting of her, commissioned by Dominique before they had left Europe, hung on the far wall. *So young then. Worlds away.* She could not recall the face of the artist, but remembered his biting tone. A cool breeze flitted through the curtains and the scent of precipitation lingered in the air. Linnet sauntered outside to the inlaid stone portico with her arms wrapped around herself. She watched as the workers in the orange grove loaded their baskets onto their horse drawn carts and departed the field.

Clouds coalesced on the horizon, pregnant with a late afternoon rain, but it was the silent mother who shed her water first. Weeping alone under the billowy canopy, not just for the journey that her son was soon to make, but also for the journey that she had undergone and would soon embark upon. The future was wide and terrifying and Linnet did not know if she was ready for the challenges that it offered. She felt tired and wanted Dominique home. *Sometimes, all one had to go on was faith, and other times… blind luck.* Linnet didn't know which one she needed now. *Faith or Blind Luck?* She huffed. *Maybe, a little bit of both. Who knows?*

Neither was what the sky needed. It ebbed and flowed, swirling to its own rhythm and finally opened up and released its bounty on the woman and the land. Linnet opened her arms wide and looked up to the falling drops of rain. Whatever was to come would come. There was no stopping time. Men and women were either led to their destiny by the circumstances of fate or they walked forward creating the circumstances as they went along.

Win or lose? It didn't matter. There were no hidden prizes in the afterlife. All that there was to do was play the game. *Day after day…*a single chain stretching back to the beginning, to the dawn of time and the earth itself, connecting all those that had walked the astral mother to today. From the first humanoids that filled their lungs with air to the young mother that now stood amid the Engenho grounds. The raven haired woman felt her ancestry, her place in the annals of actuality. The rain fell across her forehead and her shoulders, wetting her hair, lips, and breast. It was cool after the humid day. Her flesh tingled with the vibrant life thrushing through her ordinary veins. The rain was a baptism and Linnet's faith in creating her own destiny set her free.

⁂

For the returning champions of the club scene dawn was snapping at their heels as they pulled into the parking garage. Fanning tips of sunlight sparkled in the chrome of the rear bumper and Z gave good ole Mr. Sunshine the finger from the back window. The screeching whitewalls of the Caddy echoed in the cavernous concrete structure as they took turns sharply, spiraling downward.

The rubbery squeaks filtered into Ryan's consciousness as he slept in the backseat of the dust covered Austin 10. Though, it was the slamming of the Cadillac doors and Z's raunchy mouth that woke him. He emerged, to their surprise, from the late forties vehicle with his hair a mess and his determination completely intact.

"Who'd he have to screw to find this place?" Z wondered, looking at Lin.

"Not me." Lin made a face and shrugged her shoulders.

"You look like ass," Z told Ryan as he approached.

"Well, I've been one," he admitted, stopping in the middle of the bottom level. "And if you give me half a chance I'll prove to you that I can be more to you than just some stupid one night stand, or some crazy guy that keeps popping up when he's not expected."

"Yeah," Z bobbed her head back and forth. "I can see how *now* is helping with that."

Lin stifled her laugh. The ardent suitor glared at his prize, inept at catching the simplicity of the girl he came to woo. The rascally vamp cocked a sideways smirk. "There are five hundred murders a year in LA and about one third of them go unsolved."

"More like 18%," corrected Lin from behind.

"How many?" asked Z, turning.

"Eighteen percent."

348

"They've gotten better." Z reflected, impressed.

Lin nodded. "Yeah."

"Ok, what she said," continued Z with the wave of her hand. "My point is, what makes you think I won't kill you now and there ain't anybody around who's gonna cry boo-hoo over you?"

Ryan took a leap of faith and stepped forward. He was the prince; she was his princess. The dragon was dead. His face was a shroud of sincerity. "Well, if I can't be with you then maybe I don't want to live."

"Aaaawwww," Z uttered with a puppy-dog-face, placing her hands between her knees and scrunching up. "That's so cute! Did you hear that Lin?"

"Sure did Z."

"Wasn't that just the cutest?"

"Positively peachy-keen."

Z kissed him softly. It was a Kodak moment. He raised his hands to pull the delicious vamp to him, but she was already backing away.

"It's like I told you on that first night," Z said, losing her playfulness. "I don't eat where I live and I don't shit where I eat. And well..." She reached a hand into her back pocket as she took another step toward him. "Enough is enough Romeo." With a smile and her eyes deadlocked on Ryan's piercing blues, Z slit his throat with the switchblade that she lifted out her pocket with such invisible ease.

Ryan never saw it coming. His eyes rapidly blinked as he began to choke on his own wet red gurgling and his mind spun in a constant loop with a disbelieving question. *Why?* Both hands came crashing to the valley of his neck as a waterfall of rubies gushed through his fingertips. He went down weightless, like it never really happened. His brow furled pleading with the vampires to save him.

"Ya shoulda learned to keep your mouth shut," Z nastily informed the dying man, standing over him.

His blood felt warm on his cheek. He heard it pool around his ear as it clogged in his sandy blond hair. The look of death on his face was unmistakable. Lin sighed heavy, wet, and raspy. She had hoped that Ryan would have been more of a comfort to Z than the mere release of her anger over him outing her at the club, but the fact was…Z *really* liked that place *a lot*…and he'd embarrassed her. He had called her out.

In last few seconds that Ryan's soul remained tied to earth, he watched the unattainable punk step over his body, heading toward the gray painted door. His thoughts were stuck. She wiped his blood off her switchblade with the back of her pants, retracted the steel, and returned the little comfort item to her back pocket and grabbed a key from her front.

As she moved to unlock the door, she noticed Ryan's handiwork. The edge of the metal door was twisted and peeled back. "Look what that Shit did to our door!" Z was indignant. "Ungh!"

She shook her head, wanting to kill him again, and entered the small cinderblock room. She snorted at the position of the On/Off Switch, too, and shut the door to the elevator cavity with a reverberating clank. On her way to the lift, she looked over and saw Lin still standing in place, staring down at Ryan Silva.

He exhaled his death rattle, an abraded, papery grate, and Lin felt some small smattering of remorse for the man. Suddenly, it occurred to her. His name. It was Silva. Lin huffed at the irony, recalling that day, so long ago, in the São Paulo market square: Francisco's eyes, as he passed his last gasp were still there in the lock box of her memory. *Life is not without its fearful symmetry!*

"C'mon," Z urged. "I'll deal with that later."

Lin looked up at Z. She was standing with the elevator doors open and instantly it was clear to her why she made the journey east every decade since The Letter had cut into her life. Her fingers unconsciously traversed to the locket and began rubbing the well-worn silver. Her parasite retreated deeper into the body of her hand. *There was a waiting balance of forces, a center of gravity that still circulated around the massacre of the villagers during the sandstorm.* Lin felt it in her bones. *Nature conspired to move me toward some unknown destiny…and Z was a part of it. Like Alice, I've followed her down the rabbit hole.*

Lin looked down at the corpse of Ryan Silva again. His red juice inched toward her shoes on the gritty concrete. Her Jadaraa Soo twitched at the scent of decaying blood and Lin hoped that it wasn't too late. That somehow in all the tangled bullshit of the universe that she hadn't already missed her window of opportunity, that somewhere life still held open a door of redemption for her. *Devastation wasn't the only course of action.*

She heard the red headed hellcat noisily sigh and further hoped that unlike her soulless friend she would not destroy her only chance of breaking the vicious cycle of fate. Lin felt the heels of karma digging into her flesh and wanted to rise above the obvious inclination of murdering her own dreams.

"You comin' or what?" Z flatly stated, waking the vampire from her bonnet of disasters.

Lin exhaled and squished her face. "You know, that's gonna leave a stain."

"I'll use that cat litter shit that you use for the oil." She lifted her hand off the elevator doors and it started to close.

Lin scratched an itch. "I think I'm out."

Z blocked the path of the closing doors. "Then I'll go pick some up," she annoyingly explained. "C'mon. No sense crying over spilt boy."

Lin stepped over the sanguineous extermination and joined her unpredictable friend in the lift to their pad. The small metal walls of the elevator felt cramped; packed tight. Francisco's last, bewildered stare was tattooed to the inside of Lin's eyes. In unlocked her heart and the memories from the desert seized her. All those faces from the villagers that she, Ramielle, Prophet, and Jordan had murdered in the farmhouse crowded around her, riding the lift. The stench of José Onofre filled her nostrils along with the other men that she had killed during the slave revolts. The sight of Guajajara's headless body bleeding out just as Ryan had done dripped over a cascade of convenience store butcheries. The ride up in the lift felt crampt, a spiraling down, drilling a deposit of shame in the gapping maw of her brain. Death was heavy and clinging to her bones. Their ascent felt like it was taking years.

Suddenly, Lin had an urge to wash herself clean. To purge from herself the maddening guilt and strip away from her flesh the decades of destruction and decay, to spin back the hands of time and make better memories. She was nothing more than the smashed collection of lives snuffed out in the burning waste of her Jadaraa Soo. The first death the parasite had claimed was her own. The rest was collateral damage. Her head swooned. The Letter was right. The Letter was always right. *Death was the gift that kept on giving.*

1780. São Paulo, Brazil.

After the rains, evening settled onto wet grasses and leaves. With it brought the arrival of Dominique and her wards. The Engenho was alight. Bonfires were spread throughout the plantation to keep the animals confined to the deep, dark forest. Thiago and his hunting party hadn't had any luck tracking the Çuçuarana, so he thought a steady vigil throughout the night might drive the large cat away from the prospects of the barn. With the fires came song and with the songs, drinking – Linnet had designated three crates of Cachaça to be dispersed among the field hands.

Dominique found her and William among the tenant workers and joined their merriment and mirth. They were singing old songs and dancing. The joviality was exciting in its pitch. It carried far above the roof of the trees, past the hemline of the night, and the wild chances of million year-old stars. The heavens sent their twinkling lights down on them, bouncing off the wild flickering shadows. Shimmering, unseen in the thick black of the woods by the men with guns slung over their shoulders, a pair of golden eyes watched the flames dance.

The young master tried to stay awake. He really did, but all the excitement could not stay his tired body from sleep. The breadth of life at his village had worn him out. One of his native mothers handed him to Linnet and she carried him back to the house. Dominique walked beside her and noticed it immediately.

It wasn't the joy of the songs or the sugar wine that she had been drinking. She had not cut her hair or hung it in a new way, but there was something distinct and different about her. Linnet saw the woman eyeballing her and asked her what it was. Dominique found it difficult to place the new sensation into words. Linnet seemed full, like she filled her flesh suitcase with the richness of her spirit. There was always an air of ease and confidence within the young woman that Dominique had admired. Though, now it appeared to ride her bones, fitting more comfortably.

"You've changed," Jaci stated.

Linnet smiled and blushed. She shook her head, "Yes. I feel better."

"I like it."

"All the arrangements are made and I spoke with Ana Luzia today." She walked a few more steps. "I am confident in her abilities. You've chosen well with this one."

Dominique held her fingertips behind her back as she walked. The hem of her long black dress brushed against the grass as night churned critter chatter and Toucans. She wanted to embrace the woman there on the path to the house, but did not. "And when have you decided?"

"Just after his birthday. There'll be better weather for travelling."

"Yes. The winds are fair then."

Linnet leaned against her mistress, Dominique put an arm around her, and they walked the rest of the way to the Casa Grande in silence. William breathed steady and calm as the matriarchs of the land laid him on his bed. In the solitude of the darkened room they moved toward each other. Their lips perched on both sides of the canyon of space that had separated them, eager to shed their days of detachment with the comfort of a kiss. But they never made it. Shouts erupted outside from Thiago. There was a musket blast and the music abruptly stopped.

Linnet checked William and pulled Dominique outside to see what was going on. When they had reached the main encampment a native field hand informed them that the Çuçuarana had been seen in the western field. Thiago and his men were tracking the big cat there.

Deven St. Cloud, a brawny, redheaded Irishman who had joined Dominique's coven a few years previously, found the two ladies on their way to the western sugarcane field. He told them that Ana Luzia and Coralene were busy shutting up the house. He held his musket with a firm grip and a belt loaded with powder and balls was flung over his shoulder. He was eager to join the hunting party and bag the sandy jungle lion. Another shot rang out through the starry night. The air alighted with the wings of Willow Thrushes and Honeycreepers scattering from their hidden perches and Deven hoped that the beast had not already been wounded.

"You should not be out," Thiago chided both of his mistresses as they ran up to him. "The Çuçuarana is loose. You must be careful."

"We heard another shot." Deven's interest was piqued. "Did you get him?"

"No," the native regretfully informed. "We missed and she headed toward the forest behind the house."

The symbiont and her consorts turned in the direction of the Casa-Grande just as a scream curdled the luminous dark. They ran as fast as they could to the big house. Deven and Dominique got there first and met Coralene as she broke from the front doors, running across the yard.

"It's in the house. It ran upstairs and..."

"Where's Ana?" Deven asked.

"She went to check on William. I heard her cry out."

He started toward the front doors of the main house as Linnet caught up with them. Overhearing the French maid, her heart dropped. She did not hesitate and passed Deven and Dominique on the way to William's room.

"Wait!" Thiago shouted after her, following his mistress again into the full throttle jaws of danger. "Wait!"

The Irishman and the Matron of Night were close on her heels as she scaled the steps, overtaking them two by two. She reached William's room and saw Ana Luiza cowering just inside of the door holding her left forearm. Blood stained the sleeve of her dress and the hand that covered the slash marks was sanguine. Linnet and the others crowded the door. The large cat crouched and hissed.

Its ears were pulled back. Its body tense. It roared a low guttural curl and whine in the back of its throat as it lingered near William's bed. Dominique moved around to the side of the door and grabbed Ana Luiza by her good arm, pulling her from the room. She handed her to Thiago to ferry away. Linnet looked for her son, but didn't see him. Her mind raced. Her heart thudded in her chest like cannons. She did not see him! Then to her surprise and horror he pulled the bed sheet down from over his head and smiled at the menagerie of family that were gathered at his door.

"Look Mommy," he said. "A Poo-Ma."

He sat up and looked closer at the cat, grinning.

"No, William," Linnet quietly urged. "Stay where you are. Do not move."

Deven shouldered his musket and took aim. The sandy mountain lion's golden eyes flitted back and forth from all the people to the lone child near her. She was cagey and did not know where to move next. She felt confined. Trapped. William inched closer to the Çuçuarana unaware of the dangers that the frightened cat could inflict.

"You're pretty," the little boy said and lifted his hand to pet the wild beast.

"William, no," Linnet gasped.

The large cat cowered, drooping its ears to the child's touch. Linnet silently pleaded for him to move back, awed by the gentle display of the cagey feline. Dominique stood stunned. *You will know this when the big cat comes and is stayed by the hand of a child.* The words of the old Omjadda croon flitted through her head and she stepped into the boy's room, obstructing Deven's aim. The Çuçuarana reared back at the scent of the Vam Pŷr and hissed, barring the full brutality of its fangs. *You will spread the seed of our people through yours and for an eternity we shall live, one inside the other, wed.* Dominique crouched and hissed too, baring the brutality of her fangs. *After the trials of Mar we'll emerge on the other side.*

It was too much for the lost animal to handle and it bolted through the half-opened door that led out, onto the veranda. William was giggling. The jungle cat turned and cried out before it jumped to the branch of a neighboring tree and disappeared into the woods below. The men ran from the house to continue their chase as Linnet ran to her son.

"Did you see that Mommy?" the young boy delightfully asked. "She came to see me. I was dreaming about her and she came."

"Yes, she did," Linnet professed as tears streamed down her face. "Yes, she did."

"Why are you crying Mommy? Didn't you see? It was a Poo-Ma. She wanted to play."

Linnet hugged her son tightly, never wanting to let him go, thankful not to have lost him yet to the wilds of the world. Yet, the wounded child of the Omjadda did see. Dominique saw the beast kneel before the boy, and in her still beating, dead heart she knew that William would tame the beasts of war that brewed in the African tribe. He would become the bridge that would unite their two races. He *was* their messenger of peace. He had been chosen more so than Dominique could have ever devised or set in motion. Life's awful symmetry of her being as manipulative as Isabela fled from her mind as the good omen clearly came into view. She had forgotten. All those years ago, before she underwent the Ja Rů Tôk and became a blood slave, Dominique had forgotten the words that the sightless old croon of the primordial race had shared with her.

Fourteen and about to die. A rebel and too much to handle, the girl had been defiant to the last sting of the lash since they'd stolen her from the well on her father's land. The tall white brutes of the Rom Pŷr J'in were afraid that her blood would taint the Vam if they simply threw her to them to feast on as they worked the mines. So, they tossed her in the pit to be executed. Her blood spilt and wasted on the rock floor of the darkened cave. There would be no honor in her death. There could be no salvation in the mettle of her soul. The Mar child was a rueful dog that simply had to be put down.

It was the first time that Dominique remembered seeing him. *Ornn Däm Mu.* His face was still spry then with only a few wrinkles. It was long and thin like so many of his race. His crescent-moon eyes were impassive and his white skin slightly glowed, luminescent in the shadowed dark. His long jet-black hair shimmered with the inventiveness of the carnivorous beasts' non-fire light. He adorned himself with a single braid over the rest of his flowing mane, a humble attribute for his stately position as a J'in Ankh of one the seven clans. His garments were silk and embroidered with intricate markings. He stood on the balcony above the pit with the mine's Overseer and a wretched creature cowering beside him, bent and crooked like a rod. The inhuman looking thing whispered into Ornn's ear and pointed at the young child, who was simply known as Fizza.

Fizza was dirty and forced to her knees. She was ready for the deathblow from the axe in the Omjadda's hands. It was what she wanted. Since that terrible morning when the Bedouins had kidnapped her and forced her to walk an endless string of desert miles to where she was sold at an auction under the pitch of a tent to a group of shrouded heathens, the young girl had fought to escape. Her fiery spirit was first prized and fetched a hefty coin at the impromptu marketplace. Then she was beaten to make her fire tame so that she could be broken and become a blood slave. But Fizza would not break. Her damnable soul had won out and her nightmare foes regretted the day that the little whelp had entered their lives. She only left them with one choice: *the spark that can not be harnessed must be stamped out.*

As the young, arrogant child listened to the Omjaddas speak their strange language she wished that they would simply hurry her death and end this life so her immortal soul could be reborn again far away from this wretched place. Fizza had prayed to Allah long and hard while buried under the spoiled earth to make her suffering stop and carry her away. She knew in her heart that her soul was ready, but a princely subject and his minister had stayed the executioner's hand and they bartered with their evil tongues. Fizza looked up at the unwelcome guests. The Overseer did not appear pleased by what they said and he spat onto the ground, defiantly, throwing his arms up in a tizzy. She could have sworn then that the princely shade did smile.

Her spirit unwavering, only crushed more by survival, she was taken to meet her new benefactor. He was unlike the other creatures that she had seen in the two years as a prisoner. He was regal and refined. He had an air of importance about him and there was kindness in his eyes. But the crooked old rod of a woman that stood next to Ornn Däm Mu was simply unbelievable to behold. She had no eyes, nor eye sockets from which a peerless gaze could be perched. Her hair was graying and ratty, unkempt unlike most Omjadda, and sprouted from the middle of her head so that her elongated forehead protruded like a blind vessel of terror. Her fingers were bowed, spindly thin with sharp fingernail razors, and she handled Fizza roughly. Smelling her and touching her, looking her over, just like they had done at the auction. Fizza felt sick. The Omjadda witch grabbed her by the mouth, prying open her lips, and glared at her dirty, ramshackle teeth with her eyeless gaze.

"She is the one," the Jaddat spoke, sniffing her.

Ornn nodded and called the Overseer to him to barter the necessities of treatment that he wished for the child of Mar. The sightless thing crouched down and staring strangely at the young girl spoke to her in her own language.

"You will spread the seed of our people through yours and for an eternity we shall live, one inside the other, wed; after the trials of Mar we'll emerge on the other side and you will know this when the big cat comes and is stayed by the hand of a child."

The old witch touched her lightly on the nose and smiled, but she had a frightful grin with rows of sharply pointed teeth. Fizza was confused. She did not understand anything that was happening. Nor would she understand what was to follow until many years after she had undergone the blood ritual and become a Vam Pŷr, a slave to the People of the East. She did not know then whom she had met that day and whose hands in which her life now resided. Though over time she would learn. The sightless hag was named Fedah Maalj and she was a Jaddat, a seer of the people.

One could not be made into a Jaddat. One had to be born with the gift of sight in a sightless gaze. No one knew when a Jaddat would come or go among the J'ins. It was Spirit's divine will. Layal would give her people a healer and a prophet when it was most needed to them and never had there walked two upon the glade at once.

Maalj was born into the Fedah Layal J'in long before the Great Migration, during a time when the Lanz Gur Mae was withering to an untamed and hungry desert. She scattered her people among the world and tried her best to guide them, as they grew apart, healing what rifts she could as her people splintered into seven bold fractions. By the time her visions had led her to the rueful child she was mostly bent with age.

It had been over five hundred years since Fizza had heard the Jaddat's words and had her unbroken spirit sniffed out. Time felt like it was folding into itself. Dominique gazed upon the cherubic face of William, Linnet clinging to him, and the gruesome hag's prophecy rang true. The former slave felt shattered. Barely raised in the culture of her home, fraught with prayers for Allah to rebirth her with a cause to eradicate the ancient species from the face of the Earth, she was the vessel of their salvation. The hundreds of vials of black blood that she had reaped after murdering Ornn and Ele Däm Mu were preordained. *Layal, Goddess of the moon and the stars, sister/mother to the sun god, Rah – ruler of the heavens – Earth's first religion. How simple is life's grand poetry that I am to be called Jaci! Layal moves us all, sways our waters to her tide. The earth turns on its axis devilishly orchestrating each and every turn that I have fought and won.*

In the shadow of the Çuçuarana, the Vam Pŷr wanted to be angry. But she wasn't. She wanted to feel played by the universe and the machinations of time, the dual nature of the gods, and the ancient race. But she didn't. She recalled how affectionate Ornn was to her when she finally arrived at his home to live among the Tien Däm Mu J'in after centuries with the beastly Rom Pŷr. He lifted her out of their mines and gave her a position within his household.

He spent time with her and educated her about his people and their history. He lavished her with gifts, and though merely a servant to the king, she felt honored among her caste, risen by the love and praise he gave. When the Omjadda lord finally took her to his bed it was not vile and displeasing, as she would have expected. Ornn was passionate and tender – a prodigious lover. *Did he know then?* Her recollections of Maalj bending his ear loomed with unanswered feelings. *Did Ornn know that I was going to be the one to spill his life essence and spread it throughout the whole of the world, birthing my Children of Evensong?*

Looking back on it now, Dominique felt that he did. Too many things had to fit into place for her to be able to orchestrate the uprising like she had done and win her freedom from the Omjadda keep to just gamble with fate. Had Ornn not shared with her the intricate details of his people's laws and religious rites then she never would have known to call the Ohanao and claim his blood after slaying him and intercede as the clan's J'in Ankh.

Her small rebellion would have been rudely quelled before it had a chance to ignite the other J'ins' Vams with a passion for freedom if she had simply left the bodies of Ornn and Ele Däm Mu there to rot. Dominique understood it now, Ornn's hand was on her knife the whole time, but it did not make her feel any better about killing him.

Did you know that I prayed, night after unending night, for another way to set myself free and spare your life? Dominique sat down on the edge of the bed beside William and Linnet. *Perhaps, my sweet, perhaps*...the look on Ornn's face as she drew the bone blade under his chin was a fixed ornament in the castle of her soul. It rarely left her inner gaze. The mournful crunch of his brow, the way his vibrant crescent-moon eyes looked at her, it wasn't worry and betrayal! *It was pity.*

He ached for his killer with the knowledge that the Omjadda witch had given him. Her burden to carry their seed with his blood was evident the day that he stayed the executioner's hand. All of his pampering affections and gentle care with his housebound slave was nothing more than his love for his people to survive through her! *A willingness to sacrifice.* Dominique brushed her fingers through William's dark knotted hair. He was the sign that Maalj had told her about when she was just a girl. The blood of Ornn that she used to turn Isabela and others, which she hoped to resurrect in her darling Linnet, was not just the instrument of cheating loneliness and oblivion. It was the sacred vein from which salvation flowed.

Dominique thought to go mad by the sudden rush of such vivid epiphanies, but she did not. Finally, it all made perfect sense. Vam Pŷr, Omjadda, Human – *we are all one blood.* One fractured species of the divine. Maalj, Buddha, Mohammed, Zoroaster, John, and Jesus – *they are all just prophets of the One.* Layal, Rah, Allah, Ahura Mazda, Odin, or Jehovah – *all names of its singular grace.* It made no difference who the puzzle pieces were in the great cosmic shuffle – *we are all one blood.*

"Däm'Um," Dominique uttered in the ancient tongue of the primordial race, stroking the young master's hair. "Däm'Um."

We each have our part and roles to play. Dominique did not feel bitter or honored by this simple revelation. It merely was. For eons the races of the world had been broken, splintered by continents, language, avarice, and sin. Isabela was a perfect reminder of how one, unguided, could fall. Dominique could not allow her lost sheep to go unattended for too much longer. Though the wheels of Isabela's conspiracies had stopped of late the memories of them still burned brightly. There was a patch of green under a ring of Cashew Trees that never lacked for flowers or visitors.

Just as William was the bridge between the symbionts and the Tribe, she was the bridge over time. *You will spread the seed of our people through yours and after the trials of Mar we'll emerge on the other side.* Dominique could only guess at what the Jaddat was hinting at. It terrified her a little that she might one day find out. The eyeless stare from the Seer's forehead haunted her, set within her mind at such an impressionable age, with two rows of pointy teeth grinning at her like a grandmother. It sent a shiver up Dominique's spine.

Damnation or Salvation. The symmetry of the cave and William held within the snake pits of Isabela's arms came rushing back to her. *At every turn, we each are given the promise and the prayer to churn the wheels of fate forward.* It's a natural process – *painful and chaotic.* Her slavery and the wars of men were merely the universe's way of untangling itself from the myriad collections of godlight and stardust that it had spawned. It's a way for itself to return to the knowledge of One.

One breath – spread throughout all forms and shades of life.
One heart beat – knocking against the stellar knell of night.
One life – lived throughout the expanse of species and time, united by blood.

We could be a better One! A learned species lifted onto the shoulders of all those that had gone before us. Amid the countless stacks of blood and bones that the Earth had ground into its folds, birthing an Amen of dirt, so few were chosen to rise above the din and carry the seeds to the next stage of evolution. Dominique recognized her choice in the play of things and vowed that her Children of Evensong would not crumble to the same fate that the Kula Malaika Shaytan Khalid had done. Her council would see to that.

In the soft glow of candlelight, seated next to her lover and the tamer of beasts, awash in the tumble and turn of the cosmic meat machine, Dominique offered a silent prayer of thanks. She had all that she needed, right here in her arms, and they weren't going anywhere. Time, she figured, would unearth its own needs. She did not have to worry what the future bore.

Lin wiped the steam off the bathroom mirror, having stepped out from a hot shower feeling only slightly better than she did a few minutes earlier. Her etiolate features held a sullen disposition and an unsettling tremor shook within her, just above the bones, a tiny hurricane. It was not from the blood parasite. It was not from Ryan's death or from her long memories of the dead. Lin understood. She was a killer. A war-torn soul. She accepted that now. It was Z who had helped her to become one. Her eyes passed over her silver locket, spooled in a little dish on the vanity, and she knew that the clamor of Father Time had rung her bones. The miniature hurricane in her soul was that damned sandstorm in desert. From all those years ago, its dark winds clashed within her for atonement. Like the ancient Mariner from old, Lin had slain those that had delivered them from the sure death and insanity of the storm. The locket was her albatross, burdened by her insufferable fate to be born broken.

Once again, Lin knew she needed to hit the road. Find a balance of forgiveness out there, somewhere, that she could not deliver unto herself. She couldn't put it off any longer. She could not pretend to hide in her worn affection for Z or from the fear that her partner's Jadaraa Soo was dying. The fact was, Zia Jean Bell had her own things to work out. There was nothing she could do for the ruckus American. Z was slipping through the greasy cracks of time. Her fate was sealed. Death would come for her one day like a letter that she had mailed to herself.

Lin's own death lingered on the horizon. Somewhere out there amid the stars and morning glories, her eviction notice from life waited in the ethereal arms of fate. *Perhaps it would be like Z's, slow and forgetful. Or snuffed out like Ryan. Or a flambé in the sun. It didn't matter. One hundred years? One thousand? Today! We all pay the Ferryman with an ounce of silver.* Lin's silver was the trinket that she'd stolen off the corpse. She knew death would come to collect it one day. The locket was her admission into the afterlife. Lin was settled in this knowledge. She grabbed a towel off the sink and matted her hair, drying it further. *Immortality, especially for those high-falutin' Immortals, was nothing short of great PR.* The symbiont sighed, wishing that she could've been able to turn the key in the Caddy the other day.

She poked and pulled at her hair, turning her head this way and that in the mirror to view her raven's nest. She had worn it long for awhile now, and plucked the tip of a lock in front of her face. It stretched past the tip of her nose. Then she pulled all of her hair back, peering this way and that, and bent her head to one side and the other. She looked at her teeth, stretching her lips back. She wiggled her tongue between the mouth crack. *Frightening.*

Taking a pair of scissors from a drawer in the vanity, Lin began cutting. When she was done, her hair was short, cute, and kind of tomboyish. She laid the scissors next to the sink, cleaned off the hair on her collarbone, picked up the locket, and placed it around her neck. Her burden hung, tribute to wander like the unfortunate rogue in the poem, the parasite shrank back from the vile silver lining of the ornament. Lin Pevensey looked at herself in the mirror. Her albatross dangled into the cleft of her breasts, fitting and right. Her neck was two delicate curves that made her shoulders look intact.

Despite the jewel, Lin liked what she saw.

Once more, she opened the silver pendant and stared at the picture within the wings of the locket, reliving her guilt. Every line of that beautiful face was etched into the canyons of her heart. The photograph of the woman that she had killed had become so much a part of her, as was her son. Though truthfully, Lin could not, for the life of her, remember what he had looked like. She could cite his smell, his laugh, and the softness of his cheeks when he pressed them against her. She remembered the pangs of childbirth and how it felt when he suckled. But whenever Lin wandered to recall the features of her bygone little boy, she could not. The color of his hair, a glint of chin – never a complete image like the face within the locket, never the gait of him next to her. William was an impression of sightless sounds and smells from a time and an age that had passed. Lin closed the locket and went to get dressed.

She slipped into a comfortable pair of jeans, figuring that she'd be sitting in the Cadillac all night, and it occurred to her that it had been over a hundred years since she had checked up on her descendents in the African tribe. She made a mental note to look in on them once she'd returned from the trip. After she restyled her raven's nest, Lin joined Z on the couch.

The punk was watching an old black and white Betty Davis picture, one that the silent cohorts had not seen in a couple of decades. Z took a quick look at the new mop and offered a curt commentary. "Hmmp? Looks nice."

The simplicity of domestic bliss. Watching Betty Davis reminded the vampire of the first moving picture show that she had ever seen. Coney Island. A chilly Summer's day. Walking on the boardwalk. The Nickelodeons were on display. It was a grainy film of a man and a woman walking. Not together, but apart. Each was a separate reel in the nickel wind up. Two films about simple motion that possessed such incredible wonder and joy. Lin felt inspired at seeing the two tiny people move in an ordinary way, captured so extraordinarily. It spoke volumes to her. It spoke a simple truth: *Time marches on. Put one foot in front of the other. Keep moving. Keep pressing on.*

Lin's innate buzzer chimed and she knew dusk was creeping over the bright-hold places of the day. She rose up from the couch, and not making a big show of it, simply told Z that she would see her later. It wasn't until after the vampire had walked out the door, closing it with a soft click, did Z realize what Lin had really meant. She shut the TV off and flew off the couch after her.

"So that's it, you're leaving?" chided the punk as she stepped out from behind the sliding steel doors of the elevator.

Lin held the key in the door handle and was about to unlock it. She shimmied her head up and down, "Yeah."

Z appeared bothered by it. It wasn't Lin's issue and she finished unlocking her ride. Z had her own demons to work out, and one of 'em still messed up the perfect drab gray parking garage with congealing red. She straightened her stance, folded the keys in her palm, and looked at the bright colored vamp, expecting some other exchange. Z just stood there.

"I thought you said you didn't want to go," Lin threw at her after a time.

"Well..." uttered Z, crossing her arms.

"I also thought you said you were gonna clean this mess up." She indicated the corpse that still lay in the middle of the garage.

"I am," Z snapped defensively. "Just...hadn't gotten to it. It's not like he's going anywhere."

There was an awkward silence with nothing but Ryan between them.

"Well?" Lin asked after a spell, scrunching her shoulders and squishing her face.

"Lemme get my boots?" Z encouragingly appealed, wiggling her bare toes up at Lin.

Lin shrugged. "Hurry up then."

Sometimes we hold ourselves back. Sometimes we allow others to do it for us. Sometimes, we just want to shut down, crawl under a rock and die. Sometimes we can't. Sometimes we forget the past and are doomed to repeat it. Sometimes we don't and it makes us who we are. Lin sat in the bucket seat staring across the dashboard of a repeated highway, a repeated lane, driving all night to a constant destination in her soul. She warmed up the car, waiting for Z, but internally, she was already there, in New Mexico, digging through ruins. Lin was miles away, pulling the locket across its chain, drowning in the ungodly storm, choking on sand, killing herself with pride.

Keep moving. Keep going, never surrender, never give in.

The image of the man running in the Nickelodeon flitted across her brow until Z reemerged from the lift wearing her boots. She had powered down the penthouse and ducked into the tiny cinderblock room to lock the elevator. Stepping over Ryan's decaying corpse, Z went directly to the passenger side door of the vintage Cadillac. She opened it and was about to climb in when Lin asked her where her head was at.

"You forgetting something?"

"No," the rascally vamp answered with due sincerity, sliding into the seat. "I've still got my clothes in the trunk from last time."

Lin flexed her arms like an elderly Jewish woman over the curve of the steering wheel, indicating Ryan's unmoved body in the middle of the parking garage. Z sighed, rolled her eyes, and climbed out of the vehicle to finally deal with it.

Much to her dismay, Lin watched Z simply drag the corpse to the little cinderblock room and hide it behind the gray painted door. Lin took note that the punk's sole concern while dumping the body was to avoid getting any of Ryan's caked blood on her clothes. She looked herself over, from head to toe, as she headed back to the Cadillac and climbed into the passenger seat. Lin just stared at Z with her mouth hanging open. She was staggered by the vampire's arrogant refusal to dispose of the corpse and clean up the mess.

"What?" Z snapped, scrunching her shoulders. Lin just continued to stare. Words were numb in her gaping mouth.

"He's outta sight," the punk informed. "He ain't going anywhere." Z returned the unabashed glare until Lin closed her flytrap. "Ok. I'll give him a proper desert burial when we get back. Happy?" She sighed, but they still had not begun to move. "What do you wanna do? You want I should do it now or do you wanna hit the road?"

Lin hated when Z twisted her bullshit around on her like that. It made her huff like a charging bull. The ruckus American tapped out a drum roll on the dashboard and peered back at Lin, taunting her with a brazen and cheeky smile. Lin turned away and exhaled, "Zia Bell." She rumbled through the feelings, drawing the words out, as if she was writing them in the sky.

"I know. I know," the raunchy, playful vamp teased. "You love me."

Z smiled wide and it was true. Lin did love her, but sometimes... *sometimes*...Lin decided it was best to just leave it at that. She lowered the dashboard column gearshift into drive and took off into the wild blinking night of neon lights, stars, and cotton candy surprises. A trail of red taillights followed them into Layal's unmerciful embrace and the rascally vampire declared herself the Minister of Funk, staking all claims to the noise that was to join their eastward journey.

When the lights from the big city had finally disappeared in the rearview mirror, and the Santa Ana winds had kissed their tailpipe, and they reached the opened desert and cartoon Cacti that surrounded Los Angeles on nearly three whole sides, Z thought it was as good a time as any to get to the real heart of the ride. After all, Nevada and Arizona were destined for their headlights.

"We gonna grab and burn?" Z rested in a lazy position, head on the back of the seat, feet jacked out the window, feeling the rippling wind.

"Must we?" Lin wrote on the dashboard with her breath.

"I'm all out of video tapes. I gotta have something to watch. You know… mementos."

Lin turned and looked at the beautiful, soulless thing lounging in the front seat beside her. Death after all, from Z's blissful perspective, was the gift that kept on giving. "You still have all those tapes in the back seat that you *said* you were gonna clean up."

"Oh yeah," she remembered and pulled in her legs. Turning around in the seat, Z peered into the catastrophe in the rear of the car. "Huh? We can watch those when we get back." She flopped back around to the face the driver. "But what about something that says, On The Road In…whatever year it is that we just so happen to be in right now?" Z flipped her hands around, accentuating the lost sense of a calendar. "You know, they're time stamped. Says so, right here at the bottom of the screen."

Z drew a little TV screen in the air, just above the front seat, between them, and showed Lin exactly what she was talking about. *Technology! It was so neat and all.*

"We'll see," Lin finally answered, feeling her gut sink. "We'll see."

Z gave her conservative pal doe eyes and a puppy-dog-face, hamming up her huckleberry smile.

"I said, we'll see," Lin sighed, laughed, and playfully punched her compadre in the arm.

The rollicking punk chuckled, "Hey!" And returned the playful jab. She turned the song that was on the radio up and eased back into the polished bucket seat, stretching her legs out of the window into the passing night. Z began singing along with Johnny Cash as the wind from the road blew speedily through her toes.

I fell in to a burning ring of fire
I went down, down, down
and the flames kept coming higher.
And it burns, burns, burns
the ring of fire
the ring of fire...

Däm'Um:
Song of the Vam Pŷr's
LEXICON

Araci – (*AhRaa cee*) Native Guarani term for Spirit of the dawn. *South American.*

Asli – (*Ahzlee*) 1. Original. 2. The People.

Brood – (*Brood*) 1. The initiated members of one's family or coven. 2. Lesser vampires with weaker symbiotic bonds, usually deformed by the symbiotic transformation.

Bruxsa – (*Bruxsah*) A feminine vampire of Portugal. The Bruxsa is believed to transform into a creature of the night by the means of witchcraft, and goes out in the shape of a bird. Also believed to possess a normal life during the day; Bruxsas are known to torment lost and tired travelers, and feed primarily on children. *Portuguese.*

Casa del Rio Dulce – House on the Sweet River. Built in 1687 by Dominique De'Paul and Isabela da Nóbrega. *Portuguese/Spanish.*

Children of Evensong – A loose term of those belonging to the symbiont species derived from the mixing of Omjadda and Human blood.

Dalam Kha'Shiya – (*Daa Laam Kha She Yaa*) That which waits in the pitch of darkness is the traditional understanding of this moniker for the Seventh J'in (Clan) of the Omjadda. However, the phrase can also be interpreted as, *Dangerous Night Water Spirit.* The Dalam Kha'Shiya J'in is one of two Omjadda clans to emerge from the Dalam Vala'Shiya J'in after the Great Migration.
> *Dalam* = Night; Darkness. *Kha* = Danger; Dangerous. *Shiya* = Water Goddess; Ocean Spirit: Mistress/Servant of the Night Mother God/ Goddess, Layal.

Däm'Um – (*Daa'Oomm*) One Blood; first blood. *Dam* = Blood. *Um* = One; first. Other forms of the word *Dam* that have emerged into the African and Arabic Languages from the Omjaddas are: *Dama, Damma, & Dammu.*

Engenho – Local term for a sugarcane plantation in Brazil.

Eras of Slavery – Traditionally considered to range from 692 BCE to 1546 ACE. Though it is widely accepted in known circles that Vam (*Blood Slaves*) were created for the distinct purpose of human herding prior to this dating. Normac, a Vam Shiya of northern European descent, squelched the last remnants of symbiont slavery in 1546. Normac's revolt lasted nearly half a century aided in part by members of the N'um Vala'Shiya J'in. Normac is chiefly remembered for brilliantly shielding the decades long war from human knowledge by masking it with the Schmalkaldic League* and Protestant Reformation.

In total, the conflicts that ended the Omjadda's Vam trade lasted over two centuries. Beginning as modest slave revolts that were primarily quelled, no actual progress toward liberation was established until the fall of the Tien Däm Mu J'in's slavery system in 1494. This was accomplished by two blood slaves, Fizza and Ramielle Eirinhas, orchestrating a simultaneous Vam revolt with an external attack led by the symbiont, Joshua, of the N'um Vala'Shiya J'in.

> ***Schmalkaldic League** – A defensive alliance of Lutheran princes within the Holy Roman Empire during the mid 16th Century. Although originally started for religious motives soon after the start of the Protestant Reformation, its members eventually intended for the League to replace the Holy Roman Empire as their source of political allegiance. While it was not the first alliance of its kind, unlike previous formations, such as the League of Torgau, the Schmalkaldic League had a substantial military to defend its political and religious interests. It receives its name from the town of Schmalkalden, in the German province of Thuringa. German: *Schmalkaldischer Bund*

Fedah Layal – (*Fey Daah Lay Al*) The three silvery rings of moonlight surrounding a bright, full moon, can also be interpreted as *God Light*. Name of the fifth J'in (Clan) of the Omjadda. The Fedah Layal J'in emerged from a split within the Rom Pŷr J'in prior to the Great Migration.

> *Fedah* = God's/Goddess's Light. The word *Fedah* found primary rooting in the Arabic Languages to mean, silvery. Over time the '*h*' was displaced to strengthen the accentuation of the '*a*' as the language progressed with a new tonal structure. <u>*Ex:*</u> *fed-ha.*

Gai'Anâka – (*Guy ann Akaa*) The Force, essence; Mother of all things. A later derivative of this word is *Gaia*, which means Mother Earth or Plant Life. Later development of early human civilizations misused this term for a name for the Earth.

Great Migration, The – An important time in the history of the Omjadda that denotes when the ancient race was force to flee their dying homelands and venture across what are now known as Africa, Europe, and Asia. The Omjadda term for this was Rånon Ŭd'ertz (*raNon Ood'rts*); all deeper meanings are lost.

Guampa – Hollowed gourd used in traditional Yerba Maté drinks. *Spanish*.

Ja – *(Ja or Jaa depending on meaning and expression)*. Ja *(Ja)* = Source. Jā *(Jaa)* = Spiritual Essence, Spiritual Source.

Ja Rů Tộk – *(Jaa Roo TeOok)* The Omjadda Blood rite of passage that transforms a Mar into a Vam when Omjadda Blood is introduced into the bloodstream of a Mar (Human Being). This intermingling of bloods creates a (symbiotic) parasitic/host relationship in the infected organism creating a new species that is neither Human nor Omjadda, who feeds off the blood of other highly evolved living organisms.

Jaci – *(eYaa cee)* Native Guarani term for Spirit of the moon. *South America*.

Jad – *(Jaad)* Tree.

Jadaraa Soo – *(Jah Daa Raa Soo)* Omjadda term for the vampiric parasite veins of a blood slave.

Jadda – *(Jah Daa)* The Tree of Life. Deep Rooted Essence. The word *Jadda* is also used as a term of endearment to one's mother.

Jadda Asli Roh - *(Jah Daa Ahzlee Row)* Royal Blood of the People of the Jadda Tree. Modern term of the eldest J'in (Clan) of the Omjadda. Originally derived from the *Asli Pyl* tribe, People West of the Onnaki River. Ancient lore states that in the *War of No Fist* the Asli Pyl met with their neighbors, the *Om Pŷr*, People East of the Onnaki River, to do battle and that in the settlement of the conflict the Asli Pyl took the moniker *Jadda Asli*, which meant: *Original People of the Jadda Tree*. The suffix Roh, *Royal Blood*, was added after the Omjadda's first and only recorded civil war; see *The Legend of Marh*.

Jaddat – *(Jaa Dat)* Seer; Mother of the people of the Jadda Tree; Listener and Speaker with Gai'Anaka. A Jaddat is a spiritual elder born to the people. One cannot ascend to the position of Jaddat, it is preordained by birth. A Jaddat is born without eyes, eyebrows, or eye sockets, so the term, Seer, is in reference to a Jaddat's gift of spiritual sight and prophetic visions.

J'in – *(Geh'In)* Clan: Family. One's Gathering: Those one chooses or is born amongst.

J'in Ankh – *(Geh'In Angk)* Familial Head; leader of the J'in (Clan); symbol of his or her people.

Jinoo Kuntun – (*Jee nu Kūnton*) An intensely focused spiritual walk of significance. *East African.*

Kula Malaika Shaytan Khalid – (*Koo La Maa laa eeka Shay Tan Khaleed*) Cannibal Angel, Devil Immortal. A term developed by African tribes predating recorded history that describes the Omjadda Race. Arabic/African

Kulak – (*Koo Lak*) A Russian term, now part of the English lexicon, for a peasant with a prosperous farm and a substantial allotment of land that worked the agrarian parcels with the help of hired labor. In the Soviet period the term became an ambiguous Party construct with mostly negative connotations. In the mid to late 1800's, with the formation of the symbiont council, the term was applied to petitioners that wanted access into The Council's jurisdiction under the laws of its domain among one of its many covens. Over time, with use, the term developed slang undertones to reflect one's subordinate state and position among the caste of their coven's rank; usually associated with a lowly status. *Ukranian: kurkul, hlytai.*

Laahidi Buuñaa – (*Lāheedee Booyaa*) One's honor and pledge of dedication to his/her people. *East African.*

Layal – (*Lay Al*) Night Mother, the God/Goddess aspect of the Omjadda people. The word *Layal* is one of the original words passed down from Omjadda to humans that has changed very little in spelling and pronunciation. Though the word still retains a meaning of Night, all references to its dual nature of mother/sister and the God/Goddess aspects of its Omjadda origins have completely vanished with human use. In Hebrew and various Indian Languages the spelling of Layal has changed slightly. Arabic is the only human language to retain its original spelling.

Lanz Gur Mae – (*Laanz Grrr May*) Omjadda expression for *the land from here to there.* Original home of the Omjadda before the Great Migration. It is traditionally believed to be where the desert of the Senegal and Gambia regions now exist, today. Early misinterpretations of the Lanz Gur Mae with the astral body, Nibiru, have resulted in its exclusion from ancient references.

Legend of Marh, the – The modern understanding of the Arabic word, Mar, which means Human Being, has its origins based on the Omjadda legend of Jadda Asli Marh. Marh was a prince of the royal J'in, Jadda Asli. To the Omjadda, Marh and his followers were believed to be the sole source of the Human Race, however, there is no proof to that claim.

      The legend states that Jadda Asli Marh broke from time honored traditions by seeking an alliance with Layal's vengeful father/brother, Rah, who governed the day. Marh's communion with Rah is believed to have transfigured him, wherein he lost his normal bodily sheen and could now walk in both the day and the night. Marh began teaching others how to commune with Rah and gained a large following. This caused unrest and dissention among the J'ins of the time and a huge rift tore the Omjadda apart. Civil war broke out to quell these new cultural influences. This war is the Omjadda's first and only recorded blood war in their long and glorious history.

The result of the conflict led to the banishment of Marh and his followers from the Lanz Gur Mae. The Jadda Asli added the suffix, Roh, to their name, which meant, *cleansed from the golden light, retainer of the pure essence,* and all utterances of Marh and his teachings were forbidden. It was not until the encroachment of human beings, in the death days of the Lanz Gur Mae, that Jadda Asli Marh's title was resurrected. Common belief of the time held that Marh and his followers perished in the Anon *(translation lost)*. Privately among the Jadda Asli Roh J'in, however, there survived a prophecy from the clan's reigning Jaddat that foretold of Marh's return in transcended form.

The new humanoid creatures were met with speculation and wonder because they spoke with an Omjadda tongue, calling themselves Mar, for Children of Marh. Again, rumors and dissention rippled through the J'ins and it was believed that Marh, in an unholy union with Rah, birthed these creatures to be his instrument of destruction and revenge against Layal and the Omjadda people.

Mar – *(Mar)* Omjadda word for Human Being. Later development from the Omjadda term, *Pÿr Marh,* which translates to *Marh's Children from the East.* The word *Mar* developed its modern roots in Arabic and the Greek Languages. Though in Greek, *Mar* further developed into a godhead term to denote the God of War, aka *Mars.*

Mu – *(Moo)* Omjadda conjunction word used like the English word, of.

Nibiru – *(Né Bé Roo)* 1. A technical term of Babylonian astronomy, translating to 'crossing' or 'point of transition'; passage between heaven and earth. 2. Marduk's star. 3. An early name for Jupiter. 4. An astral body with an elliptic orbit theorized to have collided with another astral body that formed the Earth, Moon, and asteroid belt. 5. An undefined time of Omjadda wandering.

N'um – *(N'oom)* Dawn.

N'um Vala'Shiya –*(NN oom VahLaa She ya)* People of the Golden Treasure: fourth J'in (Clan) of the Omjadda. The N'um Vala'Shiya J'in is one of two Omjadda clans to have emerge from the Dalam Vala'Shiya J'in after the Great Migration.

N'um = Dawn, Shiya = Water Goddess; Ocean Spirit: Mistress/Servant of the Night Mother God/Goddess, Layal.

Ohanao – *(Ohān O)* The hunter's cry. Ceremonial expression of the Omjadda, traditionally used in claiming prey.

Om – *(OM)* Original Sound; first word.

Omjadda – *(Omm' Jah Daa)* Original People of the Jadda Tree. A nocturnal, humanoid species that predates all known spoken and written human languages. Early civilized writings appear to have attributed this primordial race with godhead status. Other known names: Annunaki, Nephillim, Malaika, Kula Malaika Shaytan Khalid.

Onnak – *(Oḥ Nak)* Long river. An 'i' is added when the word is used in conjunction with what it is. _Ex:_ *Onnaki River.*

Pun – *(Pun')* North.

Puun – *(Poonn)* South.

Pyl – *(Peel')* West.

Pŷr – *(Pur)* East. Later developments of the word Pŷr became known as *Son* or *Children of.*

Qamar – *(K'Mar)* The Moon.

Qamar Däm – *(K'Mar Daa)* Blood Moon. Often referred to as an eclipse or a red moon and the third J'in (Clan) of the Omjadda Race, believed to have originally sprouted as a sect of healers from the Jadda Asli and Rom Pyr J'ins. Traditionally noted to have birthed more Jaddats than any other J'in. Earliest accounts within the Qamar Däm attribute the first blood moon to the time of Jadda Asli Marh's banishment.

Quilombo *(s)* – Local term for a free-standing, indigenous village, mostly comprised of run-away Indios and African slaves, in the jungles of Brazil.

Rah – *(Rah)* Fire God of Day: Vengeful Spirit. The father/brother aspect of Layal. Believed to swallow his sister each morning and rebirth her each night. In later years with the development of human civilization the Symbol of Ra(h) was stolen from the temple of Gai' Anaka and taken to Egypt, where a vast Mar civilization flourished on its founding principles that the day is the nourishing element of Gaia, Plant Life. Through its development the 'h' was lost and Ra was elevated as the founding father and source of all life.

Réveiller Sommeil – Waking Sleep. Term used for a symbiont's natural death cycle that usually appears as a catatonic sleep state wherein one looks awake. Other terms for the Waking Sleep are Ba'al Shem Beit in Aramaic and Ůd Aỹn Mal (*Ood Aye-in Maal*) in Omjadda. *French.*

Roh – (*Row*) Developmental phrase for the Omjadda's royal bloodline. Its meanings began as *cleansed from the golden light, retainer of the pure essence* to finally arrive at the simple term, Royal Blood.

Rom Pỹr – (*Rah'M Pur*) Strong People to the East; second J'in (Clan) of the Omjaddas. In the beginning there were two distinct Omjadda J'ins. The *Asli Pyl*, People of the West, and the *Om Pỹr*, Sound from the East. Each tribe was separated by the Onnaki River, which ran through the Lanz Gur Mae, developing independently, choosing their own leaders, governing structure, and unique cultural customs. As legend goes, when the *Om Pỹr*, Sound from the East, came to war with the *Asli Pyl*, People of the West, the J'in Ankh of the Asli Pyl meet with the J'in Ank of the Om Pyr, embraced him and called him *Rom*, strong. The J'in Ank of the Om Pỹr returned the embrace thus ending the *War of No Fist* and the term Rom Pỹr was used ever since for the people east of the Onnak.

Sanglant – (*Sang Lant*) Modern term for a blood lender. Sanglants usually work for The Service and sell their precious bodily fluid, allowing symbionts to feed off of them for money. Original French pronunciation for a Sanglant is *Prêteur de Sang*.

Shrij'Tẹk Aůr – (*Shree'G Tik ArUr*) An Omjadda call for challenge. Usually delivered when one wishes to challenge the line of succession to the throne of J'in Ankh.

Tet Däm'vah (*tet Daa Vaa*) – Sacred Blood. Omjadda ceremonial term for the blessed life fluid within one's J'in.

The Council – A secret ruling body comprised of twelve members, from varying symbiont covens, throughout the world, established in 1838. The freed Vam Pỹr, Dominique De'Paul, is credited with conceiving the initial plans of the elite governing body.

The Service – Independent organization originally developed by Dominique De'Paul and Ramielle Eirinhas in the early 1800's as a way for symbionts to meet the needs of their particular feeding habits without causing harm to other individuals or raise suspicion of their existence and activity. With the establishment of The Council in 1838 the function of The Service was absorbed into the governing body.

Tien Däm Mu – (*Tee En Daa Moo*) People of blood: later, People of Ill Blood when the Vam Pŷr, Dominique De'Paul, interceded the Omjadda line of succession as J'in Ankh of the Clan. The sixth J'in of the Omjadda. The Tien Däm Mu J'in resulted from a split between rival family members of the Qamar Däm J'in just prior to leaving the dying lands of the Lanz Gur Mae. The Tien Däm Mu J'in are credited with starting the Rånon Ŭd'ertz (*Great Migration*), and renown for the *Chaya Ip.*

Vam – (*Vam*) A blood slave of the Omjadda, created when a human being partakes of Omjadda Blood in the Ja Rŭ Tộk. The use of Vam ended with the Eras of Slavery. See *Eras of Slavery* for more detail.

Vam Pŷr – (*Vam Pur*) Slave to the People of the East: Slave Son; property of the Rom Pŷr J'in. *Vam* = Slave. *Pŷr* = Eastern People; Children of. The Rom Pŷr J'in are credited with discovering the sentient properties of their Tet Däm'vah to resurrect Mar into blood slaves through a symbiotic bond between host and parasite. The modern term of this is commonly known as a *Vampire*. In the Nordic/Austrian regions of Europe and Asia the term Vam Pŷr became one word, *Vampyr*, later developing into the spelling of *Vampyre*, which was commonly believed to be a child born from the sexual coupling of a vampire and a human. Since the reproductive organs of an infected Mar no longer function normally the production of such a child could never exist. Thus the modern term for Vampyre is completely incorrect and mythical. The sexual coupling of an Omjadda and a Human is quite possible, though, to date there are no known couplings between these two races other than the creation of Vam.

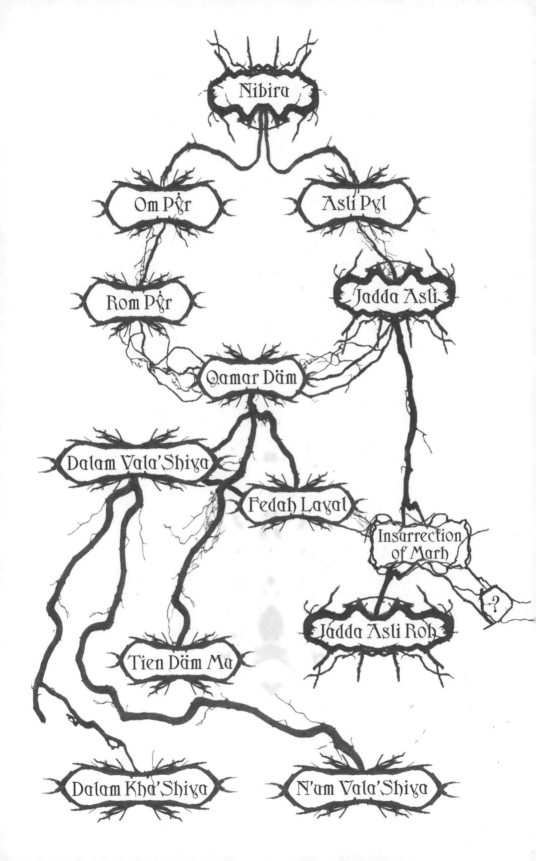

Publisher's Note

Photo: Jacquie Coté

Stavros is a writer, musician, poet, photographer, painter, graphic designer, and award winning filmmaker. In 2001, he created the Poetry Television Project for public cable access, producing eight volumes of the groundbreaking series. He helped to launch The Independent Underground Newspaper and Unpublished Magazine. He's the father of two lovely people and his favorite beer is Hobgoblin, from Wychwood Brewery. He's had a coffeehouse, an international clothing design company; and performed drums at an impromptu concert for Max, the Crystal Skull. Two of his plays have been brought to the stage and he's penned a few screenplays. He claims to like cheese and long walks in the moonlight. Though, I've only seen him eat cheese and pass out before eleven O'clock because he gets up too damn early in the morning! Blood Junky is a prequel novel to his upcoming film and book adaptation, Love in Vein. It is also the first novel that he was ever able to successfully complete. Only took him twenty years to figure out the trick, and he's warned that more books will follow!

So from all of us at CDP, Thank You for picking up Blood Junky! If you like anything about this novel, please tell your friends and neighbors; blog about it until your fingers bleed, become a beautiful walking billboard by sporting our very nifty and cool BMRH and Blood Junky merchandise, and most importantly visit us at conventions and book signings. You can checkout all of our crazy going-ons at www.bitemereallyhard.com.

Crazy Duck Press is a small, very small, artist owned publishing company and what you hold in your hands is our premiere story, in what we hope will be the first of many, from many different writers and artists. Even the tallest mountain started with a single grain of sand, so we hope you will join us as we grow and together produce stories that are different, slightly off center, remarkable, and enjoyable to read. We are also trying to make enough noise in the world to raise the attention of the film industry and turn our pages into celluloid. Blood Junky would make for a great movie! And all we need for that to happen is to sell about a hundred thousand copies. Easy, right? With your help, yes, and we can reach that goal. So please, visit us online at www.crazyduckpress.com and www.bitemereallyhard.com, tell your friends, and help us to make a great big brouhaha!

Stavros Wishes to Thank:

The Almighty – his inspiration could have landed on anyone; glad it was me! My children: One & Story; Mom, Jacquie, Dan, and Myke without whose help, guidance, patience, and support these pages would have never been written. To Lindsey, Julia, and Emily for the initial inspiration to take my vamp world and graph it to a bunch of wacky photo shoot ideas that got the stagnant ball, finally, rolling! To Trixie, who was there at the very beginning of all this crazy vampire stuff and who remains a constant inspiration. To SM & Mischa for pimpin' the film scripts and dreamin' the dreamer's dream, to Robert, Lisa, Paula, Robyn, Stephen, and Darlene; to the Fathers and Mothers at Our Lady of Kazan Skete for never giving up on me, Jonathan for keeping the faith, Grandmas for da' love, Jersey Dan for the continual word, the guys 'n gals in the Bayhill Writer's Group for critiques, Carol for being "The One", You, for reading my words, and PB 'cause in truth… All Thank Yous To Grace Pena!

Live. Love. Create.

Pick Up Your Official
One Blood Gear Today!

Sport our trendy line of
T-Shirts, Caps, Coffee Mugs, Buttons, Stickers, and Key Chains.
Visit www.bitemereallyhard.com to connect with the author, follow the continuing
adventures of Lin & Z, Download free music and art, blog, and generally enjoy
the creation of more sensational crap!

.com